THE HOUSE OF O'SHEA

The sun was warm although it was May and early morning, but as they moved down the coast of New South Wales there could be breezes off early Alpine snows. She leant over the rails and raised her face in anticipation, feeling more relaxed than she had for a long time, watching distant breakers on distant sands, seeking the sparse settlements that were all there was of human habitation in an empty land. Distantly she heard Dominic soothing Phelim – poor patient Domi for Phelim interrupted his life, his reading, dragging at his books, clinging, till too often Domi set all aside to amuse his brother. The only time Dominic dug in his heels, so to speak, was to oppose Celine. It pleased their mother. Someone must put a rein on Celine O'Shea even at going-on-five.

**Also by the same author,
and available from NEL:**

And the Wild Birds Sing
The Place of the Swan

About the author

Lola Irish was born in Sydney, New South Wales, and began her career writing short stories, radio scripts and plays, and stage plays, before concentrating on novel-writing. Her novels include the first two in the Colonial Trilogy, *And the Wild Birds Sing*, and *The Place of the Swan*, as well as *The Touch of Jade*, *Shadow Mountain* and *Time of the Dolphins*. She has twice received a one-year fellowship from the Literature Board of the Australia Council. *And the Wild Birds Sing* won her an award from the Society of Women Writers (Australia). Lola Irish has travelled extensively, world-wide as well as within Australia, and now lives in Sydney. She is a keen pianist and, when she can steal time from writing, a portrait painter.

The House of O'Shea

Lola Irish

NEW ENGLISH LIBRARY
Hodder and Stoughton

British Library C.I.P.

Irish, Lola
    The house of O'Shea.
    I. Title
    823[F]

ISBN 0 450 55105 9

Printed and bound in Great Britain for Hodder and Stoughton Paperbacks, a division of Hodder and Stoughton Ltd., Mill Road, Dunton Green, Sevenoaks, Kent TN13 2YA (Editorial Office: 47 Bedford Square, London WC1B 3DP) by Clays Ltd., St Ives plc.

For
Lindsey Jan Mulligan

Author's Note

This, the third novel in The Colonial Trilogy, is complete in itself, yet the reader will resume acquaintance with many of the characters first met with in *And the Wild Birds Sing* and *The Place of the Swan*, as well as meeting new ones.

In Australia, my thanks to the librarians and staffs of city and country libraries, in particular to those of The State Library of New South Wales and the Mitchell Library, Sydney. I would equally like to thank the staffs of city and country newspapers for their help during my years of research involving biographies, histories, newspapers, journals, diaries, letters, pamphlets and so on, amounting to hundreds of publications, in compiling the period background to my story.

My thanks also to the staff of the British Library.

During my sojourns conducting research in British Columbia, Canada, my thanks to the Vancouver Public Library, the Capilano Library, the staff attached to the restored gold rush town of Barkerville, and various museums, galleries and libraries throughout the province.

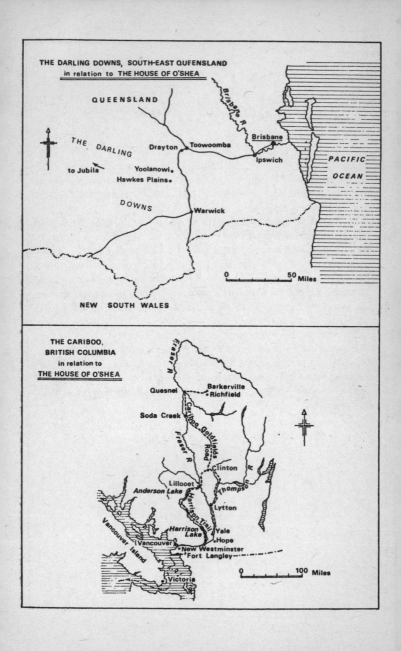

THE DARLING DOWNS, SOUTH-EAST QUEENSLAND
in relation to THE HOUSE OF O'SHEA

QUEENSLAND

Brisbane R

THE DARLING

Drayton • Toowoomba   • Brisbane

to Jubila →   • Ipswich

Yoolanowi •
Hawkes Plains •

DOWNS

• Warwick

PACIFIC
OCEAN

0   50 Miles

NEW   SOUTH   WALES

THE CARIBOO,
BRITISH COLUMBIA
in relation to
THE HOUSE OF O'SHEA

Fraser R

Quesnel   • Barkerville
                 • Richfield

Soda Creek

Cariboo Goldfields Road

Fraser R

Clinton

Lillooet
Anderson Lake

Thompson R

Lytton

Harrison Trail

Harrison Lake   • Yale
Vancouver   • Hope
• New Westminster
• Fort Langley

Vancouver Island

Victoria

0   100 Miles

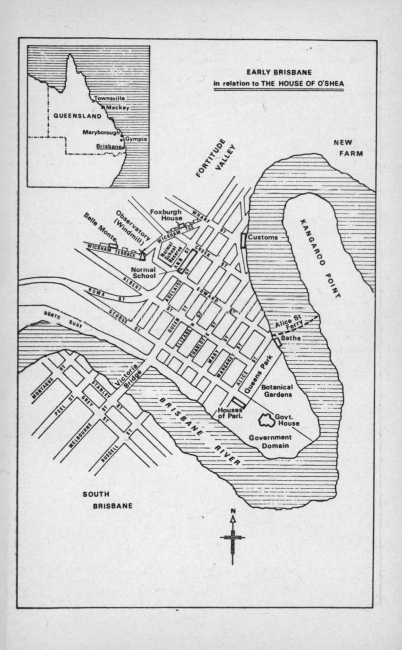

EARLY BRISBANE
in relation to THE HOUSE OF O'SHEA

QUEENSLAND

Townsville
Mackay
Maryborough
Gympie
Brisbane

FORTITUDE VALLEY

NEW FARM

Observatory (Windmill)
Foxburgh House
Belle Monte
WICKHAM TERRACE
WICKHAM TCE
Normal School Reserve
Normal School
Customs

KANGAROO POINT

ROMA ST
ALBERT
NORTH QUAY
GEORGE ST
ANN ST
ADELAIDE
EDWARD
QUEEN ST
ELIZABETH ST
CHARLOTTE ST
MARY ST
MARGARET ST
ALICE ST

WHARF ST
CREEK ST

Alice St Ferry
Baths

Queens Park

Botanical Gardens

MONTAGUE ST
PEEL ST
GREY ST
STANLEY ST
MELBOURNE ST
RUSSELL ST
Victoria Bridge

BRISBANE RIVER

Houses of Parl.

Govt. House

Government Domain

SOUTH BRISBANE

N

Foreword

The 1860s was a decade of development and expansion: a period of opening up . . . Australia boasted the new state of Queensland with, beyond its capital, Brisbane, a frontier wilderness of vast pastoral estates devoted to sheep and cattle, gold towns, unexplored bush, and the northern coastal areas of sugar and cotton 'plantations' worked by Kanaki labour.

British Columbia, Canada, weathered the gold rushes along the Fraser River that opened up the Cariboo and paved the way for the building of the Canadian Pacific Railway.

From Colony and Dominion alike the *nouveaux riches* of society, wealthy from gruelling toil or enterprise or exploitation, or a combination of all three, were enjoying new freedoms and privileges, travelling the sea lanes on the luxurious vessels of the P & O and Orient Lines to spend their wealth on the delights of Europe. At this time of change, women in particular – though most did not realise or intend it – were moving towards an emancipation and sophistication they had never known before.

Part One

Chapter One

'QUIET!'

The childish shrieks cut off abruptly, even Phelim in his cot gulping down his cries at Brick O'Shea's shout, or perhaps simply at his presence, feet apart and glowering at his children from the nursery doorway. Celine took advantage of her brother's startled loosening of her hair to twist about and thump him and protests were renewed as Domi gripped and hung on, digging his nails into her skull with a savagery unusual in the good-tempered two-year-old. Twist and kick as she might Celine could not break free. She roared in such pain that Clodagh ran to part the pair, to be kicked in the shins for her pains.

'Leave them, I'll handle it.' Shaking the floor with his heavy boots their father strode to prise Dominic's baby fingers loose and slap Celine on her small defiant bottom. Fay Witherstone appeared panting from her run from Moll Noakes's quarters, where she had been relieving Nurse Puttering, for the racket was resounding through the house. Brick plumped both children in her arms. 'Cool them down in a tub.' He flung his arms wide to embrace his household. 'I'm taking your mother walking. Settle your differences or Fay will paddle you hard. She has my permission.'

Soothing the baby, Alannah sighed her satisfaction. At least when Brick appeared he acted fast and firmly, freezing rebellion with a few words. No one else could manage Celine. At three-and-a-bit she was a tiger cub when roused, as keen a fighter as the son he had expected; the catalyst of the house behaving outrageously when her father was by, aping his moods and manners. As a toddler at nursery play she would watch the door and, at his tread, stagger on unsteady baby feet to fling her arms about his legs, squealing her delight when he hoisted her high. She had followed him like a puppy, as if her mother was no longer in the room: Alannah provided the comforts and sustenance, Brick the excitement of life. Probably it would always be so, until someone else provided the stimulus. Yet those times Brick chastised her, and he often did, she fought back. She should indeed have been the boy Brick had expected with extravagant, ridiculous, yet heart-warming eagerness; this sophisticated worldly man in his late fifties, for all his many 'affairs' and previous marriages and rich mysterious life before she, Alannah, had become part of it, boasting no child of his own. He had acted like a man possessed, wandering the rooms and halls, getting drunk now and then, Alannah suspected, while she strove with his first-born. How quickly he had stifled his disappointment, yet not quickly enough for her not to have seen it in his face as he stared down at the plump baby girl. Finally, he'd held out a hand and watched the tiny fingers attempting to curl about his own.

'She'll have a strong grip. She'll do.'

He had been assuaged somewhat by Dominic's birth, yet his son was growing into a quiet and patient child, amiable to the point of appearing subservient, turning the pages of his rag books to stare long and hard at the illustrations. 'Bookish,' Puttering pronounced, as if the child were afflicted by measles, permanent at that. 'He's scarce out of the cradle,' Brick snapped, outraged. 'Maybe so, Mr O'Shea, but one can tell.' his slight limp always pronounced when angry. Imperturbable as ever, Brick stamped from the nursery, Dominic suffered Celine's teasing and tempers, even her ferocity when she wanted something badly, with good humour until goaded enough to fight back, as today. At least Phelim, barely five weeks in the world, slept his time away.

The baby was falling into an exhausted sleep as Brick held out his hand to his wife with the conspiratorial smile that meant escape. She rose slowly. Phelim's had been a difficult birth when he should have come easily into the world, for he was her fourth − discounting her pregnancy by Brick years earlier, the child aborted through Raunie O'Shea's jealousy and revenge . . . She cut off her thoughts of Brick's former wife for they avoided mention of her. 'It's over, Alannah. Long past. It's our life now.' He would dismiss any attempt to recall the violent deaths of their respective mates, perhaps because neither wished to speak of them. She straightened her body carefully. Fay must return to Moll's bedside and Clodagh would take over the nursery in their absence; at eight, her eldest was her stand-by.

They strolled the long verandah arm in arm. It was a fine spring day, a lull before the heat of summer. She dreaded the northern summers, particularly the bustle of Christmas through the worst of the heat, but bore all as part of her life with Brick. No one would ever know how she longed for a Sydney nor'easter, even the cold winds of Burrendah, her 'Place of the Swan', when the snow lay thick on the Southern Alps. She dragged slightly on Brick's arm and he glanced at her quickly, puzzled, for he had always dubbed her 'healthy as a young racehorse'; she could not explain her weakness, more, her sense of . . . panic? Absurd, for she had help in abundance, though she missed Fay sorely during the hours the girl devoted to Moll Noakes, Brick's foster-mother, old and paralysed, a vegetable in her bed, yet somehow hanging on. She, Brick's wife, should visit Moll more often, she knew it, but the days seemed to swallow her up. In any case, Moll discomforted her even now in her helplessness, for the old eyes followed every movement about her bed. Brick made up for her tardiness, never missing his daily visit to the sickroom when at Hawkes Plains. This she, his wife, understood and accepted for the bond between him and Moll went back to events, conflicts and emotions which she knew nothing about. Puttering was bewailing Fay's approaching marriage, but Brick had welded the match between Fay and Tod Buxton, his head stockman-manager, by promoting Tod to his outstation, Jubila, where a newly-furnished cottage, slab-walled and built on logs, awaited them. There was even a piano for Fay, which had been brought by dray from Brisbane to grace the parlour.

'Of course it's bribery but worth it to save our eardrums from her appalling attempts in our drawing-room – she can drive Tod insane instead. Anyway, she should be off bearing and rearing her own, she's coddled Will too long when he doesn't need or want coddling from her or from Clodagh; at nine, our Will has acquired more knowledge of the land than I have in a lifetime; a sweeping exaggeration, of course, yet he's like to pass me by in husbandry . . . *and* at striking a bargain. He tried to sell me his bean crop and when I laughed off his price he rode over to Yoolanowi, upped the price again and clinched the deal with Cowper. He has his father's cunning, no doubt of it.'

Brick was always absolute in his certainty of Will's parentage – Jamie Lorne O'Shea was Will's natural father and that was an end to the argument! 'Even if he were not I would still have adopted the child, I couldn't leave him to the mercies of that lushy old grandmother.' Poor Fay, with her special love for the babe she'd nurtured on the long and terrible journey from New South Wales to the new state of Queensland in fifty-nine. 'If I can't depend on the father I can on the son.' . . . 'Not as you see it,' Alannah would argue. 'Will wants to be a farmer, not a grazier.' . . . 'Agriculture? Nonsense. He's just making pin money, playing about with seeds. He knows this is sheep and cattle country and that when Tod goes I'll be counting on him, young as he is, at least until Dominic grows.'

Brick was adamant. He followed instincts and feelings in shaping his own life but believed in order, discipline and a certain logic in controlling the lives of those around him, even more so for his progeny. But logic was failing him now. There was self-deception . . . Alannah's weakness was somehow enhanced by his amazing energy. He was eager to have her at his side again, riding, managing the property, making decisions, above all back in his bed. In their life together she halted him in his stride as best she could for both knew he needed the brake of her. Even so, it did not stop him from filling his days with more and more of living.

They paused at a corner of the long verandah of the homestead, unfinished and largely unfurnished, crates of fittings and shelves and books, with the artefacts Brick picked up whenever the mood took him stacked, waiting for her energy and decision to sort it all out. It was defeating her: Brick never seemed to complete one project before beginning another, with, of late, his life and plans encircling without directly involving her. Along with the building of his town house he threatened to pull down Hawkes Plains and rebuild it in stone to match the most luxurious on the Downs such as Hallsmore

6

on the Condamine and Verity House on the Macintyre. These were veritable manor houses of long-established 'Downsmen', with billiard-rooms and ballrooms and lavish cellars, where they wore evening dress for dinner and held elegant boating parties . . .

'We'll go down to the stables. I've something to show you.'

It was a long time, too long, since they had ridden together with the joy and abandon of former years, for Hawkes Plains had fine horseflesh, augmented each time Bennett Muir added to Yoolanowi's stables, or those at his Brisbane villa. It was as if Brick must surpass the man in all things, with a good-humoured rivalry she felt was only skin deep, a patina. The one thing Bennett Muir could not do, which Brick would exult, in private to his credit, was flaunt a crowded nursery, indeed any nursery. The O'Sheas, he would boast to the world at large, to Alannah's horror, were a fertile pair!

The path meandered beside the orchard. They paused on the slight rise they called the Knoll with the Downs spread around them – flat when not gently undulating, black-soiled, rich and beautiful in distant horizons where gentle English trees signified one of the hundred or so homesteads and out-stations dotting the rolling grass-land along with scattered volcanic cones and watercourses flowing through black and red loams to join the blue-grass plains of the Condamine. Small wooden towns served the three million acres of the Darling Downs, with no fences as yet, no railways or roads, only talk of them. The Downs' seven-thousand-odd inhabitants were met with only at church, special celebrations, or at shearing-time. They were a hard-working conservative lot (excepting the fashionable Bennett with his horde of lackeys) and, despite the males spending their leisure at the Ipswich Club, placing their bets and devouring their pigeon pies, all of it provided but a taste of the closely-knit life she, Alannah, had lived and loved at Burrendah, Argyle County, New South Wales.

She had trained herself, or believed she had, not to dwell on her 'Place of the Swan' though today it seemed all about her. Weakness again? Though well-managed by Ida and Dan Charlton she sometimes wondered why her father kept Burrendah for he was seldom there, preferring the life of a mill-owner and MP in Sydney, held fast by his wife, Maria . . . was she being petty again? Hawkes Plains stretched to the horizon with acres added each time she bore Brick a child – and he would keep it all, he swore, despite the threat of 'selections' and the invasion of 'cocky' farmers; there was a savage acquisitiveness in his accumulation of land and wealth and children that disturbed her. She had no concrete plans for her children other than that they should have education enough to think for themselves and so gain the freedom she herself had demanded with a heady precociousness during her first years in Australia. It was possible to cast off old ties and traditions in this country as it had not been in Ireland, a country her children probably would never see or even wish to see. She had left Ireland behind long ago yet there were times when her childhood clung, as today, when she felt herself adrift in a sea of practical, shrewd, rabidly Protestant Scots.

To the south-west the Dennings' station, Glenaire, was hidden behind gentle rises of hills. North-east towards Drayton and Toowoomba they could distinguish through its shelter of trees the roof of Yoolanowi, the Bennett Muir property, their nearest neighbour. The station was managed by Ran Cowper, for Bennett Muir spent most of his time in Brisbane. He was an absentee squatter, too recently settled to be considered a true 'Downsman' yet accepted by the Queensland Club, jumping a long waiting-list to the surprise, even shock, of Brisbaneans. Even more surprising was his intention of standing for the Legislature – but money opened all doors, whispered the malicious and the envious, for Bennett Muir owned much real estate in Brisbane including prime sites on élite Wickham Terrace adjoining his town house and an import-export warehouse on Creek Street near the wharves. Brick could match Bennett's property holdings and might even surpass him in assets, but politics? Alannah's hand tightened on her husband's arm . . .

Since leaving Sydney Brick had avoided the political world; though long settled on the Downs could he, even if he wished, win out against the Assembly's majority of Scottish burghers in view of his reputation as a radical and, even more piquantly, with aboriginal forebears on his mother's side and Irish convicts on his father's? Brick made no secret of his 'touch of the tarbrush', as the prejudiced called it, indefinable as it was in him, for colour had long died out, so distant that he and Alannah had not expected or even looked for it in their children. In any case there was no sign of it in Celine's clear baby skin and greeny-blue eyes. Dominic certainly had his father's dark hair with the promise of his strong frame, and was likely to become a man of deep passions and convictions too, although held more deeply within himself. Phelim promised to be as fair as Clodagh. Yet they were all too young to be set in looks or character; they would know soon enough of their father's origins. 'If I don't tell them others will,' Brick insisted, 'and use it as a weapon against us all.' He spoke defensively as if even now, in another state and far removed from his old life and origins, the fact of his aboriginal grandmother marked him even without proclaiming itself in his children.

Alannah had not expected such a reaction from him; it both surprised and disturbed her, for she never gave his origins a thought. He was Brick, her lover and now her husband, and that was enough. She had believed he, too, had buried the knowledge deep. Yet parenthood changed people, bringing forth facets of personality either unknown or undeveloped. It had changed Brick in many ways, nothing maudlin or sentimental, he had never shown such traits, but he was even more positive, dogged, and feverish in his plans for Hawkes Plains and his current enthusiasm for a town house. This was ostensibly for herself and the girls when they were at school, later for Dominic and Phelim: governesses and tutors were well enough but his children must learn about the world and how to deal with it; they must confront Society or what passed for it here. His speculations about Society surprised her for it was a tradition he had always despised – Bennett rivalry again? The O'Sheas must not be known as 'country hicks'.

Perhaps, Alannah mused, this change in Brick, his headlong rush towards the future, was contributing to her own sense of pressure? She cared nothing for Brick's wealth, indeed for any material status – her small legacy from her grandmother gave her pin money enough – money did not touch her directly, in no way was it part of her life or plans except that it brought the comfort of cooling fans and window screens and feather beds and warm quilts for the stinging winters. Certainly it meant valuable help with the children, reminding her that she must talk with Miss Gundy at Glenaire who took Clodagh and Will three days a week together with the Denning children. Their lessons were supplemented by her own tutoring for Will was skipping classes to tend his gardens or break in a horse, or seek lost lambs for Dominic's care. And when Will lagged, Clodagh followed. Alannah saw her eldest daughter's devotion to Will as a kind of slavery for Clodagh would suffer snagged stockings and spotted pinafores in her efforts to keep pace with Will about the property when otherwise she was as neat as a pin. She would sit close by as Will turned his soil, or carved his beautiful little wooden figures of native animals and birds for Dominic, who had a shelf of them, handing him his tools with barely a glance from the pages she was reading aloud – Will's handmaiden, Brick called her. 'It's natural. They're close in age. They've grown up together.' But Alannah knew that with Clodagh it was more than a childhood bond, the girl felt secure in Will's surety about himself and his life, a competent self-sufficient boy who never wavered in his aims; even Brick whom he adored could not budge him as he straightened from his cabbage rows, his legs planted firmly in the heavy boots he prized, to speak his mind: no longer would he answer to the name of Willy Wilberforce, it was Will O'Shea or nothing. To her mother, Clodagh's attachment to Will was too full, too rounded, too complete; they formed an oddly assorted pair, the boy foundling Brick had adopted and the shy sensitive girl with her lace collars and ribbons tied just so, her clean pink nails and slender hands meant surely for piano lessons and embroidery frames and never for the harsh pioneering life. Her clean clear watercolours were a delicate version of the world around her. 'A Brisbane school and the sooner the better,' Brick decreed. 'Clodagh must make new friends. As a matter of fact that goes for them all.'

Alannah knew his sense of responsibility to her eldest child sprang from duty and concern for her, the mother, for Clodagh did not win people, so like her father in that. Brick was right, of course; in any case she was weary of coaching her reluctant brood, no doubt another symptom of her strange lethargy, one thing added to another until all became a burden. Just as there was too much of Hawkes Plains reaching to infinity, threatening in its size and importance yet only a minute part of the state of Queensland which seemed to be closing in on her – Queensland not only stretched before her, it loomed over her shoulder to an infinity of unknown jungles of fable and superstition, of gold rushes and cannibals, of violent coasts and shipwrecks and gold-crazy men forever trudging north – Jamie with them – murdering each other for a few ounces of gold dust, those who managed to escape the cooking-pots of the aboriginal tribes – that much was true, oh yes – yet how much else was rumour? Could anyone believe the tales Fay gleaned from the station-hands to pass on to an enthralled Will, with Clodagh's little shudder at appropriate times? Alannah doubted much of what Jamie recounted on his spasmodic returns to Hawkes Plains, for refuge, to hide from pursuers, or to wheedle settlement of his latest debt from his stepfather, even from herself, when she took a perverse pleasure in refusing him. She knew Jamie too well: a larrikin, an attractive one certainly, but still the vagabond. Brick indulged the man who had always used him badly in an attempt to be fair to his adopted children, alternating between generosity and blind rage at Jamie's latest transgression, just as he tried to be fair to Will, Jamie's natural son, even if Jamie hotly denied paternity. True, he had slept with Will's mother, Dora, Raunie's scullery-maid, but so had others. Will went on his stolid determined way seemingly ignorant of the arguments that raged between the men.

'How many more of your bastards must I take in?'

'I'm farming them out all over the north,' Jamie would grin. 'Spreading myself around, so to speak.'

They had been free of Jamie for almost a year but he could and would walk in without warning to cause disruption and often chaos. 'He's been seen around northern goldfields. Around the plantations too – why? What would he want with canefields around Maryborough? I can't see him dabbling in sugar, certainly not soiling his hands at cutting cane.' Brick had paused, frowning. 'There are too many involved in the slave-trade already.'

'Aren't there new regulations to deal with the Kanakas?'

'Easy to circumvent. The luggers are still sneaking around

the islands, tricking them aboard, signing them up for three years when the poor devils think it's only for a year, landing them at secret bays up and down the coast to sell them off cheaply. No matter how desperate cotton and sugar farmers are for labour there should not be trickery and exploitation. Trouble is, Jamie will stop at nothing for gambling money. He never has.'

The path was rough. Alannah paused, longing to turn back to the house but Brick's hand on her arm firmed; he was determined on the stables. She, as the matriarch of this oddly assorted household, could only wait for them all to grow in their individual ways and in their own time and absorb Hawkes Plains between them and so take the weight of it off her shoulders; for where Brick had made himself part of it, substitute for his beloved Erins Pride, she could not. She had tried, not only for his sake, reminding herself of its splendid gifts to her, the beauty of its soil, the riches of its great vistas, yet knowing she was not akin to it and feeling guilty because this was so. She had so much – she had Brick. They had waited long for each other, now they were welded by marriage, home, children, circumstance and time . . . She stumbled in her reverie and Brick lifted her over the stony patch.

'You're too light. You need feeding up.'

'You're not used to me without my nine months' burden.'

'I know this brood of yours can be heady but you must learn to take them less seriously.'

'Your brood too,' she flashed. 'After all, it's what you wanted.'

'I wanted this chaos?' His eyes widened.

'Part of founding your dynasty. Trouble is, they're too close, it all happened so quickly.'

'I had no time to waste. I'm creeping up on sixty.'

'Fifty-nine is not sixty. And you never creep up on anything. You pound your way.'

'Even so I'm an ageing sire. You choose to forget it.'

'It's easy to forget. I doubt that if anyone heard your years they'd remember. You have that effect.'

'I remember.'

'You've begotten three, isn't it enough? Your quiver, as

12

they say, is full.' She felt a sudden resentment and a queer panic. 'I don't want more.'

'What do you mean by that?'

'Children – I don't want more children.'

'Well now, I would have thought, since you still seem to believe in that God of yours, that you'd leave the deciding to Him.'

'I don't wish more children,' she repeated tightly.

'If you don't wish it,' he said slowly, 'then I must listen.'

'You don't always listen.'

'This is marriage, Alannah. Good God, it took me most of my life to come to it so I am acutely aware of the state. Children are part of the conjugal act. Don't blame me if I've become conditioned.'

'Then I must be the one to turn from the conjugal act,' she dared, hating herself for it sounded bald and final and of course impossible.

'Which means you must turn from me.'

She felt chill. Could she live without him? They did clash, she was conscious of it of late, yet the need of him was always there as was his need of her. 'No, oh *no*. Of course not.' She leant against him with a gesture of love and belonging. 'I can't be without you, I wouldn't exist – yet what am I to do? It's just that . . . Oh, I don't know what I'm saying.'

'No, you don't.' He held her tightly. 'I waited a long time for you, Alannah, now I can't get enough of you. The only way I got through that long wait was to make plans, to leap ahead of the separation. What do you think it was like for me with you married to Aldercott and bearing his child?' He had almost said 'brat', angry with himself for considering Clodagh so. After all, she was part of her mother.

'I know. I *do* know. But I have plans too, small ones perhaps, but mine, and I don't want them swallowed by . . . well, nursery meals and swaddling-clothes over and over again.'

'There's Marion Denning at Glenaire with her sixth – or is it seventh? They're such a clump they all look alike to me.'

'One a year between putting up her batches of redcurrant jelly. Is that what you plan for me?'

'Of course not if you don't. But children come. Why not? I can afford them.'

'I can't. At least not the way I feel now.' She laughed nervously, wary of him for he could be unpredictable; besides, his life stretched behind her, vivid, wild, secretive, full of rumours and conjecture and, because largely unknown, mysterious to her. He had lived and functioned without her in those thirty years before they had even met yet none of it mattered, he was the love of her life and she was weak and moody, even a little crazy perhaps on this bright spring day. Still she persisted: 'Why would you want more children? You have your own, and Will, and "always Jamie". And Clodagh — '

'You can't blame me for your eldest,' he said dryly, smiling, yet there was something almost spiteful in the remark. He had never liked Simon.

'I'm not "blaming". It's just that I don't see the need for more.' She couldn't stifle the passion and rebellion in her voice. It broke. He turned her about to face him.

'I have no ambitions to be simply a stud but this . . .' he flung an arm wide, 'must go on, ideally to sons – oh Will will get his share, even Jamie though he's had more than enough from me already, he bleeds me dry every time he turns up with his gambling debts, and the women he thinks I should pay off or keep and for all I know more of his bastards to be thrown on our doorstep. The girls will be well provided for, you know that. But this land must be worked by my sons and hopefully loved by them. I gave up much for this.'

'I know what you gave up – you left Erins Pride. But it's still there.'

'I made my choice so enough of such talk. I gained much.' He turned up her chin, forcing her to meet his eyes. 'You're well, aren't you? Pale, a little weak I suppose, but it will pass. Doc Abercrombie assures me so.'

'I don't *want* to turn away.'

'You would really turn from me?'

In one way his surprised query was reassuring as to the security of their marriage yet he was not considering her feelings, her reaction, her problems. 'I did once.'

'Oh, *that*!' He laughed, then was serious. 'You were pregnant by me, I couldn't marry you, so you married Aldercott. We decided to let all that die and deal with our marriage now – though I confess I'm damned if I know how to deal with the way you're talking and acting.' He snapped his fingers. 'You're coming to town with me. A complete change. There are things to do in Brisbane.'

'I don't think — '

'You'll feel different once you're in the saddle again. We can ride together in Brisbane just as well as here.'

He was leading her towards the stables in a rush of words slurring into horse-talk on which she tried to concentrate. Perhaps it was impossible to make him understand how circumstances, surroundings, small fears, shaped a woman's response to a man; perhaps, no matter what one said or did or how experienced the man, the conceiving and bearing would always be woman's work and woman's conniving. Somehow, she had connived two years before Phelim. But now the practicalities of their bedding were urgent and must involve him more. The whole thing, her life, took her breath away: the suddenness of widowhood, her remarriage, her pregnancies in quick succession after her years of longing for Brick that were only assuaged by Simon's thoughtfulness, Clodagh's birth and her beloved 'Place of the Swan' – until that world had changed suddenly and tragically . . .

They had been driving home to Burrendah from Wiena, the Elston property – herself, Simon, and three-year-old Clodagh in a time of great storms. George Elston had managed to get a message through begging her to come post-haste; his wife Daisy had fallen from her horse (bound to come a cropper sooner or later, she never did learn to sit a horse properly, Hetty Witherstone of Erins Pride had pronounced). The doctor could not be found, cut off by swollen streams no doubt, and Daisy was hysterical with a broken leg and, it seemed, other injuries, with her daughters as distraught as their mother (useless pioneering stock, the only thing keeping them from disaster is Daisy's money), and Hal and Roy out trying to save stock. The rain eased a little and the wind dropped so they took the trap, with one valise for all for they must stay over till the doctor arrived. Clodagh would not be left, in any case she was a shy child and a few days at Wiena might be good for her. Alannah managed to ease Daisy's fears and calm George, noisy and ineffectual where Daisy was concerned. His sons finally turned up with Dr Marsh and all suffered the drama of setting Daisy's leg.

By that time storm clouds were banking up again and they decided not to delay but take the track by the Creek where the swans glided, cross the old bridge and reach Burrendah by the back road. They stopped at the bridge to spell the horse when, incredibly, horrifically, it happened – a flash flood, a rushing surging wall of water overflowing to wash away banks and fill the Creek with debris and logs swirling in a thick brown liquid. They had forgotten, if they ever knew, what all bush children were taught: never camp in or near a creek bed; a flash flood could destroy all before it. Water swept them from solid ground, stunning them, and all Alannah could do was snatch up her daughter and strain to reach Simon. Before they could touch, she and Clodagh were swirling in muddy foaming log-filled water, screaming for Simon, or rather it was she who was screaming, for Clodagh was rigid and silent in her arms as she struggled to keep their heads above water, glimpsing as in a nightmare the horse and trap surge past and Simon clinging to a log. He was pushing it towards them, paddling with a frantic one-handed desperation. It was then she remembered with horror that he could not swim. Yet in the end it was the whirling water that saved her and Clodagh as she clutched at passing branches, logs, trees, anything to break their rush; their exhausted bodies were swirled into a quiet pool. Simon was washed close, still clinging to his log, striving to push it near . . . Suddenly he was not there, caught up in a rush that missed herself and Clodagh. She screamed his name and went on screaming and the shivering child joined in, screaming, not 'Papa', not 'Father', but 'Simon', 'Simon', echoing her mother. The childish shrieks went on and on with more than childish strength and Alannah knew she would never forget those screams from her child that were not quite human. Nor would she forget Clodagh's unblinking fear-filled eyes. Somehow she scrambled up the bank, prised off the child and dived in again and again but it was useless, Simon was gone, nothing was there but freezing foaming water and Clodagh's screams until the child sank whimpering on the sodden earth.

The men found Simon's body next day far downstream. There was a deep cut on his forehead; that, more than the drowning, had killed him, the men were certain of it. They said he looked angry. Simon angry? He had been confused by a country he did not understand and had only embraced because of her, but angry? She had rarely seen him so. Then Brick had come and she had left all to him, she could do nothing else, and there had not been what her Aunt Delia, complaining from her management of Simon's Bridge Academy in Sydney, called a 'decent interval'. Brick would wait no longer and marry they did, Brick determined to block the tragedy from her mind. Yet it returned at strange unexpected moments, as today, while she stood beside him looking over Hawkes Plains and the Darling Downs. The shadows were lengthening. It would soon turn chill.

'The Muirs would love to have you at Foxburgh.'

'Not Foxburgh House. In any case, Phelim's too young to travel. And I couldn't leave him.'

She was stubborn and remote. He shrugged, 'Then I must go without you. The *Palliser* is due in so I'll be away at least a week according to her docking. Meanwhile, get more rest. And when I come back . . .' He kissed her hard, holding her lips until they parted under his and she trembled as she had not dared to do. 'That's better.' He smiled. 'Trust me, girl. All will be well, it shall be exactly as you wish. Now, come see your new mare. She's a beauty.'

17

Chapter Two

'HE'S A fine mount, sir! Spirited. The only thing of yours I truly envy.'

'Not my beautiful and spirited wife, Sam?'

'Ah now, Mr O'Shea, that goes without saying, for all Brisbane, to say nothing of the Downs, is desolate Mrs O'Shea's spoken for.'

'Then I'll leave you Jannali, if not my wife, in my will.'

'I'd have to wait too long for the beast,' Sam roared his delight. 'I've never seen ye more fighting fit.' At Brick's nod towards Gondola, Sam nodded back. 'Leave him, Mr O'Shea, he's used to me. I'll put him to work with the hosses.'

Brisbane was accustomed to, if always suspicious of, O'Shea's hunchback groom riding in his wake for Brick took Gondola wherever he could to keep him out of trouble. The Italian worked happily enough at Hawkes Plains, cracking his whip at the hands who thought him a great joke. Will managed him well but there were times – and always when Jamie Lorne O'Shea rode in – when Gondola disappeared, the last time to join a circus camped in Toowoomba, in search of the communal life that had brought him from Naples in the first place, to finish up in the O'Shea household. 'He'll be back,' Brick assured Will. 'He goes his own kind of walkabout, but no circus holds him for long, he knows I'll come hunting him out.'

Pleased with his day, with his stallion, and his disposal of Gondola for a few hours since Isabel Muir barely disguised her horror of the Neapolitan and Brick would not risk her antagonism today, he mounted his five-year-old. The horse was a fit replacement for Glenora who had plodded faithfully when he couldn't gallop or canter overland to the Darling Downs and was now out to stud. As they trotted into George Street Brick raised his whip in salute to Hanson, his host at the small but comfortable Belle Vue Hotel. The January heat hit him in the face and he paused a moment before resuming at a walk for he had plenty of time. The air would be cooler by the river so he turned right, then down Alma Street beside the Botanical Gardens; he would turn west along Edward Street and take his time uphill to the Terrace. The city was spreading out, a very different place from the squalid settlement of swamps and felons he had first seen, even from the rough port struggling out of its swaddling-clothes of a decade before. The river and its docks were busy, the city fathers planning bridges across to Kangaroo Point, and making a hell of a mess in the building of them. There was even an elegance about parts of the city radiating from Wickham Terrace with its fine views and breezes. He cared nothing for pomp and show, he never had (except, he smiled to himself, when it suited his immediate aims), he belonged to the land and always would, but here at the close of the eighteen-sixties his life had filled out again: he possessed a wife in place of mistresses, with children of his own – Brick O'Shea, respectable family man! Well . . family man anyway. How the assorted cronies of his rip-roaring past would laugh. Sometimes, contemplating his marital status the thick blanket of its conventions stifled, at other times he exulted in his possession not only of worldly goods but human beings of his own blood, bringing, he admitted, new urges with new powers to his life. Age lessened a man, a man shrank in more ways than the physical as he grew older, but in the place of his rambling roistering youth was a dynasty and he found the same kind of satisfaction in Hawkes Plains as he had in the roots of his early life – Erins Pride, the station it had been so hard to leave. But the Pride remained. It was *there*. And here in Queensland he had built a new station, a new Erins Pride, and all he acquired would be passed on for safekeeping to his sons.

Now he would build a showplace, not because it was fashionable to boast of a town house but for practical reasons. It would be a convenience when he must be in Brisbane to attend to banking, stock sales, supplies, shipping; again, with a home in Brisbane Alannah might favour the city more, particularly when the girls were at school, and later, the boys, for there was now a Brisbane Grammar not too distant in Roma Street, to the building of which he'd subscribed heavily. The villa site he wanted was close to the old convict Windmill, now the Brisbane Observatory. Bennett would drive a hard bargain for it but in the end they both knew he would pay. Meanwhile, they would bargain. He looked forward to the tussle.

Would it please Alannah? She had been difficult of late, elusive, seeming to shrink visibly from social contacts. She had never been a social creature but it was important that she changed, if only for the girls' sake. She did not like Isabel Muir. Few 'liked' Isabel, there was nothing as tepid as 'like' in one's reaction to her, people admired Isabel or went in awe of her or hated her outright. She was a woman who provoked strong feelings: a *clever* woman was the only explanation some could give, as if she displayed a birthmark of brain-power. But Isabel Muir was pleasant, even gracious to the mothers of her pupils, more so to the mothers of potential students, so what more did his wife want? He needed her beside him in Brisbane, socially, to employ a word he detested, but she always had some excuse – she did not feel strong enough, Phelim was too young to travel. Next month perhaps. Next year . . .

To escape a twinge of irritation he spurred Jannali, almost forcing the horse into a wagon. Irritation rode with him. Alannah was evasive in other ways too. In his moves towards his wife and their 'connubial couch', as he sometimes jocularly termed it, there was a holding off and it maddened him; his patience, certainly his physical well-being, was suffering. He could not, would not, force her, but then he had never been obliged to do so; he had never known sexual hesitation in a woman, it was something new in his life for Raunie had been an eager woman and he, perhaps more than most men, gravitated towards the sexually aggressive. Yet it was not fair to compare them; besides, he had not loved his former wife with the contentment, the satisfaction and fulfilment with which he loved Alannah – with Raunie there had been torment. Again, Raunie had not conceived by him or by any other man since she had borne Jamie; she had failed in that one thing, and maybe it was just as well although it had roused her jealousy to a terrible destructive savagery. Perhaps marriage itself brought moods: he was less than enchanted by the state yet it was necessary to provide for children, home and so on. And God dammit, wasn't he doing all possible to please her, riding through a heat barrier to do business with a hardened adversary for one of the best home sites in Brisbane to build her a house fit for a queen – like Burrendah if she wanted it so, all green shutters and white paint, furnished in Regency style, anything she liked, he did not care. He was building a dynasty and he needed her.

Nevertheless . . . he could not, dared not, plan too far ahead. It was actually a physical hurt to peer closely into the future, he did not have time on his side; fifty-nine creeping on sixty with thirty years between himself and his young wife. She would never know how often he found it daunting . . . If he shaved off his beard and cut his hair he might look younger? He put back his black head and laughed so loudly at his vanity that aborigines squatting on the corner of Queen Street stirred from their lethargy to stare after him. He was an elder of the city, a burgher, a married man, a father three times over, as well as foster-father, stepfather or whatever, to others. A man with roots and still amazed at it for until now he had never wanted children; his life had consisted of immediates, of urgent purposes, then later had emerged the deep and pungent reason why he left paternity to others: he was the 'nigger', the quarter-caste, the one with the 'touch of the tarbrush' since his old enemy, Major Merrill, father of Barbara whom he had hoped to marry, had revealed (before he, O'Shea, had known of it) his ancestry in a bid to ruin him. For a time Merrill had succeeded: he, O'Shea, had run from the knowledge until he found he could no longer hide and in doing so the fact ceased to be important, for those who knew came to accept and hold it to themselves, and those who did not know never guessed. One thing he and Alannah had agreed upon: their children must and would be told when they were old enough to understand and hopefully to accept the fact that their great-grandmother had been a full-blood aborigine. He would handle the truth for his descendants and then teach them to handle it for themselves, for in Queensland, where squatters were at war with native tribes more volatile, aggressive and savage than in the south, the contrast was greater between the aborigines and the more formally educated and Protestant settlers – Good

21

God, they were Scots! As they saw it, Blacks must be kept in their place whereas in the south there had grown healthy pockets of acceptance. He narrowed his eyes against the glare wondering if Bennett knew – but enough of conjecture. He was building a future with a beloved if presently edgy and contrary wife and a mixed bag of a family defying him even in babyhood, all but that dignified miss of a Clodagh . . . He never knew, quite, what his stepdaughter was thinking even when her grey eyes met his full on. He sensed she was wary of him, but then she seemed wary of so much and so many. He was never at ease with her; Alannah indulged her, her excuse being that the child had suffered a great shock at her father's death, which of course was true.

'She still stammers.'

'Rarely now, and then only in unusual situations or faced with strangers she doesn't trust. She'll grow out of it.'

'You hope she will, as you say of everything you haven't time or the wish to confront.'

'I've never had to "confront" children before, adopted or my own. We shall try Clodagh at Miss Muir's Educational Establishment for Young Ladies – even while I shudder at mouthing all that every time we need to discuss it.' Despite its air of pompous sobriety and inflexibility Isabel Muir's school would help Clodagh Aldercott relate to strangers in a world beyond Will O'Shea. Clodagh would never be counted among the female reformers despite her mother's early and desperate rebellions; she had Alannah's slim fairness and more than a dash of her damnable remoteness but the girl's conservatism and precise formality were her father's. He, Brick, could not visualise sharing a joke with the girl, or racing her on a favourite mare or watching her climb trees as Celine tried to do even now. Clodagh would do what was required of her for her mama's sake, for he doubted the girl cared if she pleased him or not; he felt she seldom thought of him, they were reasonable with each other – no more. She would do the right and proper thing then return to her beloved Will to follow him about, sloughing through mud or dust or whatever happened, to brush herself down calmly at the end . . . where other times she moved through life as a freshly-watered daisy. She would watch over her half-brothers and half-sister, scold them, find them when lost or needed and read to Dominic as the child turned his pages with an instinctive sense of the right moment to do so . . . At the thought of Dominic he spurred Jannali again in a kind of baffled anger. Books! He had trunks of them ready to take their rightful place in his children's life, but Dominic was his own son, his eldest, and had a destiny beyond his library. Dominic O'Shea would be groomed to take over the O'Shea properties, the O'Shea wealth, above all, the O'Shea ambitions.

But what, Alannah would ask disconcertingly, if Dominic chooses to be a seaman or an architect or, far more likely, a doctor, human or animal, for he's always tending lost lambs and other injured creatures? Or, she would add with that directness that was part of her, if he chooses to be simply a scholar hoarding useless trivia? What if he doesn't give a fig for your acres – and don't talk morbidly, she would tease, you'll live for ever. She would kiss him and go back to brushing her hair while he brushed off her queries with his qualms. All will be Dominic's with a goodly slice for Phelim and another for Will. As for 'always Jamie' . . . well, we'll settle Jamie's future when we must – or when he comes to us, cap in hand.

The firing of the one o'clock gun broke into his thoughts. Brisbane stirred from its midday lethargy, rolled over and snoozed again. 'It amuses the children,' Bennett excused the ritual as if he knew everything about children. 'And those who don't even know what day it is can check their watches.' A single flag on the flagpole meant the mail-ship was at the mouth of the Brisbane River – the flag was there. He turned on to the Terrace, the road still a dusty track each side of the Windmill-Observatory. A faint breeze tempered the day, indeed, all the villas beginning to line the Terrace caught refreshing draughts-through in summer, shimmering the gardens where trees were beginning to grow. A fine location where women were wont to stroll with their children and lap dogs and, but a short carriage drive from the town centre, hansom cabs could drive up and take young families to and from school. He dismounted and stood looking south to the low and distant hills that hid the sea. Directly below him was the thick brush of the reserve with the Normal School at its centre. Beyond it tracks meandered to straight-as-a-die George Street with its scattered cottages, and the neat fences characteristic of Brisbane. Across the river that divided his vision, South Brisbane, formerly a nothing of a place with scattered habitations and a couple of hotels, was filling up. Someone had once said that Brisbane lacked the two great essentials in scenery: church spires and snow-topped mountains. But there was water . . . 'devoid of which the finest landscape is but as a beautiful woman with her eyes put out'. A distasteful simile yet a true one.

He tethered Jannali in shade to crop what growth there was for he meant to stay only long enough to clinch the deal – and knew he was simply 'putting off'. For some reason he could never quite define he always hesitated before the imposing entrance to the even more imposing Foxburgh House. 'Native names do well enough for sheep-stations, town houses should reflect home': 'home' clearly an affectation with the Muirs for there were areas of his native Scotland, Bennett had once stated, surely in an unguarded moment, that he did not care to see again – and that went for parts of California too. 'I wonder why,' Alannah would muse. Brushing aside his hesitancy Brick went briskly up the steps to face a barrage of servants: yes, the master and Miss Muir had finished luncheon and were taking coffee. So! He had timed it perfectly, otherwise Bennett would have had leisure over the meal to attempt to distract him from the business in hand. Beyond the ornate entrance the place was even more imposing, irritating him with its opulence. Brisbane boasted too many *nouveaux riches* putting on 'fronts', hoping to compete with the south, in particular with Melbourne, though most Brisbaneans had never been there nor were they likely to go. Sometimes he wondered why he bothered with the Muirs, or why they concerned themselves with the O'Sheas, yet how, even if they wished it, could they avoid each other? Brisbane was small with its suburbs just beginning to take shape and the Downs still sparsely settled. Compatible or not they were stuck with each other.

He suffered the pomposity of the maid's formal announcement while Isabel rustled from her chair. All women rustled in these days of stiff folds and loops of skirts but no woman he knew rustled quite like Isabel Muir, part of her curriculum no doubt in the training of Queensland's privileged daughters. His own girls would learn to rustle with the best, at least Clodagh would, with Celine more likely to thump or slouch her entrances and exits from bravado or rebellion. Taffeta and velvet shimmered and Brick visualised the woman moving silkily along halls to enter classrooms, her long fingers (why did they conjure up an impression of claws?) held an instant on knobs to enable her victims to draw themselves up at their desks. Isabel was garbed for a life of inspections, greetings and goodbyes, not only at her school but here in her brother's house conveniently located so that she could keep an eye on her boarders staying on in vacation. He thought she looked particularly fine today: a thin striking-looking woman in her forties with a certain flamboyancy even while impeccably groomed. She wore gowns made by clever seamstresses and her hair was dressed by exclusive hairdressers as befitted the mistress of a select seminary for young ladies, an establishment every householder and squatter revered as preparing their offspring, hopefully, for a Swiss finishing school, and for the less ambitious or the frugal, a Belgian convent. And his Celine? Blissfully unaware as yet that she was the daughter of a native-born self-made descendant of aborigines and Irish convicts – a 'coloured' to use a term drifting over from South Africa – a man notorious for his radical views in a world of Pure Merino snobs, with the Muirs the worst of them. Damn the Scots! Why didn't they stay with their lochs and crumbling castles or whatever misery sent them drifting? If one could ever say a Scot drifted!

And what of the youngest Muir, the actress Eva, heard of but not yet seen? To Queensland's fundamentalists, actresses, even serious actresses, were not *de rigueur*. The stage was a device of the Devil – yet even believers wondered about her. At times an English newspaper hot off a ship reported her latest triumph, or a theatre magazine would be passed around, or a friend writing from London and aware of the colonial Muirs would detail her latest tour: playing Rosamund in *As You Like It* or considering the role of Juliet or aspiring to play Portia. No mediocre or common actress this, which confused even more, but an actress excelling in interpretations of Shakespeare's women. There was a current rumour that she was considering a Melbourne season with a circuit of Victorian towns before playing in Sydney – would she come farther north? Shakespeare for sailors and tradesmen at the old Royal Alexandra in Edward Street? Surely there would not be enough *petit bourgeois* to support her at the Royal Victoria in Queen Street? There had been Shakespearean productions but no actresses of her calibre. The Muirs were noncommittal; they had not heard from their sister in a long time and knew nothing of a colonial tour, giving the impression they would rather not welcome an actress into the family. He could, Brick reflected with some malice, remind Isabel that a schoolmistress, even the head of an exclusive girls' school, was but one step up from a lowly household governess.

Bennett flicked an imperative hand – a hand too smooth, surely, to have wielded pick and shovel on the fields of California as rumoured – at the maid to bring coffee. Brick bowed over Isabel's hand with the faintly mocking gesture he knew amused her while he had the feeling, often there, that he had interrupted an argument, for tension was in the room, if a careful tension. He wondered, admiring Isabel's rings, what the two were like when alone. Did they argue like careful well-bred Kilkenny cats? He had no war with Isabel, he had no feeling for her whatsoever, which was odd since all women affected him one way or another. She was simply a 'schooly' and the 'grande dame' of a residence of expensive and fashionable possessions, all fixed, heavy and immutable, as if they were there as forerunners to proclaim their owners' success and wealth – but alluring, exotic and sexually exciting Isabel was not. She returned his gesture with a faint and condescending smile and he pitied the pupil who might dare to practise guile upon her.

He drank coffee beside Bennett at the cold and empty grate, looking down slightly on the man, which gave him pleasure. Yet Bennett Muir was wide-shouldered and strong-looking, with enough good looks to be called handsome, always expensively groomed even at Yoolanowi, a quicksilver man with a wry sharp wit, easy and confident among men – with women? 'Suave,' was how Alannah described him, sometimes adding 'slippery'. That was as may be but he did make his presence felt; men were stimulated by him, women attracted, except it

26

seemed Alannah O'Shea. In a purely emotional reaction Brick resented the man's youthful appearance for Muir could give him a good ten years, more perhaps dammit, and considering the fact Brick hated himself. Bennett Muir made up his mind instantly and acted on decisions as quickly, and in dealing with him Brick played safe for one could never quite pin the man down, part of his charm some asserted, certainly his success said others. Where Brick confronted, Bennett Muir evaded. 'A secret man,' said Alannah. 'I can't explain, there's just something . . . something . . .' Curious, if one dwelt upon it, how little anyone really knew of him.

Brick's own meeting with Muir had been through dramatic and public business: one morning in July of sixty-six, the Bank of Queensland had put up its shutters. Other banks followed, repercussions of the land boom of sixty-two: until then land had been subdivided and sold as wanted and always privately, and the sudden manipulation of land brought bankruptcy to many. Brick had anticipated the crash, so presumably had Bennett Muir, for though both over speculated they had the wealth to surface and survive, indeed Brick had picked up Jubila for a song. No one seemed certain how Bennett Muir had made his money – Californian gold-mines was the logical and favourite explanation – but he had been heard to say in his cups, a rare occurrence, that the Australian colonies had been good to him, then would add with one of his grandiose gestures that the Muirs had given much to the colonies. Curiously, for he must be aware of her antagonism, he openly admired Alannah, inviting the O'Sheas to Foxburgh at every opportunity with Alannah always refusing. Brick was determined her rebuttals must cease; he and Bennett Muir were competitors with their wool but in Brisbane and its commercial life they were equals. They loathed each other, each knew that, but they were citizens of an up-and-coming if raw new state and were akin in making the most of it.

It was then that Brick noticed the portrait in an elaborate gilt frame over the mantel of a fair young woman with bare shoulders and beautiful lips. He wondered why he had not noticed it before. Perhaps it was newly hung . . . He stared, intrigued, until Bennett followed his eyes. 'Yes, it's Eva. Painted when she was in her twenties.'

'By an inferior artist,' Isabel snapped and Brick knew they were resuming the argument interrupted by his arrival, words held back until triggered by the mention of their sister.

'I can't and won't argue with your professional judgment,' Bennett drawled, 'but it was much thought of at the time. I'll admit it was an expensive indulgence but it did help Eva's career.'

'It should not be openly displayed. Certainly not here.'

'So you have told me many times.'

'It's too . . . too . . .'

'Revealing was your word. We can't leave it gathering dust in the storeroom, Eva would be offended. Come now, Bel — '

'*Isabel!* You know I detest abridged names, particularly my own, and particularly before others.'

'Before a friend?' He was amused and mocking. He turned to answer the query in Brick's eyes. 'Eva's on her way to Australia, we had confirmation last week. She'll be at sea now on the *Gerbera* bound for Melbourne. She wrote nothing about a northern tour but if she should come to Brisbane it could not be for months yet. As well, for she'll miss the worst of the heat.'

'She will have to get used to the climate. We all do. You spoil her, Bennett.'

'Difficult, surely, since we haven't seen each other in eight years.'

'I do not wish Eva here at Foxburgh House.'

'She will expect it, and so will Brisbane. She's the prima of her company and, I understand, works very hard. If she comes north she stays with us.'

'She's too old to play Juliet.' Isabel's voice took on a petulant tone. 'Juliet Capulet was only fourteen.'

'Any actress worth her salt knows how to shed years on and off stage.' He set his cup firmly in the saucer; both seemed to have forgotten Brick's presence. 'This town sees so few celebrities it will gawp even if it doesn't approve. We must do our best for her.'

'She's more a scandal than a celebrity and you know it.'

'There are always rumours involving actresses.'

'Her affair with Lord Glanville was more than rumour.'

'You cannot be certain. If true, why her suit for libel?'

'Which she withdrew. Wisely, I'd say.'

'If she comes here, Bel, I'll need you as hostess.'

'The parents of my girls abhor contact with the theatre – except perhaps the classical.'

'What do you call Shakespeare?'

'Shakespeare or not, all anyone will notice are her limbs.'

'Legs, Bel – *legs*! As I've told you many times it's all settled so put a pleasant face on it. My letters will be waiting in Melbourne. I expect you to write her a welcome.'

'I have no time to hostess levées and teas and such. Even in vacation I have students to supervise.'

'Put that lazy staff of yours to work. We must finish with a grand ball. You can vet the guest list, who better at weeding out unsuitables? Good for your school too with a chance to put your girls on display. You'll have them all a-twitter.'

'My girls make their debuts at appropriate times.'

Bennett turned abruptly to Brick. 'You must persuade Mrs O'Shea – Alannah – to visit. Bring the whole family.'

'I'm sure Alannah won't need persuading,' Brick murmured, doubting his words. He would do his own persuading, anything to distract her from her determination to take the children south; she had talked of nothing else for weeks. He had tried to reason with her; if she felt the relatively short trip to Brisbane difficult how could she face a mass migration south? Well, she'd take Meg of course, and Fay if she were willing; surely Fay would want to see her father and stepmother before she married? He was confident Fay Witherstone cared not a jot about seeing her parents, her head as full of her piano and her new home as of Tod. But his arguments could not sway Alannah, not even his assurance that all was well in the south; he received regular reports from Erins Pride as well as news of Burrendah. She would stay with Aunt Delia at the Academy for the children most likely would be too much for Papa at Brighton – meaning that his wife, Maria, would not want his family around. Was it so unusual for a woman to want to show her children – his children too – to relatives she had not seen for years? Brick knew her deepest longings were to ride Burrendah's hills . . . He was shaken out of his reveries by Isabel rustling majestically from her chair.

'I have housekeeping to discuss.'

'The maids are slow.'

'I shall attend to it.' With her hand on the doorknob Isabel paused and Brick thought her fingers even more clawlike with her rings flopping around them. 'My regards to Mrs O'Shea.' Strictly formal with the mothers of her future pupils. As she swished out the door Bennett moved briskly to the decanters.

'The sun's well over the yardarm. Brandy, I think.'

Brick nodded, his eyes on the faint cryptic little smile about Eva Muir's painted lips. Yet with his first sip of Bennett Muir's excellent brandy and his first draw on a fine Havana his mind clicked over to matters of land and finance and title deeds . . . He would need all his wits and more to as much as break even with Bennett Muir.

'You've always been jealous of your sister.' Bennett swept a stack of papers impatiently from his desk into a drawer.

'Why would I be jealous of Eva? We each have our own world and work. We haven't met or even corresponded since I saw her off to join you in San Francisco and I returned to that horrid attic in Bayswater to freeze, a time I shall never forget. You didn't offer to pay my passage to join you, you had no use for me. You and Eva had years together in America while I went from London to country vicarage and back again teaching a succession of arrogant prideful brats. You, far less Eva, couldn't imagine what my life was like in those years. You never cared. It was always Eva. *Eva!*'

'If you're not jealous you sound it. Come Bel, I brought you out and set you up in your school.'

'Because you knew I had the education to make a success of one. What would you know of the nights I burned candles over German and French, even Greek? Besides, it added to your so-called respectable career to have a sister as schoolmistress. Now I educate and launch upon society the daughters of the wealthy and I won't let you ruin my school.'

'Why would I ruin what I helped build?'

'I don't know exactly . . . only that I don't quite trust you.'

'You have no choice but to trust me. If it weren't for me you'd be out on the Downs as governess to other "arrogant prideful brats" as you call them.'

'There are other ways to involve my school and my reputation. There is scandal.'

'What are you talking about?'

'You're too open in your admiration of Alannah O'Shea.'

'Alannah?' He laughed. 'Nonsense. I'm polite, no more. After all, we are neighbours. Friends, to all intents and purposes.'

'You invite her here to stay. You're always enquiring about her. When you do meet your eyes never leave her; you are obsessed with that smug and pallid young matron, which I find rather odd; I always thought your taste ran to the exotic, even the common.'

'Alannah O'Shea stands for something in the community.' He was thoughtful and serious. 'For one thing, her father is a prominent and respected MP.'

'Ah . . . I was forgetting. You have ambitions. Furthermore, I hear she is a comfortably off woman in her own right.' She ignored his flush. 'But take care, Bennett. The lady has a jealous husband. He's a controlled man but I pity the one who crosses him, particularly where his wife is concerned. I will not have myself or my school involved in intrigue. Don't endanger us. I warn you – don't.'

Chapter Three

BRICK LEFT Moll's·quarters reluctantly yet with a sense of finality, even of relief for the old woman could not last much longer. She was noticeably weaker, yet how she clung to life, as he clung to her, perhaps simply because he was accustomed to the shapeless body in the bed, only her eyes following him as they'd followed him all his life. He would sit beside her and talk, not certain if she heard for she could not answer, only make odd pathetic little grunts. He would tell her of the children, sometimes take Phelim along, briefly, for the child grew fidgety. Tonight as he sat beside her she had dropped off and only then did he realise how late he had left his visit.

Always disturbed when he left his foster-mother, tonight he was also restless, a mood he was well aware was unfair to his wife. Alannah was brushing her hair before her mirror with long languid strokes he knew were intended to prolong her toilette; she took an inordinate time over it of late until, impatient, he would hold out an imperative hand for the brush. He hated doing so, he had never had to command her to bed with him, but since Phelim's birth it was so and it bothered him. She had taken to caring for her hair as never before, brushing it with a grace he could find intriguing, but not tonight, not now. The strokes were rhythmic, almost mesmeric, as if she had all the time in the world for all matters but himself, which not only daunted him, it halted him. If she had time to dawdle the night away he had not. She did not turn as he entered, or as he undressed and drew his robe about him loosely for the humid summer weather was hanging on, there had been a sharp storm and despite the open French doors, her throat gleamed with moisture. She put down her brush and opened her fan, closing her eyes against its gentle swish of air. The simple action broke some sort of spell, something luxurious and sensual in the cloying night and he

32

realised with a shock how unworldly and inexperienced was this woman, girl really, who loved to think she had gained emancipation and independence because she had managed to cast off a few old-world conventions, a formal religion, and the influences of a martinet of an aunt and a protective father. She was still a country girl with an uncomfortable longing, not for Ireland but for the home she had left in New South Wales. Well, he too had broken ties. She must do the same or they had no real future. Perhaps, and the idea made him shudder, not even an expression of love. He said urgently:

'Wickham Terrace catches every breeze. You'll like it.'

She did not answer. He felt disappointed and too vulnerable in the silence. She had shown so little interest in the town house that he had been obliged to go ahead with his decisions. He needed to make love to her through this long hot night, to kiss and fondle her, fill her belly to bursting with himself; yet even if he did there would be something lacking, there always was now, something not quite right, something that had been there and was mislaid. Or if there still he could not rouse it. He'd never known physical evasion in a woman; women had always been there for his pleasure, as had Alannah but now her passion was missing. She submitted, that was all. He wanted her not merely to respond but to initiate, rousing him, which was easy, and herself to a sweet physical exhaustion. He'd been forced to wait a long time for this woman, now his wife, as he'd never waited for any other woman in his life. The trouble was, he wasn't accustomed to the ways of wives despite Raunie. Alannah was occupied, even obsessed with other issues as Raunie had never been. Yet he must be fair; Raunie had not borne his children in quick succession. She took up her brush again though she knew he was waiting, and as if she resented his watchful eyes on her she said in a rush:

'The Muirs will be close. Too close.'

'You can't keep avoiding them. Besides, you may not like your neighbours wherever you live. Indeed, in your present mood you don't seem prepared to like anyone.'

'I am never at home with men of business.'

'You were at home with your father.'

'That's different.'

'No, it is not different. Moreover, you've managed to be at

33

home with me at various times.' And could not help adding with acidity, 'In the past.'

'You work on the land, Bennett doesn't. Bennett Muir is a dilettante squatter. A pastoral snob.'

'He oversees his properties.'

'Everything is an investment to him.'

'And not to me?'

'Not exactly. There's a certain understanding in what you do. A philanthropy.'

'Because I adopted waifs and strays? And ran a foundling school?'

'You did more. You gave a great deal of money and time to finding places in life for those boys.'

'Looking back it was a weakness. Few amounted to much.'

'You can't really know what they've achieved. The thing is, you took the chance.'

'Your loyalty is admirable but you talk of the past too often.' Adding cruelly, 'Certainly of Burrendah.'

'I was happy there. Is that wrong?'

'Unfortunately for us all, you do not seem entirely happy here.'

'I'm happy where you are.'

'Are you, Alannah? And put down that confounded brush.' He tossed it aside and drew her up to face him. 'Look at me – *are* you? I make allowances for child-bearing but I sometimes wonder if there are other deeper reasons — '

'Don't *say* such things.'

'I make allowances for a woman's moods too, however deucedly inconvenient to a man they can be.'

They trembled against each other but she slipped from his grasp and folded her gown about her. 'You've never lived as a family before.'

'True. We're husband and wife with three children of our own but must that alter things between us?'

'And there's where I wonder about you.' Wandering the room she picked up trifles and replaced them aimlessly.

'What do you mean?'

'You don't know your children.'

'What is there to know? They're still in the nursery.'

'I see differences even now. You expect the wrong things

34

of them, responses they will never be able to make. Dominic will never work the land.'

'He'll work Hawkes Plains.' He was adamant. 'Of course he will. He's akin to it. I watch him with the bush animals — '

'He wants to protect them. To save it all. From you, I think.'

'Land must be worked. It's what land is for.'

'He cries when you cull the native bears.'

'At three-and-a-bit that's a baby's response. This is koala country, the bears swarm, and must be kept down.'

'He doesn't know that.'

'He will learn it.'

'You won't be able to beat things into him as you did your foundling boys.'

'A paddle now and then never hurt them.'

'As for Will . . . You see Will as an asset to your property, no more. He wants to work land his own way, and he'll do it somehow. I know Will.'

'And I don't?' He knew she would resist Will for her precious Clodagh if ever it came down to it but she would be loyal and fair to the boy, then the man.

'Will's changed.'

'If you mean he's developed a temper, true. The "slow burn" as I call it. I can manage Will.'

'His so-called temper is simply impatience with the pastoral élite. He wouldn't put it into words, he's too loyal to you.'

'Is that what you think we are on the Downs?'

'I do. And you've become one of the worst.'

'Because I know and understand this Darling country? And as to snobbery, you have your own form of it . . . Anyway, I can't imagine Will letting himself be left out of anything. He can help Tod more and free me for Brisbane, so come with me, stay where you like but at least see the house building. I've had to do too much deciding.'

'*You've* decided!' Ashamed of her outburst for she knew she was hitting out at him simply because he had decided on something to give her pleasure.

'Then furnish it as you please. Another Burrendah if you want.'

'There could never be another Burrendah.'

'Well, the next best thing. I know you miss your precious "Place of the Swan" but there are things in the south I miss too.'

'Raunie perhaps.' She recoiled, appalled at her childishness, a little frightened of his reaction but he did no more than turn and stare.

'That's not like you, girl. What is it? Good God, Alannah, I'm only trying to make you happy.'

'Sometimes I wonder why you bother,' she said miserably.

'Because you're my wife and I love and need you. You agreed with me that a house in Brisbane would be necessary when the girls were at school.'

'They're still too young.'

'Clodagh's nine. I keep up with their ages, my elephantine memory. It's time she had proper schooling.'

She smiled at his use of 'proper', this man who had never been 'proper' in his life. 'Which means of course Isabel Muir's seminary.'

He made a gesture of irritation. 'You have this ambivalence. The most Irish of Irish names for them yet you insist no convent schools, no nuns or priests – fine, I agree, yet you hesitate over Isabel's school. If you can find other or better, I'll listen.'

She shook her head, not because she wanted the tight and formal education Isabel Muir would give but because Isabel's school was the best, indeed the only possible one. He was right of course, Clodagh must make new contacts giving her the chance to discover whether the bond between herself and Will was nothing more than a childish friendship. Much as she and Brick valued and loved Willy Wilberforce neither wished a match between Clodagh and Jamie Lorne's natural son, with all the complications it could bring. 'The boy's Jamie's.' Brick never wavered. 'I know the background . . .' 'You know so much that I don't,' she would complain. 'So much of your life before me.' Such varied and vast living for 'touch of the tar-brush' O'Shea as he would sometimes call himself in his ribald way, and perhaps, unrealised even by himself, he was striving to exorcise it all by planning a conventional education and Society role for their children. Brick conventional? The idea was laughable. Even so, she had heard of such changes, the shedding of former skins to reveal a new personality. Colour was not in him, certainly not in their children, they had not expected it; there was only the sense, the feeling, the *knowledge*, heightened by the savagery of native tribes pushed back to a wild and unexplored north by the clearing of the Darling Downs. Grim tales came from the wilderness, cannibalism their substance which was why, unfairly and secretly, she cherished Clodagh's Europeanness. She moved about the room irritated by her own irrationality. Brick was doing his best for her daughter; after all what would she and Clodagh have done in their struggle to recover from Simon's drowning if Brick had not come instantly and unhesitatingly to force them back to sanity and health? He had changed their world. Now he was changing it again, so swiftly it was racing ahead of her.

'No O'Shea has ever been easy in relationships.' He brushed a hand through his thick hair in mock desperation, and apology. 'And I haven't made things easier by the sons I adopt.'

'And daughters?'

'I didn't say that – though I never find Clodagh easy, you know it. She's very much Aldercott's daughter.'

She looked at him sharply. He seldom referred to Simon, indeed she often thought he had forgotten her first husband, but how could anyone looking at Clodagh not couple father and daughter; the same pale complexion, the slim figure, the innate seriousness. 'Give her time.' She tried to laugh. 'Give us all time.' They were arguing over their children like all parents. 'It's just that . . . must everything be done through the Muirs?'

'Some things. Certainly the land for the house. And I didn't do too badly in the getting of it, except of course its absurd name – for some reason Bennett prizes BelleMonte, he even put it in the contract. Do you think you can live with it? The fact that you dislike the Muirs so much, and only you and God know exactly why, makes everything damned awkward.'

'They're too acquisitive. Everything they do has a specific purpose.'

'Perhaps the reason I favour them. I know where I am.

You might feel differently about them when you meet Eva Muir.'

'I'm beginning to think she's a myth.'

'No myth. She opens at the Royal next month for a short season and will stay on at Foxburgh for a spell. There will be entertaining, so the Muirs expect you in Brisbane. As I do.'

She looked aghast. 'You know I've made arrangements to take the children south. Papa and Aunt Delia expect us in Sydney before we go to Burrendah. I can't disappoint them.'

'You're disappointing me. You can make the trip later in the year.'

'The children are already packing their toys. I can't alter things now.'

He shrugged. 'I suppose not. It's simply that I want and need you with me.' He frowned. 'For one thing, to form a united front against Jamie.'

'He's coming home?'

'Home? The only time he regards Hawkes Plains as home is when he's in trouble. All I know is that he's been seen in taverns around the Valley, gambling as usual . . . The Bennett Muirs of this world can afford to lose, the Jamies can't.'

'He gambles with Bennett? They scarcely know each other.'

'I can't be sure they gamble together, only that all gamers, win or lose, inhabit a tight-knit world.' He paused and she knew he was remembering Kurt Herlicht, his manager at Bendigo's Irish Boy Hotel and Raunie's lover – her murderer some had insisted though her shooting had been judged accidental. Would the pattern be repeated by another Kurt? 'I suppose we can count ourselves lucky if Jamie keeps reasonably free of debt, gets only mildly drunk, seduces servant-girls without leaving them pregnant and makes no attempt to mortgage Hawkes Plains – yet too much to expect if he takes up with the failed diggers and reprobate seamen who hang around waterfront dives.' He paced again. There was always a maddening daunting evasion among the keepers of 'bush' hotels. The flat of his hand struck Alannah's dressing-table and her brushes rattled. 'I swear if he drags this family into his squalid money-making schemes I'll kill him.'

'No you won't. You'll get him out of the mess as usual and take him back. You always do.'

He turned abruptly. 'You're provoking an argument.'

'Discussion. That's all.'

'*Argument*, Alannah. It's becoming a habit with you, a device to avoid the real issue of making love with me. Don't make me angry, not tonight.' He drew her close and began to kiss her, it had its physical effect and she returned his kisses and caresses in her own special way. 'Don't strain from me.' He was urgent. 'Feel safe. I haven't racketed through bordellos without learning a few tricks with women.'

She laughed a little breathlessly. 'I don't want to be safe from you, only with you.' Still she held him off. 'I've heard of things women can do . . . There are ways.'

'What ways?'

'Women in bawdy houses know what to do.'

'I'll have no dangerous practices.' He was angry. 'If that ex-madam – or close to it – of a Sophie Van Weldt has been filling your head with so-called remedies I forbid you to go near her again.'

'That's odd when it was you who introduced us, remember? She called when Phelim was born. And she's quite often at Yoolanowi; it's called "Muir's Retreat" around country kitchens, did you know that?'

'Sophie's an adventuress, no more a baroness than you are. It's simply that her husband – if he is her husband – runs seaworthy ships which is more than one can say of most up and down this coast. You'll not listen to ways of aborting my children. Nor will there be any sleeping apart from me. I may be approaching sixty but my needs are as strong as ever. Good God, Alannah, celibacy was never my strong point and never will be no matter how many years I add. I've always been a sudden man and you know it.'

'I can't deal with you when you're angry.'

'I can't deal with you at all these days.'

'I don't deny you.'

'No. You respond in the manner you regard as "duty". But you hold back, oh yes; you forget I know every fold, every indent of you and I want you entirely and completely as you used to be. Don't you want me that way? We're not meant to think when we love, nature should take over. This is marriage, Alannah, you're my wife, don't make me beg.' He was right of course, she must not make him beg for if she did he would turn from her sooner or later. For the first time in her life she envied Raunie for what must have been the woman's complete abandon. 'Is it that you think you are no longer attractive to me?'

'I don't always feel so.'

'I've never seen you so lovely. Take off that silly robe and come here.'

He was taking the initiative, summoning what was always there, if latent, their great need of each other. If you have a dozen children, Alannah O'Shea, she scolded herself, and you very well could, it cannot be helped. She shook off her robe and stood, not only accepting but beginning to enjoy his scrutiny. Stop thinking, don't hold back, stop finding words to delay. Give . . . *give* . . . Brick saw a tall and slender young woman, her belly flat and uncreased and her breasts perfect, with no change in her that he could define despite four children. A desirable woman. She entered the circle of his arms with a sigh and his hands on her were as wonderful as ever as he lay beside her. Yet she could not entirely suppress thought as she strove with him; could any woman, wife and mother, be quite the same as before? She braced her body preparing it for acceptance and the climax she craved yet, curiously, dreaded. She could never deny her holding back, she could only disguise it. Brick O'Shea was the one love of her life, she wanted no other man yet she had changed within herself: the same yet different. Life and experience had changed her. Even in the flowing and overflowing of their body juices there was a vague and awful melancholy. Even as she gasped and fought for breath against and with him the small sadness she could never explain would not go away. No matter what she did, what they did, it stayed.

Jamie Lorne, as he liked to call himself, mainly to annoy Brick, pulled up his horse. Both man and beast were weary of the saddle and the long ride; departures were exciting and full of promise but return journeys were too often a bore. But

40

the prime reason for his pause was his first glimpse of Hawkes Plains, his torment yet delight for when all else failed him it was a return to base, a focal point, the fount of all things, not because he loved it – he had no love of the land – but because it was a retreat. He didn't want to return to it any more than the O'Sheas wanted him back but he was in trouble again, this time deeply and dangerously, he knew it. Sometimes the weight of his bondage to the gaming-tables was unbearable, the same fever that had driven his mother. Now he was a hunted and driven man for Matt Burney held the bulk of his IOUs (it said much for the life of a blackbirder when the man could play for such high stakes!) and Burney was pressing for settlement, worse, threatening to gaol him for forgery – which he could do, he supposed. Damn that drunken desperate moment when he'd signed Burney's name after his hundreds of attempts to achieve the perfect signature – or so he had believed. If Burney couldn't send him to prison for debt he could for forgery. Yet the man held off – why? He was tired of the puzzle, tired of avoiding Burney every time he came ashore from parts unknown so this time he had run to the only refuge he knew, Hawkes Plains. He had lingered overlong in Toowoomba, not because it was a lovable place with its swampy depressions and red-brown mud in the 'wet' or the summer red dust turning horses a chestnut colour and giving white-painted houses a deep blush, but these days the town offered city delights beyond the pastimes of the range-people as they called themselves. It offered women other than the virginal nubiles whose papas kept wary eyes on them when they saw the likes of Jamie Lorne ride in – they locked up their daughters. He laughed aloud, scattering birds. Their precious daughters weren't worth locking up, not his style. There were servant-girls when he wanted them; he took his pleasures where he could and be damned to the world.

He was bone-tired of the north and its stinking rat-ridden luggers with their sweating half-naked Kanakas, above all of the cloying sickly-sweet molasses permeating the sugar country, clinging to the skin and cloying the hair, oozing as smoothly as Matt Burney's voice hinting – threatening – various solutions to his debts. It was as if he'd swum through a river of sticky dribbling black – at least Hawkes Plains could provide good baths. He moved restlessly, frowning through the scrub at the homestead. Much could have happened here in a year. For a start, Moll Noakes, his old enemy, could be dead; she'd been half dead when Brick had bullied them all to the plateau of the Downs, silly gullible Fay with her chocolate-box complexion matching her chocolate-box dreams, hugging the baby Willy Wilberforce . . .

He stirred uncomfortably. What would he be – twelve? About that. The years of youth seemed to add more to his own for he was almost thirty, drat it! There were women on the road, 'dacent' women as they insisted, with pudding-faced daughters, even granddaughters at their heels, who told him it was time he settled down – and he would sidle off before they could get their hands on him. Now Willy would confront him. Willy? He squirmed for the boy. The old man – as he thought of O'Shea these days – would be nearing sixty, old to be begetting a quiverful, but that's what a fellow got for bedding a young wife. Some women couldn't stop breeding. He had never liked Alannah; she had turned up her freckly nose at him from the start as if she were waiting for him to do the wrong thing, so of course he did it. Not that she was a boring woman, no, something was suppressed in her, particularly now, some energy or want, some craving, call it what one might, as if no matter how many anchors she dragged behind her or offspring she bore they could not tie her down. A restless filly. Perhaps some women were not meant to bear children, bored by the whole business, and he suspected it was so with her. Serve her right. She'd grounded herself by her own fecundity, getting herself into the old man's bed, probably on the way with another brat by now; the old man wasn't taking chances of not displaying heirs. Not that he, Jamie, cared, he usually got what he wanted, by round-about means if he must, at least until his present fix. As he rode the slight slope with the melancholy of the travelling dispossessed a small figure darted on unsteady legs from behind a tree. The horse shied and he pulled up, shouting:

'I'll thrash you for this, you wretched cripple.'

The dwarf darted ahead, pounding the path with surprising strength and speed. Jamie dragged at his whip, put in his spurs and galloped the tired horse until he loomed over the terrified Gondola. He brought the whip down on the cringing whimpering runaway. The dwarf's resistance maddened him the more. 'Run then,' he yelled. 'Run your fool legs off. Run. *Run!*'

Brick often lost himself in his forests, venting his anger on his trees, felling, chopping, digging in, cutting, for pitting himself against the strength of his timber had become something of a safety valve in his life, an ingrained habit. No matter how many trees he cut down or mangled or maimed, for he supposed that was what he did in fury, he had saved the giant blue gum, protecting it over the years, cutting into others to build his huts and stables and sheds and finally the homestead of Hawkes Plains. But this year, for the sake of his annual wood-chop, it would go he would cut down his friend, if something inanimate could be called 'friend'. He paused in axing the encircling scrub – for his cause seemed to demand his own labour – and looked about him. No Gondola. Where was the fool? He'd warned him against wandering off. There was the thunder of horse's hoofs and shouting and Gondola screaming his usual gibberish of Neapolitan and what little English he knew, and another voice shouting obscenities – Jamie! He anchored his axe, ran through the bush and crunched on to the path. A mounted Jamie was beating Gondola, hemmed in and clinging to a tree, making tiny darting efforts to escape only to be beaten back again. Brick lunged, grasped Jamie's wrist and wrenched the whip away.

'*Dammit*,' he roared, 'must you make your usual start?' He dragged him from his horse as Gondola scuttled off, howling in his bloodcurdling way.

'He near unseated me.' Jamie thrashed about in fury. 'He could have smashed the mare's leg.'

'He didn't so you'll not start on him the minute you set foot here. You always ride like the Devil. How many mounts have you exhausted this trip?'

'This one's lasted well.' Jamie retrieved his whip with an angry wrench. 'Why not? Gympie's not exactly the far north.'

'You've been farther north than Gympie.'

Jamie shrugged. 'Might have known you'd have your spies out.'

'I don't need spies. You leave your mark wherever you go, gambling, whoring, begging . . .'

'Knew it would be useless telegraphing you for money.'

'You're right. I'm not the absolute fool, I know you've been holed up in Brisbane, trying your luck as you put it.'

He shrugged. 'I win and I lose.' Then turned spiteful. 'What do you do with all your loot? Waste it on your brood? I daresay there's another by now.'

'A boy, Phelim.'

'Well . . . old men have to hurry things along. To prove themselves.' Brick said nothing, but his hands clenched.

'I thought perhaps you'd returned to see your son.'

'Still harping on that?'

'Always. No . . .' he answered Jamie's unspoken query. 'All Will knows is that I adopted him.' He paused. There was a parallel here: he had waited for the right moment to tell this man before him when a boy that Raunie was his mother and that his father had died at sea before he was born. 'If you want to dine at my table with my wife and children clean yourself up.'

'I don't give a fig for your precious table. I'll eat where I choose.'

'Ah no. The O'Sheas eat together in the nursery and dining-room of Hawkes Plains and not with the swine, so you'll suffer us at table as we suffer you. And don't wander far from the house. I've much to say to you and I'll need time in which to say it.'

Jamie caught up with the boy, Willy Wilberforce, coming from the stables and set his horse at him, swerving at the last instant with his superb horsemanship in a flurry of dust and laughter. But the boy did not swerve or even halt his stride. He paused only when Jamie dismounted and blocked his path.

'Hello Willy.'

'I don't answer to Willy now. I'm twelve so it's Will.' He was fair-skinned with dark hair curling round his ears; hair exactly like his own, Jamie thought a little wildly. The hair had always worried him. Now it made him furious.

'Will is it? Can't say I blame you for that. Even so, I'll call you Willy if I choose.'

'I won't answer.'

'You won't, eh, you young bastard?' O'Shea would never allow the word to be used in relation to the boy, too soft with his adopted, and so far as Jamie was concerned, the man was displaying a creeping senility. 'You're too cocky for your muddied boots.'

'I won't be called "bastard" either.' As if reading his thoughts.

'It's what you are, kid.'

'Nor will I be called "kid".'

'What will you do about it, eh? Thrash me?'

'I could try.'

'Thrash your own — ' He broke off, shocked at himself. It had burst from him. 'I wouldn't advise it. You *are* a kid, you know.'

'I'll grow.'

Jamie retrieved his horse. He'd deny to his last breath that he had conceived this boy for Dora had been one of the local 'lays', and he'd actually seen a male figure slinking off round the rocks the night he'd approached her on the sand of Birubi's beach, her fair hair spread around her. Who knew what had already been conceived in her body? All the same, the sight of Will tormented him. Fairer skin than his own, feasible enough, for he, Jamie Lorne, was the son of a gipsy woman, but Will's hands were plump and strong and broad, reminding him of Dora's hands . . . One was bound to have doubts for if you lay with sluts, the easy ones on the way to becoming public women, you were bound to wonder – yet for that very reason one could deny paternity; after all there was always someone before you.

'Come on, climb up. Save your energy to argue with the old man. He's in a foul mood.'

'He's not an old man.'

'No?' Jamie laughed, holding out his smooth and slender hand, a hand that had never felled a tree or worked the soil. A cardsharper's hand, deft and manipulative, a gentleman's hand, he liked to think.

'No thanks. I'll walk.'

'Then walk, damn you,' Jamie shouted. This sullen youth his son? Never. He spurred his horse. He looked back at Will trudging with his solid gait looking neither to right nor left. This stubborn mule of a country yokel his son? It was laughable. He'd deny it to his last breath.

Chapter Four

STRAT McCRAE at fifteen was working like a dog – as he had worked for his father, Sandy, all his life – in the McCrae store at Barkerville on the Cariboo of British Columbia. Since the Cariboo Road had been hacked through, finally to Barkerville in sixty-five, Sandy had competitors; even so McCrae's remained 'the store', the same hastily erected shack of whipsawed timber where Sandy had made quick money – and why not when he had demanded three hundred dollars a barrel for flour and fifty for a pair of boots, every penny squeezed from would-be miners reduced to moccasins; they counted themselves lucky to have climbed the horror trails from the coast with the last lap through mud up to their knees. Unbeknownst to any, even to his son (least of all to his son) Sandy was still hiding his gains under floorboards, in holes in trees, buried in the woods, diversions to 'foil the bastards' as he would mutter to himself, patting and digging and marking each burial place on a rough map he kept strapped to his chest, just in case, for he knew as well as everyone else that he drank too much bad whisky: the supreme canny Scot among those early Scots who had come by boat as far as Yale then braved the rapids of the Fraser River and the Indian ladders festooning its cliffs. Or taken the old fur trails. Or made their roundabout way through the jungle of the Harrison River, over Pavilion Mountain and back down to the Fraser by a goat track, over the plateau to the south of the Quesnel then eastward to Williams Creek, all to dodge the Fraser Canyon and its terrible Hells Gate. Frozen and half dead they longed, some prayed, for a decent road. There were those who even dared to dream of the miracle of a railroad . . .

At least they had their road, a wagon road at that, three hundred and eighty-five miles of it as aftermath of the new rush of sixty-two that had brought six thousand miners to dig the Cariboo creeks, creeping farther and still farther into the mountains to the one street of Barkerville set tight against its mountain, up on stilts, hopefully out of the mud, even so remaining an oozing mess of saloons and doss-houses and eating-places and breweries, yet its hotels boasting pianos hauled up on the backs of mules with fine champagne for those who could pay. The shaky McCrae store, an eyesore as it was dubbed by the progressive, was pack-jammed with goods Sandy guarded with his keen eyes, blasphemous tongue, and the old rusting musket with which he could still work havoc, worse, with his expertly wielded whip. The room behind the hut with stretchers, a table, log cuts for chairs and cooking-pots, had been the first settled home Strat had ever known, for his young life had been settlement after settlement, track after track, pausing just long enough for Sandy to make a grub-stake then move on. Sandy McCrae – as his son had heard him tell many times, for Sandy loved to talk – had joined the rush from the Californian mines on a long trek east to Jackson Creek, Oregon, where men were digging one hundred ounces of dust and nuggets a day – but still not enough for Sandy. To escape the Indian wars of the fifties he had opened a store in the boom town of Jacksonville. Sometimes Strat pondered when his own memory had begun . . . A faint scent of flowers clung when someone mentioned San Francisco, the old Yerba Buena village of eight hundred that had grown to the lawless town of thousands where he had been born, and where his father had tried his hand at gold-digging then working the lumber camps. Roses, Sandy laughed, the scent of roses at the Mission, and Strat would wonder what a rose looked like. Then Sandy (as he told it) was off again. Strat could not remember his mother's death on the road from cholera, but he often wished he could remember her face . . .

'She wasna meant for the life,' Sandy would repeat as if reassuring himself, or accusing himself for his voice would take on the familiar whine that meant guilt over something. 'I shouldna have brought her but she would coom. She would.'

Strat decided, finally, that memory had begun when he rode

his father's shoulders, clinging in terror yet never daring to show it as Sandy tramped the wild terrain of the north-west braving ever wilder Indians, turning to the coast to take ship at Portland, a small place with orchards – Strat remembered the orchards – or was it that his father spoke of them so often? Sandy, as he constantly reminded his son, could have left him behind. Instead he'd scorned the warning of concerned women that there were no children where they were bound – nor women to bear them. 'Where I go there goes m'bairn. What else can I do, leave him for the Indians to scalp? I'll not be sending ye back to kin, laddie, ye're better wi' me, young as ye are.' His thin lips and wary eyes would take on a familiar expression of cunning. 'There's gold at the end of the trail for some but brass can be made easier and quicker other ways. But ye'll learn to pull your weight, lad. Aye, ye'll pull your weight.'

How he had pulled his weight! The journey to Fort Victoria on Vancouver Island (Sandy decided there would be better pickings in the thick of things) was gruelling, the old coastal tubs so glutted men took shifts to lie down on deck to sleep. In that summer of fifty-eight – as his father would later recount around many a camp-fire – twenty thousand miners were camped about the stockade seeking a way to cross to the mainland and the Fraser diggings, with himself and his boy of five-and-a-bit making two more. Strat was set to fetch and carry as best he could for the 'Argonauts', as the forty-niners from Californy called themselves. Steam-boats, sail-boats, row-boats, canoes, anything that would float, crossed the Strait of Georgia. But those without the wherewithal for passage – as Sandy lied he was – crossed on roughly made rafts, tossed by winds and the tides, Sandy and his bairn somehow surviving. At the rip-roaring port of New Westminster – vying with Fort Victoria as capital of the west – trails met and men moved any way they could upriver to the gold. 'See and remember, laddie, the fools trudging on to nought, most of 'em, and the stores at the Forts taking in five hundred pounds a day.' Sandy's eyes had developed a permanent gleam. 'Food and grog, that's where the brass is made. Men must eat – and drink themselves paralytic, praise be.'

Six hundred miles from the coast in the Barkerville of

wretched log shacks Sandy built his store. He ran mule trains, horse trains, camel trains – Strat hated the biting kicking spitting camels, worse, their smell, but tend them he must. At seven he was not only holding horses but riding them like a young Centaur. He carried hammers and nails to the men, even drove in the nails as far as his childish muscles would let him, muscles that grew stronger each day. At nine, with Sandy always crying poor mouth, his son must beg or carry water or burn himself cooking at the great fires, or wash the men's pannikins and dishes for his own victuals, lucky to get sowbelly and biscuits – no labour no grub, Sandy decreed, and many a time Strat went hungry. And all the while he watched the men go trudging by into the Rockies. And watched too many come down again, penniless.

All the failures could do was straggle back to the Delta, ship out or stay and farm, milk cows, become river men – but not for Sandy McCrae or his lad. 'Finish up a farmer there and your life is nought,' Sandy warned, scared, Strat suspected, of losing his free help. 'At change of tide the crops are ruined. Canna get rid of the salt. Stick to the Cariboo and trade, lad. 'Tis easy to part a fool and his money when goods are scarce; if ye've something to sell there's always someone ready to buy, at any price ye set.'

Sandy must be rich, his son decided, yet they lived more frugally than ever, everything for the store. Strat still froze. He still went hungry. He was always bone-weary. He could put his fingers through the holes in his shirt, his shoes had long gone and he was lucky if he could scrounge Indian sandals. 'Sandy's bairn' had become 'Sandy's laddie', yet he still dressed as the Indians in bits and pieces of buckskin, and he still worked unpaid, hating the store's muddle and clutter, its shoddiness, its stink of venison with the choicest viands held back for those who could pay. With the Cariboo Road through, the old Harrison trail was abandoned and freight wagons and passenger coaches started up, run by the Hume brothers, a twice-a-week service from Soda Creek down to Yale to meet the river steamers. Sandy refused to pay the fares, Sandy saw no reason yet to leave his mountains, so his son could only look longingly on those going down and out into the world.

He resented Sandy's orders, his belt-strappings, and, lately, his whippings, a man who could neither read nor write beyond orders for stock or the making out of receipts. If he must slave, Strat brooded, he would have his share, money with which to buy white men's clothes such as one saw in the settlements, shoes and a choice of guns and horses. More important, a woman. His rebellion against his father was not yet a physical one but he almost turned on him when Sandy put the boot in. 'Ye're bone lazy, Stratton McCrae. Ye'll never amount to anything.'

Injustice rankled – yet how to escape? Where to go? He was known over the Cariboo as 'Sandy's laddie' and no one would take him in or give him tasks, scared of Sandy's temper and vengeance, even more of his withdrawal of credit. All he, Strat, could do was bide his time till he was grown. And hard it was for something nagged at him and would not let him rest, something biding its time, waiting for him to grow, driving him to the moment when he could do as he pleased. Life was waiting, and he was impatient to taste it to the full.

At thirteen – or was it fourteen? – his life changed. Malcolm Hume, the younger of the Hume brothers, had ordered a consignment of Sandy's best whisky, so Sandy had sent him his worst. Malcolm Hume was a fur-trader turned prospector turned timber-cutter turned landowner with valuable stock pastured at Quesnel. He had ship-building yards at New Westminster and was planning others at Burrard Inlet. Malcolm, as his brother, was rich from all ventures, with 'the luck of the Humes' as it was said. The Humes took chances – with the money to do it, said the envious. The Humes moved fast. If the 'mistake', as Sandy called his transgression, were not rectified, Malcolm Hume would come – and deuced inconvenient such a trip would be – to tear the McCrae store apart. Easy enough to do, Strat laughed, daring his father, for it barely held together under the weight of the winter snows. Sandy McCrae could huff and puff as he liked, if the malt Scotch and the refund were not in New Westminster quick smart, the Hume vengeance would be terrible. Sandy cried and ranted and raved, Sandy sent messages back and forth, he couldn't travel, his lumbago was cruel, but Malcolm Hume was unrelenting. Sandy McCrae had a son, a big fellow it was said and sharp with his sums; he would do in Sandy's place. The Humes were suppliers as well as Sandy's best customers and Sandy dared not try them too far. With instructions and warnings and the refund cash (over which Sandy wept anew) sewn into a band around Strat's waist, Sandy farewelled his son with his ticket and not a cent more. He could beg his meals or starve. Strat did not care. Right there and then he did not care if he never saw Barkerville again.

From New Westminster the thickly wooded land stretched over the slope to the northern wilderness of Burrard Inlet, a place of water and timber and saw-mills and settlers' cabins, framed by the line of mountains behind. Gazing west from its tranquil waters Strat saw in abundance what had always filled his life – trees. Timber was all he had ever seen other than the wretched log shacks of Barkerville and the Forts in between, since the time, half carried, half dragged, he had trudged the trails with his father, lucky to sleep in a tent till it was washed away and he and Sandy huddled against each other, wet and shivering, under the great timbers. In 1860, this land along the southern shore of the Inlet had been opened for settlement but with few takers – aside from the Humes – for gold was still the lure and men still plodded the trails. He, Stratton, had no desire to work the land, he wanted quick money as Sandy did, but unlike Sandy he would spend; he ached to retrieve something of the pain and sweat he'd put into his years of toil, as balm for the humiliation of his slave labour. Again, no woman of his, if he were lucky enough to own a woman, would be buried under a tree in Oregon as his mother was. Gold slipped through the fingers, Sandy was right about that, so he, Stratton, would see something for what he spent. He would lie under the great giants with the sound of water in his ears and dream . . . He had been born in America, he'd never been to Scotland and perhaps never would, he was here in a land he knew well so he would use it as it had used him. The immensity of his surroundings set his head reeling, his imagination soaring. His ambitions were endless . . . Money of his own to buy books to learn words to read about a world of which he knew nothing. He had two books: *Tom Jones*, where he puzzled over long words, devouring with difficulty its lush and savage world long gone, and *Great Expectations* by Charles Dickens, which he kept for its title, to delight in the life of an ambitious young man . . . Torn and dog-eared books kept hidden when he should have passed them on; for books were as gold to men who could read and would be passed around, grubby from fingermarks, with sighs over missing pages. Most were of murders in Whitechapel, or grim mysteries, or ghosts, or hangings in Newgate Prison, awesome lurid tales devoured by deprived and book-hungry men. Was the world really as such books described? Sandy was no help, he would sweep books off the table when he caught Strat reading by the light of the one candle he dared.

'Ye'll ruin your eyes.'

'They teach words.'

'Waste o' time. Education's useful to count profits, that's all. A man can become distracted by the thoughts of others, weary with the ideas of other men. Ye're too like your Ma for comfort, a parson's daughter with books beyond her Bible and they made her useless for the road. Use your head, laddie. The McCraes have always had sound heads.'

Strat could only heed his father for who else was there to believe? But at seventeen he had a friend, Morgan, only son of Malcolm Hume, who had sent his boy to San Francisco for an education then put him in his shipyard at Burrard Inlet, providing Morgan with the outdoor and roistering life he loved. Sandy did not like Morgan Hume. 'Fancies hi'self when he's but the son of a go-getting adventurer.' Morgan lent Stratton books from his father's library about machines and timber and the building of ships, all of which Strat devoured as best he could, reading laboriously yet taking in much all the same. Ships went places, ships carried supplies which was something Strat knew about. When he did meet up with Morgan, which was seldom, Morgan gossiped, Morgan talked of the world, and of his father's doings past and present, for Morgan envied his father even more than he admired him.

'This will be a great port when the railway crosses Canada, my father says.'

'There's been talk of a railroad since Sandy first hauled me up the trail there.'

'Real talk now. We joined Canada in sixty-seven but the Articles say no railroad, no joining up. Canada was given ten years to build it so the railroad had best get moving, my father says. Canada wants a port on the west coast to trade with the Orient again but the Americans have already crossed the continent, they have Oregon; and America will take us over if we don't watch out. They have the numbers, you see, a huge military force with nothing to do now the Civil War is over, wanting everything from Russian Alaska down to Mexico. The Americans are a driving people, my father says.'

Morgan was a parrot but in this Strat knew he was right; change was on the way, he could feel it, even Sandy was beginning to talk like a Canadian. Morgan had crossed the Rockies and knew the prairies. Morgan had lived in California. But his father had travelled the world and Strat sat enthralled while Morgan told of his father's journey long ago on his way to the Californian fields, across the Isthmus of Panama before there was a railway there, in heat and mosquito plagues and through wild jungle, half the trip by native canoe and the rest carried on the backs of natives . . . Morgan had learned much by 'knocking about', as he put it, an Australian term picked up by his father who had been to that country way down the Pacific, surviving the gold-rushes of the fifties in Ballarat and Bendigo and returning through Californy, making friends, enemies too, on the way. Strat brooded on Australia. He brooded on Morgan. He brooded on Sandy. Even more deeply he brooded on something that was happening to his body, an irritation . . . His body troubled him, he felt driven by it. He was older, stronger, and already felt a man, yet was not, quite. There was something he needed, that he must have and know, yet he couldn't put such urges into words, certainly not action for it was not much more than a flavour, elusive yet growing stronger every day. He sought things beyond his deprived existence. He sought it in strangers. He sought it in women . . .

There were no women but the Indian squaws whom his father despised and the German dance-hall girls, the hurdy-gurdies, blonde, plump and cheerful who were paid ten dollars just to dance with a man and much more for 'intimate favours', as Sandy hinted. Strat wondered if his father went to them but he suspected that Sandy, if he spent money at all, would spend it on grog. Sandy would have no hurdy-gurdy for his son so what was he, Stratton, to do? Morgan took a squaw sometimes, Strat knew that. 'Weel, ye don't,' Sandy roared. 'I'll ha'e no Indian slut claiming m'hard-earned brass any more than I'll have some fat German.' There were men, Morgan swore, who went to other men but that was an area unknown to Stratton and which he did not fancy. Women fascinated him. He wondered about them. Somehow he must get money to buy them for one paid for everything in the world – paid or begged and he, Stratton McCrae, was through with begging. In his aching need he watched the Indian women. Some were beautiful and he wanted to touch their silky skin and black hair. He wondered about the deep hollows in their throats and what it must be like to place one's mouth there. He tossed in his sleep. He sweated. One day out hunting he became separated from Sandy and watched a young girl bathing naked in the lake. His heart pounded. Odd things were happening to him, his skin tingled, he could not be still. He wanted to hold the girl, fondle her, crush her beneath him and join his body to hers. She came out dripping. He caught her, he could not help it, and dragged her close. She did not resist and he felt she had been watching him in turn. Her skin was wonderfully cool, so wet and soft his hands slipped on it. He could not let her go and pressed against her until she gasped. He tore at his clothes. But Sandy was there dragging them apart, waving the squaw into the woods and cutting his son's half-naked skin with his whip.

'Button yeself up. I'll have no grandson that isn't as pale as yeself.' Strat fought his father but Sandy and his whip were stronger; besides, curiously, even now he did not want to fight Sandy. He hated him but he did not want to fight him. That night he pounded his pillow in agony, hating the world, hating the girl he had been denied, yet she wasn't really important, she had been a shape, a form that promised relief, no more. It was the act that possessed him, ruled him, controlled him. Next morning, cutting himself a hunk of chewing baccy, Sandy said bluntly:

''Tis time ye was wed. Aye, even at seventeen. Better that way.'

'There are no free women.'

'Ye missed your chance in 'sixty-two — '

'I was only nine,' Strat guffawed, though he did not feel like laughing.

' — when the bride ship come in packed with virgins, sixty-three of 'em, all guaranteed, and all plucked up like ripe cherries from a tree the moment they set foot ashore. Ye'd have been nigh killed in the rush but I'd a fought for ye, even grabbed one for meself if the young blades had left any.' Sandy roared, his bit of crudity fortified by a dram in one hand and his baccy in the other. 'Now we keep our eyes peeled for a lass wi' strong hands and willing heart and, if she must talk, do it quick and quiet. Good child-bearing hips though, for I need grandsons to run the new store I ha'e in mind. If ye don't start begetting, it will be too late for I lose m'breath at times something awful, no denying it.' He slammed his bony knees. 'Only trollops around here so we take a wee trip to Hope.'

'Hundreds of miles just to look around?' Strat gaped. 'Besides, the store . . .'

'I'll put Benny Batcher in with the fear o' God in him and locks on all valuables. Worth the trip if we have luck on our side for there's a new lass at the Brady hoose. A teacher.'

'A governess.'

'Call her what ye like she's a woman and a Scot and that's a guid start. The Bradys won't like her plucked awa' but if we don't do it others will. She might think hersel' too high and mighty for ye but worth a try, I'd say. Think, lad, free schooling in our own parlour for our own bairns. Free!'

'What parlour?'

'Weel . . . we'll tidy up a wee bit here. Do ye up too wi' shoes and a new shirt and the rest. Attend to your manners too; women dote on manners.' He grew expansive and flushed with his generosity. 'I'll not shame ye, I'll wear the pick o' the store. And we'll take the steamboats and the coach, travel in style. How's that?'

'You'll take a bath before we set off.'

'A *bath*? I didna aim to go so far. Baths cost guid brass at Clover's Saloon — '

'A bath or I don't go. How's *that*?'

The small town of Hope, once a thriving Hudson's Bay Company Fort, lay in a bend of the river sheltered by mountains, Ogilvy's Peak towering above. The place still had a certain charm. Strat conceded in those moments he could think of anything but his coming meeting; for through cronies and connections, not forgetting their 'coachy', Sandy had contacts and had arranged a meeting at the Brady house. Hitherto Strat had done no more than pass through Hope when first coming upriver by the steamer, the *Beaver*, to start the long trek into the mountains. The town had started out as the usual fur-trading post, but with Yale upriver becoming important the place had dwindled to a church and parsonage, a court-house, a saw-mill, a hotel and a saloon, the latter the focus of Sandy's eyes. Houses of employees were dotted about, and the cannon that had awed the Indians with its boom still stood in the stockade. After finding a room (keen bargaining on Sandy's part) he appeared in an alarming outfit of shirt with tags and fringe, buckskin pants, embroidered leggings, and his hair slicked down under a fierce cowboy hat, breathing heavily with the effort of appearing respectable. Strat knew his father was about to break, as he was himself, so they'd best get it over with and quick.

What if Mary Brady put obstacles in his way? What if *she* didn't like him . . . But a new kind of excitement shook him at the sight of the woman standing beside yet respectfully a little to the rear of Mary Brady. He did not hear her name, too fazed by her for he had not seen such a white woman close and intimately since, he supposed, his childhood; he could not take his eyes from her shape filling out her tight jacket, following her curve of breasts down into her pinched waist, her body tantalisingly lost under wide skirts, his eyes probing for the naked flesh he was seeking. She was not beautiful as he knew women, yet her hair was black and rich. She had plump smooth hands holding a Bible loosely in her palms, her elbows slightly crooked each side of her waist in an ecclesiastical pose for she had just brought the Brady girls from church. She wore no rings so was not yet spoken for, he saw with relief. He fancied her eyes on him were kind for he knew he looked different, older, decked out in boots that pinched and too tight breeches Sandy had found left over from something; his nails were well scrubbed and his thick fair hair gleamed from much washing and he was tall and lithe and knew his tight clothes emphasised his strong shoulders and thighs. To his delight yet fear, her eyes never left him. Once they met his full on and held. He shivered.

'Miss Cameron is from Aberdeen,' Mary Brady explained.

He looked interested for good manners' sake, but he had no idea where Aberdeen was. It sounded Scottish but many places here did. All he could do was wonder about the body beneath the bodice and if it were for him and for some reason his mouth watered. 'Ye're a fine rider, I hear, Stratton.' Mary Brady cut into a giant fruit cake and Strat's mouth watered again for a different reason: he hadn't tasted cake for too long. 'Miss Cameron wishes to perfect her horsemanship for the girls' sake and needs an escort about the trails.'

'We're here but three days,' something impelled him to say through the glutinous fruit, from nervousness he supposed for he felt awkward, fearful, even a little disappointed; why, he could not tell. Sandy kicked him under the table.

'We're here as long as it needs.' Sandy scooped up the biggest wedge of cake dripping crumbs on the snowy cloth. He scooped up the crumbs as well. Mary sighed, confounded by this onslaught of mountain men, the old one an ignorant but wily goat, yet worse could come a'courting so if she acquiesced now she might keep Eunice part of the time. Miss Cameron was unflustered, she even smiled at Strat. 'Time enough,' Mary said, a woman of only necessary words.

They went riding on a warm afternoon, their eyes playing together in silence. She drew up her horse and dismounted. He took his cue from her. 'My name is Eunice,' she said, as if aware he had not taken it in, or perhaps it had not been told him, he could not remember. They lost themselves amid the pines, she slightly ahead, her riding skirt looped up over her arm. She paused and looked back and he wondered if she were

58

afraid too, for she stood in shade. He waited. She moved into the sun and beckoned him with her rounded smooth hand. As he came close she moved back, teasing him. She looked older, he thought, under the dark branches.

'Ye've never had a woman, Strat McCrae.' It was not a question but a statement, as if she knew or had guessed, and he felt ashamed as if he had been remiss. He shook his head reluctantly. 'Nor touched one in love.' Another statement. He shook his head again. 'By the look of ye 'tis time ye did.' She spread his palms over her belly while she unbuttoned her bodice to let her heavy breasts ooze over her chemise. His hands trembled as she lifted them to her flesh. He felt her breasts move as she breathed in, out, in, out, in a tantalising rhythm and he wanted to squeeze them as he might squeeze ripe oranges. His hands clenched. She flinched, brushed his hands aside and drew his face down so that his mouth fondled the cleft between her breasts; yes, it was as he expected and he sighed, breathing in some heady body fragrance. It must be wonderful to die of pleasure, he thought distractedly, a little dizzy. She laughed softly. 'Aye, 'tis time. But ye must wed me first.' She buttoned her jacket briskly. 'Ha'e ye a mind to wed me, Stratton McCrae?'

He nodded, speechless, fumbling for her again. He would have agreed to anything then. She laughed again, leading him back to the horses. That night his father said bluntly, 'No beauty the teacher but pious I'm told, which is as may be for she's lusty-looking, aye as any widder woman who's had a taste of it and hankers after it again. I've asked around and she can cook – guid! It's a long time since I tasted guid Scotch broth. We'll ha'e all we need lad. Guid child-bearing hips and all.'

'How would you know?' For some reason Strat felt angry.

'I know.' Perhaps Sandy did know women, and Strat realised he knew little about his father beyond being a lonely cantankerous greedy man among other greedy men. 'So we'll ha'e oursel'es a wife, eh? Produce m'first grandson an' I'll build ye a hoose on the trail out o' toon. Meanwhile ye'll get wages, not much for the store won't stand it, but enough for ye both under m'roof. Grandsons mind, and be quick aboot it.'

His father's ramblings passed over him for things seemed to be falling into place without decision. He and Eunice talked little. She let him touch and fondle her, kiss her at times till he was half mad, but nothing more. They ignored Mary Brady's complaints, her fears that she would lose her help. They ignored the stares of the townsfolk, they did not even notice Sandy reeling drunkenly along the paths. They knew nothing but their own trembling for each other and it was merciful when they were at last man and wife and could lock themselves in the room Mary had decently set aside for the 'honeymoon' as she put it, since Gerald Brady was in New Westminster and she and her girls retreated to the parsonage for a spell. Strat McCrae did not comprehend, nor did he wish to, that at seventeen-and-a-bit he had a wife, no home, a slave wage, and was expected to produce a brood of McCraes, sons at that. He had no thought of tomorrow, certainly not beyond it, his mind and body full to bursting with immediate and urgent needs.

Her body ate him up. He spent himself, lost somewhere within her, it happened, nothing was required but the making of love. His first desperation was salved yet at the same time it became more urgent, they could not leave each other alone, her eyes were always on him and when he went in to her she would be waiting ready to devour him, her hair rich and oily in long braids down her cheeks. He was spent and exhausted but delightfully so. After a time he began to need her less, his urges not so urgent now that whenever he turned over in the big soft bed she was there. The moment came when doors were opened and windows set ajar and they looked around them at their life, at each other, and Eunice grew vocal, then shrill as he had never heard her, complaining that she had a right to a house; she could not, would not, live in some hut in diggings that were not even a proper town. Why had he and his terrible father expected that she would? She was an educated woman with a good place with the Bradys. His father, Strat argued, had promised them a house, under conditions . . . What conditions? He did not, could not, explain. Meanwhile, there was the store. What store? Was she expected to run a store in the mountains? Gone was the soft and yielding woman he had enjoyed and their days and nights became a strange progression of savage tormented love-making and questions without answers.

As a favour to the Bradys she drifted back to her splendid baking and her training of Mary's daughters, with piano lessons for the children of Hope to the click-clack of her metronome – Strat heard that click-clack in his dreams. He was lost, unable to understand her or himself. He drifted. His reasons for doing things had gone cock-eyed. It had been easy with Eunice, at least the bedding part. Too easy. Perhaps, after all, he didn't want it to be easy with a woman; perhaps he was a hunter born, or perhaps, simply, he enjoyed the thrill of the chase and now that she had married him he struggled against possessiveness. She was swamping him. Perhaps he needed to bring a woman to heel, like a deer or a prairie buffalo? He spent a long time trying to understand this, and himself, but one thing he did know: there was nothing for him in Hope and in the knowledge there was a kind of relief, a relief that was almost painful when his father demanded his return. He hated his life at Barkerville yet something drew him back. His body was satiated, at least for now, and he was calm again, his needs satisfied. Now he was consumed by other thoughts, interests, queries. He took Eunice's books and her knowledge, consumed her wonderful food along with her protests, absorbed her moods and forgot them. There were times when he felt ridiculously young and eager for her. Other times he felt old with the wisdom of the world and turned from her. Life had changed for him and would go on changing, he knew it. For the first time he felt what he was, who he was – Stratton McCrae – and he liked the sound of it. He was seventeen-and-a-bit but growing older. He liked the idea of that too. No longer was he 'Sandy's laddie' – something had been added. He was a man.

Chapter Five

CELINE WAS urging Dominic to race her around the deck, a
game made difficult by stacked boxes and bales and, as usual
when Domi baulked, her coaxing turned to a childish bullying
with a thump or two thrown in. Phelim, held firmly in Meg's
arms, sensed the excitement and clung to Domi's sleeve, his
small fists red with the effort of hanging on. Dominic, hating to
disappoint him, usually managed to compromise but this time
Celine won and, wrenching himself free, Dominic was after her
to shrieks of laughter and the baby's howls. Alannah let them
be for the steamer was steady and so far the decks were empty
of passengers. Gripping Phelim hard Meg chased the two, the
baby's outrage turning to chuckles: a plump and happy child,
Phelim O'Shea. She hoped he would always be so.

The sun was warm although it was May and early morning,
but as they moved down the coast of New South Wales there
could be breezes off early Alpine snows. She leant over the
rails and raised her face in anticipation, feeling more relaxed
than she had for a long time, watching distant breakers on
distant sands, seeking the sparse settlements that were all
there was of human habitation in an empty land. Distantly
she heard Dominic soothing Phelim – poor patient Domi for
Phelim interrupted his life, his reading, dragging at his books,
clinging, till too often Domi set all aside to amuse his brother.
The only time Dominic dug in his heels, so to speak, was to
oppose Celine. It pleased their mother. Someone must put a
rein on Celine O'Shea even at going-on-five.

A faint breeze ruffled her hair, medicine for the soul, and
she let her scarf slip from her shoulders. They would dock
that evening with her father waiting, probably alone, for she
could not imagine Maria Moynan putting herself out to meet
her husband's daughter and grandchildren. How she would
feel on seeing her father after so long she did not know for

letters were inadequate, while relations between her father and Brick remained businesslike, no more. Though her father never spoke of it he knew Brick had fathered her aborted child, the occasion on which she had almost died. Yet Brick was now her husband, the relationship was different and secure, so perhaps she and her father could be at ease with each other. They might even talk of Conall, her dead brother . . . She stirred. Whatever happened, this excursion was at her own insistence for Brick had not wanted her to come, raising the most trivial of objections. 'It's the wrong time of year. You're going south into winter.' The reminder of Burrendah's roaring fires and sunny verandahs did not silence him. It was, she supposed, unforgivable that she was deserting him at this time but to be with her father and her aunt had become a need. Her return to Burrendah, her beloved home, had assumed something of a Holy Cause.

'A fine morning, Mrs O'Shea.'

She turned unsurprised for she had expected Bennett Muir to seek her out, if not quite so early, even though she had refused his invitation to dinner the previous night. She had sent a message back that she had dined with her children in their cabins, which was true. She drew her scarf around her again, a reflex action, wondering how long he had been standing there watching her.

'Mr Muir? Again, my thanks for your invitation.'

'I could scarcely expect you to accept such a belated one but we came aboard late.'

'We?'

'Matthew Burney, my Sydney manager. I have opened an office there.'

'You do not have to explain your trip to me, Mr Muir.'

'No, but I felt I would like to. You are comfortable aboard?'

'Comfortable enough if crowded, but after all it is only for one night.'

'You have had breakfast?'

'Again, in our cabins. The children are too young and, I fear, boisterous for socialising: we are rather overpowering *en masse*. I still shudder at the turmoil of our train journey from Ipswich, a new toy you see. I am beginning to wonder why I set out at all, particularly with a young baby. Brick was against it.' Why was she babbling of dull domestic episodes that couldn't possibly interest him?

'You have a nurse for the baby, of course.'

She could not suppress a giggle. 'Meg would be flattered to hear you call her so.'

'If there is anything you need please don't hesitate to ask. I know Captain Duncan well.'

'So does my husband. Actually, we have been quite spoilt.'

'And your baggage on arrival?'

'My father will meet us.'

'Ah yes . . . Owen Moynan of Moynan's Mill. Curiously, since we are both in the business of wool, we have never met – but then my Sydney business is attended to by agents. I hear more of your father's political activities than as a cloth manufacturer.'

'The mill was formerly O'Shea's Mill – but of course you know that.'

'If I can be of help when we dock please don't hesitate to ask. Otherwise, I shall take the liberty of calling before I return to Brisbane. Your husband will want to hear of your welfare.'

How stilted they were. She was tired of his questions with her own queries unanswered. He was pompous as well as irritating, treating her as one of her own children, not to be trusted to take a short trip down the coast without all falling overboard. 'Our welfare is excellent and the children more than robust,' she said sharply. Too sharply. She managed a smile. 'I am being ungracious. We are staying with my aunt, Mrs Carney, at Lucknow, the Bridge Academy in Bridge Street. A boys' school.'

'I know it.'

'I'm sure you do.' Again too sharply but she could not help herself. 'For a man so recently settled in this country you seem to know a great deal about it, and its people. Certainly its purlieus.' Something was driving her. 'I'm sure you must. cross paths with Jamie, my husband's eldest son, perhaps in gambling "hells"; isn't that what men call their favourite gaming-rooms?'

'Jamie Lorne?'

'As he calls himself.'

'We meet from time to time about the city,' he said casually. 'Queenslanders cross paths, we can't help it, we have no way of avoiding each other even if we wished to do so. We are rather an inverted society you know . . . How long will you stay with your aunt?'

'A fortnight. Then we go to Burrendah, my old home near Goulburn. I have not been back in ten years.'

He looked at her directly. 'Burrendah, I think, is what you really came to visit. There is an inflexion in your voice when you speak of it.'

'Few people notice inflexions. I suppose it does seem rather odd, this longing I have to return, particularly as my first husband drowned there. A flash flood.'

'I'm sorry.'

Weary of their formal over-polite exchange she said briskly, 'There would be few places in the world where someone has not died.' Wondering what her children were about – ah, there they clattered. Celine flew by, Dominic on her heels and Meg in pursuit clutching the squealing baby bouncing his delight. Celine stopped dead, almost sending the others sprawling, turned and stared at her mother's companion. Alannah ached to spank her there and then for insolence. Bennett smiled but the child remained stony-faced. It was plain, surely, to the man that Celine did not take to him, a child distinct in her likes and dislikes; it was to be hoped for her own sake she would not feel the same about Miss Isabel. She's wary and suspicious, as I am, her mother raged; we don't trust easily. I am unfair to Bennett Muir for today his manner cannot be faulted and if necessary I will accept his help with the baggage. Celine, conscious of all eyes on her, decided to indulge her love of display and let fly at Dominic. Domi hit back. For the joy of it they began a noisy free-for-all.

'Celine! Your game is too noisy. You bother people.'

'There's no one here but us,' the child defied, her eyes still on Bennett Muir.

'There will be others on deck soon so go down to your cabins and look at picture-books. Meg will go with you. It's time for the baby's nap.'

'I don't like the cabins.'

'I do,' Domi piped up.

'They're too small. And they smell.'

'Then you must have left food about. No arguments now. Meg will bring your lunch. Off with you all.'

Celine flounced off brushing Meg aside. In the sudden and blessed quiet Alannah turned with apologies but Bennett was unperturbed – and bored, she decided. Children were not part of his life, only of Isabel's, and even she dealt with other people's offspring. 'They are sadly undisciplined, as you can see. A fault in my character.'

He ignored the remark. 'You will find Sydney much changed. Under-populated at the moment due to another exodus to yet another goldfield.'

'There are always new goldfields somewhere. Certainly in Queensland. But then, you know the north.'

'I do?'

'I'm sure you do. You are rather a secret man, Mr Muir.' She kept it light. 'I feel you live rather a secret life.'

'Mr Muir? Don't you feel you've known me long and well enough to call me Bennett?'

'No, I don't.'

'I see. Well, if you regard me as a secret man I see you as a decidedly frank woman.'

'In that case I'll say I'm surprised to find you travelling when your sister is expected in Brisbane.'

'I'm in Sydney only a few days. In any case arrangements are in hand at Foxburgh.'

'Of course. I was forgetting Miss Muir.'

'Miss Muir? I'm beginning to think the entire Muir family has offended you.'

'I'm being ungracious again. Perhaps this trip has something to do with it. I have never liked sea travel, not even coastal. Besides . . . perhaps I am uneasy at returning to my "Place of the Swan", as I call Burrendah, rather like approaching . . . well . . . a haunted house – and I'm being ridiculous.' She floundered. 'I'm sorry to miss your grand ball for Eva – there, I do better with the Muir I've never met. Brick tells me that according to her portrait she's quite beautiful.'

'Isabel calls the painting a gross exaggeration.'

'Surely not. To be clever as well as attractive must be a devastating combination.'

'Most women would not be as generous in praise of another.'

'I am not most women. At least I've never felt so.'

'You're an unusual woman. And quite beautiful yourself.'

'Now what am I to say to that?'

'Accept it as a genuine compliment. With respect.'

She straightened. The conversation was becoming intimate. 'I hope we shall not be late in.'

'We're making good time.'

'Then I must see to the children. And the baggage. I'll not forget your offer of help if I should need it.' He inclined his head with, she decided, a mocking little lift to his mouth. She did not like it. She knew he was watching her as she walked along the deck. As so often in his company, when his eyes were not seeking hers she felt them boring into her back.

Matt Burney was what in a cheap novel would be called 'swarthy', but the description suited him, a dark man with tough tanned skin complementing dark hair and beard, and usually in seaman's garb. But in his cramped and cluttered office facing Darling Harbour with 'Melanesian Trading Co.' over the door he was more conventionally suited as he shuffled maps, papers and lists before his employer.

'. . . I assure you, Mr Muir, it will be plain sailing.' He gave his slightly crooked grin. 'With no apologies for the pun. Since the new regulations covering Kanakas, Fiji is where the trading is done. It's like this: the schooner clears Sydney with a small general cargo and in Levuka changes name; the *Myrtle*'s cap'n is an experienced trading skipper and swears it's an easy matter to convert a barque into a brig simply by unshipping the mizzen mast, nought to it. The *Myrtle* becomes the *Venture* or some such and we re-register with the British Consul, with new papers. Instead of a return cargo of pigs and coconuts we load Kanakas for the Fijian planters. They're as desperate for labour as Queenslanders but pay only five pounds a head against the Queenslander's nine, yet balance that against cost of food, and clothing – Kanakas are happy enough lying about naked – with berthing under the regulations, and you'll still come out of it nicely. Again, the *Myrtle* can carry one hundred and eight against a licensed fifty-eight. The missionaries give

67

trouble of course, always meddling, conveniently forgetting that a measles plague can wipe out whole tribes in a swoop, but I know how to handle the Bible-bangers. One snag, as I've said . . . Our recruiting man at Tanna is on the grog and tangled up with too many chieftains' daughters; the chiefs refuse to let him land any longer. All we can do is sneak him off — '

'As I've said, Burney, replace him fast.' Bennett flicked dust from his expensive jacket, eyeing with distaste the paperweight of a shrunken head on the man's desk. The place was not only dirty but raffish, as was Burney himself no matter how much he spent on onshore tailoring. Besides, he was too cocky. 'Get rid of that obscenity, I won't have these heads about the place, they're too obvious.'

Burney shot the offending artefact with a pile of wastepaper into a basket. 'Never easy to find the right fellow but I have someone in mind . . . A man has to be running from something, see, even better, running scared, needing to get out of the country, that sort of thing. My fellow is a wild gamer and these days loses his head too easily . . . He's been living hand to mouth in the north but knows the plantations and Kanakas around Maryborough; he even managed to coax 'em up to Mackay when they hate the bloody place. He's got a way with the niggers. Well, his IOUs are mounting up and I hold most of 'em. He has no hope of settling. Better still, for my — our — purpose I caught him out at a spot of forgery; excellent copy of m'name but still not good enough. I've scared hell out of him with threats of prison but haven't pressed charges and won't, I'm keeping him dangling, suggesting he work all off around the islands . . . It will take him years at the usual wages but I don't see he has a choice.'

'The name of this possible?'

'Jamie Lorne, as he calls himself.'

'O'Shea's son? I suspected it. What do his IOUs amount to?'

'Close on four thousand.'

'Whew! You're a better gamer than I've found you, or else he's a hopeless one.'

'The point is, Mr Muir . . .' Burney's voice took on a truculent tone as he swaggered about the tiny office, 'what do I get out of it? I mean, I'll be saving you wages, and you do fine at this business as it is . . .'

Bennett Muir ran a finger over a stack of ledgers, surveyed the film of dust and wiped his hand on a snowy pocket-handkerchief. Replacing the handkerchief in his pocket he splayed the edges tastefully. He knew a great deal about Burney that the man never suspected: originally in the sandal-wood trade, then as a Royal Navy seaman he'd deserted and carried thousands of Pacific Islanders to labour in Peru's offshore guano deposits . . . Like all violent men Burney was proud of his cunning; he, Muir, had no doubts at all of the man's recruiting methods but left well alone there, all he wanted were results. 'You get excellent pickings "at this business", Burney, with regular bonuses, all of which amounts to far more than you'd make elsewhere. You know it, I know it. I pay you well for secrecy, for keeping me entirely and per-manently out of your expensive legitimate "front" of a South Seas trader. Now you'll continue to keep accurate books which I'll continue to vet at regular intervals, and with this little bit of business I'll vet them more often – while you know better than to try to falsify a penny. The most you can hope for is an extra bonus – we'll see. Meanwhile, you'll sail with this fellow and see him settled in the New Hebrides. You'll watch his every move – you or your spies there for it matters nothing to me how you tame him so long as he works well. You're responsible for him, remember that. And warn him against chieftains' daughters, I'll have no trouble over women — '

'He'll toe the line, Mr Muir, I'll vouch for it. I can gaol him any time I like and he knows it.'

Bennett paused with his hand on the doorknob. 'The point is, Burney, I can buy up a stack of your IOUs any time I like – oh yes – and make life damned uncomfortable for you. Actually, you're a rotten gamer, and in this matter of Jamie Lorne O'Shea I'd say you've been lucky!'

Amid the flurry of organising baggage and children and her father attempting to greet all at once, Alannah had been relieved to find Bennett Muir at her side. Though introduc-tions added to the confusion and clamour the men seemed at

69

ease with each other. 'Mr Muir is Brick's business associate,' she found herself explaining, lamely and untruthfully. Why did she feel she must explain the man's presence? 'Business rivals.' Bennett's smile had been pleasant and his manner smooth (oily, she had always called it). 'Friendly enemies, Brisbane calls us.' Driving from the Quay her father was blunt. 'Import-export is a vague term at any time. What does the fellow deal in?'

'Wool – I suppose. Doesn't everyone? Whatever it is he's opened a branch here. He travelled down with his manager, though I never met him.' She had hesitated. Bradshaw? Bullock? Baker? She couldn't remember the man's name.

'I'd say Muir's the kind to expend his energy to the limit and show no adverse effect. Durable. What I call a hunter.'

She smiled. 'And you're not?'

At sixty Owen Moynan was still a handsome man, certainly a successful one, and apparently a contented one, indulged and cosseted by a woman he clearly adored, so he could see no wrong in Maria's veiled insults towards his daughter and family; yet so subtle were they it was almost as if they occurred only in her mind. He was delighted if confused by the children's energy; he had visited Burrendah when Clodagh was born but he would never come to Hawkes Plains without Maria. He had topped his cigar smoothly, a smooth man all round. 'You have what you want, you're where you belong. It took me a long time to accept that. As long as you realise you won't always like living in the north – and that happiness comes and goes. One can't always live on the heights. In the beginning I think you expected that.'

Aunt Delia Carney was as blunt and implacable as ever over her likes and dislikes, her wills and won'ts. 'I vowed I'd never set foot in Brighton while Maria Sparrow – you know I don't accept her as a Moynan – is there. I've always said she's no better than she should be, a hussy, and nothing will change my views. Your father calls each week for tea, we discuss school matters and read your latest letters, and that's that!'

'Papa obviously likes hussies, at least this one.' Alannah laughed it off. How simple her life would be if she were as devious as Maria and as uncomplicated in her moral judgments as her aunt. Her own emotions simmered and boiled over, she could not help it; she was forever holding herself in check, one reason why she appeared remote, a throwback to her Irish childhood with the Dominican nuns, walking sedately in crocodile through the streets of Belfast. She had thrown off that Catholic childhood with Con's help, Con the beloved brother dead at nineteen in a mob fight, the reason Aunt Delia refused to come to Hawkes Plains, blaming not only Jamie Lorne but Brick, the latter unfairly, for luring her beloved nephew into trouble. Alannah knew Conall Moynan had been more than capable of creating his own chaos.

There were little dinners at Brighton and Lucknow and at the homes of business and political social climbers eager to cultivate her father's patronage. There were teas for the children where they sat subdued before guests all hoped never to see again. Clodagh would sit beautifully straight, as Miss Muir insisted, answering Maria's probing questions politely and truthfully. Celine caused an initial stir by perching herself at the dining-table, her chin scarcely above it, and banging a spoon on the damask demanding to join the grown-ups in the '*grande* manner', pronouncing *grande* in the French way. Where, Alannah wondered, did the child hear such phrases? From her father? Surely not from Will? Jamie? It was possible. Perhaps Dominic boasted more advanced books than anyone suspected. Celine's long legs had to be forcibly uncoiled from her chair and she was dragged off protesting she would *not* eat milk puddings with the babies in the contrived 'nursery'. She was sent to bed in disgrace. 'There's much of you in that child,' Owen warned. 'Too much to my way of thinking.' Alannah could never quite manage her younger daughter and there were times in the first week when she longed to catch the next steamer north.

Things were better at Lucknow with its gardens and horses and the fish-pond to fall into – and no Maria. Bennett Muir called, to charm her aunt with his greetings and goodbyes. There were outings and expeditions in which her father joined: drives to South Head to watch ships sail in. They took ferry rides. They rode in horse-trams, even had a train ride now and then. They picnicked around the bays and drove about a city growing in an amazing manner, George Street crowded with broughams and cabs and heavily laden carts, and its wonderful Saturday night promenades. Celine was fascinated by the Chinese settlements around the Circular Quay and George Street North. She demanded to be taken to the Markets by Meg and Fay but once there escaped to wander the Chinese vegetable stalls, and the poultry, fruit and vegetable booths. She snitched a pork pie and was perched on a box, dishevelled and blissfully happy, sharing it with a Chinese boy and a part-aborigine waif when discovered by a distracted Meg.

'Your mama and grandpapa are driving Sydney looking for you, Miss Celine.' Meg's eyes were red from tears. 'You'll be punished.'

'I don't care, I like it here. I'll run away whenever I like.' This time she was spanked, warned, and sent to bed without her tea. Alannah counted the days until they could immerse themselves in the easy formality and blessed remoteness of Burrendah, her 'Place of the Swan'.

'Daisy's money keeps Wiena going, as always, with my Rob's help as always, though it's mostly advice these days for he's not getting any younger. Like the rest of us – begging your pardon, ma'am.'

'Why the formal "ma'ams"?' Alannah managed a laugh through her irritation.

Hetty Witherstone pushed her side hair up and her apron down in her old familiar gesture: dear aggravating meddlesome Hetty, grey but still indomitable, with her Bible quotes, her proverbs and her clichés as background to her pounding of scones, a little heavier these days, her bread the same. 'Well, there's some think of you as Miss Moynan, others as Mrs Aldercott, and now with a third name to remember, "ma'am" seems easiest all round. You looked a bit peaky when you arrived, ma'am, but no wonder with your youngest a babe in arms — '

'Doing his best to wriggle free.'

'And our Fay with no more gumption than she ever had.'

'She's wonderful with Moll. And she has sense enough to choose Tod Buxton, he's a fine stockman.'

'As long as he knows how to shake her out of her dreaming

spells. You would have appreciated Miss Clodagh on the trip, though Miss Celine tells us you had a friend on board.'

'Stop the "Miss Clodagh" and "Miss Celine" too.'

'Why, I had no wish to offend, I'm sure.'

'My younger daughter is a four-year-old gossip and busybody. Mr Muir is a family acquaintance, my husband's business associate — ' She pulled herself up. No more explanations, certainly not to satisfy Hetty's morbid curiosity. 'No more of this servility Hetty, or I'll be angry.'

'Miss Alannah then?'

'It always was.'

'A pity Mr O'Shea couldn't have come with you.'

'He's busy with the Brisbane house. Besides, he's always happy around Hawkes Plains.'

'And you're not, quite – begging pardon again.'

'Stop the "pardons" too.' Alannah got to her feet to finger familiar objects about Erins Pride's kitchen. 'I don't know why this restraint between us, Hetty. Once we were at ease over anything and everything. Perhaps I've been away too long.' She added defensively: 'Hawkes Plains is a beautiful place and my home.' Ill-at-ease, Hetty began talking rapidly and at random, enquiring of Gondola and Barney, even Jamie, while caring nought for any of them. 'Gondola is off at the faintest hint of a circus but always returns. The same with Barney, but Brick finds him among the remnants of the local tribes.' She paused. 'Celine can't abide Barney, she runs from him.'

'She shows sense there.'

'It's more than the man, I think. It's colour, I'm ashamed to say. She acts so with all the Blacks. I hope she won't offend them here, they're not used to it. It makes me wonder if she's heard some garbled account of her father's background.' Hetty stared for this was one matter over which they had complete rapport. Brick O'Shea's ancestry had been so long and so completely accepted in the County of Argyle it was never alluded to. 'We hope she'll grow out of it.' She smiled companionably at Hetty for it was unthinkable they should be at odds over trifles. 'Her father's answer to problems with his children is "They'll grow out of it". He doesn't know a thing about young children really, but he tries hard. As for Jamie . . .' She shrugged helplessly and Hetty sniffed. 'The

73

same wanderer, turning up now and then to make more trouble.' More quotes and clichés over Moll Noakes. 'Merciful release when she does go . . . Best all round . . .' Warming up, Hetty fell into her stride with news closer home.

'Grace was over last year, she has four and another on the way; always another on the way for Grace. Joey leaves all to her though he couldn't have left quite all now could he?' Her laugh shuddered above her bashing of pans and her stoking up of the stove. 'She can't get back quick enough to her kitchen garden and fruit trees; imagine all that out in the desert at Oorin. Ida sends her letters over. The eldest Bowes boy spells out the words and the second writes them down, with a bit of help from my own lads who've settled in nicely. They get schooling from one of the hands, a gentleman come down in the world, lots of them around these days, remittance men they call them. Grace has what she wants. I just hope Joey has.'

There were few changes at either property, both long settled and run by routine and habit; even the usual floods and droughts seemed diffused by long usage. An ageing Dan ran Burrendah, but Ida remained her practical efficient self. 'It's I who have changed,' Alannah reminded herself. 'They have just got older.' Celine was everyone's darling, charming while alarming somewhat with her enthusiasm and the agility with which she met each new day, a vocal aggressive whirlwind of a child growing too fast, her flyaway hair always out of its braids and Clodagh forever tucking it in. Celine's eyes looked disconcertingly on the world, her personality outstripping Clodagh's so sharply that Alannah's protective instinct towards her eldest sent Celine flouncing off shouting protests about 'favourites', yet her resentment was short-lived and next morning she would be ready for the new day. Thankfully, there were no incidents between herself and the Black 'boys'. Perhaps after all it was just Barney the child disliked.

Alannah's great joy, as it had always been, was riding Burrendah, followed at a discreet distance since Ida insisted, by Paddys One, Two or Three, all as nuggety and tenacious as ever if rather more grizzled. She rode to Wiena station, refusing to let Daisy Elston wallow in her 'tragedy' as she

74

called Simon's death. 'If you hadn't come to help me . . .'
'It's so long ago, Daisy. Besides, a flash flood is no one's
fault.' Daisy, the faded belle, was wispy and vague, her equally
wispy daughters still unwed, their mother refusing any faintly
interested district son as planning to retire on their dowries.
Since her girls were overshadowed by their brothers' wives
she planned to settle them in England. (Seen the light at last,
Hetty sniffed. They're useless here. All they can do is open
a school or finish up as seamstresses. In my view the local
lads have had lucky escapes.)

The children explored the district, Clodagh making her
careful dignified way on horseback and Dominic and Celine
mounted before the men. Sometimes they took the trap into
busy Goulburn. Some mornings, with Clodagh and Celine in
the next room arguing over hair-ribbons, Celine resorting to
foot-stamping or tears faced with Clodagh's quiet opposition,
Alannah would wander out to the verandah with memories
crowding. She had stood here one winter's morning long ago
waiting for Brick to ride down the slope to tell her of Conall's
death. She could not bear to be so reminded of his lonely
grave somewhere in the High Country and turned back to
her warm room. Simon's grave within its neat iron railings
was well cared for but it took her a long time to wander down
to the Creek crossing, calm and gentle with the stillness of
autumn, and recall what the water had been like when he
had struggled against it to save his wife and child.

Oddly, it took her even longer to walk to what she had
always called her 'special place' tucked between the willows
and the Creek with the remains of the old stone bridge
crumbling away. Ten years . . . how long ago it all was.
The sun shone bright and warm on the soft green hollow
where she had lived her first sexual excitement with the man
who was to become the most important in her life. She knelt
and ran her hands over the grass, visioning their entwined
bodies, and a sudden longing for Brick made her gasp; she
wanted to rush to him then and there and love him as she
had loved him here. She sat leaning against the wall with lacy
fronds of willows trailing over her body, with earthy scents
and the gentle ripple of water teasing. The pad of green was
soft beneath her and it was as if their combined weight was

pressing it down and Brick was with her and within her – yet he was not. It could not be lived exactly so again. No matter how much and how deeply one loved, life became a matter of rare brief eruptions of great happiness levelling out to a comforting warmth. She was approaching thirty, Brick soon to be sixty and hating it so much he must constantly prove himself to her, afraid of leaving her behind – she knew. He and Burrendah did not belong, they did not mate. Nor did her 'Place of the Swan' mean much to her children, they were Queenslanders, even Clodagh; but then, nothing had meaning for Clodagh unless Will was there.

She shivered slightly. It would soon be cold. She got to her feet, loath to leave but it must be so. There was, after all, only one thing to do, gather up her possessions, her maids and her children and go home to Hawkes Plains. To her husband and her love.

Chapter Six

BRICK HAD stayed a month in Brisbane to oversee the comple-
tion of his town house. Hawkes Plains was functioning well
under Tod's management, particularly since Jamie had taken
himself off, presumably north again, though Brick suspected
he had returned to some favourite dive in the Fortitude
Valley: either way with a little luck he would not cross the
paths of the O'Sheas for a while. Painters and architects
still wandered BelleMonte but it was partly furnished, the
master bedroom complete with a huge four-poster and the
whole awaiting Alannah's approval and finishing touches. A
housekeeper-elect, Mrs Plum, recommended by the Muirs and
enticed from her present situation by a generous stipend, was
packing in readiness to join the O'Shea household; otherwise
there were no servants for Brick intended Alannah to choose
her own. Meanwhile, only gardeners came and went each
morning. He had considered moving in but did not fancy
being there without Alannah and she was not due for another
week at the earliest. He fretted, impatient, irritated that she
had even taken the trip. There was nothing for him to do but
ride up each day and wander the silent half-empty rooms.

He had dined out often and well for Brisbane wore a festive
air, with hospitality all round. He was weary of making excuses
for Alannah – a prearranged trip to visit her relatives in the
south – but he found himself much in demand. At Foxburgh
House Eva Muir was an attractive and stimulating dinner
companion, with Isabel clearly averse to her – jealousy there?
– while Bennett, though solicitous, seemed hesitant, even
grudging, as if in some way his younger sister held some trump
card. Her knowledge of theatre was extensive and European.
'My Portia shocks people but I'll continue to play her so.
People do not seem to understand pre-Restoration theatre
where women's roles were played by men. I play Portia as

a man would, strong, awkward if you like, yet full-blooded
and ruthless. To many, my Portia is unfeminine.' Smiling,
defying such a façade with her natural limpid femaleness.
Brick went to her opening performance and was moved by
it; she conveyed a sophistication that could be construed by
inexperienced provincials as ribaldry, an abandon in the role of
Juliet that belonged to Renaissance Verona and never Queen
Street, Brisbane. It excited him. He did not go again. Today he
wandered idly through the spacious rooms. The outside world
was dry and dusty, a day to close windows and doors leaving
only enough opening to breathe. A day for cool drinks and,
if possible, nudity, and he loosened his shirt. Would Alannah
enjoy this view? He had spent a long time planning the house,
particularly this room – their room. But the day was too heavy
and languid to think. He did not want to think.

It was there, gazing from the French windows on to the
Terrace and a hazy Brisbane that Eva Muir found him. She
stood a long time watching him, conscious of his absorption
in the outside world. She almost felt the silence. She had come
on impulse. There was no reason why he should be here today
and alone but she had thought it probable. The great front
door was unlocked and she had wandered the silent halls and
rooms, a house empty of things and people. Now he seemed
to fill this room, or so it seemed to her, more correctly
he dominated it as he dominated everything, certainly her
thoughts and feelings since they had met. She had looked for
him past the footlights each night but had seen him only once.
She had never known anyone quite like this man though she
had known many, young, old, rich, drifters, had loved a few
and slept with more in various gradations and imitations of
love; Brick O'Shea, black-haired despite his age for he was
no longer young, had a mystique she found irresistible. She
was tired of boys, wearier still of the not-so-young trying to be
boys, but this man would not try to be anything but himself.
He was different, with something exotic about him that was
entirely natural. She had heard the rumour that there was
native blood in him and it added to his attraction; she had
always craved the exotic, had sought it in men, women, life,
hence her lifelong love of the stage: theatre gave her an
extension of living, a glamorisation of life, adding colour to

the world for reality was too often drab and pedestrian. She had always felt different from others with a need to escape the mediocre for the excitement of what might be around the next corner. She had sought this man deliberately for her life would only be complete if she knew him intimately, as a lover, and watching him from the doorway, unseen as she was, her body quickened. She had mentally despatched his pretty proud young wife even before the girl had taken herself south, in a mood perhaps, or a pet; she, Eva Muir, had no time for wives, particularly one foolish enough to let such a man out of her sight, though in the end it would make no difference: she had no intention of leaving this barbaric frontier town until she had experienced him and he her.

In the reborn successful Eva Muir, leaving behind the May Lowry pseudonym of her early Barbary Coast days, the juices of life and love and sex ran freely. Now the world was hers, certainly this outpost of Empire to which she had come to confront her brother and sister with her success. There was exhilaration in such power not only onstage but in her intimate knowledge of her brother's Californian years that she would never let him forget. Perhaps only she knew and had nurtured the truth of his life after she had joined him in 'Frisco as a desperate sixteen-year-old running from a rigid 'service' in Glasgow. She had refused to become one of his pretty waiter 'girls' (it was not done to use the word prostitute), for her chance of a new life in a new country must yield much more. She had learnt to use peepholes to watch him with his harlots, cheating in his gambling-rooms, meeting with criminals, awaiting her chance to use such knowledge. Though he had used her she had used him to gain what she wanted: in return for certain erotic favours bestowed on a powerful theatrical figure who patronised his gaming-tables, Bennett had gained for her her first part, small, but she had made it so important it had led to serious theatre, and prestige.

Goodbye Barbary Coast and its cosy expensive dives even if Bennett's had been one of the most luxurious. Goodbye (regretfully) to his sumptuous house, BelleMonte – it was a measure of his confidence in his position in this country that he had kept the name alive. She had never looked back and no doubt Bennett had hoped, indeed believed, that he had escaped her along with other reminders of his past . . . But he would never be free of the threat of her and if it served her purpose in the future she would use him. Isabel, she suspected, was ignorant of her brother's life in America but, ignorant or not, neither she nor Bennett could shake the unassailable position of Eva Muir, actress, for Shakespeare notwithstanding she was one of the 'notorious whores' of tradition, and gloried in the fact. Yet she could if she so wished ruin Bennett's rich respectable life here, the comfortable silky existence he and Isabel had built to hoodwink gullible Australian burghers who envied and admired them. Bennett had not wanted her in Australia, any more than Isabel had, for different reasons, nevertheless she had come with her 'front' of a closely nurtured and successful actress, counting on Australia's isolation and its hunger for European flavours to serve her well. The one love of Bennett's life – and of her own, she supposed – was money and the security and power it gave, antidote to their hazardous childhood spent in the shadow of an in-and-out-of-prison Scottish advocate father. Isabel? She had never known what Isabel wanted.

She moved into the room and Brick turned slowly as if still possessed by the world outside. He stared and she laughed softly. 'The door was unlocked. I walked in. Perhaps I should not have done so but I expected a housekeeper about. Or workmen. Gardeners . . .'

'There is no one else here.'

'I heard so much about your beautiful house I wanted to see it for myself. I hope it pleases your wife?' She had no interest in wives, certainly not in Alannah O'Shea, only interest in his reaction. He did not answer, just went on staring. 'It's so quiet. As if we are above the world.'

'There are no servants as yet.'

All was still, no sound at all, as if the two of them were the only ones in the world, even cut off from the world, the silence enhancing a sense of isolation for through the wide closed doors she could see a terrace leading down to more terraces and so to the gardens. He watched her remove her scarf, then her cloak, for the enclosed room was so warm that soft tendrils of hair clung to her cheeks and neck. Moisture gave a sheen to her skin, gleaming in the midday sun. The room was bathed in sun, they were dazzled by it. She put up a hand to shade her eyes and moved to close the curtains a little. 'You don't mind, I hope?'

He shook his head. He could not drag his eyes from her. He had known many beautiful women so what was there about this one that made him catch his breath? Her throat looked pale and cool and he ached to place his hands about it for it would be silky smooth. She brushed against him as she walked to the terrace doors and stood looking out. Her breasts were full under something flimsy, she always wore such clothes. He loved the dark shadow between her breasts and he felt more than any other emotion anger at his long abstinence. He wondered what he would do when she touched him as she would and soon, this outwardly calm but eager woman who wanted him and had done so from the first. He had run from her, a bizarre circumstance in itself, Brick O'Shea running from anyone, particularly a woman, but now he would not run – no more of it! Atmosphere, and propinquity, would achieve what he had let be.

'I have no matinée today.'

She moved to the door and locked it. Her action did not surprise him, perhaps she had turned many keys, a woman who had known many men for her approach was sophisticated and unfaltering, a secret woman who would not tell but simply show him. The room was dim, the light diffused, soothing yet somehow exciting. Her movements were graceful but measured and decisive; she was taking everything out of his hands – good! She moved to the bed and began to undress with the studied movements of an actress, perhaps a ballerina, dramatic and moving to cue. Her clothes were flimsy yet, he knew, expensive, and she folded them neatly on a chair. He made no move to go to her or even to remove his own clothes, not yet, for all would be taken care of, they were already certain of each other, and prepared, with no need of courting or foreplay or the weaving and strutting about of display. No pinching or stroking needed, no words, nothing. It would simply happen. As he expected she had a beautiful body. She would let him appraise her a while then would take the initiative, a woman who knew exactly what she was about; all would fall into place with the ease of two people, man and woman, who knew the world, their sex, and what they were about. She held out a hand to him.

'Come. We have all afternoon.'

All the time in the world, he thought, holding her on the bed. Something was singing in his head, throbbing. Think of nothing but the woman, not of yourself, not yet. Her lips were very sweet. He savoured them, taking his time, her arms about him, caressing him, drawing him close. He heard her sigh and felt the shudder through her as he entered her and began to explore. There was sexual shock and expectation, then a singing anticipation for she was exquisitely schooled, trained to meet his body and use it, enfold it, draw upon it with an urgency even he had rarely experienced. There was a delicious palpitation in her that he could scarcely endure. He rested, drifting between his labours, his face against her throat and warmed by her breath. He dared not kiss her again, not yet. There were some women, he mused, enchanted by her inner warmth, who were different from other women; women whose bodily energy was concentrated in a tight fierce core. A nucleus. Such a woman seemed to function independently of the man who was rousing her, as if she would be roused without him, yet at the same time must devour him. This was such a woman. Their friction resumed and gathered momentum . . . still more . . . She was drawing on him, giving, drawing, giving, drawing . . . He wanted to shout out his triumph. Perhaps he did cry out, it did not matter, he exulted in her and in himself. She was giving him back his youth, and in abundance . . . Recreating it. Now, he could no longer bear it. He put his mouth on hers, and overflowed. Spent in her he sank his elbows in relief to hold her quivering beneath him. It was a long time before they were still and he withdrew.

She had sent her cab away, she told him. There were boys playing in the bush down the slope and he sent them to find a cab. He saw her off, exchanging few words. If eyes watched he did not know, nor did she. Neither cared.

Jamie drew up his horse sharply and, dismounting, moved behind a shield of shrubs that still gave him a clear view along the Terrace. A cab waited before BelleMonte. A man and woman descended the steps, Brick O'Shea, and even from a distance he recognised the actress, Eva Muir. All Brisbane knew her by now, a woman, it was said, irresistible on and off stage. Something about the eyes . . . He smiled to himself. O'Shea, it seemed, had found her so. He, Jamie, had stood in the knot of crowd watching her drive through the city and had actually elbowed his way into a Gallery performance to see what the fuss was about only to be bored by Shakespeare: music-halls were more his style. He watched Brick help her into the cab then turn abruptly to the house. He drew his horse farther back as the cab bowled past in a cloud of dust, his protection, for even if she had noticed someone standing there she could not have seen him clearly. Wickham Terrace was empty of human life. He had been drinking heavily for days until finally in desperation he had ridden up from the Valley to borrow – a dependable word, 'borrow', signifying a paying back, which of course he had no intention of doing. He had tried every avenue – so-called friends, gold-digging mates, publicans, even madams of bawdy-houses, to find himself shunned. The same with the Valley inns and taverns for he owed bed and board at most of them. The miserable Cawnpore was the only one that would give him credit. Besides, he was having no luck at the tables; there was no one, nothing but Burney's offer . . . He shuddered as he mounted and turned his horse, looking sourly on his life turned sour. He had ridden up in the hope of finding O'Shea alone, as he usually was at his precious BelleMonte, to be confronted with . . . what? A situation. An intriguing one. Perhaps after all he had gained something more valuable than a loan, if he could have scrounged anything from O'Shea at all. Now he had something to hang on to, something solid, something he could use . . . All he would need was the right moment and instead of begging he could demand. Exhilarated, optimistic as always when he could see even slightly around corners, he rode happily back into town.

The grand ball at Foxburgh House was the highlight and culmination of Eva Muir's Brisbane 'season'. There had been extensive juggling for invitations to meet her and the principals of her company and Isabel had been sharp in her selections, a list composed of what she considered the *crème de la crème* of Brisbane Society: politicians, both elected and aspiring (of the latter only the possibles), businessmen, import-exporters, bankers, brokers, medical men and representatives of the law; but in the main it was the squatting fraternity, the long-settled landowners (horse-thieves and land-grabbers, according to how townsfolk viewed them) residing in Brisbane or willing to make the trip in who filled the ornate room with assorted wives, daughters and near relatives. No expense had been spared, the décor was lavish, the flowers extravagant and the buffet to match. Champagne flowed. The Muirs with Eva as guest of honour stood to greet the élite, many of whom she had already met, but this was a formal occasion and must be conducted so. Brick bowed over Eva's hand as everyone else in line, bored all over again with explaining his wife's absence. He chose a waltz to dance with Eva, making no attempt to evade her questions or even her eyes that had followed his every movement since his arrival.

'You have avoided me.' She made no effort to keep her voice down.

'I have been busy.'

'One finds time for what one really wants to do.'

'I have not sought you out, one reason being that my wife arrives in two days.'

'And children.'

'Of course. I have a long tail. You knew that.'

'The family man incarnate.'

'It seems so.'

'We are not to meet again?'

'Not alone.'

'It's cold-blooded. Brutal.'

'I've been called a brutal man. Perhaps I am about some matters. In this matter I call it being reasonable.'

'I don't want you reasonable. I don't want you back with your sparrow.'

'Is that how my wife appears to you? How wrong you are. She's a swan, and a rather splendid one, taking flight now and then to show off her feathers – not your colourful plumage, but then she cares nothing for decoration.'

'I would do anything you say. Anything.'

'No you would not and you know it. Nothing would be permitted, finally, to interfere with your life's work, your career. It was an experience between us, God it was, but something apart from our respective lives.'

'I could love you.'

'Don't. Love implies constancy and commitment. I don't really believe you want that. Nor do I. Not from you.'

'At this moment I hate you.'

'That's better. It's healthier. You should hate me for what I am called, a hard man. But then, you are my female equivalent. In this matter it's a good thing. Where relationships are concerned we're hard people.'

'So . . . I must return to London without you?'

'Wasn't it your intention to return? I understood so. Otherwise your brother has wasted his hospitality and your sister her quite awesome organisation.'

'You will not join me in London?'

'No. Nor anywhere else. When I'm with the English I become too Irish and I don't like the sense of a veneer . . . Don't do this, Eva. Don't try to make yourself a necessity for I won't let you be. You must remain an experience, a diversion, as I must to you so let's finish up together honestly. It doesn't mean I won't remember – as you will now and then.'

'Always.'

He kissed her hand on leaving, as others did, a courtesy, no more. But he held her hand a trifle longer than was necessary. He did not notice Isabel Muir's eyes on them, nor did he hear her distinctive rustle amid other rustles. He was too conscious of Eva's touch.

'She made a show of us as well as herself.'

'How?'

'For one thing, the way she danced. Just as she performs onstage, with abandon.'

'I'm surprised you can define "abandon" in a woman. Come now, Bel, she showed far less leg than she does with her Juliet, or even her Rosamund – but then you only saw one performance and had to be bullied to that.'

85

'She sets out deliberately to attract.'

'She succeeds.'

'I shudder not only for my girls but their parents.'

'Forget your girls. As for the parents they had a fine time on my champagne.'

'You defend Eva in everything – why? When I joined you here five years ago you never wanted to see her again, any more than I did.'

'I've had longer and wider experience of Eva than you. She can be a hawk when it suits her and not the rather splendid . . . well . . . lyre-bird she is on most occasions. Don't fall out with her.'

'I refuse to pander to her as you do.' She frowned. 'I sometimes wonder about your life in San Francisco. And hers.'

He paused in pouring himself a final brandy. 'What do you mean?'

'Don't treat me as a fool, Bennett.'

'I never have.' His voice took on a spiteful tinge. 'I treat you as a clever if somewhat grim spinster who's settled herself rather nicely in life. As recompense for the loss of other things, I imagine.'

'You've always been a secretive man, certainly over your American years.'

He laughed, sipping his drink. 'Are you actually suggesting there was something sinister about our life there?'

'I don't know. But it doesn't seem feasible that ordinary buying and selling could produce the fortune you display, even squander. You've never clearly explained it, at least not to me.'

He gave an exaggerated sigh. 'I catered for well-heeled Californians — '

'Not the public version. The truth.'

He placed his glass on the table with such force that the crystal goblets and decanters tinkled and shimmered. 'I was a dealer in gold. I traded. I bought a run-down saloon, built it up to a luxury hotel and sold it at a substantial profit. I did the same with my house there. I ran a hotel in Melbourne before I settled in Brisbane. Here I deal in fine and rare goods as well as in property. I export raw materials and import anything anyone will pay for – antiques, rare books, furnishings. I have a list of contacts all over the world and plan to travel to Europe, and the East if necessary, to suit my clients, providing they pay my price. I have plans to open an emporium to service this growing city.' He shrugged. 'If all that doesn't satisfy you, Bel, what more can I say? Don't badger me. Can't you be satisfied with what you have here?'

'What exactly do I have here?'

'A cushy life, getting cushier. I'm staking you to a fancy French master, doubtless on the run from some indiscretion, and a croquet lawn for your young ladies.'

'While I grovel to the wife and daughters of a nigger!'

The words were spoken so savagely Bennett stared. Isabel was trembling, but with anger or revulsion he could not tell, indeed he had the odd feeling that the cause was something entirely different. 'I've never heard you voice that rumour before.'

'Is it just rumour?'

He shrugged. 'There's talk. But to my knowledge O'Shea has never spoken of his origins nor has anyone faced him with specific questions. You know Brisbane or you should – leave things be, it's easier not to know . . . Perhaps the climate has something to do with it! If there's gossip in your school I'd advise you to cut it off cleanly, laugh it off if you must but get rid of it. One can't tell what O'Shea would do — '

'You don't care what he would do. Your only concern is not to offend his wife!'

Surprisingly, he was calm against her fury. 'I find it hard to separate your various jealousies, Isabel. Isn't it enough that the O'Sheas pay well for your talents? I warn you, for the sake of your precious school, even more for your precious self, don't fall out with one of the richest families on the Downs.'

Brick did not look forward to greeting his wife and children amid the turmoil of the Brisbane docks yet he had cherished a schoolboyish urge to drive them up to the completed town house and watch Alannah turn the key in the door, anticipating her surprise and, he hoped, delight at the result of so much time and money. Her letters had been cheerful,

87

and happy he thought, but she had been away two months, too long, and he felt an absurd shyness at their reunion. It was an interminable berthing. His children waved down to him, Celine bouncing up and down, even Domi, a stoic when it came to greetings and goodbyes, smiling and waving for Celine stimulated her brothers. Phelim, in Clodagh's arms, was holding out his hands. Clodagh seemed to have grown taller. She smiled at him, yet he knew she was smiling beyond him seeking Will, knowing full well he could not be there.

Even at a distance picking her way through the chaos on deck, Alannah turned his heart. She raised an arm in greeting, clutching at her large-brimmed hat flopping in the breeze while Fay and Meg and the porters sorted their baskets and impedimenta. His wife was not a beautiful woman in the classical sense yet there was always something about her that caught the attention, that caused men to remember her. A distinction . . . An air of permanence . . . She ran to him like a schoolgirl and they kissed, his children milling about, Phelim guided by Clodagh staggering on unsteady legs. 'My dear. My dearest *dear*,' she whispered. Her kiss was eager and his heart leapt for he needed her eagerness. He thought he had never seen her so lovely, so . . . melting, a silly emotional expression but it was an emotional day. He could not take his eyes from her as their heavily laden cabs bowled through the clear crisp winter's day to Wickham Terrace and BelleMonte.

North Brisbane's Fortitude Valley was once Bell's Valley until renamed for the Scottish Presbyterian immigrants brought out by the fiery preacher Dr Lang on the *Fortitude*, denied land grants and dumped by authority on the outskirts of the town in a wilderness of timber, scrub and vine. Always in fear of marauding aborigines they had cleared land and built slab and bark huts, surviving the mud of the humid summer 'wet' and the drifting tormenting dust of the winter 'dry'. Now the sons of these immigrants were leaving their fathers' farms for better land and opportunity, the mansions of city merchants dotted the hills around and settlement was creeping beyond the Valley towards the Bowen Hills and the upper reaches of the Brisbane River. Still the scrub towards the river sheltered a straggle of taverns grandly called hotels, gambling dens, and whore-houses serving seamen and fishermen, pimps, runaways and timber-cutters, as well as those of the Brisbane Establishment who rode out from time to time in search of sporting diversions of all kinds.

Brick turned off Ann Street in a chill dusk along a faint track in search of the Cawnpore, a gambling and sporting den of dubious reputation run by ex-seaman Ebenezer Mott of even more notorious legend. 'Petrie Jack', once yard-man at the Belle Vue turned fisherman, with digs of a sort near Frogs' Hollow, the unfilled creek bed leading to Eagle Street and the wharves had, for the price of two sovereigns, given Brick his best lead yet. Petrie remembered Jamie Lorne – a swaggering black-haired fellow with the air of a grandee – and Petrie had heard – only a rumour, Mr O'Shea, but he *had* heard it – that Jamie hung out at the Cawnpore. The long low shape of the inn glowed tepidly through the trees. It boasted a large uneven yard with stables in one corner and a woodstack in another. In a third corner was an odorous rubbish dump while the fourth sheltered a rough 'ring', where broken-down relics of a fisticuff's career pounded each other to bloody pulp at secret well-attended boxing nights. The whole squalid array, enlivened now and then by a horse's neigh or a scurrying rat, shone ominously in the light of a lantern hung crookedly on a post. Over all was the smell of urine, horse-dung and dry straw. Dust stung the eyes. Mosquitoes tormented. Brick tethered Jannali firmly and pushed the shaky door that had the look of having been kicked open too often. The noisy tipsy crowd ignored him and he did not have to look far for Jamie crouching over cards at a corner table in a fog of pipe smoke and fumes from the adjacent kitchen, dishevelled and obviously as tipsy as the rest. Jamie glanced up, squinted through the haze and, curiously unsurprised, grinned at his stepfather.

'At least you picked a fine night for your slumming, old man.'

Brick nodded at the door. 'Outside.'

'You know enough about poker not to interrupt a gentleman at play.'

Brick strode to the table and hauled Jamie to his feet,

scattering cards. Ignoring protests he dragged him into the yard and sent him flying against the rotten fence palings. 'When I say outside I mean it.'

Jamie shook himself free of splinters. 'Damn you, I had a good hand.'

'From all I hear you never have good hands these days. You've lost the knack despite all your coaching from your mama.'

'Leave Raunie out of it. You never loved her.'

'We had our special attachment and you know it. I'm here to settle matters with you and I'll not wash O'Shea dirty linen before sly-groggers and horse-thieves and worse.'

'They're better company than your precious nob hill snobs.'

'There's always some indefinable "they" in your life that you love to blame for your troubles. Your problems are self-induced. Why not try a job of work for a change?'

'Cleaning chamber pots and cutting firewood around here? No thanks.'

'It takes hard cash to live the life of a gentleman drifter. I'm weary of picking you out of various gutters but your stepmother seems to want to know your whereabouts every year or so — '

'You're the one who hounds me.'

'Perhaps because neither of us relishes you dumped on our doorstep battered and bleeding from your latest brawl.'

'It was my doorstep once!'

'It could be again, but not simply on a whim for sports days and kangaroo shoots. I pay no more fines or meet your IOUs or get you out of trouble with women. It's over, Jamie. You're at rock bottom, by the look of you nothing worse can happen.'

'Oh yes it can.' Bitterly. 'I owe money.'

'You always owe money. Learn to live on your yearly allowance or starve.'

'It's gone already on cab fares and the hiring of mounts. I sold my horse.'

'You'll get no replacement from me.'

'No? I rather think I will, old man.'

'That sounds like another of your threats. When you turn theatrical you sound like a bad play staged by a third-rate boys' school. Sooner or later you trip yourself up. Talk clearly or I'll take a whip to you; I trounced you as a child and I can do it now.'

'Not now, old man. I don't think you'll want your attempts at fornication known around Wickham Terrace. Or, for that matter, on the Downs. Certainly not by Alannah.'

'What are you up to now?'

'I'm not up to something, I know something. At least I keep my indiscretions — as you call them — confined to scullery-maids who don't matter for no one believes them, but you bed down celebrities — or attempt to. Oh yes, I rode up to your grandiose residence to find you strutting, or rather scuttling inside after stowing your actress in a cab — '

'Good God,' Brick exploded, 'now you're descending to blackmail.'

'At your advanced age I'd say you're damned lucky to have the chance of even a stage whore!'

Brick's fist slammed Jamie's chin and this time he went sprawling on the wood-pile. 'That was more for the reflection on my virility than for insulting the lady who, I assure you, can look after her reputation very well. If it's a matter of passing years, you're an ageing roué, or rather, an ageing larrikin, which is never a pretty sight.' Jamie lurched at him but Brick was nimble and Jamie landed on the fetid mound of rubbish. 'As for your stepmother, nothing you could say or do will harm us; I wouldn't let it any more than she would, we've come through too much together to be afraid of slander. Now get yourself out of this dive. Leave Brisbane. Leave the country for all I care. If I hear of you mixed up in crooked dealing, I'll hunt you out and kill you, I swear it.' He threw a handful of sovereigns at the figure struggling from the refuse. 'Book yourself passage somewhere. Or buy a horse and lose yourself in the north. This is the last you'll get from me, Jamie. You're on your own.'

Eva Muir had stayed in Brisbane longer than was expected. She had been treated to lavish farewells and now people were slightly bored, indeed, wives were becoming a little jealous of the adulation shown a woman who was, after all, only an actress. There was a small knot of Brisbaneans on the wharf to see her off to join her company in the south and take ship for England, but always the prima, she departed graciously and majestically in a flurry of trunks and veils. Brick was not in the crowd but that evening he stood long on BelleMonte's terrace watching the river and its lights, particularly the glow from the Sydney steamer as it took the bend and glided from sight.

Chapter Seven

THERE WERE no children. After two years of 'copious couplings' as Stratton McCrae had heard an eccentric wandering
cleric describe 'the privileges of the married state', Eunice
McCrae had not conceived, yet remained as responsive and
sensual towards him as always, despite long separation and
quarrels, both quarrels and couplings now holding an element
of desperation. Sandy McCrae's impatience, and finally, disappointment, blew up in incredulity. 'Ye're an upstanding
fellow, a true McCrae, so why have I no grandsons? Not
even a lass or two?' Strat had no answer, he did not know
why not, nor did he care, for by now it seemed unimportant,
with even a certain relief to be nearing twenty and still free
from fatherhood. 'The woman's barren,' Sandy raged as if
at a personal affront to himself. 'Too old when she married
ye and wouldna say. We're a couple o' fools. The Jezebel
tricked us.'

'You're the one who chose her child-bearing hips!'

Sandy smashed a few plates and spat out his baccy in disgust
but Strat did not care about his wife's age. Hers had never been
a girl's body and in strong light, which she always seemed to
shun, there were deep lines on her face and throat. Her body
was too full, too flamboyant, too . . . used? With his limited
and muddled knowledge of women on his marriage he had
assumed she was a virgin, in any case it would not have
mattered then and it was just as unimportant now. Hers was
an eager satisfying body that still drew and held him and on
his rare trips to Hope they made love silently, furiously, and
bitterly for there were always accusations after. Perhaps she
wanted children, she did not say and he did not ask, she
never explained or apologised, just gave him release in her
lush ritualistic way. There was no love on his part, he did
not care what she did when he left her, he did not dwell on

her for his need of her was purely sexual: he'd read of love in books, some strange rare emotion that he would like to experience: bodies joined in the usual way – he well knew how by now – but with something more, something deeply personal. Perhaps she did love him as she insisted, for when he drew apart she clung. She clawed at him.

'You're always leaving. You can't leave me.'

'I'll come in the spring. In the thaw.'

'It's not enough. I'm your wife, Stratton.' Desperately, 'Am I not your wife?'

'You are.'

'What of the years ahead? I fear for us.'

'If we shared my father's roof we could manage.'

'That bullying, degrading old man? Never!'

'If you will not come to Barkerville — '

'Hundreds of miles upriver to diggings that do not even make a town?'

'I belong there.'

'You belong with me.'

'My work is in the Rockies. You knew that.'

'I didn't know you expected me to live in the same house as your dreadful old father.'

He had no argument with that for Sandy was indeed dreadful. And it was true, they had not spoken of home and living, and now it was too late. He made excuses, a convenient barrier to separate them, admitting to himself that perhaps he did not really want to escape Barkerville, only Sandy, for he went stubbornly back for the something he was sure awaited him, a feeling that never died yet one he could not explain to himself, certainly not to Eunice; some reward, though what precisely it would be he did not know. He could, as she suggested with a half-hearted desperation, take up land, but he did not want to work the land nor did she: he had married a gentlewoman governess, his mistake, and certainly hers: their tragedy, as she called their fragmented life. She was anxious, not simply to impart knowledge but to gain it, her activities detailed to him by townsfolk intrigued, or shocked or confused by their mismated existence, some of their gossip malicious.

In general Eunice McCrae was admired for her dedicated

study of the ways of the Hope Indians at the Indian Village adjoining Hope, one long-house containing several families, a smelly place under a roof where fish dried eternally. The Indians lived on fish, berries and wild geese; they also grew splendid potatoes. They made baskets and rugs and worked silver into amulets and rings. They made blankets from the hair of their dogs, dyed with native roots and herbs. Eunice was planning to write a treatise on the Indians: it was a Christian duty, she insisted piously, to understand the native peoples. She did intend to speak to the women over their habit of flattening babies' heads, although little harm seemed to come of it. Strat did not bother to remind her that Indians abounded around Barkerville. Since he earned only a pittance she would open a school to keep them both, then he would have no further excuse not to join her; why she still wanted him she did not know for she had married a boy. A *boy*! He could only agree with her for he did not truly understand himself, his stubbornness, his cruelty towards her, his need to avoid the constant wrangling. They were coupled, each the half of a disaster, but he did not blame her, he simply wanted to escape her. Her threat to hold him struck fear into his soul.

Once he went down to the mills on Burrard Inlet to talk with Morgan at the Hume shipyard. He missed Morgan and his news and views of the outside world. There were more saw-mills and cabins now, there was even a pub. The Humes were fashioning ships' masts for there was boat-building, with the timber-saws resounding through the clearings that awaited settlers' cabins. Everywhere was talk of progress, and excited argument over the railroad creeping from the east, slowly, too slowly, indeed only a piecemeal joining-up of lines already there, mainly around the Lakes. There was a new Government in Canada, arguing as the old had done over the millions of dollars the railroad would cost, arguing even more fiercely on how best to cross the terrible barrier of the Rocky Mountains, or even if they could be crossed at all. The Humes, partners in new ventures, were richer if that were possible and Strat listened and wondered and racked his brains as to how to catch up with Morgan, let alone his father, with the world racing along without him.

'My father doesn't need more money, he just makes it,' Morgan boasted. '"Goldie Hume" they call him for he's smarter even than my Uncle James. The railroad will change everything, my father says, bringing commerce and industry to the west. He'll be in on it all when contracts are given out.'

'Contracts? What contracts?'

'For supplies. Materials . . . provisions . . . For a start there's hardwood, from the United States I suppose, and who knows, Australia? Plenty of hardwood in Australia. We sell our lumber there now so why not bring Australian timber here? And Australian meat . . . mutton for the thousands of men laying track. It could be packed in ice. Ice ships sailed there from California twenty years ago, my father says, and Sydney had cold drinks for weeks.'

'Where would they find ice in Australia?'

'Well then, from New Zealand. Plenty of icy mountains in New Zealand. Anyway, my father says someone in Sydney by the name of Mort is experimenting with ways of freezing and shipping meat, something to do with pipes and ammonia . . .' Morgan would finish with his usual amiable vagueness when faced with direct questions. Strat never knew whether to believe Morgan or not, he seemed to weave wild dreams around so many issues. 'Just think of the victualling needed.'

Stratton was thinking, for this was closer home! Who, aside from Sandy his father, knew more about store-keeping than 'Sandy's laddie'? He'd been forced to live and breathe as a trader all his life. Even so, he must know more and still more about the world and the men and women who ran it so he sat into the night over Eunice's books, everything and anything he could get, for by now he could read well. He decided he knew a great deal, but in patches, for he had never been to school, just picked up knowledge where he could, and there was deep anger in him when he considered his deprived life. Mary Brady, warming to him since he had not taken Eunice away, lent him more books, as did Morgan, for Morgan had finished with book-learning; Morgan wanted to enjoy himself while Strat envied him his easy education, his worldliness as he saw it, and Morgan envied Strat a wife, a woman always there. Morgan had got himself into a scrape with a squaw and his father was furious, the tribes did not like it, the squaw's father did not like it, so Malcolm Hume was packing Morgan out of the country for a spell, preferably to Scotland, to find himself a 'dacent gal' to marry. Strat refused to consider Morgan 'packed off' anywhere but Morgan had no money save for what he scrounged from his father and Malcolm Hume was generous only when it suited him. Morgan had little choice. They lay under the trees staring up, envious of each other.

'I'd rather Australia than Scotland. For one thing, it's far away.'

'Everywhere is far from here.'

'Australia is the South Seas really.' Morgan drifted, dreaming, heady with the spring sun and faraway places. 'White sands and bush and scrub and palms and great trees they call stringy-barks. There are natives called aborigines who eat each other and anyone else who comes by. If I work on him my father might, just might, send me to Australia.' His voice took on an excited conspiratorial tone though there was no one within miles. 'My father has a friend there, or enemy, I'm not sure which, met with in 'Frisco during the rush, by name Muir. A difficult codger, my father says, but clever – and by that he means too clever. Yet what he really means, and I know my father – it's the way he *says* things you see – is that the man was a bit of a bounder in 'Frisco — '

'Wasn't everyone in that first rush?'

Morgan laughed. 'I guess my father was too. Anyway, all I know is that this Muir codger was in partnership with my father. Now he has a sheep-station – they call ranches stations in Australia – with a business in the city. He's aiming for Parliament too. Quite the nob around Brisbane.'

'What's Brisbane?'

'The capital of Queensland, the new state. He's done better than most Scots there, and there are Scots a-plenty my father says.'

'More than here?'

'I shouldn't think so,' Morgan bragged. 'British Columbia's full of us. But Australia has Irish too, in the south, trailing their priests and papish trappings and doing their best to increase. Rule of the Church, you know, to procreate.' Strat loved the

97

words Morgan used and added them eagerly to his patois of words and phrases. 'Sydney started out as a gaol. Then they shipped the Irish: Sydney Ducks they call Irish ex-convicts who kick up a rumpus in Californy.'

'I'll go to Australia with you,' Strat said impulsively.

'With your pa watching your every move?'

'He can't do that for ever.'

'And you with a wife?'

'There's nothing to that any more.'

'I thought that might be the way of it.'

'The Bradys don't want to lose her. I think they influence her.'

'Then Australia it is. The farther the better eh? For both of us.'

Excited, they talked only of ships and shipping-routes. They pored over timetables and maps sent from 'Frisco or left behind by wandering diggers still embarking in the south for the Cariboo, pushing ever farther into the Rockies. Australia became an obsession, Strat dreamt of it, wondering what it was really like, for after all Morgan had never been there. First to 'Frisco, not easy since shipping was rough and spasmodic, but once there it should be easy to take ship across the Pacific – with some time in 'Frisco to themselves, and why not? There was a shivery excitement in them and their talk, it gave them something to hold on to: two young men seeking escape, one from a dangerous liaison, the other from a pointless suffocating marriage during which there were times Strat thought he would go mad. Each was afraid to stay.

'You have no money,' Morgan would remind him.

'I'll get it.'

'How?'

'You'll see.'

So Strat McCrae began to spy on his father. Sandy was becoming more secretive, more furtive, at the same time more garrulous. He was, his son decided, getting old for he forgot important matters and Strat found himself taking over areas of the business he'd never before been permitted to handle. Even so, Sandy was not yet too fuddled to let the financial reins out of his hands. Strat ran the teams, ordered supplies, bargained with confidence and aplomb.

He felt there was nothing he could not do yet still Sandy would not let go, talking incessantly of the past, leaping from subject to subject, tale to tale, far-fetched stories surely not to be believed. He talked of his long dead wife, of life on the trails, anything and everything to coax his son's head out of a book. And there were more than books to worry him, there were maps spread out on the rickety wooden table.

'Ye're like your ma, she wanted to know things. She liked big cities. She went to plays and the music-halls, and saw famous paintings and talked about 'em. Made her own clothes too, neat as a pin.' He would brood, sulking, resentful of being faced with matters beyond his ken. He grew nervous and irritable because Strat would not speak of Eunice. 'She's your wedded wife, lad, and that's the trouble, with the right to the name of McCrae so we canna break the bond. We're stuck wi' her wi'out grandsons to take over the business. There's no more I can teach ye, ye know it all but when I'm gone ye won't keep it going here, I know that. All wasted. *Wasted!*'

Strat had nothing to say, poring over his books or piling invoices and supply lists and letters and notes, for nothing escaped him now. He'd spent his life at the lowliest, dirtiest tasks for no reward, now he would lie like Sandy, cheat and manipulate and use people like Sandy did; he, Strat McCrae, needed social and financial advice, help if he could get it, and who better to give it him than Morgan's father, a man of wealth and influence? Malcolm Hume would be liaising with the railway company that would consume meat and timber and all else that men would need along the track. If the Humes were in on it all then he, Stratton McCrae, would be in there with them. He had met Morgan's father but once, yet the man had not seemed unimpressed. He stole a sheet of fine notepaper from stock and wrote in his best hand requesting – yet without suppliance – an interview, if possible at the man's hotel in Yale. If granted he would make the trip, do or die.

One night after a feverish day's work Sandy was tossing wood about, straining and puffing and blowing as he handled the heavy pieces. It had been an angry day altogether as he argued with all around him – the Indians, the boys, the squaws at their bargaining. He had berated Stratton yet in the end refused his help, so unusual in his father that Strat decided it was an ominous sign and escaped to his books on Samoa . . . the Solomons . . . the Hebrides . . . Absorbed, he was conscious of silence. Then a grunt, a strangling sound and a thud from behind him. He swung about. His father was slumped on the floor gripping the bench, breathing heavily, trying to drag himself up, but as Strat leapt Sandy fell and lay still, his eyes open and staring. Strat felt his pulse – nothing. He tore open his shirt and put his ear to the gnarled brown chest – nothing. He pounded the chest, but he had seen too much on the fields; his miserly old skinflint of a father was dead. He rocked him in his arms, Sandy's eyes staring up at him until he closed the lids in despair. A stroke? Possibly. He had worked his heart to death with toil, yet greed had eaten into him. If there had been a doctor close he would not have consulted him. 'Only fools waste good brass on the sawbones.' A doctor was useless now even if one could be found and if he bothered to come, for there was too much death on the Mountains, they were used to it, the ground around Barkerville was well spattered with miners' graves. He would fetch Angus Gordon, lawyer, and leave all to him.

Something scraped Strat's arm as he lay Sandy flat. Unbuttoning his father's shirt he saw something strapped to his chest – a thick, carefully folded wad of paper. Accounts? More likely a wad of gold dust. He unstrapped the paper carefully for it was damp with sweat, and with the years by the look of it, unfolded it carefully and spread it out. It was a map of some kind for there were markings, tiny crosses radiating out from a centre square resembling a house . . . There was a water-butt, but three windows instead of the usual four indicated their own lopsided store. He was intrigued by tiny sketches of recognisable objects – the old man could draw, no doubt about it, how little they had really known of each other. Here was Barrell's Saloon, no doubt of that. Murphy's stables and Murphy's vegetable patch. He recognised a clump of crooked trees unique to the town, and an abandoned cabin a quarter-mile in the woods because of the trickle of a stream behind . . . It was undoubtedly a map of Barkerville and surroundings. The floorboards where he sat were clearly marked and his eyes bored through his father's body. He covered it with a rug for he could not bear a defenceless Sandy; whatever else his father had been he had died a fighter. He had never known him go to banks so there could be but one explanation for his carefully drawn map: he had buried his fortune all over town and beyond. Now Sandy was dead and he, Stratton, was his son and so his heir. Here in his hands was what he had long been waiting for.

Angus Gordon brought a doctor from somewhere so after the town had clumped past Sandy's body, muttering or coughing or clearing their throats to wander off again to get drunk, Sandy was taken away. Strat knew he could do nothing till the funeral was over and the town settled down, but no matter how hard it was or how long it took he would unearth every bag of gold dust, every nugget, every artefact or gem paid over Sandy's counter in return for the necessities of life. Sandy had never mentioned a will, and he and Angus found none, which meant that authority would take over – well, authority could have the store and the stock along with the unpaid debts for he, Strat, never wanted to see Barkerville again. Meanwhile, he must move quietly and with caution for let an inkling of fortune leak out and some vagabond, misfit or wanderer would kill him for it, and gladly. On the other hand, it was well known in the town that Sandy McCrae had squandered his wealth on gambling and booze, and although he, Strat, had never heard gossip concerning his father and women, he had little doubt that Sandy had spent on the hurdy-gurdies (grumbling all the while at the cost). Barkerville would not expect Sandy McCrae to have left great wealth. Holding back just enough for his needs he could dole out Sandy's money to banks in New Westminster and Victoria, even farther afield. He trembled at the possibilities . . .

So began his furtive silent search, by the light of a shaded lantern where possible, otherwise by candlelight. Sometimes he was forced to probe in the dark. The map did not fail him. It led him back towards the early diggings of Richfield, then he retraced his steps through Barkerville – or Middle Town as some called it – and on to Cameron Town below, the three settlements straggling the creek for a mile or so. He dragged his wealth from holes in trees, from the soil, from water-butts and from behind wall-boards, for Sandy had stored as a squirrel hoards nuts for winter. Why? Surely not to leave his son rich, or anyone else for that matter. Simply to die wealthy? Or, incredibly, to squander the lot on a glorious binge in San Francisco? No one would ever know. Now it did not matter.

Totalling his fortune from hundreds into thousands of dollars he made his plans. He would leave Sandy's grave decent then no more lifting of boxes and sacks and measuring flour to the last ounce. No more hauling or chopping wood in freezing dawns. No more Eunice . . . He would send her money from time to time but it was all over, finished. He found a large strongbox with a sound lock in Sandy's 'office' and stored his loot. He ransacked the store for his wardrobe, had a bath and haircut at Clover's Saloon and bought his coach ticket. With the legalities safely left to Angus he stowed his padlocked strongbox under his seat and planted his feet firmly upon it – his personal effects it was understood – and he was off without a backward glance or a regret. He would spend a few days in Yale for Malcolm Hume had answered his letter making an appointment – the last Monday in the month, at eleven in the morning. He booked a room at a good hotel, saw his box stowed in the hotel safe and appeared at the Hume hostelry with minutes to spare, not too early to seem eager or too late to appear irresponsible. He was shown into a well-furnished study with much stuffed fauna about for the Humes were avid hunters. He was staring at the mounted head of a grizzly when a voice came from behind him.

'Y'like m'trophy, lad? Took a week to stalk the beast but I got him, had to, it was him or me.' Malcolm Hume plumped his heavy body in his fine leather chair, a dark imperious Scot with shrewd eyes that scarcely left his visitor. Unlike Morgan in every way, Strat suspected. He was given weak coffee in a small cup while Malcolm picked his teeth. No wonder Morgan is scared of him, Strat thought; I'm scared of him too but I'll never show it for if I do I'm done for. The toothpick was held poised while the Hume eyes probed. 'Ye're no' like your Pa.'

'I believe I resemble my mother – and Sandy's dead.'

Malcolm sucked through his teeth, swivelled his chair and folded his arms on his desk. 'So I hear. We didna like each other but relished a spat over business. Naa then! If I decide to send m'lad to Australia for a spell could ye pay your own way wi' him?'

Strat gulped at the bluntness of it – canny old Scot – but did not hesitate. 'I could.'

'Guid.' Malcolm slammed his desk and, heavy as it was, it shuddered. 'Steerage will do if ye canna manage more, guid for the lad, take him doon a peg for if I don't the Australians will. Schooling hasna taught him sense or gi'en him a head for business. Ye've a guid head for business, laddie.'

'My father insisted.'

'Ye canna insist on what isna there! Could ye collect a debt noo?'

'I collected debts for my father.'

'Aye, but this is a goodly sum. Forty thousand dollars.'

'Forty thousand?' Strat gaped.

'Forty – I'm charging the rogue interest. I dinna care how ye get it short o' murder and if ye decide on that keep me oot of it. The less Morgan knows of the real reason for sending ye both the better, but he'll carry letters to one Bennett Muir, m'partner in a hotel and saloon in 'Frisco in the fifties. We sold well but he skipped with the brass, aye the lot, to parts unknown – and how smartly it was done doesna matter noo. I've had spies out for years. Now I've found the bastard.'

'You want to prosecute, is that it?'

'Couldna do it, gentleman's agreement, no proof, only our word, so that's where ye come in. Muir will be uneasy when he reads m'name on a letter but he willna know how much either of ye know so he'll take ye in to find out – I know the mon. That's where your front of a trader – which ye are – comes in. Lumber. Softwoods.' Exhilarated, he shifted in his seat. 'No harm in killing two birds with one stone; if we put our minds to it we could beat Seattle at the lumber game, even 'Frisco, for we've enough in BC to build the world. Fine stands of timber on the Island, to say nought of the mainland and the Cariboo. Could ye beat the Yankee pedlars at their own game, lad? Y'know their spiel.'

'Well . . . I've dealt in lumber, grown up with it. I know just about every tree in the mountains for I've slept under most of them. I know wood from wood — '

'Ye've got spunk, I'll say that for ye.' Malcolm's picked-clean teeth gleamed. 'And polish. Rub it off on m'son, show him some fresh fields, as it were.'

'Woods.'

'Eh?'

'Fresh woods, Mr Hume.'

An expression of distaste passed over Malcolm Hume's heavy face. 'Morgan tells me ye're bookish . . . Weel noo, there's m'plan: get a foot in Muir's door, butter him up, get his confidence and prise m'forty thousand – not a penny less mind – without fuss or fight on his part for his own sake for if I don't get m'brass in cash or kind – and y'know the value of gems and gold – I'll take the next ship out to blow the bastard's cushy life to smithereens. I've sworn it on the Good Book. The point is, bluff and bluster as he will he knows I'll do it. I could bring others in too. The rascal had a young sister, a beauty as I remember . . .'

'One question, Mr Hume. Why not collect the debt yourself?'

Malcolm shrugged. 'No finesse – I'm like to blow the bastard's brains out before I collect a farthing. Besides, daren't leave m'business here, don't trust m'brother. Can ye do it, lad? Time is of the essence.'

Wondering where the man might have heard the phrase Strat took a deep breath. He would be on his own in a strange country, keeping Morgan amused and ignorant while dealing with a hostile adversary, manipulating and blackmailing – for it amounted to that – the former friend now enemy of this shrewd and grasping man who was, he had no doubt of it, as big a rogue as the other. 'I can try.'

'Not guid enough.' Malcolm's hand smacked the desk again. 'It's yea or nay, and if it's nay there's the door.'

Strat took another deep breath. 'I'll get your money, Mr Hume.'

'Guid. Set forty thousand pounds before me and ye'll not find me ungrateful. What shall it be? Ha'e ye a mind for land at the Inlet?'

'To own it maybe. Not work it.'

'Spoken like a true Scot and a capitalist. We believe in land rather than love it.'

'I want my own business.'

'Ye ha'e one.'

'I'm finished with Barkerville. I want a contract with the railway company. Victualling.'

'Ye'll throw in your lot wi' a project that's taking years to get off the ground?'

'If I don't get in early others will. I hear you're throwing in your lot, Mr Hume.'

'Morgan talks too much,' his father grumbled. 'Ye're aiming high. They're a canny lot in Toronto, e'en more so in Montreal.'

'I mean to go beyond food. I'll contract for anything and everything the Canadian Pacific might need. I'll travel the world to get what they want. I know I can do it.'

'Ye'll need capital.'

'I'll get it.'

'Weel noo, all I can do is try for ye.'

'Not good enough.' Strat struck the desk in a daring mockery of the other but Malcolm Hume seemed to have worked himself into a good humour.

'I'll do m'best. As to the other matter, if ye've a mind to vamoose with m'brass halfway here I swear I'll find ye, as I found Muir, and tear ye apart. Understood?'

Strat got slowly to his feet and height. 'I don't like to be threatened, Mr Hume.'

Malcolm Hume lumbered awkwardly from his desk. 'Nor do I, lad. Nor do I. I havna much to m'credit but brass, but when I gi'e m'word, I keep it. Ask around the Cariboo.'

'I have.' Strat grinned, sure of himself. Malcolm Hume's laughter boomed. Strat found it a scary sound.

'Keep your letters and papers tight. And keep m'lad in line, he goes mad when he sees a woman. And put the fear o' God and Malcolm Hume into that bastard, Bennett Muir, may he rot in Hell!'

The first craving of miner or backwoodsman when he descended on San Francisco by ship or by road was a bath, followed by a haircut, new clothes and a woman. Stratton McCrae emerged from the first three (the woman would have to wait) in an aura of shaving-cream and pomade, of gleaming stick-pins and velvet lapels with a new and glorious confidence. He made a healthy deposit at substantial bank interest for his future use in 'Frisco then set off to book passage on the first tub that would take them across the Pacific to Sydney, even better, Brisbane, though he held out little hope of the latter. Morgan had disappeared with a list of gambling dives and hook-shops compiled by friends and added to from a purloined diary of his father's, but Strat knew enough of 'Frisco to realise it was no longer young: the old riproaring areas of the city boasted at least a veneer of solidity and respectability, covering the hills and scattering rocks and seagulls in the building of palatial homes. He booked on a freighter, a poor thing, but it sailed in two days; otherwise they must wait a month and in that time Morgan could get himself into no end of trouble – as he, Strat McCrae, could do with more time on his hands. No sign of Morgan so he treated himself to the most lavish dinner he'd ever had in his life – pheasants stuffed with prunes and chestnuts, Oysters Casino, Fillet of Beef Wellington, and so on – enjoying the admiring glances of women at the big blond fellow in the expensive wardrobe yet with something oddly boyish about him . . . No Morgan that night or next morning so Strat sought him in various bars. He searched the waterfront, then old areas that had something depressing about them in their look of careless transition. No Morgan. Back at the hotel there was a message in his room with two words 'Collect friend' scrawled above an address – a well-versed and discreet hotel this! He took a cab to an old block that had seen, as the saying went, better days, which also went for the flashy woman who confronted him as if he were to blame; neither Spanish Maisie nor her girls would stand for such brawling – or for other things she could mention. 'Found the hotel card in his pocket – when we found his pocket. You've taken your time.'

'I've been searching the town.'

'Now you've found him you can have him. Where did he pick up such tricks? From the Injuns? Or them Froggies up there in Canada?'

'He's been without women a long time.'

'Made up for it in ten minutes.' She dragged Strat to a room where Morgan snored on a chaise longue, his wild hair violent against the baby blue brocade. 'Can't rouse him. He cleaned out m'stock of champagne. He's rough done up in silk.'

'Not really.'

'You ain't seen him with m'girls, a regular bull. I run a good house, see.' Her voice and stance took on a certain primness. 'Select parties. He's been raving about his pa . . . If his old man performed the same he'd have been out on his ear, even in the old days.' Morgan was stirring, mumbling, blinking at the light.

'Cleaned me out . . .'

Spanish Maisie inspected her nails. 'All lies. They all say it. Wild spenders lose count of their money. My girls don't need to rumble clients, they're sitting on fortunes as I keep telling 'em and I won't let 'em sell themselves cheap. I run a good-value house, all know it, just plain old-fashioned fucking but plenty of it for the price. Of course I keep a room upstairs for gents who want special services, but I won't supply Arabs and Englishmen, they're the worst.'

'I'm a Scot.' Attempting to balance, Morgan was shaky but indignant.

'You're a Canadian.' Strat held him upright with the flat of his hand.

'Not keen on backwoodsmen either, their dirty boots ruin m'carpets and sheets.' A couple of burly negroes were shuffling Morgan out to a cab, Morgan's plump, rather stupid face engaging even in drunkenness.

'We sail for Australia in the morning.'

'Don't know where it is but God help its whore-houses if they have to service the likes of 'im. I'll not have him back y'know.' Maisie was working herself into a pious fury. 'Not if he were to stuff a thousand-dollar bill down m'girl's stays.'

'Frankly – madam – I can't see your precious house providing any service worth a fraction of that.'

He left her open-mouthed but, mercifully, silent.

Morgan snored so heavily Strat went on deck to the early-morning fog. All he had seen of 'Frisco had been through a blur of Bay fog, bar fumes, and a procession of sluts and their madams – Morgan, he decided, had rotten taste. But he would be back. The world was full of cities he would pass through but return to devour and, hopefully, conquer. First he was off to murder the career of a socially prominent citizen of an expanding colonial city in return for his own future. He had no qualms about it. If he didn't take it on, someone else would. All he must do was make certain Malcolm Hume did not renege on their bargain. The sun strengthened and the fog slowly dissolved as they steamed towards the Golden Gate. He stayed on deck a long time watching the land and the shape and sense of San Francisco slowly disappear, well-satisfied with the reborn, re-garbed and well-prepared Stratton McCrae. Even more, with the rich Stratton McCrae. There was nothing, surely, he could not achieve.

Chapter Eight

'I WANT to grow things.'

'Dammit, Will, you *do* grow things, and well. We eat most of what you produce, and you have a demand for the rest.'

'Not just vegetable gardens. I want to grow crops in a big way. I want to grow wheat.'

'Wheat was tried around Warwick, you know that, just as you know the Downs is not wheat country; the rainfall's too uncertain and when it does rain it falls at harvesting time, not at planting when it's needed. Wheat gets rust – but this is elementary, why do I bother to repeat it?'

'I know I can make a go of it.'

'Not on my land, boy.'

'I am not a *boy*.'

'You are to me.' Brick was beginning to shout. With an effort he controlled his voice. 'No, you're not a boy and I shouldn't treat you as one, you're seventeen. But that makes you old enough to listen, to be reasonable. This is sheep and cattle country, too valuable for experimentation. Just because a band of Moravian missionaries at Moreton Bay and the *Fortitude* migrants grew cotton — '

'Successfully.'

'Because the American War focused attention on cotton. It created a demand for it.'

'Maize has been grown. Other crops too.'

'Agriculture is all those people know. Here on the Downs we must suit the terrain. Besides, there's another aspect of it; if large tracts of the Downs are sold for agriculture – as is happening – and capital sunk, a labour problem is created. A big one. Land must be worked, there's no available labour, so we get blackbirding – and I won't condone forced labour at slave-wages. All my life, though I'm called a hard man, I've advocated coolie, aborigine, white man, Kanaka, all the same, fair wages for fair work. The answer is don't create the problem, the unnatural demand. Agriculture must go elsewhere.'

'Then I'll go elsewhere.'

'You'll what?' He was shouting again.

'I'll go to the foothills. There's a farm selling near Drayton. Twenty acres.'

'The Rankin place – I know it. There's no stock. No implements.'

'But six acres cleared and all fenced. With a place to live.'

'A humpy.'

'It will do till I build better. They're asking two hundred pounds, cash. I have one hundred.'

'Where did you get one hundred pounds?'

'I saved it. From my marketing. I make customers pay.'

'I've noticed.'

'If I don't get the other hundred I'll lose it.'

'And you expect to get it from me?'

'Why not? I'll pay you back, and with interest. There are farms around Drayton now, Toowoomba too, small farms that one man can work.' There was a steely look to him. 'If I lose the Rankin place I'll find another, somewhere.'

'Your work is here.' Brick was equally steely. 'You know I must spend more time at Jubila, it's just picking up after the drought. The new chums Tod hired haven't found their feet or bearings yet, they lose themselves in the scrub along with the cattle. I depend on you.'

'I know, but I can't help it. This is my chance.'

'Then take your chance, damn you. But I won't help you. If you walk out of here you're on your own. And don't come back.'

To his horror he stumbled and in anger found the path. He could not stay and face a defiant Will. Not now. He had not considered the boy growing up, or if he had he'd suppressed the idea. His own sons were still children, Dominic not yet ten. It was too late, this breeding of sons, a bitter fact. He had worked Hawkes Plains into one of the finest stations on the Central Downs, starting from scratch with only the land and a rough shelter. He had built the homestead for Alannah with only casual help, living with the thought that she would come, how or when he did not know, only that she would come: illogical – yet not entirely for she was very young and somewhere there must be a life for them together. She would bear his sons; the conviction had kept him going. These last years had made up for their long wait – as Will had made up for Jamie's transgressions, cared for by Fay then by Alannah, with Will and Clodagh close companions until Celine was born: years of fulfilment for him and, he had believed, his wife. Now in his rage and frustration he swore at his world, tramping the track to the fork where he had left Gondola with the horses, feeling every one of his sixty-six years and conscious of his limp, slight as it was, as he had never been. He would forbid Will to leave. Will must get over his rebellion, he was young and could wait a few years until Dominic was grown. After all, Willy Wilberforce O'Shea would have had no rights at all in a foundling home. Will owed him something.

Mounting Jannali he patted Gondola on his tousled head. We are both growing old, he thought. Age terrified him. There was a heaviness in him since he had buried Moll as if she had taken a part of him with her. Their life together haunted: the beginning of Erins Pride, the building of his career, her delight at his planned marriage to Barbara Merrill then her despair at the girl's death. Her hatred of his marriage to Raunie and Moll's bizarre housekeeping at the Pride when Raunie refused to live there. Her long decline at Hawkes Plains and her death, mercifully in her sleep. Moll Noakes had shadowed his life if not entirely ruled it, an old convict woman who had been his mother's friend and support through the terrible early years of military rule and convict suppression, now blessedly gone. What was left was a new life in a new state that, if Moll could have shared it, she would never have understood; all she knew was her own brutal long-ago world. With Gondola trailing he rode to Hawkes Plains, took his sharpest axe and went out and down to spend his terrible pent-up energy of rage on his trees.

Clodagh Aldercott had never liked Miss Muir's Educational Establishment for Young Ladies, she had endured it. As Miss

Muir reported to the girl's mother, folding her hands (Brick was right, they *were* clawlike) with the rapt expression she considered essential where value for money must be assured, Clodagh's French was adequate, her German slightly less so, her music tuneful and delicate, her dancing proper if uninspired, while her spare and sensitive paintings of the Darling Downs and Brisbane showed artistic promise. Clodagh could be depended upon for definite results in life whereas Celine . . . Miss Muir unfolded her hands with the faintest of sighs. An imaginative, robust – certainly robust – child with no interest in anything but the Romance subjects. A flick of a bony finger and Miss Muir dismissed Celine O'Shea to the jungle of the fashionable world. If the child cared to improve her manners very possibly she would marry.

Clodagh was dressing for dinner at BelleMonte with her always tightly held terror of formal occasions for she would never grow accustomed to self-display. Despite her recent 'coming out' when she had moved through the motions of a formal debut by training rather than spontaneity, garbed in white but managing to avoid the worst of frills and bows and escorted by a young army cadet, of 'impeccable family' as she was frequently reminded, she had been affable but certainly not as inviting as Miss Muir would have liked. Since she and Celine had become weekly boarders at Miss Muir's, Mama made trips in to arrange weekend picnics and teas and dances – Papa had decreed it! Clodagh made an effort for Mama's sake but she had no small talk and if she tried too hard her stammer returned. She felt herself too tall and thin rather than slim. She felt awkward even if she were not, knocking things over when nervous and she was often nervous. She refused elaborate hair arrangements, brushing her hair till it shone and rested smoothly each side of her cheeks, pale no matter how she pinched them. 'If I cannot be beautiful, Mama, I can be neat.' Alannah was resigned to her daughter's plain skirts and blouses with no ornament but a locket, sometimes her precious cameo, but on occasions such as tonight she insisted on formality.

Social events were overflowing from Foxburgh House in the entertaining of the Muirs' guests from America – Canada, Papa corrected – before they were taken off to Yoolanowi.

Tonight Clodagh must descend BelleMonte's regal stairs alone and mingle with the guests assembling below. She must converse with Jimmy Marr – James since he had set up in Brisbane as the protégé, it was said, of Mr Muir himself. All that ever sustained her through such ceremonies was the anticipation of Hawkes Plains where she could ride at her own pace, following Will at his mustering or felling of trees or working about his gardens . . . She made an experimental coil of hair round her finger then let it drop. It hung straight as a pencil stick. She could not manage without Meg and Meg was needed below; Meg Willis was needed everywhere since Nurse Puttering had gone as children's nurse to Glenaire. Thankfully, Will never cared if her hair curled or not, perhaps he never even noticed. She had sat, back to a tree, mending his jacket as he weeded his garden grown to a large experimental patch. She knew his every mood, or believed she did, as she knew her own, but he was preoccupied in a new way. She made a further attempt to distract him.

'Mama says you're back at regular classes with the Dennings.'

'Our mama decreed it. For my part it's a waste riding back and forth for penmanship and the chanting of tables when I can learn all I need right here.'

'I never wanted to go to Miss Muir's school.'

'Our mama decreed that too.'

She smiled. 'One never knows, quite, whether Mama or Papa O'Shea does the actual decreeing.'

He leant on his spade, amused. 'You can't go on calling him "Papa O'Shea" all your life, Clo.'

'Oh yes I can.'

'He's your father.'

'He's not and you know it.'

'Well, a stepfather can be the same.'

'Not to me.' Miserably, for she hated to disagree with Will.

'Anyway, it was time you left here for a spell. Just as it was time for Celine. She's growing up fast.' His head was down so she could not see his face.

'She says if she gets into any more scrapes at Miss Muir's, she'll run away. She will, you know.'

'She'll be hauled back.' He straightened, grinning. 'Even so I think she'd try.'

'I miss so much, Will. For one thing, watching you wood-carve.'

'Little time for that these days. Besides, you've other things to watch and do. You might even become a famous painter.'

'My simple little landscapes?'

'Phelim chatters about your parties. And your beaus.'

'They're not *my* parties. And I don't have beaus.'

'You will. Better start one of those hope-chest things that girls fill with knick-knacks for marriage.'

'I have no plans to marry.'

'You'll marry.'

'No.' She was urgent and definite. 'Not unless it's to some-one I really want.'

'No one would make you do otherwise.'

'They might. Mama will choose a lawyer like Jimmy Marr. Or a doctor – someone in the professions. She says I'd be useless on the land. Yet I love painting it . . .'

'You're not useless around me.'

'I never feel so. You have patience.'

'Everyone marries sooner or later.'

'Miss Gundy doesn't.'

'Oh well . . . Miss Gundy . . .' Will's way, less cruel than most, of saying Miss Gundy must face the fate of a bluestocking governess, even more, the fate of one with sun-spotted hands and a burgeoning moustache that fascinated Celine so much the child could not take her eyes from it and had to be kicked under the desk to distract her. 'Everyone who can, that is.'

'Do you want to marry?' Feeling foolish at a foolish remark but holding her breath for his answer.

'A man on the land needs a wife.' Will was always hon-est with her, as he was forthright with others: dependable hard-working Will as he was known. Yet when Celine was around something happened to Will, he was different. He laughed and joked with Celine with a closeness, a mateyness, that provoked an actual physical ache. Celine amused and stimulated Will, even at age ten, but then Celine O'Shea

114

amused everyone while exasperating many with her bizarre adult mishmash of talk, her mixture of frankness and pseudo-sophistication that involved her in so much trouble with Miss Muir. Celine never considered life's tomorrow, it was always today. Something cold touched Clodagh when she saw Celine and Will together, not jealousy, who could be jealous of a child, but a sense of fatality, something she knew she could not halt for Will's eyes followed the child growing in so many startling ways into a beauty. 'Anyway . . .' Will flung rich black soil on to his new patch, 'I can't marry for years. I must make my way first. I've found a property I want, a farm near Drayton. Trouble is, the price is two hundred pounds.'

'Would it be any good for that? I mean, I do know something about values. Papa talks values all the time.'

' "Papa" eh? We're improving. It wasn't so hard to say was it?'

'It's easier with you.'

'The farm is run down but I can build it up. I've saved half the money.'

'How?'

'By selling my produce. Now I'll have to sell more . . . I might do well at Yoolanowi now the Muirs are entertaining – I wonder what people eat in Canada? Besides, I can take odd jobs, do carrying, join the shearers now and then. Even better, beat the Chinese at making cabbage-tree hats . . .'

'You couldn't work harder than you do. Is there no other way?'

'I've no collateral to put down at a bank.'

'There's Papa.'

' "Papa" again? Keep it up. The idea doesn't suit our Papa.'

'Why not?'

'I'd rather not say.'

'Then what would you say if . . .' She paused then thrust words between faintly trembling lips praying she wouldn't stammer, 'if I were to get you the other hundred?'

'Where would you get one hundred pounds? Bake and sell your pies round the stations?'

'If I needed to. But there could be another way. If – I say *if* – would you take the money?'

'I'd take it any way I could get it. I know what I want, Clo. I always have.'

She would, in a way, be sending him from Hawkes Plains, yet Drayton wasn't exactly a world away . . . Whatever he wanted she wanted, whether a run-down farm or, in time, Celine. She turned his coat inside out to stitch the torn lining, bending over the work, shading her eyes burning from her held-back tears.

Her hair was flopping where it should not. She peeped cautiously round her bedroom door. 'Celine!' Hoping her hoarse whisper reached the girl crouched at the top of the stairs. Then she stood poised at the look on her sister's face, the child's eyes alight and mouth slack as she gripped the rails and stared between them at the guests below. Celine brushed aside Phelim's hand plucking at her sleeve for Celine always knew who people were and all about them, even if she made up most of it: Celine told wonderful stories. '*Celine!*' Clodagh hissed. Her sister scrambled to her feet and, uncaring if she were seen from below, flounced along the landing and into the room. Clodagh closed the door. 'It's a small thing to ask. I'm late and my sash won't sit right.'

'Oh, bother your sash. You look fine, you always do.' Celine gave an impatient tug to the bow. 'I wish I were sixteen and going in to dinner.'

'If you were sixteen you could take my place and gladly. But don't wish your years away. You've plenty of time to grow.'

'Everyone's always telling me that. There's no time for me.'

'What are you talking about?'

'He'll be leaving soon, I know it, and I'll never see him again. My heart will break.'

'There you go being silly again. Ten-year-old hearts don't break.'

'Oh yes they do. I don't want to sit on the stairs with the babies and watch him in the distance. I want to fascinate him.'

'Fascinate who? And stop using showy words.'

116

'I like showy words. They're grown up. I want to grow up, I want people to notice me. No one takes notice when you're only eleven.'

'You're ten, Celine O'Shea, so stop exaggerating. People do notice you, believe me. They can't help it.'

'He doesn't. He doesn't get the chance. He's always being dragged away somewhere.'

'*Who* doesn't get the chance? Stop being cryptic.'

'The tall fair one. He's so beautiful.'

'You don't call a man beautiful. Handsome perhaps.'

'Must you always be so . . . so . . . *precise?* I call him beautiful because he is. Anyway, to me.'

'If you mean Mr McCrae, as I suppose you do for his friend is darker-haired — '

'He's red.'

'You're exaggerating again. They're guests at Foxburgh House.'

'I won't call him Mister. He doesn't look a Mister at all. He must have another name.'

'I hear him called Stratton.'

'I like that. Strat's even nicer. Friendlier. I'll call him Strat.'

'You'll do no such thing. It's disrespectful.'

'Why is he in Brisbane?'

'No one seems to know exactly. You're so good at putting ears to keyholes I'm surprised you don't know everything about him. Perhaps he's here for sheep, or more likely, wool. Even timber – I hear he's returning to Canada to help build a railroad.'

'Domi says Canada has plenty of timber.'

'It may not be the right kind for railway sleepers, the strips that hold the rails together. They'll need thousands of sleepers — '

'I know what sleepers are. I know more than you think.'

'You know too much, at the same time too little. It all comes out in a weird and dangerous muddle.'

'Well, I can't hold things in like you. It spills out.'

'A trait that could get you into much trouble. Just be careful.'

'Of what?'

'Life, I think. It can hit back.'

'That's a silly answer.'

'I suppose it is. I'm being silly because I'm nervous. This is an important dinner.'

'Perhaps Strat is here to view our trains.'

'I shouldn't think our little railroads would interest him. He'll be working on a long and difficult one crossing the Rocky Mountains.'

'The Rockies are in America too. Domi has books about them.'

'Domi seems to have books on everything.'

'Is he married? Strat I mean?'

'Mr McCrae. I believe so, though it's not our concern. Certainly not yours.'

'He doesn't look married.'

'People don't *look* married.'

'Oh yes they do. Mrs Denning looks married.'

Clodagh laughed. 'Marriage isn't always a matter of being pregnant so stop chattering nonsense and pass my cameo.'

'Why do you always wear this woman with her nose in the air?' Frowning, Celine passed an exploring finger over the cameo relief.

'She's a sibyl, one of the special women of antiquity, inspired with the gift of prophecy — '

'She looks like a haughty schoolmistress. Like a podgy Miss Muir.'

'Pin it *there*,' Clodagh indicated impatiently. 'And don't stab me. You could learn many interesting things about the ancients if you would only listen in class. I'm sure Miss Muir tries.'

'I don't care about ancient things, I like now. Sometimes Mama looks married. So does Papa. Sometimes Papa looks awfully married.'

'Perhaps because you worry him so much.'

'I don't mean to. I love Papa.'

'You're too young to talk about men the way you do, Celine.'

'I'll get older. I'm growing every minute. If only the boys wouldn't follow me around all the time I might get to talk to Strat. Have you talked to Strat?'

'Only at dinner parties. And a riding party beside the river.'

'You're allowed because you're sixteen, not because you can ride. You're a rotten rider, Clo.'

'I know.'

'What else do you know about Strat?'

'Well . . . his father was a trader in the Rockies. His father's dead.'

'Did he leave Strat lots of money? I like rich men.'

'Don't talk so. It's his business if he's rich or not.'

'What's his wife like?'

'I don't know. He doesn't talk about her.'

'What else do you know about him?'

Clodagh took a deep breath. 'He and Mr Muir talk a lot together, business I suppose. Perhaps he's studying import-export. Or victualling . . . something like that.'

'I never hear you say "something like that". You're always definite. Perhaps Mama thinks riding with Strat will make you stop mooning over Will.'

'I don't moon over Will. It's just that . . .'

'Will's in love with the land – and a bit with me, which is a shame I suppose for you're a really good person, Clo, everyone says so.'

'You must stop talking about love all the time, Celine. And I don't feel a good person or even a kind one at the moment, I'm in too much of a hurry. Will my hair do?'

'Let it hang here and there, it's softer. Why do you drag it back as Miss Isabel does, all glued up?'

'They must be in by now.'

'They're still milling about down there, I can tell.'

'How can you tell?'

'My sixth sense.'

'You're talking nonsense again. Stop listening to Meg and her ramblings about the occult and evangelism and mesmerism and such.'

'Meg only talks, she doesn't do.'

'Mama will be livid and Papa furious if I'm not down.'

'The other way about; it's Papa who gets livid.'

'How do I look? And don't say elegant. That's all you ever say – elegant.'

'Will "serene" do? That's an elegant word. Do you think I'll see him again?'

'Mr McCrae and Mr Hume,' Clodagh said carefully and distinctly, 'will be at Yoolanowi for the shearing and at Hawkes Plains for the sports day. Both look as if they can easily chop trees.'

'Strat could win, but Papa must. That's how much I love Papa.'

Suddenly Clodagh was all efficiency. 'Send the boys to bed, they've been wandering the halls long enough, gawping. And go to bed yourself. Do as I say, Celine, or I'll send Mama up.' She opened the door a crack. 'Now I can hear them moving.'

'Make your grand descent just as Miss Muir commands: "Shoulders back, girls, don't slouch." You won't stammer, Clo, I know you won't.'

'Don't even think of it.' She was trembling. 'They're such smart people.'

'They're drones.'

'Who told you that?'

'I made it up.'

'No you didn't but I've no time to argue. Sometimes I think you're growing . . . well . . . strange. Open the door wide and pray I don't trip.'

'I never pray, you know that. I always feel as if I'm talking to myself.'

'Pray this once. *Pray!*'

When Brick was at Jubila for weeks at a time Alannah was quite happy to stay on at BelleMonte, particularly as Clodagh was taking art lessons from Mademoiselle Desnée at Miss Muir's school, now moved to larger premises with staff and reputation to match the city swollen in the seventies by bumper immigration and exports. Bennett Muir had returned after almost two years in Europe with a lavish Savile Row wardrobe and crates of precious *objets d'art* to grace his luxurious Golden Emporium in Queen Street, which was managed by yet another protégé, a Monsieur Luffet (though Alannah suspected his name was his only Gallic connection for he spoke a rather comic stage French). Bennett had been eager to talk of London 'doings' but surprisingly, news of his sister had been almost dragged from him; Eva Muir had returned to London after a successful American tour of risqué Restoration plays ... Though rumour had it that Bennett still planned a political career he showed no haste to mount the hustings, presently occupied in entertaining young Canadians who had turned the heads not only of Brisbane debutantes but of their mamas. Mrs Plum ran BelleMonte so efficiently that Alannah could not find excuses enough to refuse the stream of invitations to tea and gossip, or rather scandal, that obsessed Brisbane matrons, particularly those domiciled on the Terrace. One of her favourite escapes was to what she grandly called her conservatory, off the morning-room, with a piquant view of the changing city and the river busy with scurrying ferries. The surrounding bush was disappearing, villas climbing the slopes below. At least the conservatory was green and cool and soothing to the eyes in hot weather though she had no interest at all in 'potting'; it seemed one more trivial pursuit. Yet making a pretence of it protected her for an hour or so from the keen eyes of her forbidding housekeeper who made her think of a plump domestic Isabel Muir. It was a relief when Clodagh appeared and she could remove her gardening gloves and push aside her damp, soil-clogged little plants. 'I hope you've come to take this over. I'm not very good at minute gardening.'

'You're very good at things that interest you, Mama.'

'Aren't most people?'

'I want to talk to you, Mama. Seriously.'

'You always talk seriously, Clodagh.' Then, sensing a need in the girl to confide, an unusual occurrence, she added quickly, 'Shall we go inside?'

'It's nice here. It's private.'

'It all sounds rather ominous.' Lightly. 'But I can't imagine you with guilty secrets, Clo.'

'Don't joke, Mama.'

'I won't if it's so important.'

'It's very important.'

'In that case wouldn't you like to talk it over with Papa as well? He'll be joining us at Hawkes Plains next week.'

'No. Oh *no*, Mama.'

'I see. What is it then?'

'I want you to give me one hundred pounds.'

'One hundred . . .' She paused. 'You get your allowance, Clodagh, a generous one, and for anything else that's needed we discuss it with Papa.'

'I know, but this can't be discussed with him. I don't want him to know anything about it. Please listen.'

'I am listening. But I must know what such a large sum is for.'

'It's to buy a farm.'

'You want a farm?'

'Not for myself. For Will. There's a farm for sale near Drayton and he wants it badly. He's saved one hundred pounds, think of it, but Papa won't give him the rest, or even lend it though perhaps that's just as well for Will would have an awful time paying interest as well as the capital. You have your own money, Mama, so please give it to him. He's worked so hard and saved over so many years and it's too bad no one will help.'

'Why did your father refuse?'

'Will wouldn't say. He never says anything against Papa. But I know the reason. Papa O'Shea — '

'I refuse to listen to that absurd name you give your father, Clodagh.'

'Papa then. He doesn't want Will to leave Hawkes Plains. He wants him to go on working for him, which isn't fair for Will works only for wages and has to grow things to earn extra. And now he has the chance of his own place — '

'Your father is overworked. He goes back and forth to Jubila to help Tod, a long trip. As for Hawkes Plains, it's a big property and good hands are hard to find. Do you really think it's right and fair for Will to leave him now?'

'Papa holds him too tightly.'

'Does Will know you're asking me?'

'No. It's just that he'll die if he loses this farm.'

'He won't die. He'll plod on working and saving and finally getting what he wants. It will just take a little longer, that's all. Will can afford to wait, he's young. In any case, I don't like going against your father.'

'If you don't give Will the money I'll get it for him somehow.'

'Don't talk nonsense.'

'I can work. I can make things and sell them. I'll give him my allowance; I don't need money or new dresses or party things, I have brushes and paints enough and really don't need expensive lessons. There's the musical box you gave me for my birthday, I can sell that. I did as you wished, Mama, I paraded down the red carpet and bowed to the Governor — '

'Stop it!' Angry, Alannah stood over the girl. 'You must stop this . . . dedication. It's unhealthy. You can't baby Will forever or make his decisions for him. You can't shape his life. He'll get his own property in time.'

'He wants it now, and he wants this one. You of all people should understand about a certain place, it's the way you feel about Burrendah. What's wrong with me wanting Will to be happy?'

'You can't arrange happiness for others.'

'I want Will to have what he wants.'

'Because you think it will make him care for you the more. He does care for you, and greatly, it may not be exactly the way you want, that's all. You must face the possibility that Will might want a life entirely without you.'

'If it makes him happy to have Celine some day then I'll accept it.'

'Celine?' Alannah moved exasperatedly about the small space crammed with ferns and plants. 'Stop talking so about a ten-year-old child, even if she is growing up quickly.' She knocked over a pot-plant, picked it up and thumped it on the bench. 'You're all growing up too quickly, or wanting to, becoming possessive about things, about life, about each other. You're obsessive, as if you've all suddenly become aware of each other in a new way. Your father's right, he's seen all this before I have, one reason he insisted you spend time apart and away from Hawkes Plains with the chance to do varied things in different surroundings.'

'No one has to remind me I'm sixteen if that's what you mean.'

'It seems I must remind you that Will's seventeen, in

many ways a man, and farmers marry young. It's necessary.'

'That's what he says.' The girl sat hunched on the garden seat with her hands tightly folded. Her mother seated herself beside her but did not touch her; in this she must not comfort, Clodagh must find her own ways out of involvement.

'Will needs a wife to work with him his way. You can't do it. You are being trained for a different life.'

'What life am I being trained for, Mama?'

'What all women are trained for whether they like it or not – marriage.' She sighed. 'Almost everyone marries sooner or later and with you it should be what your grandfather would call a suitable young man.'

'Who would you call a suitable young man, Mama?'

Alannah plunged. 'James Marr has excellent prospects.'

'I don't want Jimmy Marr.'

'Then don't have him.' Her mother got to her feet. 'I chose my own man and so can you. I don't know the right one for you, Clo. I only know it's not Will.'

'Because he's illegitimate?'

Alannah swung about, surprised. 'I've never told you that. Nor, I'm sure, has your father.'

'If Will's mother abandoned him and no one knows who his father was, it's reasonable to assume he was born out of wedlock, as it's termed. You're all so . . . snobbish!'

'I won't let you accuse us so. We love and respect Will, he's your father's adopted son, just as Jamie is. It's Will who makes the divisions.'

'No one knowing Will could doubt his father was a fine man.'

'That's not necessarily so.'

'Will's strong and kind and ambitious. I won't let him be looked down upon just because his mother didn't want him and he's never known his father.'

'Oh, Clodagh, *dear*, you're distorting something you know nothing about. Your father regards you all as equals in the family. He's good to you, he's good to Will, and heaven knows he's done more than enough for Jamie who's used him badly all through life. He's not young any more and if he refuses to help Will at the moment it's because he needs him badly – don't you consider your father at all? There are always two sides to things, you must have learned something of life between the Latin verbs and the dancing classes. Will would have been in a foundling home at best but for your father and Will should consider it. Can't you reason with him? Can't you continue with him as the brother he's always been?'

'He's not my brother and I never feel that he is; he's no more an O'Shea than I am. But you won't have to wean me from him, if that's the term, for Will doesn't want me. He doesn't see me in any light but as a friend.'

'Then it's useless you going through life being intense about him.' The girl did not answer. Alannah stood looking down on her bent head a while then suddenly raised her hands and let them drop helplessly. 'Very well. I'll give Will the money.'

Clodagh's head shot up, her eyes shining. 'Oh, Mama!'

'Don't thank me. I will have to contend with your father's anger, for he will be very angry when he finds out, as he will sooner or later.' Silence again. 'You will have to pledge Will to secrecy; he can say he borrowed the money somewhere, I don't know where, but as you can see we will have to lie all round. Your father won't really believe it so finally I'll have to confess. It will all fall back on me. It seems you don't mind that either.'

'*Can't* mind.'

'I see . . . Will's a minor so will need my permission. He'll also need money for legal expenses. We leave for Hawkes Plains at the weekend, there's much to be done before your father's precious "shoot" or wood-chop, or whatever he's decided to call his festival this time . . .'

'Domi gets upset. He always does. He hates the shooting.'

'Dominic O'Shea had better get used to it, and to other things, if he means to wander Africa one day,' she said tartly. 'And don't look at me so, I'll talk to Will as soon as we get back. Have I ever broken a promise to you?'

'No.'

As Clodagh still hesitated Alannah turned her back on her to stare from the window. 'Leave me be, Clodagh. I refuse to discuss the matter further now. Just leave me be.'

Chapter Nine

'DON'T STAND on ceremony, please Will. Don't you want to sit down?'

'I've been with the pigs. I might spoil your fine cushions.' He grinned. 'The place has grown rather grand, you know.'

'Not near as grand, as you put it, as the Brisbane house which you've never seen. Why not, Will?'

'A rough-booted farmer like me hobnobbing with city swells?'

'Stop that. You're our Will wherever you are and whatever you do. It's you who draws a dividing line, from the time you insisted on living in the men's quarters instead of here where you belong.'

'It's easier that way. For work, I mean.' He looked so contrite she laughed. There had always been intelligence in Will, and despite his solid frame a certain delicacy, reminding her poignantly of Raunie's golden skin, black hair and easy gipsy grace – Raunie this youth's grandmother? As he stood looking about him, awkwardly aware of his stained farm clothes, she felt as certain as Brick that Jamie had fathered this youth. 'The Brisbane house was built for us all, just as this was. Sometimes I think you don't want to be part of us. And now you want to leave us altogether.'

'I'll be around when needed.'

'In letting you have this money I'm going against your father's wishes.'

'I can't help that.'

'You must want it very badly.'

'I do.'

She paused, then said abruptly, 'Do you ever hear of Jamie?'

He showed no surprise. 'I hear talk. Rumours.'

'If you know his whereabouts you must say. We haven't seen him in over six years. He could be dead.'

'He's alive and sailing round the islands, trading – at least it's what I hear.'

'Your father hears rumours too.' She moved restlessly. 'In this matter of the money you must suffer my authority. You're under-age.'

He shrugged. 'I never thought of that. I'll pay you back, with interest.'

'No interest, no complications, just the purchase carried out promptly and legally.' She paused. 'You have a good friend in Clodagh.'

'I know.'

'Well then! Bring the trap to the front tomorrow at eight o'clock. It will take three days but, luckily, I have shopping, as well as business with Mr Crutchley. He'll attend to everything for you. We must be back before your father arrives from Jubila . . . Remember Will, this matter is strictly between you and me.'

Clodagh stood watching the boys disappear with their sick animals to cosset before the kitchen fire, Dominic struggling with his ailing lamb and Phelim's arms full of a baby native bear. Cook would object and order the creatures to the barn but Phelim as always would manage to sneak them in again. She turned back to where Stratton McCrae waited with Gondola and their mounts for they were riding to where the men were clearing in readiness for fencing. She wondered why Mr McCrae chose to ride with her instead of joining his friend and Papa O'Shea in the sheds; she fumbled so over many things and was gauche (one of Miss Muir's favourite expressions) on horseback, unlike the women of the Downs competing to entertain the two colourful Canadian 'backwoodsmen' in their showy 'Frisco wardrobes and broad hats – particularly the blond Stratton McCrae who towered over the men and made women feel feminine and helpless when they were not. Wonderfully, when they talked she shed a little of her shyness, and so far had not stammered once.

'Hard on them, weren't you?' He smiled. He had very white teeth. She admired good teeth.

'Mama's afraid they will bother you.'

'They don't. As a matter of fact they're teaching me – in their different ways.'

'Very different. Domi's head is usually in a book when he's not rounding up stray animals. He has a regular zoo in the barn with birds and a wallaby and possums orphaned when trees are cut down – Domi hates to see the trees go – and cockatoos. He probably has snakes too; he knows how to handle them, or rather how not to.'

'I've seen his assortment, most of it strange to me. As a matter of fact, my head was always in a book at his age, when I could get my hands on one, that is.' They were walking their horses to the track, Gondola following with his beloved hack and murmuring a Neapolitan melody under his breath. 'He tells me he wants to be a missionary in "darkest Africa", his own term.'

'I doubt if he knows what missionary means. He's not religious, none of us are. Papa O'Shea wouldn't let tutors or governesses put "nonsense in our heads" as he calls it. I suppose we're heathens. Mama says the Reverend Sharple despairs when he visits, for only Domi listens. But I'm talking too much,' she finished, in awe at herself.

'It's good to talk. I spent years trying to talk to my father without either of us saying anything really.'

'Papa O'Shea won't take Domi's ambitions seriously, he laughs and calls him "our infant humanist" when he binds cut knees or massages turned ankles, or when the men come asking for remedies for this and that for Domi seems to know what herbs and potions will help – it's uncanny really. He learns from the Blacks, you see, in particular from Barney Cook when he's around. Barney's a rogue but he's a tracker and knows a lot. Mama says that if Domi wants to be a missionary he'd better be a doctor first so he can look after himself before others.'

'Perhaps he'll be a missionary-doctor. Plenty of them in darkest Africa. In other countries too.'

'Papa O'Shea — '

'Don't you ever call your father simply Papa?'

'Mr O'Shea is not my father.'

'Oh?'

'He's my stepfather.'

'Even so . . .'

'I can't seem to call him Papa, not to his face, I mean. I find many things difficult, you see, like talking to people. I get nervous. Sometimes I stammer.'

'No sign of a stammer now.'

'Anyway, I don't know what Papa O'Shea would like me to call him.'

'You could ask.'

'Perhaps I will . . . My father was a schoolmaster. He was drowned saving Mama and myself from a flood at Burrendah, our old home. I was three.'

'I'm sorry.'

'No, you're not. Not really. How could you be? You never knew my father. I didn't know him myself; I mean, I don't remember him, I only heard about him. Can you remember when you were three?'

He frowned. 'Nothing clear . . . or in sequence. I remember being on the move, always along some trail, to where I never knew, with tall things above and around me – trees. Always trees. And there's a vision . . . misty and vague . . . of a woman bathing my scratched knee. The water in her basin was bright red. Everything red. I hate the colour red – because of that, do you think?'

'Mama says you've travelled the world.'

'Not yet. There's a great deal of it I haven't seen.'

'Do you want to see it?'

'Of course. Don't you?'

'Not really. I don't want to be far from Hawkes Plains.'

'Or from Will, I imagine?'

'Will is my friend.'

'I'm sure he is.'

'He's always been here, as I have. He loves Hawkes Plains, as I do. But now he wants other ways. He wants to work the land differently.'

'And you?'

'I hate school in Brisbane and the entertaining at Belle-Monte, which makes things difficult for Mama, you see. But I remind her that she wants to be at Burrendah, her old home, though she'd rather die than let Papa suspect.

129

Why do we all want to be some other place than where we are?'

'Perhaps because we feel sure we'll find happiness some other place.'

'Will you find happiness some other place?'

'I don't know. Perhaps it's one reason I came to Australia; sometimes there are reasons hidden even from ourselves as to why we do things.'

'Like Papa O'Shea laughing when he's really unhappy over Domi going to darkest Africa to cure the natives of horrible diseases. And because Phelim will follow wherever Domi goes. Phelim wants adventure, and company, that's why he bullies Domi out into the world to "look around" as he calls it. Phelim is . . . is . . . '

'Gregarious?'

'Yes. You know words, don't you?'

'Some. But not always how best to use them. Or to say them correctly.'

'You use them well with me . . . My sister, Celine, just wants to fall in love.' She laughed softly, wickedly. 'As a matter of fact Mr McCrae, she's fallen in love with you. She's ten.'

'I've never affected ten-year-olds in that way before.'

'Celine's intense. She wants to skip years.'

'One can't, so don't worry. Isn't there an older brother?'

'Jamie. The "thorn in our side", as Celine calls him. I don't know where she picked up the phrase, I can only think the Reverend Sharple. Jamie's the son of Papa O'Shea's first wife. He adopted Jamie. Papa O'Shea's always adopting someone. He adopted Will. He adopted me. We're a complicated family, you see. A mixed bag, Mama calls us.'

'An interesting mixed bag.'

'I'm talking too much again.' It bothered her as well as amazed, and she went on rather stiffly. 'I should listen to you, Mr McCrae, for you're the guest. Where would you rather be?'

'Mister? You do have difficulties with names, don't you Clodagh – may I call you Clodagh?'

'It's my name.'

'Where would I rather be? Nowhere but where I am, riding the trails — '

'Tracks, we call them.'

'Tracks. Talking to a charming girl who'll be the belle of any ball she attends.'

'Oh no.' She was as much shocked as surprised. 'I'm plain.'

'With that shining hair and fine manners and elegance – yes, elegance. It's a state of mind, no one can give you elegance, or take it away.'

'No one's told me such things before. I mean, no man.'

'You've never been sixteen before.'

'It makes a difference?'

'Always.'

'Then I'm glad for Mama's sake. And for Miss Muir's – she's our headmistress. You wouldn't know it, Mr McCrae,' she went on thoughtfully, 'but this very minute everyone is wondering about us.'

'Who is everyone? And what are they wondering?'

'Everyone is Miss Muir, and Meg, Mama's maid, and Fay Buxton at Jubila, and the Dennings at Glenaire, and Mrs Plum at BelleMonte. Everyone is wondering why I would waste a morning riding with you when you're married; they consider I should be riding with Mr Hume because he's a bachelor and eligible. To cultivate him, you see. I don't think Mr Hume is interested in marriage, do you? Certainly not with me. I'm not supposed to know what goes on around me, and perhaps I wouldn't very much if it weren't for Celine. She listens at keyholes.'

He chuckled. 'She seems a bright lass all round.'

'Too bright sometimes. So I think it's pleasant that we can ride over the "trails" not caring what people are wondering about us. We don't even have to like each other. It's so restful.'

'Very.'

'We can talk about your railway.'

'It's a big subject.'

'I'd like to hear about it, Mr McCrae.'

'Couldn't you manage Stratton?'

She smiled, again wickedly. 'If I did you might find it all too much. You see, Celine intends to call you not only Stratton, but Strat.'

He laughed loud and long. 'Do you know, I can hardly wait to meet this sister of yours.'

With Yoolanowi as base the young Canadians rode the Settled District, fêted from station to station, staying on where they pleased. Now they would stay at Hawkes Plains to take in the end of shearing and the sports day, intrigued by an Australian wood-chop, wandering the bush discussing Australian flora with the hands and arguing together when and where to cut down. By devious means and a tightly held excitement that made her as taut as a spring, Celine O'Shea managed to follow Strat McCrae at a discreet distance about the stables and yards, the dairy and wool-shed, everywhere but the men's quarters which were forbidden her. She ignored Morgan Hume who spent much time playing cards with the men in their leisure hours, a happy-go-lucky fellow who laughed at his own jokes and teased the servant-girls; she had seen him kissing Clara behind the scullery door. Hidden by brush or peeping from behind trees she watched the tall one with the bright blond hair that gleamed in the sun. He had a lot of hair and, she thought, a wonderful face under his beard and moustache. He trailed Morgan as they tramped together but everyone knew it was really he, Stratton McCrae, who led. She had never seen anyone like him; he was, she decided, what a god must be like. Or the Prince in 'The Sleeping Beauty'. He lifted things easily and could walk miles without losing breath while she puffed and became red in the face tramping from wool-shed to machine-shop to kitchen garden keeping him in sight, dodging Meg when she came searching or Clodagh who would marshal her back to the house for lessons or some boring chore, as if she were a *child*!

Today she hung about the verandah steps waiting her chance to talk to the young god, though he wasn't really young, twenty she'd heard . . . She liked older men, mature men – a lovely word, *mature*. Sooner or later he would take his morning stroll so she planted herself in view, smoothing her wrinkled stockings and picking grass seeds from her pinafore. Now here he was, stamping about the verandah, peering up at treetops, and the sky with its faint sprinkling of cloud. She said brightly, with assurance:

'It's going to be a fine day.'

'Thanks for the certainty.'

'I've come to walk with you.'

'Have you now? Celine, isn't it?'

'You know it is,' she said crossly then thought better of angering him so early in the day. 'Would you rather go riding?' Rashly, for she wasn't dressed for it. 'We all ride, though Clodagh never really learnt. She's a rotten rider don't you think? She won't say but I think she's frightened of the horses.'

'Even a rotten rider, if she is, can amble the river paths. I'm on a shoot this morning.'

'I can shoot.'

'That's hard to believe.'

'I can shoot well.'

'Then you should not at your age.'

'I wish you wouldn't say "at your age" like that. I'm getting older. I'll show you how I can shoot, if you like.'

'I don't like. Your papa wouldn't like it.'

'Papa wouldn't know if you don't tell him. He doesn't have to know everything.' She made little runs to keep up with his long strides. 'Will taught me to shoot. He's a wonderful shot. Will will do anything for me.'

'Poor Will.'

'He's not poor Will.' Indignantly. 'He's enamoured of me.'

To her horror he laughed. 'Do you know what "enamoured" means?'

'Of course.' On her dignity. 'It means he wants my body.'

'*What?*' He stopped dead, staring down at her. 'Where did you pick that up?'

'In one of Jamie's novelettes in his trunk in the storeroom. The key sticks but I can turn it.'

'I'm sure you can.'

'Jamie's books tell grown-up things, with words like . . . well . . . wanderlust. That's what Papa says Domi has – wanderlust. It sounds like an awful disease. We'd be *desolated* if Domi died.'

'It's not a sickness that kills. It means wandering the world.'

133

'I like the last part best – lust. What does lust mean, Strat?'

'Ask your mother.'

'I'd rather you told me.'

'Tell me about your Uncle Jamie.'

'He's not really our uncle, he's our brother but not really our brother either. Will's our brother too but not really, see?'

'It will take time for me to unravel that.'

'That's why it's all right for Will to love me all his life, though I don't tell Clodagh that, it would break her heart.' She fell into step beside him, managing to keep up, afraid he would leave her behind. 'It's sad really. For Clodagh I mean.'

'Adult love is beyond you yet, Celine.'

'Oh no it's not. I'm telling you about Will to make you jealous.'

'Why?'

'Because I'm going to love you all my life and I want you to love me back.'

'You must stop talking so. You're only ten.'

'Eleven.'

'Ten. Your sister was definite.'

'Clodagh's always snitching on me. Anyway, I'm growing fast, see? My legs are shooting up. And my arms . . .' She held them out proudly. 'I wish I had the wanderlust, I could travel with you.' Her words tumbled over each other so that he wouldn't become bored. 'I'd like that.'

'No, you wouldn't. Mine is a tough life.'

'I'm tough.' She paused to look up into his face. 'You're sweating – Mama makes us say perspiring but I like to say sweating best.'

'You're born to this sun.' He strode out again. 'Acclimatised.'

'That's a good word. I know the words but they sound different when you say them.'

'It's called accent. I'm Yankee-born tempered by Canada: we overlap. But backwoods or bush, upcountry or backcountry, it's all the same really.' He glanced at her keenly. 'Yes, I think you could be tough. You're already precocious.'

'That doesn't sound a very nice word.'

'It doesn't have a very nice meaning so let's stick to travel, it's safer. Travel becomes an itch making you want to go farther and farther into the world. Perhaps to get away from things.'

'What things?'

'In my case, hard slogging work since I was a youngster.'

'Do you miss your home?'

'Canada? It won't disappear. That's the wonderful thing about a favourite country, it's there for your return.'

'Are you going back?'

'Yes, I'm going back.'

'Domi says you have pine forests.'

'Lots of pine. Dominic's the studious brother, isn't he? A kind of oracle?'

'Nurse Puttering says Domi should be a priest and Papa gets red in the face because he doesn't like priests and won't let them roam around here getting at the men. Do you think Papa's a dictator? Mama says he's a dictator about Domi. I can't see why Domi can't do what he wants when he's grown.'

'Perhaps because he'll come into this property some day and will be expected to work it. We can't always do as we want, Celine.'

'I'm going to do as I want.'

'You very well might. And break your Mama's heart.'

'Mama's too sensible to break her heart over me. Over any of us really. I want to know everything you know, Strat.'

'You don't know me, Celine.'

'Oh yes I do. I watch you all the time. Some day I'm going to marry you.' He laughed, and angry and baffled she stamped her feet. 'I am. I *am*.'

'I'll be an old man when you're grown.'

'I don't care. I like old men. Tod Buxton's old and I like him.'

He roared laughing. 'He's in his thirties, from what I hear.'

'That's old. Jeb Whaley's so old Meg says he's decrepit. He wants to marry Meg but she says they have to prop him up on his horse so what hope would they have in bed?'

'Oh, *Celine*!' She thought he would never stop laughing, but finally he sobered. 'I'm married.'

'She might die. She could be dead right now and you've not heard.'

'Don't talk that way.'

'Why not?'

'Even if she were, heaven forbid, I wouldn't want to marry again. It's not all it's cracked up to be.'

'I suppose not. Things happen, don't they? People die and leave each other. Or fall out of love. It would be terrible to stop loving someone. Worse, having someone stop loving you.'

'You know nothing about grown-up love, young lady.'

'I'm not a young lady, not like Clodagh. I don't want to be like Clodagh. I'm going to be different. I only know about other people's love yet and I want my very own.'

'Your papa's right, you *are* precocious! What looks like love at age ten often is not.'

'What is it then?'

'Indigestion perhaps.' He seemed to think it all a joke. '*Mal de mer*, an urge to throw up. Any number of things.'

'You shouldn't laugh.' In injured dignity, she stared him out until he sobered.

'No, I shouldn't. It's all a matter of growing up. Your mother will explain.'

'I'd rather you did.'

She fancied he sighed. 'You're not like your sister.'

'Half-sister. The same mother, see.'

'A very charming mother.'

'Not when she sees through us. She sees through me all the time. I can't get away with things for long with her.'

'I should hope not. Don't you like Clodagh?'

'Of course I like her. I mean, we're related so *expected* to like each other. But not in a sloppy way, Clodagh couldn't be sloppy if she tried. She's just not adventurous, she doesn't *do* things, she hangs around here looking after Dominic and Phelim, and me when she wants to be bossy, but most of the time she looks after Will, cooks for him – she's a spiffer cook – and rides all over looking for him and when she can't find him leaves the pies and puds with the men who gobble them up.'

'Clodagh's a good friend to Will.'

'She wants to be more. She wants him to love her and marry her and live happily ever after; she doesn't say so but that's just her pride. Does anyone live happily ever after, Strat?'

'Very few, I'd say.'

'Mama and Papa want to.'

'Then they well might.'

'I think girls like Clodagh think everything will be sure and safe when they marry so they don't have to do any more about living.'

'Marriage means a lot to some women.'

'I think Clodagh's afraid of what the world might do to her, you know?'

'Perhaps she shows sense. It's a pretty frightening place out there.'

'Everyone says that all the time but I'm not going to be afraid of it. Nor of love. I want everything to be exciting and wonderful. I think love must be spiffer. If I weren't sure of that, I'd know, wouldn't I?'

Her logic made him temporarily speechless. 'You *are* precocious.'

'Is love wonderful, Strat?'

'I don't know much about it, really.'

'You married someone.'

'It's not always the same thing. What kind of books does Dominic collect?'

'All kinds. Mama has books sent out from Brisbane and our grandfather in Sydney sends books for birthdays and Christmas. Domi loves to riffle through Papa's trunks of books; Phelim knows where the keys are kept and puts them back so Papa won't know — '

'You're all pretty crafty with keys.'

'That's what Nurse Puttering calls Phelim – crafty. Mama and Clodagh read us all about Africa and the Boers and the native wars and things like that, and all the books go up on Domi's shelves. He dusts them all the time. He's a funny boy, don't you think?'

'I collect books on engineering and timber-cutting and ship-building and victualling — '

'They sound terribly dull.'

'Not to me.'

'Well, if they're interesting to you I'll read them.'

'You are a funny little thing, you know.'

'You're not going away are you?'

'Soon. Brisbane for another spell, then Sydney where I'll meet your grandfather and look over his mill. Then take ship to 'Frisco and up the coast to British Columbia.'

'I wish you'd stay at Hawkes Plains for ever. Don't you like me, Strat?'

'You take my breath away.'

'That's no answer.'

'I can't find a better. Let's just say you're making an impression by persistence. You're growing on me.'

'Where's British Columbia?'

'Western Canada.'

'Is it big? And important?'

'It's very big. And once the railway is through it will boom. I'm going to be part of that railway.'

'Mama says railways will soon be all over the Downs.'

'I don't doubt it.'

'Will you write to me, Strat? I'll write to you every week.'

'What could you find to write about every week?'

'Lots. I'll tell you everything that happens. Please Strat.'

'I'll be travelling.'

'*Please*, Strat.'

'We'll see.'

'What's that around your neck? Shining . . .'

'A charm. The Indians fashion them of silver.'

'Can I have it? To remind me of you. Something in memoriam.'

'You say the darnedest things.'

'I'll keep it for ever and ever and ever. *Please* Strat.'

With a resigned sigh he took the charm from about his neck and placed it in her eager child's hands.

'Blackmail, that's what it is. Blatant bloody blackmail!'

'Nothing of the kind. It's the legitimate collection of a debt.'

'Bloody hell it is. How old are you?'

'Twenty.'

'A pretty cocky twenty.'

'I learnt to be.'

'I see it now: the son arrives with entrée letters, but the son doesn't know enough to come in out of the rain, too occupied with the local frails, so you're along with the front of a trader to talk timber and mutton at my table, with no intention of doing business — '

'Afraid not. We can get all the timber we need from Oregon. We could use your mutton but can't get it over intact, unless this fellow in Sydney can freeze and ship it.'

'Damn the meat. Damn the timber. The point is, you duped me. Duped us all.'

'And the point is, Mr Muir, you skipped 'Frisco with forty thousand dollars.'

'It's a lie. A damned lie.'

'Well then, thirty, half of which belonged to Mr Hume. Now he's claiming it all, as some return for his expensive years spent hunting you out. With interest of course.'

'You've no proof. It was a gentleman's agreement. No legality.'

'We all know that. But Mr Hume makes no secret of his life in San Francisco; you do. You have everything to lose.'

'What's he paying you for this blackmail?'

'A nasty word, Mr Muir. It will only be blackmail if persuasion doesn't succeed. Persuasion will succeed, we all know it. As to my payment . . . A contract to supply the Canadian Pacific Railway.'

'You trust that mountebank of a Hume?'

'No. I'll see the contract before I hand over the money.'

'Damn you, McCrae, I don't have forty thousand dollars!'

'But you have Yoolanowi station, and your Brisbane mansion, and a thriving business by the wharves, and an emporium glutted with valuable goods.'

'Mortgaged to the hilt, the lot of it. You'll ruin me.'

'Hardly more than make a dent, I'm thinking. The thing is, unless I return to Mr Hume with forty thousand dollars in cash or kind – and I know precious gems and can weigh gold dust – he swears he'll be out by the next ship to raise hell. We all know he'll do it. Moreover, he mentioned a young sister with you in 'Frisco . . .'

'The bastard.' Bennett Muir was looking apoplectic. 'The bloody bastard!'

'We leave Brisbane at the beginning of October. Meanwhile we preserve the status quo – and a pleasant status quo it promises to be.' Strat McCrae, sure of himself and his ultimate success, decided to be generous. 'A month, Mr Muir. One month, no more no less.'

Chapter Ten

THE SHEARERS were dribbling off to New South Wales, some to go on to Victorian sheds as work got under way in the south. A few would stay for the sports and the wool-shed dance, an end-of-shearing celebration usual in some form or another all over the country, reminding Alannah poignantly of Burrendah. She called the event Feast Day, sometimes laughingly Holy Day, a pilgrimage of male strength and bravado, a showing-off, a mateship in which the local bloods, old hands, new chums, anyone who could wield an axe could compete. The young planned reunions and their mothers packed pies and cakes to escape from steaming kitchens and meet old friends and exchange gossip. This year the festivities were centred around the Canadians, or Yankees as they were vaguely called, for few Americans came to the Darling Downs, fewer still from Canada, the latter a country Queenslanders knew little about, only tales told by forty-niners settled as station hands. Dominic O'Shea wore his wary look that so annoyed his father as he tended his pets, growing quieter as the men talked of guns and marksmanship.

'Where did he get this religious bent?' Brick fumed. 'It's even aesthetic at times.'

'Humanist, I've heard you call it. From you, I suppose. You were always a man of causes.'

'I still am; different causes that's all. But the land always came first with me and I expect the same of my sons. Phelim talks too long and loudly of adventure in far-off places and Dominic is obsessed with this African missionary idea — '

'Doctor, rather.'

'Doctor . . . missionary . . . who in his right mind would embroil himself in the slaughter of Bantu by Zulu or the other way about, with the Voortrekkers annihilating the lot if they can? Leave them all to murder each other.'

Barney Cook had wandered in with his tribal cronies to camp by the Creek. To Alannah's dismay Celine avoided them, particularly Barney, and the others she had known for years; she was not outgrowing her distaste, her fear perhaps, of the natives. 'There is nothing sinister about black skin, Celine. It's all around us. Back in time skin had to adapt to climate, that's all. You're fond of Emmy Walsh – her mother was a full-blood.'

'Emmy's our cook. That's different.'

'It is *not* different. Sometimes you're as arrogant as you are imperious and I won't have it so, nor will your father. All Europeans feel as you do at first. I did. But we get over it.'

'I can't help it. I can't, Mama.'

'You must help it. The world is full of dark-skinned people. It will do you good to travel.'

She covered up for the girl when her father was about for there was tension in him enhanced by tiredness from rebuilding and restocking Jubila after the devastating drought and his long rides back and forth for he would not leave her or Hawkes Plains for long. He was short of temper, particularly with Dominic, even with herself, which was unusual for he was always master of himself, only Jamie really shattered him. The week before the sports he seemed everywhere at once with an expenditure of energy even beyond his marvellous reserves of strength, finalising the wool-clips, paying off the shearers, seeing the wagons away, even erecting the marquee when anyone could have done it . . .

'We cut the big gum tomorrow.'

'Your precious tree.'

'It will build a house for the Marlowes. I promised them a new place, they have six children.'

'You're limping.'

'The leg's fine. Do I complain?'

'No. But you would not no matter what trouble it gave you. Why push yourself at your — ' She broke off.

'Say it. Age.'

'Very well . . . age. You've won every year, you can afford to leave this chop to others.'

'To the young bloods, you mean?'

'Why not? Stop while you're ahead. Why risk . . .' Again she hesitated, she could not hurt him.

'My life? I won't take a seizure, girl, but if I did I can't imagine a more satisfying way to go.' He grinned. 'Unless it's to expire in your arms. I have only one real competitor, the McCrae fellow, he's used to the great firs but he'll chop into our logs as savagely. He's a giant with an axe even if he doesn't know all the rules yet.'

'If you must do it, take care.'

'I'm used to it.' He kissed her long and deeply. 'I want you there as close as you can safely be.'

'Aren't I always? After all,' she teased lightly, yet with relief in the idea, 'this year you might get soundly trounced. I wouldn't miss that for the world!'

Two days before the sports Jamie rode in. The Canadians were at Glenaire and would not be back before the morrow. So Brick had gathered his family for a late dinner, a rare occurrence, when Clara appeared, startled and apologetic, to be brushed aside by Jamie dumping a duffel-bag at his feet and leaning against the doorjamb. One hand was roughly bandaged.

'Jamie!' Alannah broke the stunned silence, startled by a vision of this man as a youth leaning just so against the doorjamb of Birubi, the O'Sheas' Sydney house, one New Year's night long ago, with his mother hurrying to greet him.

'Who else?' Jamie laughed as the boys stared at this mysterious older brother, uncle as they called him, identified only by name, returned as if from the dead, a man heard of but whom they did not know. Celine might dimly remember, but Dominic, no, and Phelim was staring intrigued for the man was spectacular, burned almost black by the sun, bony-thin in seaman's clothes, his black hair thick and long and wild, a graceful, raffish, exotic gipsy-man. Clodagh remembered him too well and sat folding and unfolding her napkin, her eyes on her plate.

'Your hand,' Alannah murmured. 'You've injured it.'

'There's blood on the bandage,' Dominic pointed out in his formal way.

'I caught it at a saw-mill.'

'You've actually been doing a spot of work?' Brick spoke for the first time.

'I'll rebandage it. Clodagh will help.'

'Stay where you are Dominic,' his father rasped. 'That goes for all of you. Clara's serving dinner.'

'Wrap it in this. It will do for now.' Alannah passed over her table napkin, anything to weave around this unexpected and dreadful situation. 'You're hungry, of course.' She tried to smile. 'You were always hungry.'

'The same.' He slid into the chair beside Clodagh and watched her with his sly little smile as she wrapped his hand. She did not look up.

'There's roast mutton.' Phelim's eyes did not leave the colourful and fascinating stranger.

'It's always roast mutton.' Jamie grinned at him. 'Comes with the place.'

'You've got rings in your ears.' Celine pointed when she had been taught not to. 'Like the sailors in Domi's books.'

'They're pirates.' Domi watched his father. He watched him a lot hoping to please him yet rarely succeeding.

'It's what I am, a sailor home from the sea. You're Celine, of course, who else? I remember you as a snotty-nosed kid of four or so.'

'You tell lies. I'm never snotty-nosed.'

'Enough of such talk. We're at table.'

'Well, I'm *not* snotty, Papa,' she dared. 'Clodagh makes me take a clean pocket-handkerchief every day. Did you bring us presents?'

'This for a start.' He dived into the bag and plumped a shrunken head before her napkin holder. Brick's chair crashed as he leant across to sweep the hideous thing into a corner. 'I will not have these obscene things in the house!'

'Then don't say I never bring gifts.' Jamie shrugged. 'I suppose you all thought me dead.'

'It crossed our minds.'

'Haven't I always turned up for your macabre log-chopping ritual?'

'Not in six years,' Alannah reminded him. 'Aren't you going to explain where you've been?'

'Before the children?' He slopped bread in his soup and gulped all down as if it were the first meal he'd enjoyed in a long time.

'You shouldn't speak with your mouth full.'

'Enough! It wouldn't surprise me if you'd been in gaol.'

'Came close to it now and then but I fooled 'em. Got any new books, Domi? I've brought you herbs and remedies and stuff from the islands.'

'You'll not bring witch-doctor superstition here!'

'That superstition, as you call it, saved my life a couple of times.'

'You've been racketing through Melanesia. Don't lie.'

'Why should I lie? There are no laws against trading.'

'There are laws against illegal dealing – Kanakas for instance.'

'Laws don't stop blackbirding. Everyone's at it. Lucrative – or so I hear.'

'You could have been eaten by cannibals.' Celine looked glassy-eyed at the prospect.

'I'm here aren't I, eating at your table? Our table, rather.' He glanced about. 'Isn't there one missing?'

'Will has a property of his own,' Alannah explained. 'A farm.'

'Has he now?' She thought he looked relieved. Celine shifted about and opened her mouth to speak.

'Not a word, Celine,' her father boomed. 'Eat your dinner.'

'Good idea.' Jamie concentrated on his mutton. 'Pass the salt, Phelim – it is Phelim, isn't it? I know you if you don't remember me.' He smiled his most ingratiating smile at his stepmother. 'You're right, Mrs O'Shea. I'm hungry.'

Jamie had ridden to Hawkes Plains in an expansive and triumphant mood. He handed round curios and carvings and shrunken heads while Celine purloined the one from under the dining-table to scare Meg witless with a lighted candle beside it, baring its horrors until Clodagh snitched and Alannah marched in to sweep the thing away between thumb and forefinger. He joined Morgan Hume and the men at cards, exulting in his change of luck, he argued trees and logs and the sharpness of his axe with Stratton McCrae, the child Celine always in their way, while Phelim O'Shea followed him about demanding exotic island tales. He had not yet been alone with Brick, but when they did clash he would be quite unconcerned about it. Matt Burney was dead and his years of servitude to the man were over. Burney's threats had been rendered harmless and Melanesia remained as a series of violent ingenious episodes devoted to 'recruiting labour': the sheer cliffs of Mota in the Banks group . . . Lush beautiful Tanna with its smooth brown girls compensating for loneliness for his own kind . . . Starting fires at dawn in the bush behind sleeping villages to drive the panicking Kanakas into an ambush on the far side . . . The ramming of canoes then enticing islanders aboard with gifts and clapping them under hatches . . . Crashing a length of jagged iron – the dreaded Eye-Drop – when a canoe came under the stern . . . standard practices throughout the Pacific since sandalwood and whaling days. And the best ruse of all – the missionary trick: the crew would stand around on deck singing hymns while he, with his smattering of the language and disguised in white coat and bell-topper, spectacles and umbrella, was rowed ashore. Missionaries were welcome and crowds would gather for the scraps of paper they thought were tracts and he would lie about the Bishop being aboard and wanting to see them . . . Every trick, all of it, carried out under the shrewd and greedy eyes of Burney, or his bully Norton, vetting Jamie Lorne O'Shea's every move, for he had been enslaved as rigidly as the dark-skinned men he cajoled. He'd jumped ship a couple of times but they found him and dragged him back. They made seven hundred pounds for a couple of months' work, two-and-a-half thousand a trip – no wonder Burney would go to any lengths to recruit. But finally Burney had gone too far: a violent and sadistic man, he'd battered a recruit to death in a long rhythmic fury with nothing more than a stick and the natives had taken their revenge in the dreaded green and impenetrable jungle of Malebula, the Evil Eye of superstition, their spears swift and true. His own precious luck had held and he'd escaped. With Burney dead and eaten, and Norton disappeared, dead too no doubt in some other jungle he, Jamie

Lorne O'Shea, was free. The boredom and expectation of the thousand miles of open ocean between the islands and the Brisbane River, with seasickness and dysentery plaguing them until at the end of it he had walked off with naught but freedom and some scraps of personal plunder to show for his years of exile . . . He was in the stables tending his hack and admiring the stallion, Milbong, when his stepfather found him. He prepared to brazen all out.

'It's a while since I've seen such fine horseflesh. I'll try him out tomorrow.'

'I've other plans for you. I've been chewing over a certain name for a long time, now I can spit it out.'

'Still spying around the wharves, eh?'

'Over six years of it, with one name surfacing time and again – Burney. Matthew Burney. As I heard it, he's skipper of the *Venture*. It's never dropped anchor in Brisbane so it must skulk in and out of northern ports — '

'Burney was never skipper. Not that it matters for he's dead, eaten too, in the New Hebrides, so can tell you nothing.'

'He doesn't need to. You've hinted enough of your press-gang activities without having to be precise about them. I swore if I caught you blackbirding I'd finish you off.'

'You can try,' Jamie laughed, 'but you're six years older and ageing fast – old man.'

Brick's right arm was still strong enough to send the other crashing against the horse-stall setting the beasts quivering but Jamie leapt to his feet and Brick's head shot back with the force of a fist toughened by village fights all over the Pacific. For the first time in his life Brick struggled to rise, in shock, then terror not only for his helplessness but in his fury against this man, a disgust driving him to subdue, punish, annihilate; to revenge not only his treachery but his mockery and contempt. Jamie stood over him watching him struggle. 'You've taken whips to me in Sydney, on mountains and the plains, and when no whip was handy, your fists. No longer, old man. I came back because I chose to. And if I choose to kill you here and now I can do it – old man.'

'Do it then,' Brick gasped, clinging to the stall uprights, struggling not only to rise but for his breath. He could not rise, not yet, for a terrible and unexpected weakness, a crippling of the body, held him back. 'Kill me if you must,' he gasped. 'If it's what you want, kill me, I can't stop you. Do it, damn you. *Do* it!'

Legs apart and firmly planted Jamie stood looking down on his lifelong adversary; in the pull and tug of their years the one who had always been the stronger. Now both knew who was master. It was more than enough for Jamie Lorne O'Shea. Turning abruptly he walked confidently away.

For some reason she could not quite define Alannah dreaded the coming sports, particularly the wood-chop that surpassed even the kangaroo shoot in creating fevers of anticipation. There were six formidable entrants coming from as far as Warwick and Toowoomba and since it was an open day Hawkes Plains would be crowded. The trees remained as stumps, great creamy sentinels in the bush beyond the wool-shed, the brush around each cleared for the cutters, and the onlookers who would gather at a safe distance from flying chips. The men had been sharpening their terrible axes for weeks, while brisk betting 'books' had taken over in the men's quarters, the Canadian Strat McCrae and O'Shea of Hawkes Plains the favourites. Umpires, supporters, barrackers and various hangers-on argued happily about timing and clocking and handicaps with a couple of genial fist-fights to keep things going. That night Alannah woke to Brick restless beside her, breathing heavily, his forehead hot to her touch in the cool night. He sweated. With a long-drawn-out sigh he turned over to her, half woke and struggled up on one elbow with a curious supplicating gesture. He did not speak. She cradled him in her arms as she might one of her children until, finally, they slept.

When she woke next morning he was dressing. He seemed calm, even composed, but that disturbed her the more; she would rather he lost his temper with her if he must. 'It's early,' she protested.

'There's much to do.'

'You've plenty of help.' Then lightly, 'You can always put your sons to work.'

'I have no sons.'

'You have four.'

'Don't call that vagabond of a Jamie my son!'

'Well, you suspected — knew really — what he was up to all these years.' Loyalty took the place of her sweet reason. 'Will should be here.'

'Will walked out.' He was angry. 'He can't walk back.'

'You're unfair to him. He's making a go of the place, getting rusty machinery to work, building up his soil, fencing, all on practically nothing.'

'I won't have Clodagh staying with him weekends. I don't want her riding to Drayton at all.'

'She goes to do what she's always done, look after Will, mend his clothes, cook something beyond his monotonous mutton and pumpkin — '

'You spoil her. You always did.' He was savage. 'Did you love her father so much?'

She gasped. 'I never loved Simon, you know that. I married him because you were lost to me, I didn't even know where you were. For all I knew you might have deserted me.'

'Alannah!'

'It could have been that way. Simon was a good man. When he guessed, or somehow knew, that the child I lost had been yours and not his it made no difference. Would you have done the same?'

'All right, I'm unfair. I'm growing old and cantankerous and talking instead of doing, an ageing man with a beautiful young wife and jealous of everyone who looks her way. I want this contest, to prove something I suppose . . . to the world, more so to you.'

'That's juvenile! The aim of a boy.'

'I know. All the same I must do it.'

She slid from the bed, padded barefoot across the room and clasped her arms around his neck. 'Let Will take your place. He'll come. He'll do anything for you.'

He brushed her aside. 'Will lied to me. Tricked me. He told me he borrowed money for the farm when he had no collateral — where did he get it? If I knew who advanced it I'd tear the bastard apart. I don't believe Will even had the one hundred.'

'Oh yes.'

'How can you be sure?'

'I know.'

'How do you know?' He turned on her. 'You're hiding something from me. Ran Cowper at Yoolanowi advanced it, didn't he? I've suspected it for some time.'

'Ran Cowper? Nonsense.'

'Why nonsense? Ran's always helped and supported Will. I'm going to face Cowper with it — '

'It's not Ran, it's . . . If you must accuse someone, accuse me.'

'You?'

'Don't look that way. I gave Will the money. I couldn't stand by and see him lose the place for the sake of one hundred pounds. I gave it unconditionally and without strings and got the sale through without a hitch. I'm telling you because you're tormenting yourself with what you imagine is Will's treachery, worse, accusing Ran Cowper. I've always hated keeping secrets from you — '

'It would have been better if you'd kept this one. At least you could have talked it over with me.'

'You wouldn't have listened. You refused Will in the first place.'

'You've let me down.' His tone was flat and lifeless. 'You went behind my back.'

'I had no choice. What you won't see is that Will would have gone with or without my hundred. He would have found some way to get his farm. It had to happen, can't you see that?'

'What I see is that I've been too generous in letting you manage money. I see that clearly.'

'It was my *own* money, left me by my grandmother and added to from Con's estate. My *own*, to spend as I please.'

'Only because I allowed you to control it. It was not a trust, and I could have argued it out with lawyers, even in a court of law if I'd wished.'

'You would do that to me?'

'I never have. Perhaps I should have done so.'

She was aghast. He had always been the most generous of men, not only to herself but to all around him. Now anger piled on disappointment was making him mean and petty. Her own anger followed him to the door. 'Don't go out in this mood. And don't take on that wood-chop tomorrow. *Don't!*'

Ignoring her he closed the door after him, but quietly where she'd expected him to slam it. Her pleas died with his footsteps. She was as angry as he, but she was also afraid.

That night she slept alone. It had never happened before for no matter their differences they always shared their bed. Pride kept her from seeking him out; he must resolve whatever simmered within him alone, or at least without her. She fell into a fitful sleep. Towards morning she woke to rain and went to the window to a short sharp rainstorm that would clear in the day but leave sodden grass and dripping trees to steam under the sun, if there were sun. It was early when she woke again to hear him moving about his dressing-room; at least he was here and preparing for the day and all she could do was talk of trivia, anything to ease his mood for in an hour or so most of the Central Downs would be jostling each other through the gates. Meg brought their tea, in a rush to finish her morning chores, and Alannah sipped hers in bed watching her husband move silently about the room not even looking her way. She must check bedrooms, she told him, Marion Denning was not the only expectant mother who would want to rest . . . Celine must stop following Strat McCrae about, the man was altogether too patient with the child . . . Yoolanowi's people were always the first to arrive, would Bennett come with them, or later? No one seemed to know . . . He went back and forth to Sydney so often she wondered why he kept a manager there . . .

'Manager? What manager?' At last she had his attention.

'The manager of his Sydney office.'

'What Sydney office?'

She frowned, striving for clarity, for it seemed important to him. 'On my trip by sea that time Bennett told me he was travelling with his manager, though I never met the man — ' She broke off, startled. 'Matthew Burney, that was the name. I remember now – Matthew Burney.'

'Burney?' He was staring at her. 'Are you sure?'

'Quite sure. "We came aboard late," Bennett said. "Matthew Burney, my Sydney manager. I have opened an office there." His exact words. Isn't it odd, one can't recall a name for years then suddenly it's there . . . What is it? You look so strange. Is it important?' She set down her cup and saucer for there *was* something strange in his attitude and she searched for the right words. 'Can't you forget Jamie . . . Will . . . everyone and everything that is bothering you just for today? We'll have people wandering through the gates any minute — '

'Stop chattering,' he shouted at her. 'Damn Jamie. Damn Will. Damn Muir. And damn *you*!' Choking over the words he stumped out the door, banging it, leaving her shocked and confused – what had she done? Something was wrong, very wrong, something beyond Will and Jamie, even beyond herself. One thing only was clear: the day was off to a bad start and she had the sinking feeling it would get worse. The sooner it was over and done with the better.

The sun broke intermittently through clouds tossed by a fretful wind. Boots were caked with mud and the ground about the logs was a trample of slippery grass but it had not rained since early morning and, in any case, seasoned woodcutters made light of weather, eager to be wielding their murderous axes. Handicapped as at local shows, as a courtesy – though he had not asked for the privilege – Strat McCrae would be first away. He had been chipping and chopping for days, working from one side of a tree to the other, cutting out wedges to slide in his standboard, getting the hang of it all. Stragglers were already wandering down to the logs but something held Alannah back; not until the thing was under way – and inevitable – could she bear to watch. She stayed with the women and children, rearranging pies and buns, slicing great wedges of plum cake and setting more cold meats on already overloaded platters, all to be carried to the tables in the wool-shed when the contest was over. She talked and tidied up and ordered children out of her way, she smiled and sympathised and gave orders, with all the time at the back of her mind a persistent unexplainable sense of dread.

Jamie had wandered aimlessly but happily all morning, no part of the activity about him for he had no interest in tests of physical strength which had always seemed to him so much wasted energy – he'd wasted energy enough these past years. He'd sold his bric-à-brac on the wharves and in dockside inns and his pockets, if not exactly jingling, were comfortably heavy. He would have liked to be riding the stallion, Milbong, but had decided to avoid O'Shea's anger, which meant avoiding O'Shea; he was quite happy to let the man stew. He could of course go and torment Celine but she followed McCrae so closely and the fellow's height and speed and muscle-power exhausted even in the watching. He'd managed to shake off the amiable clod of a Morgan Hume who spent much time arguing with McCrae about leaving the country; Morgan wanted to stay but Morgan's tycoon of a father had sent for him and McCrae had booked ship for the first of the month. Now Morgan had gone seeking a place to watch his friend mangle the bush and he, Jamie Lorne O'Shea, was alone with its silence.

The silence was broken: Strat McCrae was off! Soon others joined in with the sharp thud-thud of axes on wood and through the lattice of trees the flash of blades, pinpoints of light against the coloured shirts of men and the print dresses of women intent on holding back their children. Jamie trudged on, slipping and sliding in mud and brushed by branches and dripping leaves. To his left Strat McCrae was chopping strongly and on his right O'Shea cut with his usual precision, the pair an impressive sight to those who cared, which he did not for truth to tell he was bored by the spectacle. But what he did note, and clearly, was Bennett Muir standing back from the circle about O'Shea and partly screened by bushes, intent on the man's performance. As he walked on the thud-thud grew in intensity, it took over, it was all there was – but suddenly all changed. There was the flash of a spinning axe, and shouting, and glimpses of men running . . . And he was running with them to the clearing where his stepfather lay at the foot of his log with blood soaking his shirt from a deep wound in his side. Men crowded, trying to staunch the blood. Yet even in the confusion he saw something else, and that clearly – Bennett Muir walking up the slope to the homestead of Hawkes Plains; walking steadily and strongly and without once looking back.

Even before the other women Alannah knew what the distant shouts could mean and she ran as she had never run before.

153

She had always been able to run; as a child she had sprinted beside Con at country races in Ireland, now she stumbled over roots and long grass to the crack and crunch of undergrowth and shrubs but she did not fall, she must not fall. The deserted stumps shone brightly in a flash sunburst as with an exhausting final sprint she reached the men kneeling beside her husband. With desperate blows she pushed them aside and dragging off her blouse she held it against the gash in his side. He stared up at her, his lips moving, then his lips were still. She held him in her arms rocking him against her almost naked breasts.

'Alannah – don't.' Someone was trying to lift her to her feet. It sounded like Jamie – could it be Jamie? 'He's dead.'

'No.' She pushed him away. 'We must stop the bleeding. He'll live if we stop the bleeding.' Now someone – a child – was screaming; where had she heard such screaming before? A tall blond man was gripping her by the arm.

'It's more than the wound,' he said. 'It's a stroke, we think.'

The screaming went on and on and she could not bear it. She slapped the child, hard, and the screaming stopped. The men were drawing her away and she stumbled along with them, hating them but knowing she could not fight them longer. And after a while, softly and to herself, she began to cry.

Some time in the next few days, during the sessions of subdued talk, or the sad little meals picking at the mounds of largely untouched food, or even her father's burial amid the graves shielded by willows and safe above the waterline of the creek, Celine O'Shea ran away. The horses were all accounted for so it was decided she had wandered off, aimlessly perhaps, as far from the scene of her father's death as she could trudge. Horse parties fanned out to the north-east but Will, who had more or less taken charge on his arrival from Drayton, decided to explore the country to the north-west, so familiar to them as children; besides, there was an abandoned hut some four miles out, once the Marlowes' home till Brick had moved the family closer in, used as a storeroom for years until, mouldering away, it was left to rot. The rain was now beyond a drizzle and even in shock Celine must seek shelter. Strat McCrae, returned from some solitary reconnoitre, insisted on joining the search and though Will knew the man only slightly he respected him as an experienced backwoodsman familiar with much local folklore. They decided to explore on foot, with one lantern. It was dark when they reached the hut, a lopsided lump in the dimness, its half-open door off a hinge and stuck fast in the broken dirt floor. As Will expected, Celine was curled up behind it asleep. When he touched her she sat up with a start, muddy and dishevelled, one foot minus its shoe, bare and bloody in its torn stocking.

'It's all right, Cel,' he soothed. 'It's Will.'

She whimpered, huddling against him. 'I'll never see Papa again.'

Lifting her in his arms he held her close. 'All the same, you should not have run away.'

'Mama slapped me.'

'She didn't mean anything by it. I don't think she even knew it was you – not clearly.'

'I wanted to walk, just walk, you know? But it started to rain and I lost my shoe and cut my foot and could only limp. I remembered this hut where we used to play but the door wouldn't shut – there's someone with you . . .' Strat McCrae held the lantern high. 'It's Strat. Oh, *Strat*!' With a ferocious wriggle she freed herself from Will and held up her arms to the other man, rain soaking her hair until it hung in black streaks down her cheeks. 'I can't walk. You'll have to carry me.'

'Looks like it.' He wrapped his jacket tightly about her.

'Don't go back to Canada,' she murmured, burying her face against his shirt. 'Don't go away.'

'Go to sleep,' was all he said, blundering along the wisp of path. Will knew the man would need light and guidance and the knowledge pleased him greatly. But for some perverse reason the rickety hut door irritated him. Why had no one bothered to right the thing? With an angry wrench he lifted it on its hinges and closed and bolted it. The simple action seemed to relieve somewhat the sight of his beloved Celine in the arms of the self-assured Canadian . . . Yet she was safe, and would be well, and soon Stratton McCrae would sail for Canada, never, he hoped, to be seen again. Lantern in hand, Will O'Shea set off after the pair through the sodden dripping bush.

Part Two

Chapter Eleven

ALANNAH MUIR was dressing for her wedding anniversary dinner – her fourth. Each year Bennett insisted on a family celebration, the grandest ritual among many observed at Foxburgh House arranged by Isabel with her thinly veiled air of condescension since Alannah need no longer be treated as the mother of pupils but merely as her brother's wife. Alannah tucked away a wisp of hair for there must be no stray ends when Bennett appeared, on the dot, with flowers and his self-satisfied (smug she called it to herself) expression that would ready her for her gift jewellery presented with aplomb at dinner, each year surpassing former pieces in ostentation. She cared nothing for jewellery and put each piece quietly away hoping he would not notice their absence but sooner or later he would enquire and scold her in his clipped jocular way that yet seemed to hold a threat . . . She breathed in deeply, holding her breath as Meg pulled on her laces; at least she had managed to keep Meg through the general changeover of servants. She let out her breath in relief. When had she ceased to struggle against Bennett? Perhaps at the time she had ceased to struggle against Isabel. She had not been able to dislodge her sister-in-law; no hint of taking rooms elsewhere, even in her now spacious school, had the slightest effect. Isabel Muir clung to the prestige of Foxburgh House, and Bennett, and though she and her brother disagreed violently at times, Bennett clung to her. It was Alannah, Bennett's wife, who felt the outsider.

Meg smoothed the gown carefully over her mistress's still-slim hips while Alannah stared at herself in the long mirror. Bennett insisted she appear in the most fashionable clothes and coiffures even though she knew they did not suit her. She looked sleek . . . oiled. A sleek oiled-down lady! She had never regarded herself as beautiful no matter how many compliments came her way, she was irregularly featured, and too fined-down to suit the current vogue of well-padded and tightly laced women overflowing their stays. She could not keep pace with *La Mode* no matter how much Bennett spent on her; he was extravagant yet at the same time would query the most trivial household account, so much so she found it less wearing to meet much of the housekeeping herself. She swivelled about, seeking Alannah Moynan Aldercott O'Shea behind the façade of Muir for she must still exist; her freckles were there beneath the powder, her fair hair, misty with grey, was there too under the glued and sculptured coils adorned with a pearl spray, and even at forty-three she knew her skin was still fine under the paint . . . Her husband insisted she be ready and waiting in good time so, corseted and uncomfortable, she moved to the French doors to look out on the view, almost identical to the one she had enjoyed from BelleMonte.

Her life with Bennett was comfortable, pleasant and safe. Too safe. All was taken out of her hands. Even in his love-making he took the initiative; he did not expect response as Brick had done. Brick had demanded unison, but it seemed enough for Bennett that she was in his bed to receive him when he needed her. There was something curiously detached, even mechanical about their unions for his needs were regular, abrupt and routine, so much so she found them a little . . . monotonous. Alone, she would giggle over it for she had never expected to find Bennett Muir monotonous, yet she had the impression that any woman in his arms would serve his purpose, that he expected certain responses from a wife, others from mistresses — if he still kept mistresses. Why, in the end, had she married him? She had asked herself the question frequently of late — was there an answer? None that she could define just as there was no explanation as to how she had survived the years after Brick's death, tossing, or lying taut in the bed imagining him coming from his dressing-room to laugh with her, indulge in argument, sort out problems relating to their 'various family', or simply to love each other. Abruptly and tragically he was gone by a combination of accidents, not only the bleeding from the terrible gash in his chest caused by a slip of foot, the axe catching and twisting, but a stroke . . .

There had been nothing the doctor could do when he came, Brick was dead when they carried him to the house; he had died in her arms, only his lips moving, and she would never know what he had been trying to say.

He left a great deal of money and property, herself as executor with Crutchley and Marr, a tribute to her good sense – Brick had always credited her with sense – to be held and managed on trust for his family of minors. Hawkes Plains and Jubila went to Dominic. Without being asked Will had left his farm in the hands of tenants and moved back to Hawkes Plains to run it until he came into his own inheritance, or Dominic was old enough to take over. There were substantial legacies for the girls, now invested, and for Phelim, Erins Pride, which Rob and Hetty Witherstone would run as long as they could. There were bequests for servants, for Fay, Gondola was to be cared for and Barney watched over. Joey Bowes at Oorin station had not been forgotten. Even Jamie, after all, had collected a quite presentable sum and had promptly set about squandering it, making little forays back to Hawkes Plains or BelleMonte to bully Will, tease Celine, mock Clodagh and, from long habit, attempt to borrow from his stepmother . . . She had tackled the awesome prospect of dealing with 'always Jamie', yet Bennett did better with him than Brick had ever done; in some odd way the two seemed to control and complement each other. She had been left BelleMonte in her own right, perhaps Brick had known she could not bear Hawkes Plains without him, and a great deal of money came with the house making her a wealthy, certainly an independent woman if she so chose. Her father and her aunt had begged her to come to Sydney even for a time but instead she had married Bennett Muir – perhaps because in the end she did not care?

Why had Bennett married her? For her money? She knew many people, including her own children, thought so, yet why should Bennett Muir, reputedly one of the richest men in the state, need her fortune? True, he was secretive, he had no small talk with her and was as reticent about his income and its sources as he was about his past which did not interest her in the slightest. He was just as secretive about his life now which was also hers. He gave no explanation of his frequent trips to Sydney and she wondered about his work there, his 'office' if it still existed, remembering Brick's reaction when she had mentioned it. He would alternate extravagance of jewellery, clothes and furnishings with a sparseness of daily living. Perhaps he needed money for women . . . She suspected he had been involved with Sophie Van Weldt, widow of the Dutch shipowner, but she sensed it was over, if it had ever been, for after Brick's death he would stay at Yoolanowi alone, riding to Hawkes Plains where she was attempting to resolve Celine's despair and hostility to offer his help and advice. Fighting her lethargy born of shock she began to stay for long periods at BelleMonte and need only voice a wish and he would be there to fulfil it. He was solicitous of her family's needs when she saw little rapport between them, yet even Celine's open dislike did not deter him. After a time she found herself depending on him, even agreeing with him on some issues, so much so she met with calm if not eagerness his proposal of marriage.

'I expected slightly more enthusiasm. After all, it can't really be a surprise.'

'A proposal of marriage from you *is* surprising.'

'Why not marriage, Alannah?'

'I've always thought you the kind of man who indulges himself with mistresses.'

'You don't know what kind of man I am. Not yet.'

'Any more than you know me as a woman.' She smiled. 'You've been rash; for all you will ever know I might have considered an "arrangement".'

'You don't consider me capable of permanency?'

'I can't say. I wish I could for I have a distaste for promiscuity. Annoying of me, I know.'

'At least it's a definite view. I like definitives.'

'You have been very kind since Brick's death but you gave me no indication you wanted to marry me.'

'Because I haven't attempted intimacy? Come, we're playing a game of evasion so let me put my cards on the table, something I do expertly when I wish. I've asked you to marry me for many reasons, not the least because you're a handsome and competent woman, born to be a wife — '

'I've never regarded myself as so.'

'Oh yes. Again, we both require comfort, security and privacy and Foxburgh House can furnish all that provided it has the right and proper chatelaine.'

'Isabel is not right and proper?'

'Isabel should give more time to her school.'

'Oh, I agree. But I think your sister prefers to manage Foxburgh House.' She could not help the barb. She had dismissed Mrs Plum from BelleMonte only to find the woman installed at Foxburgh; Plum was obviously as difficult to dispose of as Isabel Muir.

'It is my hope, Alannah, that you will try to understand Isabel as she does her best to understand you . . . The truth is, my business interests are growing and I should entertain even more than I do so a wife does seem to be necessary.' It sounded not only pompously self-satisfied but cold-blooded. 'I have always felt you were not entirely happy at Hawkes Plains and that you preferred living in town, therefore Foxburgh could be an extension, albeit a most important one, of the life you live here at BelleMonte.'

'There's one bit of country I love.'

'Ah . . . Burrendah. I would be willing to take you for regular visits. Another aspect of our marriage is that your family needs direction – a master.'

'My family would scarcely appreciate the term.'

'Well then . . . a father.'

She giggled, she could not help it. 'I can't imagine you in the role.'

'A ready-made family might be pleasant, certainly a badge of respectability.'

'Respectability concerns you greatly, I know.'

'It does not concern you?'

'Not particularly. I have never had much taste for the social round.'

'You've never tasted it with me.'

'I'm relieved you feel so about a "ready-made family" for I do not wish to bear more children – even if I could – and in fairness you should know my attitude.'

'Then we shall not produce children. I confess it eases my mind, for providing heirs is not my reason for matrimony.'

'Nor, by the sound of it, is love.'

163

'Love?' He smiled. 'Come now, a juvenile emotion, more suited to your daughters who, from all you tell me, nourish a wealth of romantic notions. But there is more than love, as you call it, between man and woman, there is passion.' He said it dispassionately, matter-of-factly, but it quivered between them. 'Important and necessary to a man. I have always been attracted to you, Alannah, you have dignity, poise, elegance, all qualities I would require in a wife. You are also . . .' his smile was thin, 'stubborn. Yet I do not find it daunting.'

'Disconcertingly stubborn, my father says. But isn't stubbornness, as men call it, nothing more disturbing than a woman knowing her mind? I have often thought men do not like women to exercise their intelligence – but then of late I do not feel sure of anything, I seem to drift . . .'

'As my wife you would not be permitted to drift. Come, you're too youthful and attractive not to marry again so why not Mrs Bennett Muir? You can have anything in the world you want – within reason of course.'

Which meant, she knew, what he considered she should have. She had disliked him greatly in the past but now he was different, or seemed so – could people change? He was generous and attentive yet could she sleep beside him, partake of his particular form of 'passion', a man she had not only disliked but distrusted? There was attraction, she had always been aware of him behind their formal verbal exchanges – but a third husband? She was no *femme fatale* yet men wanted to marry her, she seemed to fall into the married state; was he right in that she was born to the wifely role at the same time as rebelling against it? Besides, what could he give her that she had not? . . . Escape perhaps from Hawkes Plains and her life there that only Brick had made happy. She had never been able to explain the feeling, intensified since Brick's death, that it was an alien place to her – odd, when she had loved him so and her children had been born there and even while they strained for other climes it remained part of them, a refuge to return to. In the end she could find no valid reason to refuse Bennett Muir, there were gaps in her life to fill and it might as well be he who filled them. He had taken her hand in his, a commitment, but his grip had hurt. It had been hurting her ever since.

His soft tread along the hall and a whiff of expensive hair oil. His flowers were overpowering and she admired them dutifully, wondering where to pin them, but as usual he settled the matter without discussion. Quite unfairly she decided his gift jewellery would be vulgar, when he had never been so, but lately he had taken to seeking bargains, as the born trader he was. He looked elegant in his dress-clothes, a man 'born to please his tailor', as he put it, whereas Brick had worn such plumage as a duty, a camouflage, looking dashing and dramatic yet always the bushman – and she realised with horror that she was comparing husbands.

'Was it necessary to invite Will?'

'I invite him every year but this is the first time he's accepted. Perhaps Clodagh persuaded him.'

'More likely he jumped at the chance to feed his eyes on Celine. Whatever the reason he's out of place.'

'Will's never out of place. If he appears so then so must I. To all intents and purposes I'm his mother.'

'You're talking nonsense.'

'As you say, I often do. He'll stay only a few days, and at BelleMonte with the boys; he doesn't like to leave Hawkes Plains for long.' How glad she was she had kept BelleMonte for her sons on their free weekends as a discreet escape from their stepfather, with a room for Will when he needed it, even one for 'always Jamie', for oddly enough, Phelim could manage Jamie. 'There's no sense in you keeping the house on.' Bennett had been at his most persuasive. 'I'll invest the proceeds for you.' He had met her refusal with a stinging anger and they had argued desperately over it, but the house was hers and she had had her way. Now she was on the defensive over Will. 'After all, he doesn't have to go on managing Hawkes Plains, he's been financially independent for over three years. He stayed because Dominic wants it so.'

'Your precious Will's down there mooning over Celine. You're a mooning family.'

'All men are in love with Celine O'Shea,' she shrugged, smiling. 'She says so.'

'At least it will set Clodagh back on her heels. She makes a fool of herself over Will.'

'Women often make fools of themselves over men.'

'What is that supposed to mean?'

'Isn't it time we went down?' she evaded. 'You insist on punctuality and they do their best to please you.'

They were assembled in the drawing-room, all except Jamie and Celine, Celine deliberately late to annoy her step-father. Jamie might possibly ride up from his rooms at New Farm overlooking the river and close to his old haunts in the Valley, but he studiously avoided formal family gatherings. She hoped the dinner would go well for they had come solely for her sake: her two handsome sons, Dominic dark and Phelim fair, one serious and the other so outgoing yet both with their father's strong frame. They were being polite to Isabel, her face flushed from the attention as she fingered the little pile of letters and cards to be read out at table; there would be one from Eva Muir, there always was, bright sophisticated greetings quite different from her curiously intense letter on the occasion of Brick's death. Eva had lately returned to London from an American tour, extending her repertoire from Restoration to contemporary plays, and become the daringly innovative toast of New York. Clodagh, tall and growing out of her awkwardness (and her stammer) at twenty-three, was talking to Will and giving scant attention to the hovering Jimmy Marr.

'Please don't invite him, Mama. You know I will never marry him, just as he knows it. I've told him over and over I will not marry at all.'

'Mr Crutchley cannot come from Toowoomba to attend so Jimmy represents the firm in Brisbane. It's a courtesy invitation, that's all.'

'He won't be snubbed. He really believes that the more successful he becomes the more attractive it makes him to me.'

'Don't set out to be unkind, Clodagh. Such devotion is not so easy to inspire.' She did not add: 'As you well know.' She just wished she had the brutality to say it.

Celine literally dashed in, ignoring Bennett's frown and colliding with Dominic as they joined Will, the latter in borrowed dress-clothes, probably Domi's, talking crops and fertilisers and rainfall, land talk to which Dominic O'Shea listened with respect and little enthusiasm. He was far too dependent upon Will, but then everyone in varying degrees was dependent upon Will. One could not blame him for making the trip to be with Celine for, scorning white, she had settled upon a pinky-cream that unconsciously highlighted her hair coiled about her head in her casually exotic fashion – she hated her black hair. Yet she looked equally exotic in old riding breeches, shapely on her beautiful figure, dreaming over her little pile of letters bound with ribbon and tucked in her glove drawer amid gloves she never wore except under protest for she had beautiful hands with long fingers and loved to show them off. The carved silver medallion – charm, as she called it – that Strat McCrae had given her glimmered on its chain, her most prized possession together with his letters which came from all over the world, lately from Canada where his railway (it was always *his* railway with Celine) was creeping across the prairies. Writing to him and willing him to answer had become her life since writing her first letter to his bank in New Westminster, British Columbia, and since then Alannah had shared her agony:

'He does answer, Mama. Not often because he's moving around with his railway, but he *does* answer. He goes to England often, and Europe, I don't know exactly why, he doesn't say, to buy goods I suppose. I write three or four letters to the last address he gives me then there's this silence . . . This *awful* silence . . .' I know those silences, Celine, I live with them. 'I think about him in the snow and the cold, drinking too many whisky toddies and lonely enough to think of me and write, and after months – I count them – there's a letter, from Saskatchewan or Manitoba or Alberta.'

'He'll be different now, Celine. Older.'

'I'm older too. I'm eighteen.'

'Seventeen still. I believe you genuinely forget your age so you can jump ahead.'

'Perhaps. So that Strat will love me as I love him.'

'He remembers you as a ten-year-old child, that's all. His life has nothing to do with you.'

'He might write his wife is dead.'

'I won't listen to such talk. It's indecent. In any case he might have other women, have you thought of that?'

'I've thought of it, and I don't care. I won't let him forget me. I *won't*.'

Stratton McCrae was Celine's obsession – but wasn't all love precisely that? Alannah's gift brooch was presented with a flourish and in her eyes it was indeed vulgar; oh, valuable no doubt for it was studded with large Black Forest garnets but it was too big and flopped about, dragging at her dress. She hated it. 'Wear it on our next duty visit to the McCreadys, Mama.' Celine hated the McCready women. 'They'll envy you. They love flashy gems.'

Bennett's wineglass slurred on the table. She knew the brooch was an investment with him; everything he bought seemed an investment these days. The talk round the table was soft and disjointed and she knew they were waiting for her to lead the conversation. Quite suddenly their collective prejudices and foibles became unbearable. Brick had left her financial security but a wealth of personal and emotional problems, with Celine at the core of them. There was an added edge to her these past years, a girl on the defensive. She had run in one afternoon from Miss Muir's, flushed and angry, to confront her mother.

'What now?' Alannah sighed. 'I'm always expecting you to be expelled. Or at the very least, ordered discreetly to leave.'

'All I did was defend Ada.'

'I see. Well, I expect you to stand by your best friend. Was it serious?'

'Papa said to bring rumours into the light, to make them truth or dispense with them altogether.'

'He did.'

'Ada's so clever, Mama, where I'm not clever at anything really. She helps me push up my wretched marks. I don't care if she is illegitimate.'

'It's only a rumour about the Fremonts, Celine. And one rumour that should be left in darkness.'

'And the one that her father, her real father, is a gaol-bird and only her Grandmama's money keeps her at Miss Muir's?'

'The part about her grandmother is definitely true.'

'Miss Muir's ruby ring disappeared – you know how she flashes her rings, it's a wonder they haven't all been stolen long ago – and she more or less accused Ada of stealing it, right out in front of everyone, and there was the most awful row. Then it was found – I think she got scared the way we all stood up for Ada and decided to produce the ring herself. But later she said to me, again in front of everyone she was so furious, "I suppose I couldn't expect anything but collusion between a girl born out of wedlock" – that's how she put it, Mama – "and the daughter of a man who, no matter how rich and successful, is descended from Australian aborigines." Is it true, Mama?'

So it had come. Celine was fourteen and had a right to know her background. The matter concerned only Brick's issue and somehow it seemed fitting that she gather them in the big drawing-room of Hawkes Plains with its skin rugs and hand-crafted furniture and fittings, its grand piano and shelves of books, a room she had deliberately transformed to save the homestead from being rebuilt. Dominic would not care about his forebears, perhaps he would feel even more akin to the Africa that fascinated him, and it would mean nothing to Phelim, Phelim would go on being himself, but Celine? She did not *hate* the Blacks, she assured, and her mother believed her, it was just that she was happier away from them. She could never explain her aversion; perhaps she was daunted by their lethargy, perhaps the flavour of an alien culture, perhaps it was simply a physical distaste; whatever the reason it was there. And now she, Alannah, had no choice but to add to it.

'There is something important I must tell you. Your father should have done so perhaps, but we both thought you too young.'

'You're going to tell us Father's real name,' Phelim grinned. It was 'Father' now, no more childish 'Papas' for Phelim O'Shea. She laughed.

'No one knows your father's real name, I don't think he knew himself, though there was some rumour that it was Sean. No, it is something more important and significant, yet in the end unimportant.'

'That's cryptic. That's the right word, isn't it Domi? Cryptic.'

There was, after all, no other way to tell them but honestly and bluntly. 'Your father was a quadroon. A quarter-caste aborigine.'

They were silent, until Dominic said quietly, 'We know what quadroon means, Mama.'

'Then it should not worry you for colour dies out in the Australian aborigine. It was not apparent in your father and it is certainly nowhere in you. In the south people knew of it for your father never hid the fact. Many have known of it here. After all, it's happened to so many . . .'

'You mean . . .' Celine's voice shook, 'that we're like Barney Cook? And the others?'

'Of course not. Barney's a half-caste. Your father's grandmother, your great-grandmother, was a full-blood working on what became his station, Erins Pride. His mother married an Irishman who died before your father was born. It's all so long ago it should be let die.'

'Then why tell us at all?'

'Because sooner or later someone would reveal it – which is exactly what has happened. Besides, it would have been dishonest to leave you in ignorance, would it not?'

'I'm glad you told us.' Dominic was always sure of himself. 'I don't mind. Why should I?'

'It's not you, Mama, who has to live it out. It's not you that will pass it on and on –'

'There is nothing to pass on, Celine. It's gone, vanished. You loved your father, do you love him less now? He's bequeathed you so much – health, wealth, protection and love – and if you do not like his legacy complain to the trees, to the air, but not to me for I will not listen.'

After that Celine's letters to Strat lapsed for months but eventually the pattern resumed and her mother could only hope the girl had accepted her background; even so, she did wonder at times . . . Now she looked at them talking with animation, Celine and Phelim arguing happily as they often did, Clodagh's absorbed conversation with Will interrupted by the cocksure Jimmy, Bennett at one end of the long table and herself at the other in the family formality he insisted upon – even though he had no affection for her children, nor, she sometimes felt, for herself; quite simply he liked to control when and where he could. In return they tolerated him, no more, with Celine hating him, flaunting his orders or keeping zealously out of his way.

'The Boers did not invade: the Bantu crossed from the east and the Dutch from the Cape and they clashed somewhere in the middle. They should all have the same rights.'

'Please Dominic,' his mother put in, 'no politics. Not tonight.'

'I say hang the Boers and the Bantu and all the rest. Why not India instead? Now there's a place I could explore, riding elephants in style while you weep over your leprous beggars.' At Phelim's outburst, Clodagh set down her knife and fork in disgust and Bennett his wineglass.

'If you must cite misery while we're at table, Phelim, there are sores enough in Australia.'

'The Missionary Society needs doctors. I've made my commitment to Africa and you know it.' Some girl some day would love Dominic deeply, his mother thought, for a woman loves a man with a cause as long as the cause can embrace her. But whoever the woman, she will need to love him unreservedly for she will only be a small part of his life. Dominic addressed his brother but all at the table knew they were being chastised. Dominic was determined on a medical degree from Sydney University and once gained he would be off, Phelim trailing, for neither wanted to work the land. 'Will knows what's best for Hawkes Plains,' Domi would hedge. 'He's shaping it.' . . . 'Your father did that.' She was sharp . . . 'Of course. But Will's making improvements. I might even finish up handing it over to him altogether, who knows?'

'Africa!' Bennett snapped, taking up his glass again. 'You should be running your own acres. However . . . if you MUST pursue this crazy idea it might as well be with the Dissenters, they're innovators as well as survivors – they expose themselves to native arrows without qualms – and absorb one's mental energy even more than the physical. Extraordinary people. But enough of this!' He held up his hand for attention, his Buddhist gesture, so like Isabel's that Alannah saw a smile flit over Celine's face. 'Now that the toasts of the

171

evening are over I have something less formal but equally as important to say. Next year I am taking your mother to London.'

Alannah stared, the silence broken by Celine letting out her breath in a sigh. 'London!' Phelim hit the table with the flat of his hand, a favourite gesture. 'Just like that?'

'Not quite like that. There is much to arrange for an extended stay. We will leave late summer to arrive in the English spring.'

'You've never even hinted . . .' Alannah could only gasp.

'I must be there for the wool sales; everyone goes who can. Then to Paris for art and antique showings – but why the shocked expressions? Surely it's reasonable for a husband to take his wife abroad?' His thin smile swept the table. 'At least it's smartened you up, you're inclined to lounge at dinner tables. You'll have plenty of time to get used to the idea; finding suitable rooms in London for six months, perhaps a year, won't be easy.'

'I won't let Mama go without me.' Celine stared him out.

'You have no say in it, young lady. Your mama is my wife and knows her duty.'

'A year?' Alannah couldn't seem to do anything but gasp.

'Why not? Everything will be left in good hands.'

'I must go, Mama. I *must*!'

'Please Celine, not now. We'll discuss it later.'

'*Now.*' The girl's chair scraped as she stood to challenge her mother. 'I've wanted to go to London for so long, you know that. Domi will come too, he can get his degree there, and Phelim will follow, school or no school; anyway, Phelim knows so much already . . . I'm eighteen, Mama, and will do as I please.'

'You're seventeen and cannot do as you please until you're twenty-one. And even then . . .' Bennett shrugged, leaving it hanging in the air, like a threat.

'There's no law against choosing age any more than there is in choosing a name one likes.'

'There is plenty of time ahead to discuss details.' With a cool flick of his hand Bennett indicated his glass to be refilled. 'This dinner has been prepared with much thought and care so I insist we finish it without further argument. Sit down, Celine.'

She hesitated a moment then flopped into her chair to ignore her food and look straight ahead. Alannah could feel the rebellion around the table but finally, taking their cue from Dominic and Clodagh, always the reasonable ones, they were silent, the only sounds the tinkle of cutlery and the gentle swish-swish of the serving-maids.

'Celine's fixation on that fellow McCrae must stop. It's an embarrassment.' Bennett slid into bed beside his wife. 'You don't seem to care for the reputation of your family.'

'People do fall in love, even children. Celine has never faltered in her feelings for Strat so perhaps a meeting with him in London would resolve the matter one way or another. In any case I couldn't go without Clodagh; she won't want to leave Will but if she knows I need her she'll come.'

'Need her? You will have your husband.'

'London would be wonderful for them all.' She could not suppress a mischievous smile. 'When Jamie hears of it he'll want to come for the music-halls. And of course the gaming, but he gambles wherever he is.'

'Who goes or stays is your concern, not mine. It certainly won't be my expense.' He raised his hands in mock acceptance. 'Bring them all – why not? You can afford it.'

'It does rather depend on Mr Crutchley and Jimmy.'

'I've never known you to fail with that ill-assorted pair.'

He was feeling for her, distracting her, weary of talk of the O'Sheas, bored by them. His kisses were demanding but without warmth and when he turned over on to her in his imperative and heedless way she felt, as so often, part of an obscene act in which she remained alone and unsatisfied. More obscenely, she ached to slide from under him, to separate herself from this man who was not Brick, only some stranger in command of certain 'rights' to her body. The prospect of travelling alone with him in England and Europe without the familiar hedge of her family was already beginning to terrify – for all their hostility towards their stepfather they helped by their very presence to make the marriage endurable. Her

173

intense longing for Brick, even while in Bennett's arms, or perhaps because of his love-making, had become a sickness. When he turned from her to sleep she held the sheet against her mouth and her body rigid, so that he would not hear or even sense her soft crying.

Chapter Twelve

THE GOLDEN EMPORIUM was in a quiet area of Queen Street where Brisbane matrons could alight comfortably from carriage or cab and be greeted by Pierre – Monsieur, as they delighted in calling him – Luffet with his exaggerated Gallic airs and escorted through ornate doors to explore the lavish salons of valuable furniture, paintings and artefacts. Bennett Muir, having made a rare visit to take personal delivery of a unique eighteenth-century roll-top bureau, for which he had buyers competing, paused in the glare from his front windows before drawing blinds. It was summer but the dust of winter still drifted, dimming the pale silks and taffetas of shoppers to a dull brown while veils were drawn over mouths and nostrils and sunshades held at protective angles. Across Edward Street crowds had gathered at Hunter's Sales since Brisbane's unpaved roads created a huge demand for footwear. The only improvement was strips laid in front of certain shops and offices, as he had done before the Emporium, to protect customers from the mud of the summer 'wet' and the packed-up dirt of the winter 'dry'. Tram tracks would be laid next year over the scarred and neglected thoroughfares, roads incongruous against the imposing banks and insurance and newspaper offices that were the pride of the civic fathers.

He ran a finger along a sideboard to find it dust-free. The girl, Julia, did her work well, bullied no doubt by Pierre. He wandered the rooms glowing from polished wood and gilt-framed mirrors and glass-fronted cabinets, satisfied as to how his stock – his 'collection' as he preferred to call it – had built up mainly from deceased estates; he would make the initial inspection, ascertain (more bribery) likely bids at auction then send Pierre to clinch the deal, for trade, even in beautiful objects, was considered socially beneath eminent Downsmen. He had almost lost the emporium in his bitter

175

undignified scramble to raise the forty thousand dollars to pay off Malcolm Hume through his astute young blackmailer, McCrae: instead of a further mortgage on Foxburgh House he had sold a slice of Yoolanowi, had thrown in gems hoarded since his 'Frisco days, then gold dust and nuggets and his own diamond stick-pins, McCrae weighing and valuing and calculating – still not enough. He'd added Isabel's finest rings (to her protests and eternal hatred) but in the end it was his Melanesian Trading that had saved him, as it kept him going now despite vigilant government regulations and policing of the Pacific. After Burney's murder, of which he'd received only garbled and diverse accounts (Jamie Lorne O'Shea would know the truth but he, Bennett, left well alone there to preserve his anonymity) he'd found a substitute – there was always a substitute – in one Oliver Hickett, rid himself of the *Venture* and kept its successor confined to ports in the far north. But his smartest move was his marriage to Alannah O'Shea . . . He had walked away from O'Shea's dead body, escaping at last and forever the shadow of a man descended from Irish convicts and aborigines yet arrogant before a Scot from a Georgian square in Edinburgh – even if his own father had been a gaol-bird Bennett Muir's day had come! He had turned on his heel and walked up the slope to Hawkes Plains and finally into the arms of O'Shea's young widow, a triumph that, no matter the fluctuations of their marriage, he did not regret.

She would never of course forget O'Shea. He knew that each time he made love to her; often he was barely conscious of her sexual responses they were so light. But she was not expected to be a voluptuary; sexual excitement had not been his reason for marrying her, her function was to be a showpiece in his house, an ornament, a symbol of prestige like all his possessions. And she fulfilled her allotted role with dignity if not alacrity, her deeper emotions reserved for her proud and secure young who stung his marriage as mosquitoes might his skin on a cloying summer's night. Celine did not like him, nor he her, yet her beauty troubled him . . . it startled, though she cared nothing for fashion and let her hair hang freely, and seldom wore paint or powder or jewellery; she needed no decoration, she glowed, particularly now, excited by the

176

idea of London and the man, McCrae. Stratton McCrae nagged at him even though he had managed to avoid the firm of McCrae and Hume when last in London; he needed McCrae even less than he needed the O'Shea progeny for he had only one real need in life – money. Money to finance the political career that would otherwise continue to evade him, money to support his exclusive and expensive clubs, money to supplement his cellar and stables and his card-playing and race-meetings. As for women, that other sport, rather to his surprise after four years Alannah still held him. He could not touch the O'Shea fortunes, their trusts could not be broken, so Alannah remained his one real asset: she was his wife, vulnerable as all women faced with the intimacies and tensions of the marriage bed. He flattered himself he was a persuasive man. He was also, he firmly believed, irresistible where women were concerned.

He paused once more by the windows. Brisbane was squeezing itself in and out of Hunter's in puffs of dust. It was an exhilarating day. Europe was already possessing him, exciting him as later he would be stimulated by Europe's varied and sensual pleasures while his wife occupied herself with her offspring and sightseeing. He did not want the O'Shea family in London but they would come: Celine, always at war with him, Clodagh in her role of family companion (and deuced hard to marry off), the two confident and distinctive sons who with luck might lose themselves in Africa or, for all he cared, at sea – and the ubiquitous mocking Jamie, scrounger and hanger-on, always hovering on the outskirts hoping for handouts, still unaware of the connection between himself, Bennett, and the dead Burney – and he would keep it exactly so! BelleMonte would be closed for the duration, Isabel would run her school and, resentfully, a near-empty Foxburgh. Will would manage Hawkes Plains and Jubila while keeping an eye on Erins Pride, in place of their young absentee overlords. Yoolanowi – what was left of it – would function under Ran Cowper, and Luffet would continue to spread his false but lucrative charm over the Emporium – all of it, everything, supervised to the last penny by shrewd old Crutchley in Toowoomba and Jimmy Marr in Brisbane . . . Solicitors, overseers and managers became expensive necessities and money, or rather the lack of it, remained his continuing problem so even the sale of a roll-top bureau was important. His clients were due. He drew the curtains against harshness. The diffused, rosy, faintly distorted world of gilt and wood and mirrors soothed him as always and he smoothed his expertly tailored jacket and patted his tie. The half-lights of life had always been to his taste.

'I don't give a jot for your African Wars or the state of the natives in Bechuanaland or anywhere else.' Phelim's energetic gestures sent books flying. 'There are enough in Africa already trying to solve its problems. Too many, I'd say.'

'Missionaries are there to save souls, as they see it.'

'Don't you believe it! Those earnest gentlemen of the cloth embroil themselves in politics as soon as they land, and you'll do the same, you won't be able to avoid it, there's no clear demarcation line.'

'My concern is for the sick and helpless. I want to clean up the wells and the dams, the drains too, if they have drains.'

'And patch bodies till the next onslaught smashes them up again. Our Papa —'

'I prefer "Father".'

'Father then . . . said wars grow out of religion with a natural progression to politics. He also said war is murder that can't be solved, remember – or was it Mama who passed on his words? I was scarce out of swaddling-clothes, as it's so delicately put, when he died. Anyway, I see land as the root of war; if land is for the taking someone will fight over it. The native tribes despoil and erode it, the whites build it up and make it productive then the natives want it back. Damned if I know why we're getting involved in such a debacle.'

'You don't have to come to Africa.'

'No – except that it all sounds a bit of a lark. While you're agonising over misery I'll go canoeing up – or is it down? – the Zambesi. There are islands along the lip of the Victoria Falls, they actually overhang, a great place for picnics I'm told – if one can dodge the native spears.'

'Another Romantic notion to add to your climbing of

Kosciusko and paddling the Amazon – the Murray too for that matter – and taming the cannibals of South America.'

It was a long speech for Dominic, filling boxes with his precious books leaving little room for clothes, but clothes were as unimportant to him as they were to Clodagh. He had penned his goodbyes to schoolmates and was collecting letters of introduction and recommendation from Queensland clerics to influential pundits in Britain. As a last resort he would camp on the doorstep of the London Missionary Society ready to go in any capacity – teacher, apothecary, dispenser of pills and potions (white witch-doctor as Phelim called him) for he could gain his medical degree at any time. He was also an excellent shot and a splendid rider and knew the bush even if he had not yet experienced the African veld. His quiet confident enthusiasm was so infectious Phelim constantly reminded him that his plans – their plans – depended on their mother even more than on Crutchley and Marr, for they were under-age damn it! 'It's a wonder we don't hate her, controlling our purse-strings.' Phelim shifted about, as impatient as his brother but for different reasons.

'Hate Mother?' It was 'Mother' these days as if Dominic O'Shea had taken a giant leap beyond Hawkes Plains and his youth to face the world. Phelim never saw himself as serious or particularly astute or capable of sound judgment, when he pondered on himself and life at all which was seldom, but from association and habit he saw his brother more clearly than others did.

'I want to splurge on tropical gear and guns and safari equipment, not to mention Savile Row suits to cut a dash in London,' he grumbled. Watching his brother move effortlessly and surely about the room he added: 'Missionaries and doctors take wives with them when they go out, to avoid temptation, you know? But I suppose a wife is too much to expect of you at your age. You'll just have to struggle with temptation as best you can – not that I've noticed you wrestling with flesh and the Devil. Don't you ever notice girls?'

'Of course I notice them,' Domi laughed. 'How could I not with so many growing up at Glenaire?'

'And filling out.' Phelim drew a diagram in the air with his strong flexible fingers. 'An earthy lot, particularly that

179

Susan . . .' He looked reflective. 'I've kissed her you know, thoroughly too, but the last time she pushed me away – yet she didn't run, she didn't do anything, just stood there watching me as if waiting, expecting more, something else, something *specific*. Well, she didn't get more, not of anything; I got cold feet. I mean, I knew if I made another move she'd take a grip on me so to speak, pin me down, commit me to some sort of "honourable intention" and I'd be done for!' He looked glum. 'There are so many Dennings to marry off and we're the nearest and I suppose the most eligible, and it's scary for I mean to avoid wedlock as long as I can. To enjoy the world my own way.'

'Africa can be your escape route.'

'True. Yet sometimes I think we're both mad!' He flung an arm at the window. 'Look at it. It's yours as far as you can see. Doesn't it mean anything to you? Won't you miss it?'

His arms full of medical journals, Dominic stared past the vines shading the verandah where his parents had loved to stroll, past the trim lawns to the kitchen garden and the roofs of the dairy and barns and stables and shearing-shed until his eyes lost themselves in distance. 'Of course I'll miss it. It's where I was born and grew up and learnt to ride and shoot and muster and all the rest. But it will be here, waiting. Will knows how to run it better than I, he makes it thrive. He cares for the Blacks as I wish; those few left about here. He understands the Chinese too.'

'Not many Chinks left either.'

'You know I don't like them called Chinks. Don't do it.'

Phelim hated to be chastised, particularly by his brother, and assumed his sulky expression. 'Chinks or Chinese, they've learnt to look after themselves pretty well. Look . . . I'm called a selfish bastard to want adventure and pleasure and stuff, but you're the one ignoring our mining settlements and banana and pineapple plantations and sugar refineries, with nary a doctor to be found in their dusty bush towns.'

'You never go near Erins Pride – how do you defend that?'

'As you said, it will always be there,' Phelim mumbled. 'We're gentlemen squatters, brother, without the current wherewithal to enjoy our inherited status and if I can't

180

survive in style until my majority, well, I can sell the place.'

'I think there's something in Father's will that says you can't sell it. Erins Pride was the beginning for him, you know.'

'Trusts have been known to be broken.'

'Not ours. Watertight. Besides, there's Mother, and old Crutchley with his eagle's eye, and Jimmy hanging on Mother's every word in case she influences Clodagh against him.'

'Then we'll borrow from Clo. She'll refuse at first, you know what she's like – the cautious protective older sister – but in the end she'll dip in. Better than trying to put the hard word on Will.'

'Will's doing enough for us as it is.'

'Oh, I don't know . . . he likes the rural life, he's adding acres to his own property as if all he has to do is dig them up.' He frowned. 'Don't let that saintly name of yours turn you into a pompous ass. Sometimes I think you belong in the cloisters and should have taken the cloth.'

'I belong in the world mending shattered bodies, not praying for sins. But it wouldn't do you any harm to attend a service now and then.'

'Perhaps I shall in London; some fashionable and public display, a real show, you know? I might even go the whole hog and take Communion in the Abbey.'

'You can't. You were never confirmed.'

'Is that a fact? Poor Mother – since you prefer the title – can hardly be blamed for a certain amount of religious confusion: Grandmama Cassidy Moynan a religious fanatic; Mother dumped with the Dominican nuns in a divided Ireland; her father and brother Protestant; her first husband a pious Wesleyan; her second a roistering pagan – and Father was all of that even if we weren't around in his heyday. Now she's married to Bennett whose one god is money – and he'd sink his claws into ours if he could get a good grip. Good old Jimmy Marr, astute in all but courting Clodagh, though I still say beware of love-besotted lawyers.' He stood and stretched his powerful frame. 'I suppose it's useless expecting you to join tomorrow's shoot? It's our last here for a while.'

'You know my feelings on blood sports.'

Phelim heaved one of his dramatic sighs. 'You'll be glad of me in Africa, I shoot anything that moves. I'll be the one with the burden – a do-gooder brother with a Holy Cause.'

'You're twenty-three. Don't you care if you go through life an old maid?'

'And don't you care that you're eighteen and still making silly prosaic statements?' Clodagh, folding and patting her favourite blouses and skirts into boxes, stared at them thoughtfully. 'Actually, twenty-three feels exactly right. As to marriage, you know I would only wed someone I love.'

'Yet you won't understand about Strat and I.'

'Strat and me,' Clodagh corrected from long habit. 'There is no Strat and you, Celine. It's only in your mind.'

'It wouldn't be if I had your money and could go off and find him.'

'I won't advance you a penny in travelling expenses. By the time you come into your legacy you might have changed in your feelings.'

'Never!' She looked sly in the way Clodagh hated. 'People get divorced these days you know.'

'Rarely. And when it does happen it's expensive.'

'All the same, Strat might have got rid of his wife.'

'And taken another.'

'Never!' She was always awesomely sure of herself – and Strat. 'He's waiting for me. I've written him three letters telling him we'll be in London in May and I'll die if he's not there waiting. And I'll keep writing him times and dates, and the name of our ship when we know it; Mama doesn't even know it, yet I'm sure Bennett does and is teasing us. I hate Bennett's teasing. I hate him more every day, he's so secretive . . . I don't think he and Strat like each other much.'

'Men don't have to like each other to do business. It's like politics.'

'One thing I do know: when I meet Strat again I won't act the lady, I'll throw myself at him.'

'Mama won't let you behave so. Nor will I.'

'You throw yourself at Will.'

'That's a cruel thing to say. I would never embarrass Will. And don't talk about Stratton the way you do, what would Miss Muir say?'

'Pooh to Miss Muir. What would she know, she's never been in love. Anyway, she's no longer our schoolmistress, just Mama's sister-in-law.'

'She's given me introductions to people in London – galleries and art collections, that sort of thing.'

'I should hope so.' Celine permitted herself a rare burst of generosity towards her sister. 'You're clever, we all know that. I don't know much about art, I sometimes think I know very little about anything except how to love Strat, but even I know there's something . . . well . . . different about your paintings. Something distinctive. They seem to talk . . .'

'It's what I intend. I want them to say things that I find hard to express in words. I try to put down in paint all I know and feel about our trees and streams and hills, everything that's around me. I've had little tuition so I suppose I'm what is called a primitive, and perhaps I should stay that way – oh I know it all sounds silly, but it's how I *feel!*'

Such a display of emotion from Clodagh was unusual and Celine shifted uneasily. 'You talked to Strat when he was here.'

'Perhaps because he listened.'

'I hope he listens to me.'

'He might if you didn't talk nonsense.'

'He seemed to like my nonsense. He laughed a lot.' She moved impatiently about the room. 'Why are you packing those straight-laced old blouses and skirts? You can afford the latest London fashions.'

'I'm comfortable in these.'

'Odd, isn't it, I can't wait to get to London yet you don't want to leave the familiar things of home?'

'No, I don't. But Mama won't make the trip without me, she's afraid not only of what you might do but that the boys will refuse to listen to her and Bennett and stow away to Africa or somewhere.'

'Why should they listen to Bennett? I don't. I don't trust him, I never have, but Mama doesn't seem to care about anything much since Papa died. I mean, she gives in . . .'

oh she's strong but with her the man is always stronger. It's the kind of man she chooses.'

Clodagh stood poised with an armful of clothes as if reluctant to add them to the others. 'The only reason I ever want to leave the Downs is to visit Burrendah.'

'Mama should not have gone back that time, it made her restless. She's never really been happy here, you know.'

'She was happy with Papa.'

'Of course, but that's in the past. Now she has a new husband . . .' She added abruptly: 'Why do you think she married Bennett?'

'Perhaps she just likes men.' Clodagh resumed her folding and patting. 'She seems to like them better than she likes women.'

'She's always paying for things. I'm sure she's paying for this trip with her own money, perhaps even some of ours.'

'Bennett is supposed to be rich.'

'I know, but I sometimes wonder . . . So many rich men seem to over-invest and come awful croppers.'

'Have you been listening at keyholes again?'

'You should try it, it can be illuminating.' Celine nodded seriously. 'There's talk around the stations that Bennett Muir has lost a great deal of money, yet he still spends . . . What we need is a man in the family with a finger on the city's pulse; if only Dominic would hurry and grow up – but even when he does I doubt if he'll be much use, all he thinks about is Africa's coloureds, he says they're just coming out of their misery and need help.'

'He'll make a fine doctor.'

'I suppose so. He's so very sure of himself and what he wants. You're all so sure – Will, and Jamie in his peculiar way, while Phelim doesn't give a damn what the world thinks of him. Even you have always known what you wanted – Will, your painting, the independence to live exactly as you wish, while I . . .'

'You mean you're uncertain about Strat McCrae after all? That it's all just talk?'

'Of course not. But the fact is . . . I *act* assured, and hope I look it, yet I'm always a bit scared, ever since Papa wanted a boy and I turned out to be a girl.'

'Oh, *that!*' Clodagh laughed. 'All men want sons. It's the heritage thing.'

'And I'm still afraid of the Blacks. I don't know why, there's no reason to be . . . And now I'm one myself and scared Strat might hate me for it – and that's the truth!'

Clodagh turned to stare at her. 'And here we are thinking you'd accepted the fact. You must, you know, or you'll have no peace. And why should Strat McCrae criticise you for something you can't help, a worldly experienced widely-travelled man who, for all we know, has fathered half-caste papooses all over the Rockies? One thing I am sure of: whatever happens to you in Europe, Celine O'Shea, it will help you grow up, for if ever a girl needs to broaden her mind it's you.'

'You shouldn't live here alone, Will.'

'Alone? With a kitchen full of women and the men's quarters choked with station-hands?'

'You know what I mean – without a woman of your own, I can't understand why if you won't marry you don't just take one. Clara would fall into your arms – if she hasn't done so already.'

'Don't talk that way. It sounds brittle.'

'I am brittle, I'm told. Of course I don't mean just any woman.'

'I don't want just any woman.'

'You're twenty-four and the male urge is strong, quite terrible at times I believe. I know all about men.' Celine nodded sagely, the wisdom of the world in her voice. 'It wouldn't surprise me if Bennett went to others now and then.'

'Don't talk that way, I said.' He was angry. 'It's not only brittle, it's flippant.'

'Why so shocked?' She laughed. 'After all, they say Ran Cowper has sired every child born on Yoolanowi. You don't believe it?'

'Well . . .' He shrugged, then grinned. 'Maybe one or two.' He ran his hand along the new fence separating Hawkes Plains from Yoolanowi, a last ride out for Celine before she left with her brothers and sister for Brisbane then Europe. It was a hot summer's day and he watched her remove her wide-brimmed hat, shake her hair loose and wipe moisture from her forehead. 'You've never been to Narengee to see my new house. I think you'll like it. I'm improving the property all round, I can afford it now.' He stopped staring and joined her in leaning on the fence looking out to the hills. 'I wonder if you realise how beautiful you've grown,' he said softly and seriously. She laughed it off.

'I'm not beautiful. Not really. My nose is too retroussée, a European nose, not Australian at all. Someone once asked me if I were French – imagine? I suppose it was because of my black hair. I hate my hair.'

'It's beautiful hair.' He put up a hand to caress it but she moved aside.

'I never thought about being beautiful when I was small. All I wanted was to be the boy Papa hoped for when I was born, he made no secret of it, so I started to say outrageous things.'

'You still do.'

'I copied the men, and Cook when she lost her temper, so Papa would notice me even if he didn't approve. I miss him so.' Her voice caught.

'So do I.' He heard again, and clearly, O'Shea brushing aside questions, as always when he, Will, probed his parentage. 'I've told you of Dora, your mother. As to who fathered you, what does it matter, you're here, alive and hearty, with all this . . .' Scooping up a handful of soil he had let it dribble on to Will's palm. 'The earth cannot be manufactured or truly destroyed, just rearranged, so once you have it never let it go.' It had been a hot day such as this as they lopped trees and O'Shea had staggered slightly and for the first time Will had seen his ageing father, a tremendous man, falling away. 'I used to wish I were his natural son,' he went on, 'but not now. If I were I couldn't marry you.' She said nothing but he saw her hand clench on the wood and he ached to know what it meant. 'All the same, I wish I knew my true background to set before you.'

'There is no need to apologise for your parentage, Will.' Her voice was hard. 'After all, I come from a long line of Australian aborigines.'

'In blaming your father for that you're unfair.'

'I know. The boys don't seem to mind: Domi says it will bridge gaps where he's going, though I don't think the Boers will appreciate it, they despise the native tribes.' She slammed the top of the fence post with her palm. 'I *know* I'm illogical. I *know* I follow my feelings too much.'

'I wish you had feelings for me.'

She turned to him, contrite and passionate. 'Oh Will, *dear*, I have. You know we all love you.'

'Not in the old way – another way.' He was equally passionate in taking her hand and trying to draw her close. 'I can speak this way now, I have something to offer you.'

'I don't care a fig for your money, you know that.'

'Because you've always had money. You were born to it.' She dragged at her hand but he held it tightly. 'Will . . . listen, *please*. Remember the time I ran away and Strat found me?'

'I found you. McCrae carried you back to the house, that's all.'

'Even so . . .' He was drawing her closer and she could not break away. 'Even so . . .' she grew breathless, 'you must have known that I loved Strat.'

'How can you love the man? You were only a child and you haven't seen him since. That isn't love.' He held her firmly, pressing her against him, and their bodies seemed to melt into each other. She resented it. She resented this new and different Will so alien to the brother, playmate, antagonist, friend, of her childhood. He was kissing her, trying to hold her lips, and she became rigid with a kind of . . . distaste. Distaste for Will? It was wrong, even more obscene than their embrace, and she hated herself for feeling so. In her miserable confusion she threw back her head and pressed her hands hard against his chest.

'Don't do this, *don't*. It makes me feel . . . strange. As if it's a kind of . . . incest between us.'

'*Incest?*' His eyes widened, not in disgust but in anger, and his hands dropped from her. Instead, he slapped her face, a stinging blow, and she staggered with her hand to her cheek. 'How dare you say that.' His strong stocky body quivered. 'As if it's an aberration. We're man and woman, Celine, and

187

free to love each other. I've always loved you and always shall. You don't love Strat McCrae, you couldn't, and you'll get over whatever you think you feel for him. You must get over it.' Anger was so rare a thing in Will she found it frightening and held her hands over her ears in an attempt to blot out his words, swaying as if from their force. He dragged at her hands but she fought him. Breaking from his grasp she ran, stumbling, to her horse. She feared he would follow her but he did not, only his voice, loud and decisive, even threatening in the otherwise empty silence, pursued. 'I can wait. I've waited for most things in my life so I can wait for you. I'll be waiting for you to come back – do you hear me, Celine O'Shea? I'll be waiting!'

With desperate fumbling movements she turned her horse and galloped off leaving him standing, shouting her name to the winds as a man demented.

Isabel Muir, unduly restless, had wandered the deserted rooms and halls of Foxburgh House now empty of life except for herself and a skeleton staff. The house looked . . . sad, a word she rarely employed, a romantic emotional word, she would have explained to those of her girls advanced enough to understand definitions. It was three days since she had watched the steamer disappear down-river: from Sydney the family would sail on the luxurious *Orient* via Suez and would be in London under forty days. Now there was nothing to be done but bear somehow with servants grown lazy without Bennett to support her discipline and the further irritant of early winter winds, sharp from the south-west, which could blow for a week. Her skin scraped when she ran her fingers over the back of a hand; she hated the dry sound, as she hated the brown spots growing there and spreading. Nothing would rid her of them; she could not erase them no matter how much cream she smoothed in in daily massage. Age spots, they were called, and the phrase terrified for in her mind it signified decay. She had taken to wearing gloves about the house to the amusement, she was well aware, of the servants, particularly Plum who had become insolent now that the true mistress of Foxburgh was absent. Each evening, with her kitchen neat and smelling of carbolic, she would carry her crochet to the drawing-room where an early fire blazed and plump herself in a comfortable chair to indulge in a 'little chat' as she called it with the master's sister. But the 'chat' became a monologue about Nellie the chambermaid and her warts that nothing, simply nothing, would burn off . . . and Lizzy near violated by the wicked old gardener since disappeared – yet Lizzy was such a liar and the old man so slow one could not believe he could have caught the girl if she'd really wanted to escape. Then there was Kate, deposited in the convent laundry to bear the fruits of her shame amid clouds of steam and flapping sheets. Plum even dared to remark, with a sly glance over her pince-nez, that the young masters could not be blamed since the hussy was with child when she took service. As if she, Minny Plum, could not count!

That evening the winds about the house sounded loud, which they were not, and the pendulum of the ormolu clock overly persistent. Against the background of Plum's heavy drone Isabel's eyes returned again and again to the empty space above the mantel that had held Eva's painted likeness; for the day after the family had sailed she, Isabel, had ordered it to be removed to the storeroom, wondering what Bennett's wife – Alannah was always 'Bennett's wife' in her mind – thought of it over her head as she sipped her after-dinner coffee. But Alannah may not know . . . She plucked irritably at the fingers of her gloves – know what? After all, what was there to *know*? She rose abruptly, cutting off Plum's opinion of the Hardwick family farther along the Terrace, and announced that she was retiring for the night, delighting in Plum's resentful waddle through the door. She moved aimlessly from chair to chair, to the windows and back again, suffering her loneliness until the walls seemed to be closing in on her and there was no escape from them. She could not bear to look at her hands and drew on her gloves: clothes hid her ageing body but her hands were public and flamboyant, intact virginal hands never giving or receiving except in service to others, as uninvolved in love as her unused body; never now would they enfold, caress, touch, weave about the body of a man. She remained unwanted and unloved while Eva . . .

He had loved Eva – yet could she be quite certain? She

could only remember them dancing together looking into each other's eyes while she had stood surrounded by her young ladies, young faces that came and went in her life, always moving on and leaving her, disappearing to make way for others. For all her own rich gowns and coiffures and false curls and jewels it was Eva who possessed the beauty and fame and love – O'Shea's love at that. Why, after all, would it not be true, as much a fact as the marks of age on Isabel Muir's hands? She saw again his dark and brooding face, a little heavy as he grew older yet even more fascinating to her. She felt again his kiss on her hand; his teasing exaggerated caress that she must pretend amused her when it had meant everything. The touch of his lips clung even now.

A fury was growing in her, a consuming anger against her brother, her life, above all against Eva her sister, an anger that must somehow be appeased before it destroyed her entirely. With quick jerky strides she hurried to the dining-room and took the largest sharpest carver from the dresser drawer. The house was quiet. Even so she did not risk turning on lights and with only the soft glow from a candelabra to guide her, rustled along the hall to the small flight of steps leading down to the conservatory and the adjoining storerooms. She flung open the door of the smallest, seldom-used room. It smelt musty, which seemed to suit her mood. She swept the cover from Eva's beautiful tantalising gaze. Destruction could, happily, be blamed on some disgruntled servant-girl, or even on a mischief-making housekeeper. She would find a way. She began to slash, digging in the knife-point; it was hard work but she gained strength from hate. She cut, cut, cut into the canvas until distortion pleased her. She cut on, deeply and methodically, until recognition was gone and pieces of canvas hung obscenely; until the twisted mouth and face had entirely disappeared and nothing remained but havoc.

Chapter Thirteen

BY THE Autumn of 1883 the railway track from eastern Canada had passed the old Hudson's Bay Fort and cluster of squatters' tents that was Calgary on the plains and was pushing up the Bow River towards the Kicking Horse Pass, leaving in its wake scraps of line separated by haphazard and maddening gaps, the rails laid by Swedes, Hindus, Irish, French Canadians and any other body that could face hardship, with immigrants already plodding the trails and hugging the patches of rail; would-be settlers clinging to the line as if it were salvation itself despite no telephone or telegraph; and mail incongruously routed through 'Frisco, Victoria, Harrison and Yale then to the east and back again, when its original destination was only a few hundred miles distant. At the same time, the two hundred and fifteen miles from Savona's Ferry on Kamloops Lake through the Fraser Canyon to Port Moody on the Pacific Tidewater was a mess of steamboats unloading steel rail, of bridge skeletons and tow roads and tunnels, tunnels, tunnels; the forbidding cliffs of the Fraser swarming with 'Onderdonk's Lambs', as the hated and unwanted Chinese were called, but without whose cheap and plodding labour the railway could not be completed. In bizarre contrast to this sleazy madness there were steamboats fitted with electric light, spring beds and velvet drapes for those who could afford luxuries – and with corruption a way of life there were many waxing fat on the building of the Canadian Pacific.

Now, three years after its first trembling to the might of nitroglycerine, a regular burning down of its wooden shacks to be replaced by higgledy-piggledy restorations, daily riots and a railway building on the cheap, Yale's one street of brothels, saloons and workshops, with a couple of hotels doing their best to appear respectable, wore not only an exhausted look but an abandoned one: amenities were being moved up to Savona where, it was hoped, the lines from East and West would meet. Or thereabouts . . . Meanwhile, Yale was expiring, indeed parts of it, like gangrenous and useless limbs, were already dead and buried.

Strat McCrae had spent the summer up and down the makeshift towns and camps of the Fraser using the steamboats between Soda Creek, Quesnel and Prince George, what rail was in operation, the coaches, his own supply teams, and finally, canoes and rafts if nothing else offered to cover the remote rough-and-tumble of the great rivers. But not once had he returned to Barkerville despite the fact that these days the place was considered quite civilised; he sent his men, for Barkerville belonged to his gruelling past. He had long ago branched out from basic victualling to fulfil eclectic and difficult contracts, each one a challenge: rice the staple of the Chinese coolies, nitroglycerine, illicit whisky (Canada was dry along the line of the railway and if he did not supply some imitation of spirits others would), livestock, particularly horses, and the hunting out of rolling stock. Yale's one carshop could not produce enough so he had found second-hand stuff in Nevada and since 1881 had been bringing it in by steamer. Landing the machines was a tricky procedure needing a gang and three yoke of oxen and block and tackle to move the engine from the river-bank up to the tracks. He could not leave the job to his men but with luck he'd be out of Yale in a matter of days and on his way to Burrard. This year he'd left their European operations to Morgan Hume, covering up for Morgan's indiscretions, and with a keen vetting of the books not for Morgan's sake but for his own since Morgan's father, for all his moods and tempers, was still his prime contact. Law and order in the mountains was erratic and desultory, functioning mainly in the summer months, so most of the time he, Strat McCrae, did things his own way. His own way, with Malcolm Hume behind him, had netted him another fortune, not simply as contractor and supplier but from investments during the feverish Winnipeg land boom. And further, when the railway reached the Pacific coast Burrard Inlet would be wide open for plunder . . .

Tonight he had bathed and wrapped himself in a gown before dressing for the best dinner the dining-room below could provide, with cards later perhaps. In Yale contacts, friends and enemies came together over faro and poker, chuck-a-luck and dice, those with sense staying clear of the con man's three-card monte, wary in this beaten-up rotting town redolent of drills and blasting powder, salmon and sawdust, tobacco smoke and black powder, with nought to do but get drunk or wench where one could, rolling from the saloons to a shut-down Sunday, meandering to church or joining the trek to the illicit whisky sheds. He poured himself a drink; no Chain Lightning or Injin Killer, a fearsome mixture of water, bluestone, oil of smoke, a dash of good liquor, spiced and coloured with black tea. He drank, when he could, the quality stuff, the best imported. As he took his first gulp there was a knock on the door. Irritated at the intrusion he wrenched it open. His wife, Eunice, stood there.

He could do nothing for the moment but stare. It was three years since he had seen her and then formally in his lawyer's office in New Westminster to finalise the purchase in Hope of a house where she could run her own school. Twice a year he sent her an allowance but the house had been something of a buy-off; in return for her financial independence she would leave him alone, free to live his life as he wished; she would not bother, harass, or come near him – yet now she was at his door. As he stood, frozen as it were, her dark eyes devouring him and attempting to hold his, lumber men on their way downstairs squeezed by, grinning.

'Are you going to leave me standing in the hall to be stared at?' she flared. 'I'm your wife, Stratton.'

Her age-old cry. Her constant reminder. A shop-keeping pair he recognised came from their room, no doubt changing their minds about him for they had been pushing their daughter at him for years though he made no secret of his marriage. It was odd how so-called respectable folk judged a man with a wife as more acceptable than one with a whore, for who could tell, married men could suddenly become widowers and so, eligible. He cared nothing for the judgement of shopkeepers but a need for privacy in this wretched ghost town made him draw her in roughly and slam the door.

'You had no right to hunt me out.'

'I have every right.'

'No. You made a bargain with me.'

'An unfair one.'

'How did you know I was in Yale?'

'I heard.'

'You're always spying on me.'

'Don't . . . please, Stratton.' Her eyes looked too big in her face. Damp pools. She plucked restlessly at her collar. 'I'm not well.'

'The doctors can find nothing wrong with you. I took you to one myself.'

'I keep having spells . . . This awful weakness.'

'You make yourself unhappy. You want things you can't have.'

'I want you, I make no secret of that.'

'You can't have me – how many years must I go on saying it? We're separated. And if divorce were possible it would be so, I make no secret of *that*.'

'Don't say it. Not divorce.' She looked pale and ill which only fed his anger against her, against the whole awful lingering situation. Because of youthful sexual needs and a greedy dominating father he was tied to this woman, perhaps for ever for maybe divorce would never be possible; she was the devoted and loving wife, he the deserter. 'Divorce would be a sin against God,' she reminded him primly for she was, as always, pious. 'Besides, I've never given you grounds for it.' Always shrewd and tenacious. 'Why can't we live together again? Why not, Stratton?'

'I offered you the only home I could but you refused. I know it was a miserable place but all settlements are; this is a country in flux and we'll be dead before it settles to some kind of permanency. It's a backwoods country and if you want otherwise go back to where you came from. I won't be part of your life again, I've made my own.'

'With other women.' She was sharp and bitter. 'I hear.'

'There's little to hear.' Resenting her he swung about. 'What else do you want of me? I bought you a house and school. Do you want a carriage? I'll get you a carriage.'

'I want a husband – you.'

'Take another man.' He was equally sharp and bitter. 'I don't put restrictions on you.'

'I don't want any other man. How can you not care what I do? Don't you care about me at all?'

'No. Will you never understand? *No*.'

'I've never wanted any other since I first saw you as a youth.'

'I am not that youth any longer – *boy* as you called me. I never loved you. I married you because I needed a woman, a mountain boy buried in a goldfields town watching others take what women there were yet not wanting it that way for myself; I wanted my own woman, a commitment – at least I think that's the way it was, I can't really explain because I didn't understand myself then, not at seventeen. All I know is that you served a purpose at the time, you were suitable, but no more. Now it's over. *Over*.'

'It will never be over for me.' With desperate little gestures she tried to touch him, hold him. 'I'll do anything to make you love me, even to have you pretend you love me. Anything.'

He held her off. 'Don't do this Eunice. You've made me hate you enough.'

'Hate me then, hate me, but at least notice that I'm alive and breathing. Feel for me, something, anything . . . Oh Stratton, this separation is unbearable, sometimes I feel I'm dying, and I don't want to die. I want to live for you and with you.' She was dragging at her clothes, clawing at them as if they were choking her and with distaste he saw her demure schoolmistress's gown fall around her feet revealing the full curves of her breasts above her tight bodice. She was as he remembered her, full-bodied and full-fleshed, a physically desirable woman in her forties, forty-five he thought, for she must have been close on twenty years older than he when they had married. It was seven years since he had been alone with her like this for he had always made certain they met in company, now she was invading his room, breaking down barriers, halting his life once again. Half-clothed before him she was supplicating and yielding, sexually inviting. Too conscious of her and furious because of it he scooped up her clothes and dumped them in her arms.

195

'Damn you! Dress yourself and get out. Have you no pride?'

'None where you're concerned.' She threw the clothes aside. 'I love and need you, that's all I know.' Undressing, she came to him to brush her naked breasts against his chest in a way that once he had adored but as she felt for him a nausea made him push her away.

'For God's sake, Eunice, stop it. Get out.'

'I won't leave you. I can't. I belong here. Don't make me leave you.' She clung to him, whimpering, begging, running her hands over him, and anger at her invasion spilled over and with a savage blow he sent her spinning against the door. She crumpled to the floor, breathing heavily, her eyes closed and a bloody gash down the corner of her mouth. God, had he killed her? He had never hit her before and did not want to have to do it now. A spark of compassion, or was it fear for himself, made him drag her to her feet and support her, limp in his arms. He lifted her easily and placed her on the bed, dampened a cloth and washed the blood from her face. Her eyes opened to his. Moaning, she held him close.

'You can't find me unattractive. I'm the same woman loving and wanting you.' For all her supposed weakness she was surprisingly strong, drawing him down to her, whispering and cajoling, her hair enveloping him until he could scarcely breathe, and it was as it had been when he was a boy, lost in his first taste of a woman. 'I want you now just as I always wanted you. You can't forget those first days at Mary Brady's when we locked the door on the world and loved each other. You loved me then, I know you did. You *did*. Don't draw away, stay with me.' He felt he was smothering and in a kind of terror strained against her, clinging consciously to the sounds of the raucous dump of a town beyond the stained and dirty windows where other men and women were making what they called love, drawn together by need as he and Eunice were. 'No matter what you say I'm your wife. I want to be your wife, just as it was at first. Don't draw away from me, I can't bear it. Come to me. Come . . .' She was whispering, urgency in her voice and body and he could no longer halt the growing sexual excitement in himself. It was too long since he had made love to a woman, he thought bitterly, hating her yet lost in her with a quickening he could not control. He could no longer resist or rest and they began to move in unison, breathing as one while she urged him on in her triumph of repossession, bent on satisfying herself, and him so that he was no longer master of himself. 'We're happy again, oh yes, yes . . . *yes*. Everything's all right, see?'

But it was not all right. It could never be. Impossible, he thought hazily, that this was love for he hated her even now. With a gasp of despair more than satisfaction he turned away from her to bury his head in the pillow, staring into the dim void of the room with its worn boards and shabby strips of carpet and scattered clothes. He had wanted to kill her while she throbbed beneath him murmuring and slobbering her joy; despite the quivering and overflowing and physical relief of the ritual sexual act that could, after all, be slaked by any woman, he hated her for seeing their couplings, this one in particular, as unique and precious. It had been nothing. This was not how he would live his life, this spasmodic bedding with a woman who possessed him legally but no more. Hating her he hated himself. Worse, he retrogressed, for his marriage created squalid situations such as this where she could and did invade his life. This must not occur again. Somehow he must achieve a precise and final cut-off for no woman should want a man who did not want her, who used her as he just had because she was eager and available. If she would not leave him alone there was only one thing for him to do: create a barrier of distance that she could not cross. Somehow he must achieve sexual escape from this neurotic, ageing, unhappy woman whom he had not freely chosen but who had been there at his time of great need. She was turning over to him, wanting him again, but he brushed her aside and dragged on his clothes.

'Get dressed.' He flung her clothes at her. 'I don't blame you for what just happened, I was part of it, but it will never happen again. I swear if you come near me again, Eunice, I'll kill you. I mean it. Get dressed I said.'

She made no move so, struggling with her, he dressed her forcibly. She fought him but he won, at least until she looked decent enough to leave the hotel. 'Get out and stay out.' He threw her from the room, locked the door and stood firm against her pounding, her pleading and imploring, then her threats, not caring if the hotel, the whole town, heard her. He was silent, waiting for her to tire. Finally, she went away.

His house was on the Kitsilano shore, an area becoming popular with successful British Columbians in proclaiming their new riches. It was one of a number of substantial homes and gardens distinct from, yet adjacent to, Gastown – Granville as it was officially called – a settlement in a state of flux since there was no decision yet on the railway terminus, only that it would be on Burrard Inlet. Track rested at Port Moody at the Inlet's end but the General Manager, William Van Horne, on his exploration of Burrard Inlet during his visit in August, was rumoured to favour Coal Harbour as the end of the line, with a town to be named Vancouver, and knowing what he did of the man Strat McCrae had no doubt that Van Horne would have his way – Vancouver it would be. Although investors waited nervously he himself had no hesitation in speculating in Gastown, here at Kitsilano, and across the Inlet at Moodyville where scattered roofs were appearing amid the pines, and smoke curled from sprawling timber mills.

His house was a large one with a long balcony off the main bedrooms giving extensive views of shipping approaching the First Narrows and the long line of mountains on the opposite shore where vast pine forests dripped streams down to the Inlet. The hot summer had slid gently into fall and with the distinct seasons of the Northern Hemisphere fogs had obscured the town, ships sliding towards him like wraiths, appearing and disappearing with warning lights glowing. Now fog was giving way to drifting cloud and dripping rain, and the first snows were reported on the Cariboo. Winter threatened. Chin, his Chinaboy, originally a coolie from the Kwang Tung province, who had worked on the railway for a dollar a day, had jumped at the chance of working for him and, honest as all the Chinese, managed his house and staff in his absence.

Now he brought him a bourbon and his mail. Such a day of dripping rain seemed a good occasion for both.

He picked out an envelope of a delicate pink covered with the scrawl of the Australian child, Celine O'Shea. Child? He laughed at himself for still thinking of her so, even though a faint scent drifted from the envelope, as always, and he visualised her brewing rose-leaves and sprinkling her envelopes with the brew for her letters were always slightly crinkled; at least if they did not immediately catch his eyes they did his nose. Feeling rather foolish he opened a desk drawer and took out a bound pile of her letters – at least he hadn't tied them with ribbon! Why had he bothered to answer such letters written by this lovesick child who was a child no longer, eighteen – nineteen perhaps – a woman, as she kept reminding him? He felt a stir of the genitals at the vision of her black hair and clear skin and the graceful careless movements of her shapely limbs even at the age of ten – was it actually eight years since they had first met, or rather, since she had bombarded him with her stimulating presence and questions? If he were any judge of women she had grown into an eager, vivid, spoilt – yes, even though the indulgent father was dead – beautiful girl for how could she fail to be so? She was most certainly a brash one; Australians were known by the trait.

A restlessness set him pacing the long room opening on to the verandah with its wide and splendid views of the Inlet and the far shore. The clouds were lifting, shredding across the high pine forests that would soon be snow-capped. Her letters had always found him sooner or later and the fresh eager sense of youth they brought had brightened many lonely moments round camp-fires on freezing nights with the wolves howling. Youth! He needed youth in a woman. Yet what was she really like now, growing up in the years since she had walked or rather bounced beside him on his strolls about Hawkes Plains, keeping his attention by her chatter, her sheer physical vitality? There had been something . . . seductive about her, if one could call a child seductive, something unforgettable and irresistible, something inviting . . . Amused, even a little disturbed at his thoughts, he opened her letter, surprised at his eagerness, to read at random:

'If you're not in London to meet me I shall die . . . I've been waiting for this all my life . . .' London? In earlier letters she had hinted at England but he had put it down to the dreams of a schoolgirl. 'We arrive in London in May, that's all I'm certain of as yet . . . Mama won't go without Meg – you remember Meg, her maid?' He frowned – ah yes, Meg the treasured servant. 'Nor will Mama leave Clodagh, they're so close; of course Clodagh doesn't really want to go but will do so for Mama's sake – and to keep me in line, as she puts it. She can try.' A mind picture of Clodagh, intent yet serene, a frightening combination, then an even sharper one of her mother: Alannah O'Shea, now Muir, with her fair dignity and air of remoteness, or was it abstraction? Yet his most vivid memory of her was as the heartbroken woman at her husband's death. Somewhere in her earlier letters Celine had detailed her mother's remarriage to Bennett Muir, a con of a man whom he, Strat McCrae, had successfully blackmailed out of forty thousand dollars in cash and kind to earn his chance of a fruitful career. He and Muir had met occasionally and reluctantly to do business in antiques, a matter of expediency and profit to both, but Bennett Muir a family man? The idea was ludicrous. His sharpest memory of Bennett Muir would always be of the man walking up the slope to Hawkes Plains' homestead on the day of the fatal wood-chop, away from Brick O'Shea who lay dying under the trees. He had not run as others had run to help; as he, Strat McCrae, had run – no, he had turned and walked away. Did his wife know what he was really like? Speaking casually of the O'Shea family to Malcolm Hume, Strat had mentioned the marriage. Malcolm, always the cynic, had ceased picking his teeth to stare then laugh his unpleasant laugh: 'Weel naa! Ye canna expect live and let live from that bastard. A rich widow did ye say? Muir will fall on his feet mon, ye'll see, ye'll see.' Strat went back to his letter.

'. . . Jamie threatens to scrape the fare together and join us by a later ship. Mama hates the idea for he's bound to cause trouble, as he always does sooner or later; a real *beau reste* as Mama calls him. We're talking French to each other these days though there's no mention of going to Paris, it's all terribly vague since Bennett is making the arrangements. Anyway my French is so bad nobody knows what I say so

200

don't expect me to talk French to you. Eva Muir, the actress, is Bennett's sister and is "taking us on" as Phelim puts it. But no Court Presentations. Clodagh absolutely refuses to be "displayed at the marriage mart" as *she* puts it, while Domi says the whole thing is a pretentious and wasteful exercise when people are starving; Domi just wants to improve the world, starting with Africa – though how abstaining from being presented at Court will fill the world's empty bellies I don't know. Phelim says he wouldn't take on the peerage, they're debt-ridden for a start, and if he ever does take a wife she'll be the indulged offspring of a filthy-rich brewer, the money's certain-sure. For myself, you know I'll never marry anyone but you so you must come to London and rescue me. Bennett won't say what ship we'll sail on but knowing Bennett he'll go on teasing us while it suits him. We're all going, you see – what an entourage! – all except Will; we just can't imagine Will anywhere but looking after the properties. As soon as I have more details I'll write . . .'

Her frank phraseology, her childish eagerness, touched him. Was this child-woman who insisted she loved him to be his escape, his solace and his stimulation? Too often when people met after many years the magic was lost. Perhaps she'd be disappointed in him. He did an uncharacteristic thing: he paused before the long wall-mirror to appraise himself. He seldom considered his appearance in relation to others for he cherished no competitiveness or vanity, he was as he'd always been, a man who from long experience understood his body and what it could do. He had been a physical being since the age of five when he had survived the mountains, even more importantly, his father. Now he was surprised to be studying himself so. He saw a large man, unusually so in a country of strong and hardy men. His thick blond hair, perpetually seared by the sun, had a bleached look. His skin was burnt brown yet was still smooth and clear. He was twenty-eight and, he supposed, physically at his peak. He ate in spurts of sparse and plenty, a habit of his mountain life, for one ate and drank what one could get or could afford, and he could still go long spells without food and drink and he expected the same of his men. He ate well at good hotels when they came his way, like a soldier sleeping when and where he could.

It was the same with women. They turned to him but he had taken one rarely through the years . . . In San Francisco where he had settled for a while to fulfil a contract for four hundred mares and stallions he had enjoyed – and alternately despaired of – an intense affair with the wife of a rancher, one Amy Mendarez, an exotic creature of Spanish descent marooned in a sea of sand and cacti. He was, she had assured him, her gift from God for she was a passionate mystic devoted to daily Masses and confessions until they, and their bedding, became inextricably mixed; he felt certain she attended Mass before each coupling and said prayers for his soul afterwards. The fervour of her responses along with some odd and disconcerting sexual aberrations became entangling and uncomfortable, for in too many ways she reminded him of Eunice his wife. Still he lingered for she made no real demands upon him, clinging to the security and, in her eyes, sanctity of her marriage, whereas single women expected to be wed, which duty he could not fulfil. Next there was Kitty, wife, or perhaps mistress, it never seemed quite clear even to Kitty, to a horse-breeder. She was an easier bedfellow, pretty, grateful, ordinary, and comfortingly stupid. Otherwise he lived for himself, obsessed with escape from a wife he did not want, with his work and above all, his future.

Now what precisely was his future? Was his life to be entwined with a young girl still, he assumed, a virgin despite her outrageous talk? He could, to use a cliché, find himself in deep water for Celine O'Shea was no demimondaine, no servant girl, no bored wife or widow; Celine was the daughter of a large, privileged and protective family, with a suspicious mother, a duenna of a sister, and a stepfather as feudal-minded, he had no doubt, as her brothers. Furthermore, virgins were for husbands, it was an unwritten rule, and he could not be her husband only her lover – how would her world accept that? Not easily, he feared. So there was only one way . . . They must contrive as others contrived. They must run away.

He caught his breath. Italy. He had sailed from Marseilles to Naples, then on to Rome, working on commissions with unlimited funds from *nouveaux riches* politicians and industrialists, men trying to outdo each other in opulence. But it was

Florence that had held him with its antiquity and atmosphere, not the least his small pensione in the Piazza D'Annunziata where his room had looked out on a little courtyard and a magnolia tree in bloom . . . His hand shook as he put down the letter. The girl was exciting him even at a distance yet he could be anticipating something that might not come about; the schoolgirl virgin could have grown past and beyond him even in the months since she had written this letter. He had to know. One way or the other he *must* know. He had made no more than brief frenetic trips to England, alternating with Morgan, now he must do things differently. Besides, a lengthy stay in London would put a world between himself and Eunice.

He shouted for Chin and another bourbon. 'I go to London in the spring,' he told his man, drinking quickly as he paced the floor. 'The house – and the railway – must manage without me for a while. I plan a long stay.'

Chapter Fourteen

'THE CITY's too small, too crowded. Half its population should emigrate. We need cane-cutters back home. Develop their muscles.'

'London's a great metropolis,' Dominic reproved. 'Must you talk like some brash ignorant colonial?'

'I suppose that's what I am – a brash ignorant colonial.'

In his cheerful heedless way Phelim had startled the porters at the Albemarle on the morning of their arrival and had been shocking its occupants ever since. Their rooms faced down a St James's Street alive with hansoms and the comings and goings of the fashionable world of the *fin de siècle*. The hotel was patronised by the diplomatic corps, the army and navy, the nobility, and even royalty, Bennett assured them smugly; a fact which impressed Alannah and Clodagh not at all but sent Celine peeping round doors and creeping along passages, returning with tales of this young officer or that emerging from this or that bedroom, until Clodagh put a stop to what she called 'keyhole peeping'. Alannah knew Bennett would prefer the all-male existence of Long's or Stephen's, more like sporting clubs than hotels, but he was already planning a trip to Paris which did not seem to include her, for which she felt relief, swamped as she was by invitations and drawn into Eva Muir's busy preparations for a revival of *As You Like It* at the Lyceum. Though much revered in intellectual circles Eva had influential friends from all strata, including the popular, and 'racy' (as Phelim called her) Lady Constance Matthews – or had Bennett furnished the connection? Alannah wondered . . . In those first weeks he was out late and often but she decided to leave well alone for, quite simply, she did not wish to know his movements.

The London 'season' was in full swing. Days were fine and bright after misty windless mornings and even the occasional dull spell was warm with the sun bursting through clouds, golden late afternoons fading to long and lovely twilights. At least the pile of invitation cards to garden parties, dinners and teas took Celine's mind, if temporarily, off Strat McCrae and the fact that her mother – and not she – had received his letter: he would be in London at the end of May staying at the Langham in Portland Place. 'Who'd have expected such swank from a Canadian backwoodsman?' Phelim boomed; he had taken to shouting from room to room when his exuberance spilled over. 'The Langham has ascending rooms – lifts if you like.' He spent much time frowning over the set of his collar and the sheen of his riding boots, alarming his mother with his mounting tailors' bills; she was as swamped by accounts as she was by invitations, one seemed to grow out of the other.

'It's not fair, Strat writing to you instead of to me,' Celine persisted, beside herself.

'He wrote before we left Australia asking the name of our London hotel. As soon as I knew I answered him.'

'You never even mentioned his letter!'

'It was private correspondence, Celine. We are here in England as a family and the man is showing good manners.'

'He's coming to London to see me. *Me*.'

'On business too, I'm sure. He keeps a branch of his firm here.' She smoothed the letter under her daughter's envious gaze. 'He hopes we will all honour him at an initial dinner . . .' The cold formality of it brought indignant tears to Celine's eyes for she cried easily, at least where Strat was concerned; how dare he ignore her after so many years of writing and waiting and longing.

'I don't want my first meeting with him to be with family. Domi will argue over the war in the Sudan and Phelim boast about his new riding gear while I just sit there, dying.'

'You're always dying over something,' Clodagh snapped.

'This is London,' Alannah was firm. 'It is how things are done.'

'Well . . . I refuse to wear white. And stupid rosebuds in my hair.'

'You're a young unmarried girl. You can't flout convention so.'

'Why not? You always have. Why are you so proper all

of a sudden? I will not keep proclaiming my virginity all over London; it's embarrassing enough to still exist in that state.'

'*Celine!*'

'Well, it is. Ranked with all those simpering chattering nubiles — '

'Where *do* you pick up such expressions?'

' — *If* they are still intact. I sometimes wonder.'

'You frighten me when you talk so, you seem to set out to embarrass. If you don't stop this ribald talk I'll ship you home without you meeting Stratton at all. I can, you know.'

'I'll run away first.'

'Then run. You won't remain "intact" as you put it for long out there in London and it will be in a way you won't relish.' Relieved yet exhausted by her candour she took a deep breath. 'And expect Dominic to run after you, he wouldn't let you play the fool, he has a keen sense of the fitness of things.'

'If by that you mean he's prudish, he certainly is. And smug.'

'Come now . . .' There seemed nothing left but reason. 'Is this how you want Stratton to see you? As a sullen sulky girl from the Australian bush?'

'One thing I do know: if he wants me to go away with him I shall.'

'No girl should chase a man so, particularly a married man, must I remind you of that?'

'And may I remind you that his is not a real marriage? He hasn't seen her in years.'

'He may tell you that but married people come together. They must. And even if he has left his wife it could be for another woman.'

In the midst of arguments over maidenly muslin and roses in coiffures Bennett announced he had leased a house in Chelsea, a Bohemian area certainly with public-houses and little shops in side-streets, but close to his sister's small but luxurious home. The owners of Number Five, Elysian Place, were in Rome for a year but the house was fully staffed with a mews behind with stables and horses and a carriage, an ideal arrangement and location for Eva to launch them on London Society. 'I believe there are still some large estates left in Chelsea. Market gardens too.' The idea of a house was tempting to Alannah, bored as she was by the confinement of hotels, while Celine's eyes glowed. 'Meg tells me there's a fine drapery on the King's Road.' The house turned out to be a substantial one of bright red brick and terracotta, many-gabled in the style of Pont Street Dutch, four floors with two rooms on each, with smoking-, guest– and dressing-rooms, and a study facing the street. There was a neat back garden.

Alannah had mixed feelings concerning her sister-in-law: Eva was making them welcome and their stay exciting and it was not that she actually disliked her, she simply did not know her and did not feel at ease with her. This worldly sophisticated woman of the theatre and fashionable London made her feel, despite her maturity (and three husbands), hopelessly provincial. Alannah liked driving about, she loved riding through London's parks, but she found Eva's friends arrogant and proud, even decadent, most of them inhabiting the aloof languid world of the aesthete, discarding tight waists and bustles for clinging flowing garments of vivid greens and yellows, with hair *à la Grecque*. But what disturbed her more was that Eva was drawing Jamie into their social round: he had taken rooms at Stephen's living, she feared, on credit and expecting her, his stepmother, to buy him out of financial scrapes that would ensue as surely as the sun rose. He had contacts in London, as he had everywhere, in this case fast-talking, fast-living young rakes like himself who made a play for Celine and regarded Clodagh (so she insisted) as a somewhat elderly sister or maiden aunt. Nevertheless, they carried Clodagh's paints and brushes, admired her sparse stylised sketches, escorted her to the Royal Academy, to view the paintings offered for auction at Christie's and to Hampton Court to see the Romneys. They whisked both girls off to tea at Richmond or to picnic along the Thames and just as cheerfully guided Phelim on a round of cricket matches and race-meetings. Domi never had much to say to Jamie but Phelim was loud in praise of the man's wardrobe and insistence on escorting them to the opera when he would rather be at a music-hall. But one and all loved the daily parade in Hyde Park, taking the air in the carriage, or on foot, the girls properly escorted, along the old Route de Roi – Rotten Row. Most of all they preferred to ride, even Clodagh happy to prance on a quiet mount while Celine displayed her prowess and stared at those beauties indicated with a sly grin by Jamie as the *'grandes horizontales'*.

They were all a little breathless with this exciting new world, Alannah resigning herself at grand functions to the row of elegant gold-backed chairs around the ballroom floor, enduring the inanities of their dowager occupants for Celine's sake; Celine forgetting (she hoped) Strat McCrae for at least a few hours as she whirled by in the arms of yet another young officer or flirted with the young bloods lined up to dance with the O'Shea heiress and her half-sister Miss Aldercott. The latter had already come into her fortune but was rumoured cautious over it, no beauty but handsome enough, wielding her fan with grace and an air of authority.

'You promised no matchmaking, Mama, remember? At least not for me. They are pleasant and polite and that is all I require of them. I came to keep an eye on Celine, and the way she's acting she sorely needs it. She's a shocking flirt. But then she's a born poseur. And at the moment, over-excited . . .'

Letters absorbed and dominated their lives: Clodagh's letters to Will and his rare answers . . . Will's letters to Celine of which she divulged nothing as, irritable and irrational as she was these days, she searched each batch of mail for a letter from Strat. Dominic awaited orders, or at least offers, while Alannah frowned over letters from her father: Aunt Delia was poorly and had been so for some time. 'But do not fret. It is no worse a disease than old age.' Letters from Hetty Witherstone with news of Erins Pride and Burrendah, reminding Alannah poignantly of home! Rob Witherstone wasn't getting any younger (but Hetty had been making that statement for years). Dan Charlton was poorly but Ida was as usual. Grace and Joey had been over from Oorin, their sons bushmen born and bred . . . Letters from Will reporting on Hawkes Plains and Jubila: Dominic's menagerie was growing. Bushfires had surrounded Brisbane and there were floods in the north. Gondola had disappeared, this time he feared, permanently . . . Isabel Muir's letters were brief and terse; difficult women, the Muirs, or was it herself who was the difficult one?

As for Bennett . . . she seldom heard from her husband, travelling rural France on a tour of country châteaux, antique

sales and exhibitions, seeking *objets d'art* to ship home. She felt
no guilt at not missing him for he did not seem to be missing
her, his last letter consisting almost entirely of the gastronomic
delights of Lyon. She suspected he had timed his absence to
avoid Strat McCrae; nothing to put her finger on, only a
suspicion of mutual hostility – her imagination? After all it
was eight years since she had seen the man who had made such
an impact at Hawkes Plains, for this was 1884, her family was
grown, and her girls each attractive in their own way, Clodagh
slim and serene (and unhappy), Celine on the threshold of
some crisis, something which she, her mother, was unable to
halt. And, after all, had she the right to moralise when she
herself had loved and conceived by a man who was not at the
time her husband? Celine was disturbing enough but her sons
were equally so, Phelim noisy and strutting his dandy wardrobe, Domi browsing London bookshops for more 'teasers' as
Phelim called his radical library, returning with Schreiner's
The Story of an African Farm and Shaw's *Universal Socialist*, with
pamphlets detailing The Fellowship of the New Life, becoming
known as the Fabian Society. He would lock himself in his
room to read until literally dragged forth, when coaxing failed,
by his brother for a night around the music-halls or to dine at
the Café Royal awed by alabaster and marble dadoes, gilded
Corinthian capitals and Venetian mirrors. All very fine he
would agree when pressed, before donning his new eyeglasses
that made him look more scholarly than ever to return to his
books and his letter-writing. He had presented his letters all
over the country and, like Celine, was simply waiting.

'You're too young to wander the world.' How often had
she told him so?

'I'm eighteen, Mother.'

'Phelim's even younger.'

'I've never asked him to follow me.'

'Even so he will. I can stop you both, you know.' A silly
superfluous threat, as were her threats to Celine, for what
after all could she do to reinforce such rules? Besides, threats
brought what she dreaded, Dominic's respectful but distant
look, the same he had worn as a child when she had interrupted
his reading. At such moments her longing for their father's
presence and support became an actual ache.

'Don't try, please Mother. We'll be going to a mission station, as a group, and I'm sure there'll be a place for Phelim if he wants it, he's so versatile. I must get a start somewhere and the sooner the better. Trust me to know what I want. I'll go sooner or later, you know.'

She did know. Bennett's taunt of 'All they want is your money' made Dominic even more determined, with a further straining from the fashionable London life he despised. The eyes of young girls followed his handsome brooding face but he took little notice of them. 'A frivolous lot. They all look alike to me in their frills and flowers, like a bunch of chattering peonies.' At least, in following Dominic, Phelim would be separated from Jamie who dragged him from one night haunt to another. Jamie was forever moving hotels, each more bizarre and lower in the social scale than the last, always on her doorstep swinging his cane with his hat at a jaunty angle, proffering flower bouquets or bonbons signalling his old game of 'putting the bite on' as he called it. They could never entirely escape Jamie Lorne O'Shea, he was even included in Strat McCrae's dinner invitation.

'He's sure to bring some tart with him to shock the hotel.' Phelim, reading over his mother's shoulder, sounded faintly envious. 'I'd rather hoped for supper-rooms, to watch actresses at play.' Phelim O'Shea was much taken with actresses, he'd met a few even if they were only in the singing and dancing chorus.

'Stratton McCrae would not invite your sister, or myself for that matter, to public rooms and you know it. This is to be a formal dinner.'

'It's as if I don't exist,' Celine wailed. 'I should go to his hotel.'

'I'll lock you in your room first.'

'You're still treating me as a juvenile.'

But a letter did arrive for Miss Celine O'Shea: 'I look forward to our meeting . . . I hope you enjoy the dinner, and the hotel . . . I intend we shall be very gay . . .' Little else but time and directions as if everything, everyone, even Strat, were conspiring to keep her out.

'I must have a new gown.'

'Madame Barteque will advise on something suitable.'

'I don't want a suitable anything. I want . . . want . . .'
The awful thing was that she did not know what she wanted,
not really, except of course Strat's presence and awareness. 'I
want him to notice me.' She felt the need to shock. 'Did you
know the demimonde wear superb negligées costing thousands
of pounds each just to *greet* their clients?'

'Then we're grateful for financial reasons alone that you're
not a demimondaine.'

Celine was tired of Mama's crisp unfeeling remarks and felt
hemmed in and possessed by family. She needed someone else,
some other woman who would understand, a woman like . . .
yes, like Eva Muir who wore beautiful and elegant clothes
that were . . . well . . . *different*. If Strat saw her dressed like
Eva he would surely know that she had grown up. Excited
at the idea she refused an invitation from Lady Constance
for her mother, Clodagh and herself to take tea, with the
excuse of essential shopping – of *course* she would take Meg,
of *course* they would take hansoms. Her excuse sounded lame
and Mama looked dubious for days but Mama could not
force her to go, and Mama would never refuse and so perhaps
offend Lady Constance; Lady Constance had been kind, for all
Phelim's assertion that she was cultivating them in the hope
of an invitation to Hawkes Plains to trap a 'sheep-farmer'
as she called them. Lady Constance, Phelim insisted, was
impoverished gentility selling her name and patronage to
gullible colonials – Phelim had become a gossip as well as
a dandy. Perhaps Bennett was buying them in, he grinned,
then guffawed at the idea of Bennett squandering anything on
his stepchildren. A series of little notes went back and forth
between Eva Muir and Five Elysian Place, until the afternoon
when Celine saw her mother and sister off in the carriage,
Mama reluctant even then, looking back and waving until
the carriage turned the corner. Bribing Meg to secrecy (Meg
had become extremely bribable surrounded by the fleshpots
of London) Celine took a cab to Eva's sumptuous little house.
She could have walked the distance easily but at least no one
could criticise the formality of her arrival.

Dressing for the dinner party at the Langham took even
more ingenuity but Celine had long ago perfected the skills

of deviousness and contrivance and managed to make Clodagh so exasperated at her tardiness that finally, pink spots of frustration on her usually pale cheeks, her sister swept down to join the others in the hall, Celine flew to complete her toilette with a final dash to the hansoms drawn up before Number Five, clutching her cloak tightly about her. Each time they paused under lights she felt her sister's eyes turn to her but Clodagh said nothing until they were assembled in the foyer of the hotel:

'I thought so.' A sharp click of her fan. 'Feathers and pearls in your hair!'

'So that's why you kept us waiting. I'm very angry.' Her mother's voice throbbed with the effort to keep it low.

'You don't look like our Celine,' Phelim hissed.

'I don't want to look like your Celine. I never want to again.'

Mercifully, argument was postponed while they were escorted grandly and formally to a private dining-room with the table a riot of greenery and baskets and bowls of brilliant hothouse flowers amid the silver. Vaguely Celine sensed maids hovering to take their wraps but she had eyes only for the man at the end of the room giving orders to the waiters: it was eight years but she would know him anywhere; older of course, sleeker and better-groomed, close-shaven now with trimmed and oiled sideburns, he no longer looked a mountain man but the rich and successful man of the world she had so often pictured in her mind. She shivered with delight that he was here before her and she could not wait to be close to him, to touch him . . . A maid was removing her cloak and she knew she could not postpone the moment longer. With a defiant gesture she let it slip from her shoulders to reveal a heavily beaded gown of scarlet satin and velvet. Too large for her, it had been taken in, which made its décolletage and bustle even more evocative. It was Phelim who broke the stunned silence:

'Jumping Jehoshaphat! You've got yourself up fit to parade the Haymarket.'

'This is no time for jokes.' Their mother's voice was icy. 'I suppose I should have expected something of the kind.'

'She doesn't need to tell us where it came from.' Clodagh's fan sounded as if it would snap in two.

212

'How *dare* she put you in stage clothes – and with no time to change.' Alannah Muir turned with a slightly desperate smile to the man hastening down the room to greet them.

'And nothing to change into,' Celine retorted. 'Strat will love the way I look, you'll see.'

But Strat McCrae did not even glance at her, not at first. He bowed over Mama's hand then over Clodagh's pink and polished nails, then somehow her brothers got in the way, deliberately she felt certain, in an attempt to hide her – or rather, her gown. Even Domi was talking intently, as if resuming some long-ago conversation for they had always liked the Canadian. But at last Strat was holding her hand.

'This can't be Celine, this grown-up beautiful woman – but then you were always beautiful.'

'Even at ten?' She glowed, waving her fan, but she had never been able to use one elegantly. She could not be coy.

'Although I never would have believed you could tame that hair.'

Now he had spoilt things; she hated her black unruly *aboriginal* hair. She began to talk rapidly and at length, monopolising the conversation until all in all it became a terrible dinner. Under his scrutiny she was miserably conscious of her glaring shimmering scarlet, remembering suddenly that Clodagh had told her he hated red – how could she have forgotten? She talked on and on for Mama said nothing beyond answers to questions, only her eyes alive and smouldering on her younger daughter. All Celine could think of was escape with Strat to . . . where? The sea? Brighton perhaps . . . Everyone went to Brighton. Even the wine she was permitted didn't help as they ate their way through interminable courses, Clodagh with her delicate application, Phelim with his usual gusto. Turtle soup . . . cod with oyster sauce . . . pheasant . . . lavish side-dishes at which she only picked while male conversation drifted about her: hunting trips . . . the building of Strat's railway . . . the merits of P & O liners against Orient . . . blood mares . . . and Africa, Africa, *Africa*.

Bored and angry she reached too hastily for her glass and her beaded embroidery caught and the glass went over spreading its red wine over the snowy cloth. She tried to mop it up while waiters fussed and between them they made the stain worse. Her gauzy scarf sent Dominic's wineglass flying and wine dripped down her skirt. She heard male laughter, or thought she did – could it be Strat? She fled, her chair crashing, he scarf trailing and catching and she heard the sharp tinkle of glass. She stumbled through a room of diners, all male, turning to stare at the girl in the flame-red gown creating chaos. There were startled and angry murmurs as she bumped into tables and more wine spilled. On the verge of tears she flew out of a door and into the streets of London.

She had no idea which direction she was walking or even were she was, she just walked. After a while she realised it was raining a steady drizzle, that she had lost her scarf, that her eyepaint was running and her hair escaping from its pins. Wheels splashed her, as did horses' hoofs, her hem and train were bedraggled and she hooked the latter over her arm as best she could. She thought she must be in Oxford Street, then decided it was Regent Street, for it was bright and busy and wide. She took shelter in a doorway but men paused to stare and one, half drunk, grasped her arm. She shook him off and moved on hastily. There was nowhere else to go but on, she could not go back.

'Celine. Wait. *Celine!*' The hand under her elbow held on. Of course it was Strat. 'You can't walk alone like this. Besides, you're getting damp. Take my arm.' He tucked her arm firmly in his.

'I made a fool of myself.'

'We should not have laughed.'

'Why not? I look a figure of fun. Besides, you hate red.'

He shrugged. 'It looks rather wonderful on you. Sets off your hair.'

'I *hate* my black hair.'

'You're just not what I expected, I suppose.'

'That's the trouble. I don't know what you expected. And my hair's coming apart!'

'Let your hair fall, you'll be more like the Celine I remember.'

'I don't want to be that Celine. I want you to know me as I am now.'

'Look . . . we're almost at the Circus. We can't just wander

214

around like this; we'll take a cab and drive about until you're ready to go back.'

'I can't go back.'

He said nothing until they were in the shelter of a hansom with his evening jacket about her shoulders. 'You're still running away from things, I see. That's not very adult, is it?'

'Is that how you remember me? I ran away once before didn't I? When Papa died.'

'And I brought you back.'

'But Will was the one who found me. So he says.'

'Ah . . . Will.'

'I don't know what you mean by "ah . . . Will". He's changed. We've all changed. Except me in loving you.'

'And Clodagh's devotion to Will, I'm sure.'

'I dressed like this to impress you, to make you see that I'm no longer ten; I'm nineteen this month and old enough to run away with you.'

'And have your brothers, young as they are, come chasing us?'

She laughed. 'Domi's too lazy and Phelim would think it a great joke.' She paused. 'Will might imagine himself in love with me but I don't return it; I've told you that. I've written so much to you . . .'

'I imagine every man is a little in love with you, Celine.'

'I don't want other men, I only want you.'

'You're still saying outrageous things.'

'Why won't you believe me? Look . . . I'm still wearing your Indian charm, see? I wear it always.'

'We must go back to the hotel,' he said abruptly.

'Mama will never forgive me.'

'Probably not but you must face her – not to mention my glacé ices melting away.'

'I'll go back if you take me to Brighton tomorrow,' she said bluntly.

'Brighton? Why Brighton?'

'Because I want to see Brighton with you.'

'After this chaotic night?'

'*Because* of this chaotic night.'

'Well . . .' He shrugged. 'It will probably be a rainy London tomorrow. Perhaps the sun will shine on Brighton.'

'I don't care if it does or not. Oh Strat!' She flung her arms around his neck. 'You've never even kissed me, not once, and if you don't kiss me now I'll *die*.'

Brighton's afternoon parade – its British *passeggiata* – was in progress. They had strolled long and far so in East Street they bought French chocolates and bonbons and stared back at ancient dowagers in sealskin jackets peering at them through double eyeglasses. They punished themselves further by walking the seafront, their hair and her cloak swirling in the wind that was clearing the rainclouds away. The piers were crowded about by steamboats and rowboats. They had left London early in a hired trap, passing south London's rows of symmetrical villas, negotiating carts, coaches and bicycles, stopping briefly for breakfast before winding through the leafy reaches of the Sussex Downs. The previous night they had returned to a subdued dinner party, subdued but for Phelim, always irrepressible in spirit as in his love of food; Jamie and his 'tart' had come and gone, which was just as well, he informed them, for the 'tart' had a cold and sneezed over everyone and everything. Dominic was in earnest conversation with a waiter who had been to Cape Town. Clodagh and Mama appeared calm but Celine knew retribution would come; at least Bennett wasn't there to add to the tension. Strat had firmly and with authority announced that he was taking her, Celine, on a sightseeing jaunt on the morrow and they might even reach Brighton. Home again she had locked her door and kept silent through Mama's knock and demands to be admitted. Sooner or later she must talk to her mother – but not yet. They paused to watch the sharp little waves breaking over the pebbles. She shivered slightly.

'It's a lonely sea, don't you think?'

'All seas are lonely.'

'Are they? I know little about the sea – except the trip over when we spent most of the time in our cabin; Clodagh suffered badly from *mal de mer*. I know very little of your life altogether and I want to know it all, to be a part of it.' She turned to him and said coolly and calmly, 'We're not going back to London tonight.'

'Do you know what you're saying?'

'Oh yes. I've thought it all out.' She dipped into her cloak pocket and slipped a plain gold band on to the third finger of her left hand. 'This is Bennett's – I think. Mama wears Papa's ring most of the time. She says — ' with a strangled little giggle, 'Bennett doesn't really know the difference. She only loved Papa, you know.'

'I guessed that.'

'I love you like that.' Her voice broke and she put a hand to her mouth as if to steady it. 'Don't you want me, Strat?'

'Ah, Celine, how could any man not want you?'

'Then everything's all right, isn't it? I have no reservations you see, no pride, I just want to belong to you. I'm sure there must be some little hotel . . . I mean, I you surely know how to manage things?'

'I can never marry you.'

'I know that. I have grown up after all, you see?' Tears glistened in her eyes and she gulped, gripped by deep emotion. It transferred itself to him so that he could no longer bear it. Both knew they must be satisfied. He took her hand firmly in his.

The hotel was small, quiet and discreet-looking, a little back from the seafront yet with a sea-battered look about it: he'd had experience enough to know and judge one place from another. The housekeeper asked no questions nor did she even glance at Celine's ring. They giggled over the fact, then were serious for the room had the much-used look of having sheltered many lovers. It pleased them so they ignored its seediness. She stood by the grimy window, across the room from him but not looking out, as if she needed space between them. She began a nervous patter. 'I don't know anything about this part, what I must do, I mean. There's never been anyone before you, you see, so you'll have to teach me. I don't know how to make love, well, not really, except by listening to others but I don't want others to have to tell me. I've imagined what it could be like with you but I might have thought it all wrongly.' She gulped, choking on her need and desolation. 'I'm scared of not doing it right, of not pleasing you – and don't laugh at me.'

It was a childish wail and it touched him. Horrified, he prayed he had not shown amusement. She turned towards him. 'But the first thing . . . surely . . .' She undressed quickly without guile or timidity until she stood before him naked but for the Indian charm glittering against her smooth skin. 'Well?' She could not bear his silence and moved her limbs into an awkward pose, evocative, almost obscene.

'Don't,' he said sharply. 'You have no need of that. You're perfect as you are.' He strode the room, picked her up and placed her on the bed. 'Isn't it awful?' she was babbling. 'I don't know anything really in spite of growing up among barnyards. But this is different, isn't it? Oh Strat, what do I *do*?' She clutched at him, half laughing, half crying. 'Be still,' he murmured, massaging her breasts, squeezing them, taking each nipple in his mouth in turn until she felt a wonderful tingling warmth. He knelt over her and brushed aside her springy black pubic hair to reveal the pink cleft widening as he parted her legs and bent each to place her feet outside his hips. 'Don't look away.' Sharply. 'Celine! Look at me.' She turned her head and met his eyes, her own moist and inward-seeming, hazy as if gazing on some inner vision. He kissed her long and deeply. She closed her eyes and, as if unconsciously tutored and driven by centuries of initiates before her, folded her hands behind his neck and clasped her fingers tightly, tilting her hips towards him. 'You see,' he smiled. 'You do know.' He knew she was ready for him.

At first there was no pain, only a sweetness that went on for a long time. Then the hurt began, a hard pounding hurt deep inside her, possessing her body then her senses, creeping to her fingertips, clutching at her throat in its intensity. Yet she did not cry out, she made no sound at all for oddly she wanted the hurt, it was part of this, part of him, part of them. It went on till she could not think, she existed only in pain, cruel yet at the same time exquisite, but at a deep and final thrust her body seemed torn apart and she could no longer stifle a cry. He ceased the rhythm, held her tightly and turned her face against his chest.

'It's all right,' he gasped. 'Everything's all right.'

She lay against him conscious of her aching belly and their still entwined and sweating limbs. She became aware of the shabby room beyond the bed. And the cold. She shivered.

'I think . . . I feel . . . I'm bleeding.'

'No.' He wrapped her in a rug and held her close, warming her, smoothing her tangled hair from her cheeks. 'I know when to stop. Go to sleep.' After a time her breathing was quiet and even and he knew she was asleep. Distantly, if he listened, concentrating beyond the room, he could hear the tides swish in then out . . . in . . . out. There was no sound in the room but her soft regular breathing and the sea. Finally, he too slept.

Chapter Fifteen

EARLY ON the morning after Strat McCrae's dinner party
Alannah took the carriage to Eva Muir's house without telling
anyone her destination, not even Clodagh who was in any
case sleeping late. While an anxious housemaid scurried off
to announce her she waited with impatience, a long wait
as it turned out to the ticking of the ormolu clock on the
drawing-room mantel, so long she began to pace, striving to
control her anger. But the drawing-room décor only added to
her stress with its harsh yellow curtains and ceiling glittering
with painted dragons and a brilliance of peacock feathers.
Great bursts of sunflowers in ornamental vases stood in corners
of the room, real or fake she did not know or care. Altogether
there was too much light, sun, bamboo furniture and bric-à-
brac, making her head ache more cruelly than when she had
awakened with a start and hastened to knock on Celine's door
to be met by silence, as on the previous night after she had
heard the girl come in and her bedroom door click. Now Meg
reported that Mr McCrae had called early for Miss Celine . . .
So that was that – Brighton. Celine's 'running off' with the
Canadian would soon be all over London via various servants'
stairs, and Alannah's anger, illogical and unfair as it might be,
became centred on Eva Muir. When the woman swept in in
exotic green draperies and floating scarves she seemed only
to enhance the glare and as always in her presence Alannah
felt not only too formally dressed but drab, and today on the
defensive when she needed to control the situation.

'We shall take chocolate.' Eva floated to the bell-pull. 'A
habit from the past, but a pleasant one I think.'

'Thank you, but no.'

'Surely you haven't breakfasted? You must have set out in
a hurry . . . You know, I believe you are here to complain.'

Alannah removed her gloves with as much composure as

she could manage. 'Is it so obvious? You're right of course. I'm here to complain of your interference in my daughter's life.'

'Ah . . .' Eva's faint smile. 'The red gown.'

'And other things.'

'Celine came to me for advice, and help. She was troubled.'

'My daughter had no sound reason to be "troubled" as you put it.' Alannah slapped her gloves on the table in anger. 'Life to Celine means leaping from one crisis to the next as a mountain climber jumps from precipice to precipice rather enjoying the dangers involved. You insulted us all in your selection of a gown for an eighteen-year-old girl.' She knew she sounded pettish rather than outraged.

'Nineteen, she tells me.'

'Not quite. Celine always anticipates.' If only the woman weren't so coolly self-contained!

'She also tells me you refuse to accept the fact of her growing-up. A mistake, for if her emotions are still immature, her bodily needs are not.'

'What would you, an unmarried childless woman, know of my daughter's needs, physical or otherwise? I am her mother.' She had come resolved not to behave like a harridan yet could not hold back; it was Celine's secrecy, her going-behind-her-back to this woman coupled with her capacity to persuade – wheedle as Phelim called it – when she wanted something that was not only intimidating but hurtful. They were silent as the maid set refreshments before them but as the door closed behind the girl Alannah added tightly: 'I have the right to be angry, Miss Muir.'

'So it's "Miss Muir" now is it? All I did was lend the girl the gown she wanted.'

'An unsuitable one. You made a fool of her.'

'Well, I don't intend to apologise – why should I? I feel I understand Celine very well; such an impulsive sudden girl.'

'Sudden? A strange word surely?'

'Oh I don't know . . . Her father was a sudden man.'

There was something intimate about the phrase, more so in the way she uttered it as if she knew more of Brick O'Shea than his wife had known and Alannah felt the urge to run from the place yet at the same time stay. 'You speak of my late husband as if you knew him well.'

'One need not know people long to understand them.'

'Your visit to Brisbane was brief.'

'Knowing a man is not really a matter of time.' Her cup slurred in the saucer, the only sound but for the ticking of the clock and the remote clatter from the Embankment. A sheltered house, as pampered and exotic as its mistress yet Alannah did not feel sheltered or at ease or even safe for there was something, even in the bright tinted glare, of menace. She thought she would never know this woman – would anyone? 'She's like some prima donna warbling at a dungeon door begging forgiveness, except she doesn't warble and she'd never regret any of her actions,' Phelim had once described her with an interest and insight unusual in him, while Clodagh had smoothed a wisp of her perfectly-groomed head. 'I wish I had her presence. Mine is such a veneer it wearies me.' . . . 'Brick,' Eva was saying, 'was a very sophisticated man.' Alannah stirred at the 'Brick': how dared she speak of him with such familiarity!

'My husband was a bushman before anything else.'

'As to the "anything else", he must have had a varied life before he married you. After all, he was a good deal older.'

'Thirty years. I was not concerned how he lived those years, it was his life not ours together. I did not probe.'

'There are few men who could boast such a tolerant and accommodating wife. And after your marriage?'

The insolence of the woman! 'If there was anything "after" it was not important. Brick always returned to me.'

'The perfect wife. Wycherley dramatised you in his play *The Country Wife* – dwindling into a wife, he called it. Yet one need not wed to understand the role of a wife.'

'You speak from experience?'

'I always thought you a fool to leave such a man alone.'

She said it so unexpectedly, abruptly, and with such passion Alannah stared then felt a little chill as if confidences she had not expected and certainly did not seek were about to be revealed. 'Yes, we were lovers,' Eva went on. 'Briefly, if that's any satisfaction to you. But I would have persisted . . . Yes, I would have persisted.'

The woman's certainty in her powers stunned. Yet Alannah could scarcely blame her for she was quite fascinating with her fair hair gleaming in the sunlight and her shapeless draperies unable to conceal her lovely figure. Even so, she refused to be daunted and set about having the last word, or words. 'Even if you are telling the truth Brick is long dead and whatever happened between you is over and done with. I am uninterested in the details. You know . . .' she drew on her gloves slowly, smoothing and smoothing the soft kid, 'every intelligent woman knows that men are not only sexually curious but more sexually adventurous than they: a sharper sense of self-protection holds a woman in check. Men crave variety, we all know that, but experimentation is all it is . . . "We are sexually impetuous bulls," he told me once, "and women just have to put up with us." Sooner or later men return to the core of their lives. You won't admit it of course but I'm sure you have found this to be true. After all, you are alone – and ageing . . . You have been helpful to us in London, Bennett's orders I suppose, but we would have done very well without you: colonials are a resourceful lot. You and I need not bother each other again nor do I wish you to see my family. In any case we shall soon be returning to Australia.'

'Bennett has said nothing to me about returning home.'

'Our length of stay here is not your concern.'

'Yet I seem to be involved in the somewhat chaotic events of Bennett's family.'

'*My* family.'

'Bennett seems to regard them as his: schoolboys preparing to wander Africa, Celine to live in a *maison à deux* without benefit of clergy – oh yes she told me her plans. As for your eldest . . . well, I have done my best for that gauche, even rigid maiden – in which state of grace Clodagh is likely to remain.'

'Dignified rather than rigid, and gauche, never. Whatever my children decide to do I shall return to Australia, it is my country. Meanwhile, I must ask you to keep out of my affairs.'

'Celine will want to see me.'

'Perhaps. But as her mother I share the same roof with

223

her; spasmodically certainly, but even so it does give me the advantage.' Struggling against a verbal descent to the language of some wronged unpaid demimondaine she moved briskly to the door and instead gave way to the feelings of a Billingsgate fishwife by banging it behind her so hard it shuddered a vase of sunflowers balanced on a hall pedestal. The thing continued to shudder then sway and it needed only a push with the tip of her finger to send it crashing, to the open-mouthed stare of the maid. Alannah stepped calmly over the debris of soil and flowers and swept from the house, reflecting that she might never again experience anything quite like the exhilaration of that moment.

'Who'll buy my blooming lavender, sixteen branches for a penny?'

The girls were wandering London's streets and squares, their baskets trailing fragrance with their sweetly plaintive cry that signalled the end of the London 'season'. Yet summer continued full of events even if there were those packing for their country estates, talking crops, the opening-up of rooms and shedding of dustsheets, and boasting of daughters already suitably betrothed. Alannah moved restlessly from window to window of her house, pausing to gaze on the square with its centre garden, glimpsing a maidservant with her shopping basket, a nursemaid with a pram, an old inhabitant being taken for a 'push' in her chair, or a grande dame walking her poodle: the safe secure British scene except that she did not feel secure or even contented. Australia possessed her, she dwelt long and often on memories of spring in Queensland and the anticipation of it at Burrendah and Erins Pride. Sometimes she felt she had lived in London for ever although the house, even London, could never be home to her. She was much alone of late with Dominic – Phelim trailing – haunting the Missionary Society rooms, Clodagh at her art lessons and Celine with Strat at Brighton: she supposed it was something that Celine sent her cards now and then, cards she did not answer for quite simply there seemed nothing to say. Sometimes she felt the subject of the latest music-hall ditty, something about life in gilded cages that Phelim was always whistling for he was currently rapt in music-hall life; he was becoming a problem in his latest urge to travel the Home Counties with Jamie, no doubt a jaunt around county racetracks. She refused to finance the trip. He was too often in Jamie's company.

She struggled with her old feeling of exhaustion: why, she kept asking herself, illogically and with a touch of panic, did she keep marrying? Circumstances had dictated the first marriage, a necessity at the time and in return she had given Simon loyalty: besides, he had fathered Clodagh. Yet there had been only one man she had wanted then and for ever and now he was dead and nothing was important any longer and if she had three more husbands (heaven forbid) it would be the same. Her father was writing more frequently, of Sydney, of Melbourne where he went often, always querying their return for he did not want his grandchildren to forget him. Besides, pupils of the Academy past and present enquired after her . . . Delia's friends remembered her – poor Aunt Delia, her mind wandered these days. Ida wrote of Rob Witherstone's death from pneumonia. Dear Rob . . . She longed for Burrendah's uncomplicated cocoon-like friendships as Clodagh never wavered in her hunger for Will. Nostalgia cemented the bond between mother and daughter as they endured dress-fittings, coiffures and the constant boring teas, resentful and intense in their longing for someone . . . something . . . to spark release.

'You're here, I think, not as our Canadian friend but as my daughter's lover.'

'I'm here because I hoped I could be both.'

'You certainly haven't come from Brighton to ask permission to seduce my daughter – and in that I know I'm not being fair for knowing Celine there was no seduction on your part. Well, since it is done why are you here, Stratton McCrae?'

'Out of respect – I want you to believe that. And to tell you our plans.'

'You surely don't need my permission to carry them out?'

'No. But I'd like it.'

'You want my permission to drag my daughter about the

world as your mistress to ridicule and insults wherever you may go?' For a dreadful moment she felt her own moral fanatic of a mother peering over her shoulder; besides, what right had she, Alannah Muir, to meet this situation with outrage when she had claimed such freedoms with Celine's father? Yet she had not openly defied moral codes . . . Moral codes? Celine had mocked the term: this is Europe, Mama, it is 1884, women are demanding change, they are making their own decisions. Laws are being altered for their benefit, slowly, but it *is* happening. She looked closely at the man before her, young, yet mature and experienced in so many ways, a man who was in love with Celine: she, her mother, certainly hoped so. 'I know I can't stop you. I couldn't stop Celine in the past and I can't now. But sooner or later you must settle somewhere.'

'We haven't thought so far ahead.'

'Then you must. Do you intend drifting from hotel to hotel, country to country, proclaiming your relationship to a world which, I assure you, will exploit it to the full?'

'We are being honest about it.'

'Honesty and arrogance are often the same thing to the world, and the world doesn't like arrogance, it will hit back and Celine will be hurt. She never thinks far ahead – except where you're concerned – so you must think for her.'

'I'm taking her to Italy. It will be easier there than in England.'

'And after Italy? Scarcely Brisbane; mistresses exist but discreetly. Brisbane is bourgeois and provincial. Besides, we are well-known in Queensland as a family and Celine would experience in full fury the cruelties inflicted by Australian Society.'

'We will settle in Canada. I have built a house there; we are building a country as well as a railroad, you see. Perhaps we'll experience your furious cruelties in Canada, but among people I understand I'll know how to deflect them. I love Celine and there will be a life for us there, not a conventional one but a life all the same.'

'Your wife is in Canada is she not?'

He nodded. 'Eunice lives in Hope, a town on the Fraser River. She has her own house with a well-equipped school where she teaches, a carriage and an income, all provided by me.' He spoke briskly and clearly as if he had long rehearsed such a reply to awkward questions. 'Actually she is well able to provide for herself for she is Scottish-hardy and religiously inclined and well fortified by the Church of Scotland. She is admired for her work among the Indian tribes but as her husband I found little of Christian charity in her disposition. She is my wife, Mrs Muir, because of a boyish impulse at the age of seventeen yet she will never divorce me. Celine knows this and must accept it, for my life and my future – with Celine part of it, I hope – is in Canada.'

'I see.'

'I came from Brighton not only to see you but to arrange our journey to Italy. Celine will see you before we leave, I'll insist that she does.' A long pause. 'Neither of us can promise more.'

Bennett walked in one morning as Alannah and Clodagh were at a late breakfast: they heard the thump of boxes and bags in the hall then the room became pungent with some sickly-sweet hair pomade and his complaints about the stupidity of cabbies, the shocking state of the Dover Road, the barbarism of the travelling public and the insolence of porters. As usual with her stepfather Clodagh nodded briefly and made her exit, this time with the legitimate excuse of joining Phelim and his friends on an excursion to Windsor. With a brief kiss on her cheek Bennett presented his wife with a glazed shepherdess, bought at Versailles he emphasised, but to her it was simply one more awkward valuable item to be packed for Australia. He sported the latest in continental tailoring with a curl to his hair and she was forced to suppress a giggle; Celine would say he looked like a French dancing-master. He was irritable, and spiteful in his criticism of Celine for he'd met Bruce Mackintosh at the coach-station, an old woman of a gossip, who'd seen her strolling the Brighton seafront with a young man. How long before it was all over London?

'She's in Brighton with Strat McCrae,' Alannah agreed briskly.

'The girl's shameless. It will reflect on the family — '

'She's my daughter so what she does reflects on me not

on you. She's chosen to be with Strat and you cannot come between them. No one can. They won't let you. I'll ring for your breakfast.'

'I've breakfasted all I want. Don't evade the issue, Alannah, the matter must be discussed.'

'If you've eaten and are not tired I'd rather discuss my situation – or rather, ours.'

'What situation?'

'We've been in England almost six months, it's autumn, Clodagh worries about Will and wants to go home.'

'Then send her packing. She'll be more productive out there than she's ever likely to be in London.'

'I want to go with her. I want to go home.'

'Home? Where is home?'

'Australia of course.'

'Where exactly in Australia? You've tried many homes. You seldom went to Hawkes Plains of late years. You don't seem to like Yoolanowi. Is it BelleMonte you want? It certainly isn't Foxburgh, you never seem comfortable there.'

'Foxburgh House belongs to Isabel rather than to me.'

'Well, she is my sister.'

'And I'm your wife.'

'So you are – but a circumstance you frequently forget.'

'If I live at Foxburgh I have the right to manage it.'

'You have no feel for the place.'

'What holds you here, Bennett?' she asked abruptly.

'Business.' He was equally abrupt.

'What business? You've always had an agent in England to do your buying.'

'The man has let me down. I can't trust him so I must work up the Emporium myself. Things haven't been going well out there, it's a matter of finance, of cash in hand. It's costing a small fortune to ship out what I've already bought.'

'Why should you have financial problems? You've sold so much of Yoolanowi, and Will writes they've had good seasons with the price of wool excellent — '

'If you prefer to take the word of a bushwhacker farmer over the advice of experienced managers and bankers then do so!'

'I won't have you speak of Will that way. He's holding

everything together. As well as everything else, you've borrowed heavily from me.'

'I would hardly call it "borrow" between husband and wife.'

'We are scarcely husband and wife these days, you're so seldom here. You haven't answered my question. Why must we stay on in Europe?'

'I have my reasons.'

'That's exactly what I mean: you never explain. There are things behind things, matters behind matters, reasons behind reasons. Financial problems or not, you still gamble.'

'You begrudge me harmless flutters at the races and the card-tables while ignoring your own extravagance and that of your sons?'

'You know I must account to Crutchley and Marr for every penny advanced to the boys.'

'Phelim will squander his fortune on expensive tailoring and music-hall tarts and Dominic will waste his on Bantu, Zulu and Hottentot, with God getting what remains. As for your own fortune —' His fist thudded the table in frustration. 'You could buy half London and still have a fortune left.'

'Why exactly did you marry me, Bennett?' she asked calmly. 'I often wonder about it. You don't beat me or insult me or curse me or swear at me, you are infinitely polite even in our bedroom, but it is as if you are playing a part, something you are required to do; let us say you display a gentleman's code of good manners. Did you marry me for my money?'

'Well . . . you are a very rich woman and husbands have other rights than that of the bedroom. I can make claims on your money, Alannah.'

'No. Not any longer. Do you think me an absolute fool? I have always had a good friend in Jimmy Marr —'

'Do not weary me with the manoeuvrings of that eager aspirant for Clodagh's money.'

'Jimmy knows the law. He's also intuitive, a rare quality, and has written me concerning a new Act which is coming into force in Australia, and if I need to know more about it his contacts here will explain it in full. You're too late, you can't touch my money, you can only have what I'm willing to give you – and I've given you a great deal which I don't doubt has been spent on gambling and wining and dining and, for all I know, women. No more, Bennett. Nothing.' He did not answer, just stood staring from the window with his back to her. 'As for this house that could have been a home for us but is not, I shall do with it as I please. I shall also leave it when I choose. After all, I'm the one who pays the rent!'

She couldn't recall later why she decided to wear her ruby brooch to the opera for she liked it even less than the rest of Bennett's gift jewellery; certainly the rich colour would offset the creamy lace and satin of her gown. She felt an equal distaste for the miniature juggernaut of a jewel case, heavily carved and unwieldy, that Bennett insisted accompany her everywhere. Meg took the key from her and unlocked it. Alannah turned from the mirror at the woman's gasp; it was empty but for valueless baubles scattered on the pink satin. No Whitby jet, no tourmalines, no pearls or diamond earrings or sapphires – certainly no ruby brooch. Meg's eyes rounded with alarm.

'I locked them away last night as usual, ma'am, and returned the key to you – remember? Oh ma'am, I hope you don't think — '

'Of course not.' Alannah smiled at her as she closed the lid with a snap. 'How foolish of me to forget . . . Mr Muir took them to be valued, something about insurance. In any case the brooch is too heavy for lace, I'll wear flowers instead.'

She did her best to look unconcerned for Meg was always eyes and ears. The lock had not been forced and Bennett had the only spare key. That he had taken the gems meant nothing, she hated the pieces, but her husband must be in worse financial straits than he had admitted. She did not care. Not another penny. It was time to call a halt.

To Jamie Lorne O'Shea – the O'Shea flaunted when he considered it might open doors, particularly financial doors – London was nirvana itself and he had no desire to be anywhere else, except perhaps Paris as Bart Scobie told of it. But London would do, London excited him. The twist of fortune that had caused his mother to leave England as a girl-bride to his father, who had died before he was born, gave him in a roundabout way a thread-like communion with the city – yet the metropolis demanded well-lined pockets to enjoy it to the full. It had taken cunning and flamboyancy to keep up with those shipboard cronies who had not moved on to Rome or Paris or Madrid, according to the indulgence of parents who considered the nineteenth-century equivalent of the Grand Tour essential for a young man before settling to marriage and 'something in the City'. Well he, Jamie, had no parents, indulgent or otherwise, only hostile kin so he had spent recklessly in lunching fashionably at Gows, consuming his chops and peas in little cubicles with sand and sawdust on the floor. He'd 'done' the Song and Supper Rooms and Evans's in Covent Garden, the Coal Hole in the Strand and the Cider Cellar in Maiden Lane. He had come to know intimately the well-defined world between Piccadilly and the Strand, a world of champagne and the heavy morning head, rooms with silken sheets and wall-hangings, of clubs and gambling 'hells' and a surfeit of *tableaux vivants* and *poses plastiques*. He clutched delightedly at the wealth of pornographic literature available and never ventured out without his little books of hints for disease prevention and cure with their convenient pockets for French letters made from animal intestine. He loved this lush hedonistic existence, now slipping from his grasp.

Life had always been an up-and-down seesaw experience for Jamie with excitement in its uncertainty, but now the seesaw was down and he was forced into the company of those like himself, scratching about to pay tailor, vintner, barber and hotel, borrowing from each other when flush, living for the day but more importantly the night. He was often in the company – in the hands, he was beginning to think – of Bart Scobie, except that Scobie, as he was usually called, sported apparently unlimited funds, always willing to lend but at interest and sharp over the transaction. He wondered about Scobie: bland, plump and well-fed (there were those who dubbed him 'oily') and evasive concerning his life other than that his father was a butcher near the Brisbane wharves. He hadn't fancied the trade himself so had branched out along 'other lines', first in Melbourne then in

231

Sydney before returning to Brisbane to run rooming-houses, money in 'em with all the migration to Brisbane these days, and if one knew how to cut costs . . . Scobie talked a flat broad Australianese sprinkled with Cockney. Scobie was sly, often cruel, and obviously a rogue; Jamie despised him but suffered him for his support and advice on London. If Scobie dodged questions he asked a great many, mainly about the O'Sheas which puzzled Jamie for he thought all Brisbaneans knew the family, as they must know their offshoot by marriage, Bennett Muir.

'Never 'eard of 'im.' Scobie bit deep into a pork pie. Scobie was always eating.

'You must know the Golden Emporium in Queen Street? Furniture, artefacts, and so on?'

''Eard o' that.'

'Muir owns it. And a station on the Downs and a warehouse by the wharves and a town house on Wickham Terrace.'

'A rich 'un, eh?' Gravy ran down Scobie's fat chin. Jamie squirmed.

'They say he could float another Crystal Palace alone if he chose to,' Jamie boasted, exaggerating rather, but why should Scobie, a butcher's son from the Brisbane wharves who ate like a pig, patronise him? In such moods, when the seesaw seemed permanently down he would turn to his kin, edging his way into their good graces again for he was the vagabond, the larrikin, the outsider, in any case far down the scale of consanguinity now that there were heirs of O'Shea's own blood. He regarded Dominic as a bigot, a mean one at that, but he'd always managed to scrounge something from Phelim. Now even Phelim was hedging:

'Scarce a penny to spare old fellow, all I have comes through the largesse of dear Mama and she's tight-fisted these days. Doesn't like the idea of this African junket y'see, so all I might manage is a couple of guineas. Rotten way for our dear papa to leave his fortune but perhaps he anticipated what we'd be like, eh? You could take a chance with us on Africa – that's if the scheme ever comes off – fortunes to be made in such places these days, gold, diamonds, stuff like that; the place can't be all mud huts, with psalms and hellfire from the clerics, do you think?'

Jamie avoided Clodagh's penetrating gaze as he avoided the pox while Celine seemed to have disappeared into some permanent love-nest. That left his stepmother. Alannah Moynan Aldercott O'Shea, now Muir, was always in the background controlling their lives in her calm soft voice that held so much authority: hard to equate her with the shy convent-bred (yet spirited when pushed into a corner) girl he'd first met at his mother's house in Sydney. They had clashed over her hot-headed brother, they had clashed on the Darling Downs and through their Brisbane days and his years back and forth to the sugarcane north and on his return from wandering the South Seas – but how she could ride! A vivid picture crossed his mind of her galloping her small cream mare over Burrendah's hills, her hat off and her hair flying in the wind – even he had not been able to ride like Alannah. London seemed to have tamed her – or had Bennett? He doubted that even Bennett Muir could dominate her completely; there had always been a resilience, an inner strength about her that daunted. Even so, if he must beg to survive, he and Alannah would face each other squarely, they understood each other. Anything rather than face Bennett Muir's cold grey eyes.

Bennett locked his study door to reread his latest mail from Australia. Isabel's letter began as usual with a detailed account of Brisbane's scandals, Foxburgh's domestic crises, and the shocking behaviour of today's schoolgirls . . . Eva had written out (whenever their sister wrote to her it was to impart something malicious) and this time it was to say that Bennett planned to sell Foxburgh House . . . As if she, Isabel, would permit it! Immigration officials had called at Foxburgh enquiring his whereabouts. She had not of course given his London address, she had said simply that her brother and his family were travelling Europe (which for all she knew could be true) but what should she do if they called again? The other letter of import was from his accountant, the chapel-going Elwyn Evans, well paid to make any column of figures look good. They had removed the books of Melanesian Trading – he did not explain who 'they' were. 'Hickett's somewhere up north, I can't locate him so you must write, better still cable orders.' There was more: Captain Maher of his vessel *Elmtree* was to be hauled up in Townsville Court for the kidnapping of ninety-eight natives . . . He tossed the letters aside in exasperation. Fools. *Fools!* Evans was a fool for letting them take the books, Maher was a fool for getting caught, he himself was a fool for leaving everything in the hands of men he believed he had chosen shrewdly then paid through the nose to keep silent. His Melanesian Trading was doomed, he knew it, for sooner or later they'd squeal to save their necks.

He, Bennett Muir – yet no more than others – had broken every law pertaining to the importation of native labour; it had made him a rich man but the halcyon days were over. The decade of the eighties had started badly with Melanesia worked out and the regulations a mess, operating according to the bribability of government agents, officials and magistrates, with the further irritant of the political wranglings and manoeuvrings of the sugar barons of Maryborough and Mackay who had only one cry – labour! They would do anything, pay anything (well, almost anything) to get it. They had tried Coolies until the scheme had fizzled, they had tried Chinese from Hong Kong till the British administration had objected to conditions. Everyone objected to conditions, but how else could one make a decent profit? In desperation the cutters and schooners, his own included, had risked the shoals, tides and atolls of New Guinea to be hamstrung not only by German recruiters but by fiery Wesleyan missionaries at war over souls. Now the bubble had burst and his yearly income of some ten thousand pounds in return for a piffling outlay of beads, pipes, fish-hooks and a couple of leaky old vessels, was over. The newspapers would hound him, the London papers take it up . . . He could not go home, yet where in London, in England for that matter, could he hide? How could he live as the gentleman of standing he was with only a pouch of earrings and brooches and rings? One thing certain, he could not be seen about London peddling his wife's jewels, they were too well-known not to create gossip, so secrecy and a certain cunning would be needed to turn such gems into the thousands of pounds they were worth. The sale must be managed discreetly, with finesse, and to his advantage . . . He relised how little he really knew of London and its business, he had spent too long in France, therefore he must find the right kind of man, a man who could get the job done quietly and without fuss. If necessary, a man without scruples . . .

Jamie Lorne O'Shea. The black sheep of the O'Shea family would do anything for gambling money. Jamie had wriggled his way out of trouble on the ships and throughout the South Seas. He'd survived the slave trade. He'd survived Matt Burney while remaining ignorant of the important fact that Bennett Muir was the power behind Melanesian Trading. At first he dispensed with the idea of Jamie as not only absurd but monstrous: an extravagant rake to be trusted with such a project? Yet the idea persisted as he paced his study in the safe anonymity of Five Elysian Place, as he avoided friends and acquaintances, as he strove to awaken passion in a hostile and resisting wife, as he made desperate excursions to distant murky areas of London in search of obscure gambling 'hells' in which to recoup his losses. The idea of Jamie possessed and obsessed him. The idea took root. Finally he convinced himself that Jamie Lorne O'Shea was the only way.

Chapter Sixteen

'THE PILLOWS are *hard*!' Celine thumped them then, irritated, threw them to the floor.

'It's the Italian way. We could try another room.'

'And lose our magnolias? Oh no.'

The heat was so fierce they lay naked on their bed through the deadness of siesta, too languid to move from it until the cooler atmosphere of evening; the game of love was languid, too, like swimming in a thick and hazy pool in which skin slid moistly from skin. With one finger he would trace the reflection of window bars across her gold-tinted body till the lines curved and lost themselves in the tumbled sheets. They took long baths in the tepid water until the streets gained shadows and they could sit at their window overlooking the small dusty garden, an odorous patch smelling of rubbish and trodden-in leaves and refuse and a dead cat now and then, all redeemed by the tree that brushed their pane from time to time and whose flowers scented the room, permeating their entwined legs as they made love. 'I don't suppose there's a better way to describe what we do,' Celine would giggle with her new confidence in her responses, her timidity gone – or she assured herself it was – yet ashamed, even a little fearful of her secret jealousies growing with her possession of him. 'Nothing at half measure, Celine O'Shea, that's you!' Strat knew the hotel from past visits and she ached to probe the circumstances yet dared not.

Sometimes their solitude was invaded by the clatter of arrivals along corridors, or whispers from where they never could define (perhaps there were hidden oubliettes, Strat murmured), so many whispers, their own included. Sometimes they joined others for breakfast beneath the Gothic mediaeval ceilings painted white and grey: maiden ladies on pensions or meagre allowances who spoke in genteel tones of

'Room' as the English called Rome, and glided, or trotted when in a hurry, with genteel books under their arms. There were mothers with pale ageing daughters and students with vague expressions and young smirking couples and professors soaking up knowledge if not culture, one a busy Scot immersed in a study of the Pitti Palace who harangued his sons over keeping his notes up-to-date. How the British invaded if not loved Italy; it was more than the cheapness of living, it was the mystique of a country where one could safely nourish a delicious sense of stolen time under a pagan sun.

Their pensione, grandly called hotel, was small, discreet and Florentine-seedy, fronting the Piazza D'Annunziata, a true Renaissance square with a statue of the Grand Duke Ferdinand the First at its centre; and opposite was the foundling hospital, the Ospedale Degli Innocenti with its wonderful frieze of Della Robbia medallions of babies that not even centuries of grime could obscure in their wonderful blue. They would go out in the evening cool to small trattorias where they ate pasta, sometimes veal, and peaches, and rolls without butter for Italy was bathed in olive oil. They drank *vino* from great jugs, sometimes too much *vino*, then picked their way happily through streets and alleys of grimy slime-encrusted cobbles, dodging the beggars; Celine could never hide her distress at poverty: 'Florence is a beggars' city,' Strat would explain. 'The Italians beg, spit and smoke too much but you must bear with it all. It is not Hawkes Plains.'

'I want to see the orphan babies,' she said one morning as the bells rang for early Mass.

'Why?'

'I don't know really. Perhaps I need the *experience* of children.'

'You never struck me as as the maternal type.'

'I could be I think, with the right man to father them. You, of course.' Eunice had not borne him children, he had told her once abruptly then was silent and she wondered sometimes, fiercely and jealously, over the bond between husband and wife for bond there must be of a kind. 'We must be careful,' he reminded her. 'Or rather I must for

there cannot be children; you and I are one thing, we know
what we're about, but an illegitimate child is an unfortunate
thing.'

'We'll marry someday.' She was always disconcerting in
her certainty. 'People do get divorced.'

'In my case there are no grounds.'

'We're providing grounds.'

'It will make no difference. You know the situation Celine,
so leave be.' So sharply she did not persist, forcing herself to
live for the day, even the moment in a foreign country that
dismayed even as it enthralled. They were lovers condemned
to wander the world, seeking privacy, and anonymity if possible, their homes pensiones or discreet hotels in California or
Rome, Brighton or Canada – no, not Canada, not as Strat's
mistress in his home country. Wife was what she wanted
and needed to be, not for any moralistic reason but because
without marriage she was afraid she would not keep him.
She was afraid *not* to marry him. 'What is to become of
us, Strat?' she begged out of the dark bed. He held her
tightly.

'You come with me wherever I go.'

'To Canada . . . I suppose?'

'Of course. Eventually.'

'It's not what I want.'

'What do you want?'

'I want you to come home with me.'

'To Australia?'

'Why *not*? They all know and like you there. You could
run Hawkes Plains beautifully, you could run everything –
wait please . . . listen. We walked out on it, all except Will,
acres and acres and thousands of sheep and houses and all
the rest. We ran away.'

'Without a backward glance,' he agreed cheerfully. 'To
spend the profits.'

'Everything back there seems floating; no one will part with
any of it yet they can't or won't go back, leaving all to Will's
management, and it's not fair to him.'

'No, it isn't.'

'You could keep everything together.'

'Hawkes Plains belongs to Dominic.'

'He'll never run it. He'll not even live there, we've always known that. It would be wonderful, so absolutely right, to have you with me; I'd go home tomorrow if we could go together.' He said nothing though she knew he was awake and her hand slid from his unresponsive shoulder. She was anticipating. Pushing. All she could do was wait.

Sometimes of a Sunday they would drive the five miles to Fiesole to drink tea, other days they would take picnics of hard little sausages and peaches and grapes and wander the hill overlooking the olive and cyprus trees and vine-shaded villas of the Val d'Arno.

'You're different, you know.'

'How different?'

'More European, I mean. You can make yourself part of this where I can't.'

'I have been back and forth a bit.'

'You're not really Canadian any more.'

'Do you know what being Canadian is?'

'I suppose not. I don't really know what being Australian is. It's just that you've been to so many places and know so much.'

'Snatches of things scrounged from books as a boy. No formal schooling.'

'You've learnt a great deal since. I still don't know all you do except get rich – you are rich, aren't you Strat?'

'Very.'

'That's nice. I have no money except my pin-money allowance yet people tell me I'm rich.'

'You will be. You're an heiress.' He grinned. 'You'll be beating off fortune-hunters with sticks.'

'Are you after my money too?'

He laughed. 'I might be if I needed it but I don't, so you can keep every penny. I've taught myself how to make money, or perhaps the times are right for plunder, or perhaps luck is with me. However or wherever it comes I grab, as compensation I suppose for my sparse youth. You couldn't know what it was like.' He held out his hands palms down. 'I can pamper them now but from the age of five I cried with cold and frostbite and hard work.'

239

'They're beautiful hands.' She turned them over to bury her face in the palms.

'They're over-used. They remind me of too much.' He pushed them deep in his pockets.

'I could stay here for ever, you know.' She leant against him. His arm went round her.

'Italy has that effect, it bemuses. There's a wonderful indolence about the country, as if it's exhausted by all that's happened to it.'

'I never want to leave it.'

'We must before long.'

'Why Strat? *Why*?'

'I've been away from home too long.' They sat rocking gently together touched by the European melancholy, a latent madness of intangible borderlines between cultures overlapping and mingling, never quite separate as in Canada and Australia, countries safe from racial pressures with space to escape others . . .

He had insisted she write to her mother giving the return address of Barclay's in Rome: on the way from Naples they had skimmed through Rome but would go back to it for a time. She argued with him over letters home, reluctant to be confined to dates and time, certainly to explanations of the world they were making together. But there was a deeper reason why she did not want contact, at least not for a while for she needed time and distance to forget the evening she had returned to the Chelsea house to pack for Italy. To her relief, though she would never admit it to anyone, certainly not to Strat, Meg reported that her mother and Clodagh were at the theatre, while her brothers . . . heaven only knew where they were, Meg fussed. 'Everything's topsy-turvy these days, Miss Celine, no one stays around long enough to talk to each other. Except your mama, that is.' Celine refused to be drawn into pointless discussion so dismissed Meg and set about her own packing until she sensed someone standing in the doorway watching her – Bennett. She was not aware he was back from Paris, indeed she had not even considered his whereabouts. He was flushed, as so often these days, too much port, too much of everything she suspected, resenting him leaning against the door staring as she moved about her room.

'I forbid you to go off with this fellow,' he said abruptly. 'I've already had it out with your mother — '

'"This fellow" has a name. It's Stratton McCrae.'

'I'm aware of his name. Well aware. Furthermore, I know all about him, more than you know.'

'He'll be here soon. I'm in a hurry.'

'Did you hear what I said? I'm your stepfather and you'll listen to me.'

'I can't help but hear what you say. You're shouting.'

'You were always an arrogant crazy kid.'

'I don't like to be called "kid". And Mama understands why I must go. You are not my father to order me about. I'm no longer a child.'

'Nor a virgin, I take it. No, you are not a child,' he added slowly. 'Certainly not with that figure, and don't think I haven't noticed.'

'I don't want you to notice me at all.'

'You have your mother's sharp tongue. I don't know what you gained from your father except his touch of the tarbrush — '

'Don't talk about my father that way. Don't talk about him at all.'

'Then I'll talk about your lover: he's a Canadian adventurer, a fortune-hunter, and a blackmailer wherever it might bring him in a few pounds or dollars, so watch your fortune, girl, you may not have it long.' She had been forced to listen to his spite many times but this was more, a venom, a hate, as if he would spring at her and through her at Strat McCrae. 'As head of this family it's my duty to stop you making a fool of yourself. Someone must keep sluts in line.'

She struck him, beating at him, pounding, hitting hard and rhythmically until he held up his hands against her blows. He managed to evade them long enough to grip her arm and drag it down but instead of striking her he did an unexpected thing, he kissed her. He held her against him while she continued to fight him, kicking out until she wrenched her mouth free. She did not shout or scream, just bent and dug her teeth deep into his hand, so deeply and violently she drew blood. At his oath she wiped her mouth calmly and went back to her packing.

'Explain the wound to Mama as best you can. She wants to go home and I'll do my best to see that she does, and without you. You're no good for her, Bennett, you never were. You're no good for any of us. Now get out of my room.' Only then did she shout, uncaring who might hear. 'Get out, I said. Get out. *Out!*'

Florence was a city of churches and old stones and grand palaces and sly old men and sensuous smiling youths and faded but enticing beauties along back alleys and always the serenity of exquisite galleries. They would stroll beside the Arno where painters balanced easels along the banks and old couples searched the reedy patches of the river below for only they knew what. They were in no hurry to move on, the heat made them lazy and when it grew unbearable they would escape into some vast cavern of stone: the cool space of the cathedral, Saint Mary of the Flowers, or the Franciscan Church of Santa Croce which they preferred, for somehow it seemed cooler. They hid from the fierce sun, wandering aimlessly, awed by monumental splendours and unaccustomed to the Latin Church, creeping apologetically past the devout at their prayers, conscious of their rampant Protestantism, or rather their disbelief, their scepticism of things unseen and untouchable, united in their provincialism, secretly a little contemptuous of such abject humility. They grew sharply aware of decaying but precious objects around them. 'We're provincials with no history to speak of,' she whispered, wondering why she did so. The place was dark and hushed as they murmured over the wall-paintings – frescoes – she didn't have an artist sister for nothing, she boasted: how Clodagh would love the Giottos. Exhausted by splendour and subdued by immensity, the teasing gleams of light through distant glass, the golden mass of candles casting flickering shadows into dark corners, they would emerge to the normality of the streets and the space and freedom they were demanding for themselves and would never relinquish.

It was time for Rome.

Their pensione on the heights of the Via Sistina gave them a view over roofs of Roman tiles and walls of washed-out gold

and saffron and peach and rosy-red and all gradations of cream
to the dome of St Peter's. They dragged their bed under the
one window where the rays of early sun striped their bodies
and left the rest of the room in gloom. It became a sanctuary
of a kind for they were happy there, and Celine wished, even
prayed, they might stay, for here more than anywhere Strat
was entirely hers. October was a beautiful month in Rome
with trees all shades of red and gold and fat grapes both
black and white glutting the fruit stalls. Sometimes in the late
afternoon of a stifling day there came relief with the *ponentino*
– the little west wind – to bathe their faces in a freshness that
held a tang of the sea. There were, too, sudden thunderstorms
when, laughing, they held each other against the thunder and
lightning then went out to see the Tiber running fast and its
water turning brown. Letters awaited her from her mother in
which she sensed tension behind the chitchat:

'A small London gallery has bought one of Clodagh's
paintings in her new style, or rather, her new subject matter: a
woman standing watching the crowd crossing London Bridge
all bathed in morning light. I find it disturbing that she's
painting solitary and, to my mind, sad people, usually women,
against cluttered backgrounds – do you think that's the way
she sees herself and her life? I can never really equate your
sister with sadness, she's so beautifully organised and talented
and busy, she doesn't even complain when Will writes to me
and the boys and not to her, nor does she comment when
he writes so often of Emily Cosgrove – remember Emily, the
daughter of the haberdasher in Toowoomba? She worked in
the shop. I hope they make a match of it; dear Will, I do worry
about him for all he seems to do is work for your brothers.
My reasons for wanting to return home are so different from
Clodagh's, she simply wants to be close to Will, so contrary
of her for she has admirers here, while there's always Jimmy
making enough out of our legal affairs alone to make her the
chatelaine of a Brisbane mansion. Her ambition is to be a
farmer's wife, can you really see her so? Knowing Clodagh she
would compromise and become an elegant patrician farmer's
wife bandaging and patting and mixing mustard plasters and
pouring tea for callers in her old-fashioned skirts and blouses
with her little finger crooked . . .'

In a later letter Celine found the reason for her mother's verbal skating – her brothers. 'Dominic has been offered a place as teacher as well as a kind of medical orderly, anyway assistant to the doctor at Barkly Mission Station in Bechuanaland on the Vaal River, not far from Kimberley – I have heard of this river as of course I've heard of the Orange Free State and the Transvaal – but you would know more of Africa than I, I can't imagine Miss Isabel neglecting your geography. The diamond-washing at Kimberley is already fascinating Phelim while Dominic walks about so rigid I think he'll break. He says Barkly is more of a town than a mission station though what they call towns in Africa I simply do not know. They will go out with a group, some to other missions, all headed by Mr Woodstock and his wife – there don't seem to be reverends only misters – even so the boys are so young I'm still in half a mind to refuse my permission. Domi won't let me refer to them any longer as "the boys" and perhaps he's right; after all at their age I sailed thirteen thousand miles to a new country and learnt to love it. Clodagh is being practical in vetting Phelim's extravagant wardrobe, for fully half of what he's bought must be returned to the stores. I've seen little of my husband since he returned from Paris, I cannot be specific but I feel he's in some sort of trouble. I feel very much alone and unsettled, with the conviction, I cannot help it, that I will never see my sons again – is that foolish of me? One thing I am certain of, there is nothing to hold me in England any longer . . .'

'I'll still call them "the boys", it's what they are.' Celine clung to Strat that night, crying softly, not knowing exactly why she cried; could it be because an autumn rain was falling? Strat seemed to understand for he glossed over her misery with irrelevancies as to the weather:

'Tomorrow will be fine, you'll see. You know how it is in "Room".'

Usually they ate at trattorias but one night, flushed with wine and each other, they decided to celebrate something; her recent birthday was as good a reason as any so they settled on a rather grand ristorante near the Trinità dei Monti. They were holding hands boy and girl fashion when their reverie was interrupted by a solid Scottish burr:

'Weel laddie, y'seem t'be making the Grand Tour in more ways than one!' It was Malcolm Hume looming over their table, his keen eyes devouring Celine. 'And all this time I believed ye in London attending to Canada's interests.'

'Canada can manage without me for a while.'

'It's not managing too well railway-wise I can tell ye that.' He tossed his shaggy head towards a plump signora drinking champagne at a wall table. 'I'm making m'oon tour as ye've perhaps noticed which promises to be fruitful if mercifully brief. Even if I did introduce ye she'd naa comprehend, besides I niver do ken her outlandish name.' His eyes gleamed. 'I thought bookish lads like yeself fed their appetites at museums?'

'I'm Celine O'Shea, Mr Hume,' she said clearly. 'I can see you're curious. It *is* Malcolm Hume, Morgan's father, is it not?'

'Aye it is, though to m'detriment at times.'

'I remember your son on his visit to Australia. I was only ten.'

He chuckled. 'Ye're naa longer ten, lass, I can see that. Ye've filled oot nicely . . . I understand your mama married an old enemy o' mine, one Bennett Muir.' He shrugged. 'Naa accounting for a woman's tastes.'

'She had her reasons. In any case it is her business not yours. Or even mine.'

'Ye're a straight-talking lass, I'll say that.' He nodded at the wedding ring on her finger. 'So it's a honeymoon, is it?'

'You know very well Strat has a wife in British Columbia.'

'Ye're a lass of spirit to boot!'

'What news of home?' Strat put in hastily.

'Weel naa, the mountains are eating up the cash, what there is of it; the Company's doon to bedrock wi' only the government loan to keep things going. "Not a dollar to spare" is the catch-cry with already this year eight million dollars gone on essential work only. 'Tis the Selkirks eating everything up. I told 'em they'd niver cross those divilish rocks.'

'But they are crossing them.'

'More or less, by desperate devices like keeping the men in

245

the mountains with just food enough for the winter, and paying 'em by cheques they canna get oot to cash till spring when they hope funds might turn up from somewhere. Glad t'be oot o' BC for a spell. I just hope that lad o' mine is naa forging m'name over the length and breadth of Canada; caught him oot once, just as weel for he's not a bad hand at it.'

'I won't hide,' she fumed later in their room, flushed with wine and indignation and her love for Strat and contempt for his Scottish-Canadian friend, if he were his friend. Business associate then . . . 'Whatever he is he's a dreadful man. Why did he call Bennett his enemy? I didn't know they were even acquainted.'

'It's a long and involved story.'

'Men are secretive, even you at times. But Bennett's secretive all the time. He seems to hate you, isn't that strange? He actually called you a blackmailer.'

'Perhaps that's his word for extortionist. I strike hard bargains in carrying out his commissions in Mexico, California and so on.'

'I don't like secrets, Strat.'

'Men come together in business in special ways. It's a kind of war.'

'Well, I won't pretend any longer, about us I mean. I don't know why I ever did, I'm not ashamed of you or myself or the situation.' She dragged the ring from her finger. 'It can only bring bad luck in the end. After all, it is Bennett's. Ugh!'

'We could move on. Would you like Paris for a while?'

'We're not running away. We'll decide where we go and when. Let Malcolm Hume move back to his mountains and his railway and all the rest of it.'

'They're my mountains and my railway too, you know.'

Such remarks subdued her for a while for she did not want to remind him of Canada. Yet the country intruded for he would sit frowning over his mail, letters with Canadian postmarks in grubby envelopes as if they had travelled long and hazardous roads. He would toss them aside impatiently. 'Old requests and complaints and orders. Mail takes too long to reach me.' His Canadian maps spread before him made her more uneasy. 'Weather permitting, it can't be too long before they drive the last spike.'

246

All was the same between them, she assured herself yet knew that one part of him had already left her. She approached each day with a sense of dread.

'I won't let you go.' She turned over, urgent and possessive, pressing her hips savagely against him, 'I'll do anything to keep you with me.' Her voice trembled into a shaky little giggle. 'I'll weaken you with love.'

'Celine!' He gripped her hard, holding her still but away from him. 'We've been over and over this. I *must* go home.'

'Home? You've told me many times that home is where I am.'

'You're one kind of home to me, of course you are, but this is different. This is my work, my other life. Don't make it hard for me. Morgan can't carry on alone. If you won't come to the west then come to Montreal . . . Winnipeg . . . anywhere so long as you're close. I'll make you happy in Canada. I've made you happy here, haven't I?'

She turned to him with a small desperate movement. 'Don't go, *don't*.' Her words tumbled. 'I've only loved two men, my father and you, and I'll never love another man as you, never. My life began with you when I was ten, people laughed over it but I didn't care — '

'I can't stay in England. I can't live in Australia. I want to take you to Canada but if you won't come, what am I to do?'

She trembled. 'Oh, you and your wretched railroad.'

'It's not wretched to Canadians – or, come to that, the Americans. It affects us all.'

'You're going back to your wife,' she said calmly, kneeling before him, her long black hair brushing her bare hips.

'*Celine!*'

She quivered. 'How do I know you're *not*? You could be. Or to someone else. How do I *know*?'

He held her tightly. 'You know it.'

'But she's there when you go back. She's always there.'

'That's juvenile jealousy – and you are juvenile in so many ways. Too intense.'

'We're an intense family – except Clodagh though perhaps

she just manages to hide it better. And even Mama can let things drift over her when she wants. I can't. I never could. I can't now.'

'It doesn't make me love you less but you always were a spoilt brat grabbing what you want your own way no matter who gets left behind. Or hurt.'

'Do you really believe I would go so far? Is that what you think of me? I wouldn't do anything that would make you hate me – yet perhaps I would. I don't know.'

'You're quite ruthless in getting what you want.'

'Do you think it's because Papa wanted a boy? I mean, I tried to be what he wanted, you know, strong, to make my presence felt, to be *heard*, no mean feat, believe me, when Phelim was always so noisy.' She turned away, desolate. 'I can't bear to speak of Papa even now.'

'You must speak of him. It's unhealthy to avoid it. Don't turn from me, you turn away too often. For all your frank talk you too often avoid truth. One reason you won't join me in Canada is that you won't feel safe there, not as you feel at Hawkes Plains in some childhood cocoon with everyone in place while you weave your own form of magic around them. In a way you control them as you control Hawkes Plains, it pivots happily around you, and you're terrified you'll lose that dominance in a country where you'll feel a stranger. You're afraid of other things too.'

'What things?'

'Your dash of colour – as it's referred to – that simply isn't there. It isn't, you know. I've learnt a lot about the aboriginal race.'

'I just can't help it, I never could. I grew up with the Blacks around me yet I hate being near them. I can't explain it, it's a prejudice I suppose. I even hate my black hair.'

'The world's full of black-haired people who are not Australian aborigines. Call yourself Spanish if you like. Or Irish, that's valid for your mama's Irish and your papa by descent. Anyway, it's your brothers who will have the problem if there is one; they're going to Africa.'

'You may not be so tolerant if I bear coloured children.'

'We settled that long ago,' he said sharply. 'We won't have children for the valid reason that we can't marry.'

'*You* settled it. Things can happen. You could leave me pregnant here and now — '

'You are not pregnant. If you were I would have heard about it before this; you would use it as a weapon to keep me here, I know you too well. But if ever we are free to have children they will be as you and I so stop punishing yourself – worse, punishing your father. After all, he could have kept the truth hidden.'

'He did.'

'I am sure he didn't intend to for ever. He died suddenly.'

She drew a blanket about her, huddling in it for it was cool. 'Oh go to your wretched railroad. Why did I have to love a stubborn determined Scot?'

'Practical Scot. If life were left to the Irish we'd be in as great a mess as Ireland has made for itself.'

'Don't talk about us like that.'

'*Us?* When were you ever in Ireland? You wouldn't know an Irish bog from a potato patch or a shanty cabin from a mansion.'

'I don't seem to know anything worth knowing,' she agreed miserably. 'I don't know where I belong. I don't really know who or what I am.'

'I know. You're a lovely girl whom I love and want, and there's no need to cry over it.'

'I'm *not* crying.'

'Close to it.'

'It's just that . . . Don't force me to Canada, Strat, not yet. I can't think or plan beyond now when we're alone and happy.'

'I'll never force you anywhere. I know I couldn't.'

'Mama wants to go home, and she must, away from Bennett, but she won't plan anything until she sees me again, I know that. And my brothers could sail any time . . . I may never see them again either.'

He drew her close, rug and all, and kissed her. 'Then all in all it's time we went back.'

'Back? Back to where?'

'London – for a start. Don't look like that.' He grinned. 'After all, there's always Brighton.'

Chapter Seventeen

JAMIE STROLLED Piccadilly swinging his cane and doffing his hat to acquaintances for he had become something of a cult figure in certain quarters, at least when his pockets were jingling – and due to a lucky run at poker they were jingling tonight. With his usual optimism he was convinced his luck had changed, that his life was on a permanent 'up' and that tonight London was his – and in more ways than one! Whatever the motives of those who greeted him he felt secure under the scrutiny of women for his elegantly tailored body was as unpaunchy as a boy's (spells of semi-starvation forced upon him helped) while his hair was as black and curly as ever and although he was into his forties he consoled himself with the fact that maturity had only added to his personality as experience had added to his sexual expertise.

Dodging the muddle of Piccadilly Circus, now being rebuilt, he turned jauntily down the Haymarket. He could have taken a hansom but had decided to save the fare and walk through the fine evening, a balmy night with a clear sky – what one could see of sky beyond the glow of London – and London seemed out to make the most of it. Certainly the Cypriots . . . doxies . . . motts (all harlots no matter what fancy name you gave them) were out in force. He could have any one he fancied, he knew that, but not tonight; tonight would be different, a new start. Although he would never admit it, and until now not even to himself, he was rather jaded by Scobie's world that had become his world, with a yearning for something . . . someone . . . new, fresh and untried, a satisfaction he might possibly find in a Gaiety Girl: Gaiety Girls were special, the ultimate, every 'Johnny's' dream and goal. Yes, tonight could be different, at the very least it would be class. But tonight could be more: a chance to be seen once again in the right places with the right people. Tonight could be his salvation!

He couldn't tell exactly why his eyes had lingered on this girl in particular for they were all pretty and beautifully gowned and coiffed, moving rhythmically to the beat of their pretty vapid songs with only veiled suggestions in their discreet stage poses – look but do not touch! There was something about her, something more than her voice seeming to soar above the others, a clear young voice reminding him of another voice somewhere, some other time – Lily Marchand. He liked the name, it had a Gallic ring to it and seemed to fit her fair elegance, and he had elbowed his way to the head of the line of stage-door 'Johnnies' to find the crush so great all he saw was her dressing-room door closing on her fair head. Night after night he had sent in his card but no answer. He had haunted the little pinched-up entrance to the Gaiety, competing with the *jeunesse dorée* – the 'Midnight Sons' – and had sent flowers in abundance but still no response. He had stood watching the Girls sweep in en masse to lunch at Romano's (at special rates, everybody knew that) until meeting the girl became an obsession. Then suddenly he was admitted to her dressing-room with only her maid hovering, to find her even more attractive close up; charming, yet with something curiously innocent about her reminding him of some other girl long ago – but there had been many girls long ago. She spoke with a cultivated well-tutored English voice, nothing French about her except perhaps her manners, for her acceptance of his compliments was flawless and controlled. He had wondered at the time how long it would take him to ruffle that outer calm, for outer calm it would be, they were all the same when stirred as he knew how to stir them: girls in bark huts and shanties and native gunyahs and island shelters. Older women too; there were times he preferred older women. Yet tonight he longed for the untried – and memory would nag again. Was Lily Marchand such a one? It was possible, for Gaiety Girls were protected and nurtured, most of them too young to have had the time and opportunity away from a guardian or a mama to be anything else. Excitement drove him; more flowers and more cards still met by a tormenting silence. He fretted, waiting. Then it came, a brief flower-scented note inviting him to supper in her rooms, the address St

James's. Tonight, Lily Marchand, Gaiety Girl, would be his!

He waited, as the maid indicated, in the opulent drawing-room cluttered with gilt furniture, splendid mirrors and clocks. There was a fine rosewood piano. There were wall-coverings of the finest silk. Through a bedroom door he saw a canopied bed tricked out with gilt and expensive cushions: expense was all around him and he liked it. There were great bowls of hothouse flowers, his own among them perhaps? But there was no supper table set and it made him uneasy; indeed he found the silence and wealth of chiselled marble figures on mantel and table overpowering. Where was she? He heard a door open behind him and turned eagerly.

The woman who stood there was a handsome poised older version of Lily, in her forties he guessed – an aunt? Sister? Perhaps even her mama? Stupidly he had not expected to find the girl living as sheltered as a nun and absurdly the latest ditty sung by a popular sister act ran through his mind:

> We're fresh, fresh as the morning,
> Sweeter than new-mown hay,
> We're fresh, fresh, fresh as the morning
> And just what you want today.

'James Lorne O'Shea,' she read from his gilt-edged card.
'I'm here by invitation.'
'I know.'
'To sup with Miss Marchand. I have been waiting a long time.'
'I know that too. Tonight Lily is giving a benefit performance.'
'Then why did she invite me?'
'I invited you.'
'You?' No apology or explanation. It seemed he was expected to deal with this woman. Lily's duenna? Or was she actually her madam . . . She waved him to a chaise-longue. Joining him she leant back and tapped her teeth with his card.
'You haven't changed. Older of course but the same black hair. I could never forget your curling black hair.'
'You know me?'

'Anywhere. I recognised you at the theatre, only a glimpse of course from Lily's dressing-room, but I knew you. Ah yes . . .' He took a deep breath, afraid to query. In his chosen but precarious existence there was always the possibility of some woman popping up from his past to plague him – blackmail him if she could. But here in London? He'd scarcely had time to make history here . . . 'I never knew your name, just Jamie, but I knew you immediately. And, oddly, you were the only James among Lily's cards.'

'Who *are* you?'

She laughed. It irritated him; did she really find the situation humorous? 'I suppose I should feel angry at being forgotten but it is a long time ago and Melbourne far away. Perhaps you remember this?' It was then he noticed the ring on her finger, a narrow blue ring, a cheap ring; he still carried them about with him, 'a little present' as girls so often begged. Melbourne? Shock jolted him. Lucy. Lucy . . .? What *was* the silly but pretty name?

'Lucy Marigold Finney. Now Lucinda Amora.' He surprised himself, remembering. No woman had really touched him in life except this one yet he had not recognised her – well, it was over twenty years, twenty-five, perhaps more, and there had been so many since. Now the years had caught up with him. He had been touched in the squalid little hotel where he had left her sleeping, the blue ring – too big for her – on her finger that cold morning when he had hurried off to catch the coach to Ballarat. He had forgotten the occasion yet never quite the girl, so young and unworldly, so unexpectedly innocent that he had had to teach her to love him. 'I was very young,' she added.

'As I was.'

'In years, yes, but in other ways . . . Perhaps it was your assurance that attracted me, it made me feel that a door was opening on life. I was so anxious, so eager to please you, for I really believed that if I loved you completely I could keep you – wasn't that naïve? But there had been no man before you – and of course you knew that. When I awoke that morning I was cold, then not only cold but bereft because you had gone and I thought I would never be warm again for all I had left of you was the blue ring – oh, and one guinea. At the time I thought it generous for my quite inept performance; I was inexperienced, which surprised you as it would have surprised many people – the stage you know – but I could not hide my inexperience from you. Yet I felt that what I didn't know you would teach me for I knew you were well versed in women; I didn't mind, it seemed right for you. I loved you instantly, it happens that way sometimes, it must for it happened to me and I believed then that because I fell in love with you you must with me and you would come back. That was naïve too. Still, it was you for always, and now when I see you again even after so long I understand why. I always loved beauty. I always wanted beautiful things, and you were, still are, quite beautiful.'

He made a gesture, not from embarrassment for he was accustomed to being admired, but from impatience. 'It's long ago.'

'Of course. And you must have loved many women since.'

He shrugged. 'A pretence of it I suppose. It's expected. And necessary for full enjoyment.'

'That is what I had to learn – pretence.' Now there was a hardness in her voice that made him glance at her sharply. 'That morning after you'd gone all I had left were my ambitions so I went back to the stage. It was necessary for soon I had a daughter to provide for.'

'Well, I didn't think you were meant for the life of a nun. You were too pretty not to marry.'

'I have never married.'

'Oh? I see.'

'You don't, not really. I was not only unhappy after you left but in great need.'

'I didn't know that.'

'Would it have made any difference if you had? I concentrated on my stage career. It has been a very successful one, so successful I was able to give Lily a good start — '

'She is attracted to me, you know.'

'If you have a liaison in mind nothing can come of it,' she said briskly.

'Surely that is for Lily to say?'

'It is not for Lily to say. You see, she's not only my daughter – she's yours.'

He stared. 'Mine?'

'Is it so surprising?'

'She cannot be mine. She's too young.'

'She's older than she looks; all actresses are older than they look, you should know that. She's not seventeen, she's twenty-five, almost twenty-six, born at the end of 'fifty-nine. Oh, she's yours. You cannot doubt it.'

He squirmed miserably. 'Well, it's possible.'

She laughed at his confusion. 'It's true. She's your daughter and deep down you know it . . . When she was old enough I brought her to London for by that time I had entrée to many quarters — '

'Have you told her of me?'

'No. She believes her father to be an army officer killed in India; always convenient to fall back on, the army and India. And now you won't want her to know of you, it might awaken possessive feelings in her and that wouldn't suit you at all, would it? I've come to know you very well since we've been separated. But even more important, it wouldn't suit me for I intend a good match for Lily with every chance of it happening: an Eastern potentate offered to buy the entire chorus for his harem simply because he wanted Lily. I intend that she makes an advantageous marriage; no travelling about as the mistress of some jaded fop of the nobility for my daughter. Never! So you will go tonight and never contact her again. I'm sure that's what you want for otherwise it would involve you in parenthood; besides, Lily is very conventional and would expect you to marry me and even if you were so inclined I am not. Not now. We will simply avoid such a situation. Instead I am determined Lily will have the best of clothes and apartments. She will be seen at the best restaurants and hotels, an expensive process as you will appreciate. In planning her future I set myself out to learn all I could about you for if we had not met by chance we would have met very soon — '

'So that's it! You've been spying on me.'

'If you call it so, but I have many contacts in the artistic and social world. It was not really so difficult. For instance, you have a sister who paints and attends the opera with your stepmother. As to yourself, you are the son of the late Brick O'Shea, landowner, a wealthy man who must have left you well provided for — '

'I'm Brick O'Shea's adopted son, that's all, and he left me only a pittance.' His manner was deliberately airy and offhand to mask his alarm. 'With not a penny left. I live hand to mouth.'

'Nevertheless the O'Sheas are your kin and well-known in London as well as in New South Wales and Queensland so you have the means of raising money. Beg, borrow, steal if you must, I don't care how you raise it, but ten thousand pounds is to be paid us, for Lily's benefit, otherwise we must all endure an expensive lawsuit – and don't think I would hesitate for Gaiety Girls are special and I could make it a very pathetic story: Lily Marchand and her mother deserted, your child left without support, and so on and so on. I have influential friends, Jamie, and would win, oh yes I would win, then do you really think your family would stand by you? I doubt it. I could even send you to gaol. I wouldn't hesitate to do so you know.' The hardness and determination were back in her voice, so unlike the Lucy of old. Yet perhaps, after all, she had always been so. 'Ten thousand pounds for the furtherance of your daughter's career, quite a modest sum to ask I think.'

'I haven't ten thousand shillings!'

'Don't tease or I'll ask for more. After all, it's not for myself, I was paid my guinea. A lump sum, Jamie, paid into my solicitor's hands within three months, which should give you plenty of time. Then you need not see either of us again. If you try to hide from me or fail to pay up I'll seek you out. I'll pursue you, Jamie, I promise you that.' She was composed and deadly. 'An unlucky visit to the Gaiety I think, as it was unlucky you sat watching my sad little apology for an operetta in Melbourne long ago. You might even consider giving up theatre-going altogether, don't you agree?'

The hardness was still there as she showed him to the door slipping a solicitor's card into his hand as he went. Her little blue ring seemed to wink at him.

Lucinda Amora, born Lucy Marigold Finney to a mother who cooked for nearby inns, a father who manufactured shell lime and a brother who wrote rhymes for shopkeepers between bouts of petty theft, closed the door firmly behind her and leant against it with a gasp of triumph – she had carried it off. He had believed her. She had sent away a frightened man who would, she knew, do exactly as she wanted. There was no denying the pretence had been an ordeal but now worth the planning and investigations, the calculations of time and circumstance for she had lied brazenly and coolly to fool this devastating rake of a man, for rake he was, and prove herself a better actress than she had thought possible.

Her plan had begun to take shape when she had recognised him at the theatre then had plucked his card from the pile handed over by her daughter, for Lily was accustomed to her mother's management (for her own good) particularly now that she was at the Gaiety, an opportunity offered after her triumph of a provincial tour. Lily would accept what her mother gained for her, happy to look beautiful under the garish lights, sing her little songs and leave her assignations as well as her professional engagements to a mother who knew so much more of life than she did. And Lucy's plans for her daughter were for a respectable (rich if possible) marriage and to that end she had taught Lily Marchand – and it really was Marchand, if without benefit of clergy, the oddly exotic name of the corner grocer who had been next after Jamie, for after all when virginity was gone a certain freedom took its place. She had taught Lily pride and selectivity and how to shuffle offers and opportunities, everything towards the good address and the respectable (if fictitious) background, the sumptuous clothes and grooming, the singing, dancing and deportment lessons that had brought a transformation in the placid rather pudding-faced girl Lily had been when they had landed in England. For Lily to be seen in the right places with the right people took money, as did the cultivation of men with titles, even twice-removed heirs; for if she, Lily's mother, had failed to reach the ultimate, her daughter would do so, and the man who could so easily have been Lily's father would help her reach it. Her sights for Lily were set on the Hon. Bertie Allington, youngest and third son of Lord James Allington, educated at Harrow School, sometime officer in the Rifle Brigade, who had paid Lily the usual attentions but could be induced to pay more. Lucy had no intention of taking Jamie to court, an action which could jeopardise her own carefully built up background, nor would legal proceedings be necessary for her bluff would work: all she must do now was remain firm. Well, firm she would remain until Lily was married into the peerage. Jamie Lorne O'Shea would provide the means to that end and she – Lucinda Amora born Lucy Marigold Finney – would have had her revenge.

Jamie walked the Haymarket again, this time in no way jauntily with scarcely the heart to raise his cane. Who would have thought the silky-soft Lucy he had known would grow into this iron-hard matron playing off her daughter – their daughter – against him and the world? Usually he managed to wriggle out of sticky situations with women but not this time: one night with a virgin and a man was caught. Trapped! It would teach him to keep clear of chaste young girls ignorant of the world and of men, yet eager to love and be loved. So much for his dream of supping with his Gaiety Girl, of driving with her in a hansom on a balmy night, of escorting her to dinner, of propelling her in a punt at Maidenhead . . . Instead he was laden with a cruel debt he could not pay yet must make an attempt to settle otherwise Lucy Marigold Finney – Lucinda Amora – who meant every threat she had made to him, would haul him into court before the world and the O'Sheas. Perhaps – he shuddered – even into prison.

A girl brushed against him, her skirts coiling about his legs. She was bold and pretty and full-bosomed and he paused to make quick calculations: supper, a modest room with the obligatory champagne, and what he always jokingly referred to as 'overhead' – yes, he could just manage it. From now on he would stick to the professionals, the willing, cheerful, and all things considered, amazingly healthy and resilient harlots who tucked their fees down their stays with a 'Ta, lovey' and were off seeking their next victim. He twirled his cane, doffed his hat and proffered his arm. It was done!

The flowers looked expensive and Alannah did not need to read the card – Jamie. He was waiting in the drawing-room, Meg informed with a proper disapproving set to her lips yet with the suppressed excitement common to female servants when Jamie descended upon the household. She would see him presently, Alannah agreed, waving Meg and flowers to the servants' quarters. He was here for money, what else? He was certainly too late to farewell his brothers now on the high seas. Celine had come from Brighton and though never sentimental siblings they had all softened over the prospect of a long separation and bade each other emotional farewells before Celine was off again, evading direct questions other than to say that Strat was fussing over Canada.

She took her time pinning Grandmama Moynan's cameo brooch, the only piece of value left to her, at her throat. The looming Christmas season could have something to do with Jamie's visit, she reflected, for without money to ease the cold London would be unbearable while the Chelsea house was ablaze with coal-fires and its kitchen aromatic with Cook's steaming soups and pies and pastries. She had ignored Eva Muir's invitations, wanting nothing further to do with the woman (or with Isabel if it came to that) and if Celine did visit Eva on her visits to London she, Alannah, preferred not to know the details. She had refused as tactfully as possible all invitations to country estates for if she and Clodagh were doomed to an English winter – and they were for she must stay until Celine had decided on her future and her sons had arrived safely at their destination – Five Elysian Place would be their haven and Bennett could do as he pleased. The monotony of Jamie's perpetually empty pockets was a burden that sooner or later fell to her to dispel and if she didn't settle this latest crisis, for crisis it would be, he would go on wasting his borrowed money on flower bouquets. She puffed up her hair, smoothed her finely embroidered bodice and went down to tangle with her stepson.

Bustles were back in fashion and Jamie had to admit that they suited Alannah, gave her shape for she had always seemed straight up and down to him whose taste ran to the curvaceous; at least she didn't go in for over-decoration, for with some you never knew what was under the dead birds and fox-heads and bits of fur and flowers women loaded themselves with these days. Rather, there was a Clodagh-like severity about her, a variation from the usual until he realised what it was – she was almost bare of jewellery. Alannah invariably wore jewellery, blatant exotic pieces quite unsuited to her personality, yet valuable pieces, ah yes . . . set one down on a gaming-table and a fellow's credit would be limitless! He smiled his quizzical yet winning smile but she did not return it. So! It promised to be more of a battle than he had expected.

'What is it this time, Jamie?'

'Now what kind of a welcome is that? Can't a fellow call on his family to enquire about health and well-being and so on without being quizzed like a schoolboy?'

'A fellow can but seldom does and never unless he's after something. You're never out of character you know, so what other reason would you have for being here but the need of money?'

'You're harsh on a fellow.'

'I don't think so. Your debts are never-ending, we settle one and another takes its place, like those worms one cuts through only to have them grow again . . . Not another penny, Jamie. Not one.'

'Not even a loan?'

'Nor that. Your loans are never repaid and your gambling gets worse.'

'Phelim always did let the cat out of the bag . . . So what do I do?'

'You could work. You could go home and help Will with the properties.'

'Help Yokel Will? No thanks.'

'Don't speak so of your son.'

'Son? That, dear lady, is something you cannot prove.'

'Maybe not. But Brick was convinced.'

'I'm no good at working the land. Never was.' He shrugged. 'In any case I'm staying on in London.'

'Well, I won't finance your life here.'

Anger at her self-possession, at the power her wealth and privilege afforded her shook him. He was sick to his teeth of begging! 'I need ten thousand pounds.' He spat the words at her. 'I must have it.'

She turned slowly to face him. 'Ten thousand? Are you mad?'

'It's to save my skull.'

'You have a gambling debt of ten thousand pounds?'

'Well . . .' He achieved a watery grin against her stare.

260

'It's a kind of debt.' He decided to change his tactics; after all, truth just might do it. 'Actually, I've been confronted by the accusation that I'm a father, and this time for various reasons I accept the fact.'

'You expect me to be sympathetic as well as surprised? I assure you I'm never surprised at what emerges from the maze of your tortuous life.'

'There is pressure on me to maintain my offspring.'

'Then you must find some other charity besides the O'Sheas. You've done your best to bleed us dry. You haunted your father; he sent you away time and again but you always came back — '

'You've never approved of me, I know that.' He was bitter.

'Nor liked you – why should I? You caused Brick no end of trouble.'

'The old man and I understood each other.'

'Don't call him the "old man". He was in his prime despite what the doctors diagnosed.'

'I know. That's what made his death so ironic.'

'What do you mean, "ironic"? You're up to your old tricks, hinting, suggesting, putting suspicion about. You enjoy making mischief, Jamie; you made it between Brick and myself and given the chance you'd make it between myself and Bennett. He is my husband you know.'

In his desperation he realised he had a weapon to wound. 'You're the one who has to live with that. In the circumstances.'

'What do you mean – "circumstances"?'

'I wonder what it feels like to bed down with a man who had such contempt for Brick he did nothing to prevent his death.'

'How could anyone have prevented Brick's death? He took a stroke.'

'But no one knew that when the axe slipped. Bennett didn't know it when he stood watching Brick bleeding and unconscious.'

'Bennett was nowhere near Brick.'

'Ah, but he was. He was close, very close, and if he'd rushed to staunch the blood Brick might have pulled through. He just might you know. "We must stop the bleeding," you kept saying. "He'll live if we stop the bleeding." Don't you remember?'

'No. I remember much, too much of that terrible day, but not that.'

'Well, I remember. I ran through the bush and as I ran I saw Bennett, partly shielded by trees, standing, just standing, staring at Brick lying on the ground. Then quite suddenly he turned on his heel and walked up the hill to the house – just like that. He left Brick to die.'

'I don't believe you.' Her words were harsh and staccato. 'You're lying. You have always made trouble for the love of it, you are making trouble now — '

'I could tell you more about Bennett.' He was savage in his fury. 'Things you wouldn't like. I could tell you about his actress sister and what she was up to when she was in Brisbane . . . Things about her and Brick — '

'Stop it!' She held her hands over her ears. 'I don't want to hear. Get out of my house and stay out. Keep away from us all. Get out of here, Jamie. Out. *Out!*' She stood trembling, fighting for composure as with a shrug and his defiant swagger he slammed the door behind him. She knew he was unrepentant, he would never change, for when he wasn't lying outright he was twisting facts to suit not only his moods but his current aims. Yet what he had said about Bennett could be true; there was so much of her husband's life she did not know and perhaps would never know – so many secrets. Celine was right: Bennett Muir was no good for them, certainly no good for her, his wife, and this was the end of something; if she were not yet free of commitments in England she was free of Bennett, and that night she locked her door against him. After his first imperative knocking there was silence, he did not persist, and in the ensuing calm she sensed he was as relieved as herself that an intolerable situation had been resolved. Now all she had to do was tie up loose ends and she and Clodagh could go home.

The pea-souper fogs that plagued London from November to March for three to four days at a time spread a yellowish-brown vapour over the city, distorting the outlines of linkboys lighting the way before horses, of people groping hand over hand along railings and lamplighters spreading a flickering magic over the gloomy streets. The fog was simply another misery added to Jamie's many for he had been turned out of his rooms for unpaid rent and, hounded by creditors, had been forced to make the move to the area every young buck down on his luck dreaded – the East End. So far he was managing to teeter on the edge of it through the largesse of Bart Scobie who had acquired interests in not only rooming-houses but accommodation houses – *maisons de passé* as he called them in his appalling French. At first he had made half-jocular suggestions that Jamie find himself a place as 'fancy man' until Jamie's fury silenced him; Jamie always kept the upper hand with women, let a woman keep you and she bullied you. So finally he had settled himself in as the male bawd of a house in Primrose Court, too close to Whitechapel for his liking, for Whitechapel was an area of squalid courts swarming with Jews, French, Germans and Irish, the only relief in its grimness the music-halls and gin-palaces of the Whitechapel Road, a world apart from the elegant spendthrift London he had formerly enjoyed. He was learning bitter survival in a London of thieves and cutthroats, and brawling harpies who went through his pockets with a deftness even he had not thought possible. He could only cling to his habitual optimism: something surely would turn up! All he had left was hope.

Meanwhile the cold gripped his bones. His room cherished pockets of it so that in moving from one corner to another seeking relief icier hands than his own seemed to grip and hang on. He would go without breakfast for an occasional fire which did little to halt the rising damp. His rage at such penury, at his whole miserable situation was only partly assuaged by the knowledge that Lucy would have difficulty in finding him. Sometimes in his dreams, or rather his nightmares, he had visions of a Spain he had never seen, a warm sunny place remote from cold and creditors and this London that held him as in a gaol. Remote too from Scobie, for Scobie was always around with his dubious companions – pimps and bookies' runners, music-hall touts and actors from the Penny Gaffes, all living on their wits, as he was from one minute to the next. There were days he went hungry, other days when scrounging a shilling or so he would eat at the Holborn Restaurant, a cheap place where he was glad of the cheapest on the menu: consommé with Italian pasta at tenpence, whitebait at a shilling, and if he could manage the one-and-sixpence, pigeon and peas – a red-letter day indeed! It was at a time when he was in his lowest spirits, with the winter at its cruellest, his pockets empty and all but a few clothes pawned at the dolly-shops, that he received an invitation from Bennett Muir to dine at Bellamy's Supper-Rooms in Holborn, the note sent on from his old rooms and, by the look of it, much-handled in the interval. Furthermore, Bennett's letter hinted at an advantageous bit of business to be put in his way, details to be discussed over dinner . . .

Dinner! Jamie's hand shook not only from cold but at the prospect of decent food and wines for he was so hungry everything else faded before the anticipation of warmth and a decent table. He had never liked Bennett Muir, few did, he would prefer to have nothing to do with him, but he felt the man liked him, he even called him Jamie in an affable way that masked for an instant his usual predatory air and the hint of threat underlying every word he uttered. Yes, Bennett Muir liked him for why else such overtures? The reasons for the meeting did not matter, what did matter was a chance to escape this miserable existence in which he sank deeper into oblivion every day and shivering night; this could be his chance to claw his way back to the silken sheets and perfumed rooms of Mayfair. The man wanted something of course but Jamie Lorne O'Shea wanted something too beyond meat and the wines to match. He wanted escape from his present existence. He wanted a second chance.

On the day of the dinner he skipped breakfast – such as it would be – and bought himself a buttonhole, bullied one of his harridans to brush down his one decent suit, stole enough from her to pay for a cab, and did his utmost not to arrive early.

Chapter Eighteen

'You MUST know London well by now. Its hidden nooks and crannies, highways and byways, that sort of thing?'

Though it was said with a smile Jamie found something curiously menacing in Bennett Muir's half query and stiffened, as wary and alert as when he had arrived, too early after all and had ordered the cheapest wine – cheap wine looked just as good in the glass – and sat absorbing the familiar brassy glitter of Bellamy's Supper-Rooms. Until now the dinner had been relaxed and casual, almost offhand, with Bennett lavish with champagne and making exotic menu suggestions which his guest passed over in favour of solid platters of fish, fowl and beef, as if he would never see the like again, which was possible if he did not handle the night to his advantage. Bennett had eaten sparingly while skirting the reasons for their meeting, accompanying each course with a resumé of world disasters: trouble in the Balkans . . . worse trouble in Russia . . . the horrible fate of General Gordon in the Sudan . . . Africa in general – no news of his brothers so far as he knew – and the changing face of London; matters of which he, Jamie, was ignorant and about which he cared nothing. He had felt warmly tipsy leaning back with a liqueur and cigar but now he pushed his glass aside with one finger, an impulsive cautionary gesture to himself for he would need all his wits about him in dealing with this man.

'Well enough,' he evaded.

'Enough to know leading London dealers?'

'I might.'

'"Might" is not good enough. I haven't the time or money to waste on costly dinners so start dissecting your list of contacts.'

'Contacts? You do enough travelling to know every antique dealer in Europe as well as in England.'

'This matter has nothing to do with antique furniture. It involves jewellery.'

'You mean you're looking for a fence?'

'Nothing of the sort. This is my own stuff I want to sell.' He flushed. 'And don't try to act smart with me, Jamie Lorne O'Shea, you always were too cocky for your own good – and not simply around the gaming-tables. I can go elsewhere you know.'

'Jewellery, eh? Precious gems you mean?'

'Of course. The finest. I want a quick sale without fuss or delay, the way I like things done, so I'm willing to take somewhat less than their worth. I have a hunch you can put me in touch with the right party and if I get a good price and all goes well there'll be something in it for you. Something substantial.' His eyes travelled over his companion. 'By the look of you you can do with a leg up.'

Jamie squirmed, hating the man – arrogant bastard! Even if he did look down-at-heel with everything but what he had on in hock and he'd actually found grey hairs in the black that very morning, no colonial upstart was going to patronise him. The man had already patronised him by not inviting him to a West End club when he had the entrée to so many, even Motts where the doorman was astute at separating nobility and royalty from upstart *nouveaux riches*. It was obvious that Bennett Muir chose not to be seen entertaining the scapegrace member of the O'Shea family for their table was secluded and he'd warrant Muir had given a false name to waiters; altogether there was an absurd air of mystery about the proceedings. Well, incognito or not Jamie reflected, helping himself to Scandinavian cheese and hothouse grapes, he could run up a bill here in Holborn as easily as in the West End; for he knew his way about Bellamy's, a popular rendezvous even in the winter months, or perhaps because of winter, its dance-hall lined with mirrors reflecting its brilliant lighting and excellent orchestra while discreet alcoves and subdued lighting in the gallery and the usual private rooms provided seclusion for those who could pay: altogether a lavish expensive version of the gin-palaces lighting up the East End. In his flush days he had come here with Scobie, Bellamy's was a great favourite with Scobie, but he'd told Scobie nothing of tonight's dinner;

266

this was not Scobie's business and if Scobie should walk in he would ignore him. Bart Scobie didn't own him – not quite. Not yet.

'I'd have to see the stuff first.' Playing for time.

'You have seen the "stuff" as you call it. Your stepmother seldom went out without wearing a piece.'

'I'll need time.'

'No time to spare.' Briskly. 'A few days perhaps, all right a week, then I'll come looking for you, which neither of us will relish if you're frank about your address; I'm not wandering London's back lanes flushing you out. Contact me through the Langham – and soon. Understand?'

It all sounded so contrived and devious, so smacking of schoolboy espionage that Jamie felt the urge to laugh in the man's face. He stifled the impulse, he'd had quite a lot to drink but then so had Bennett and one never knew what the man might do in his cups. 'Given up your Chelsea house, eh?'

'Not at all. A hotel happens to be more convenient at the moment. Remember, I want discretion over this matter.'

'Because you're selling Alannah's jewels without her consent?'

'It's *my* collection. Besides, I think my wife will be relieved to be rid of it all, not her style. Damned if I know what her style is these days.' He was fretful and, Jamie sensed, slightly offguard. Clearly the man could not hold his liquor as of yore. It was then he saw Scobie at a table with two men, strangers, and the usual 'ladies of the *pavé*', for Scobie had never been selective in his choice of women, certainly he had never aspired to a Gaiety Girl! All the same these were pros, habituées of the 'dancing academies' and he eyed them with envy for they were women who knew what they were about and it was too long since he had been able to afford those with skills to manipulate nerve-ends to exquisite hurt. He would not touch the drabs of Primrose Court, nor, when they did turn up, the dollymops, the amateurs, the Lucys who sought romance for the love of it and became ecstatic over cheap blue rings. Scobie gave no sign of recognition or made a move to wangle introductions and drinks, he just sat staring at Bennett Muir until the persistency of his gaze irritated, an overlay to the droning irritation of Muir's talk of sapphires and diamonds and rubies, of values and origins and possible prices.

Jamie had no idea how he would carry out the job of go-between yet he knew he must do it for this was his chance to escape his miserable room and crawl back to the West End with money in his pockets, to pay something on account for Lucy's silence, then leave England even for a time for somewhere warm and dry . . . He began to drink steadily, anything to drown Bennett's voice detailing hotels and meeting-places – more schoolboy stuff. Yet serious schoolboy stuff . . . He was fuzzily conscious of being poured into a cab then tipped out at the entrance to Primrose Court – the doorman at Bellamy's? Scobie? More likely Bennett Muir wanting rid of an embarrassment. Somehow he found his room, fell on his bed, and snored.

He woke to a vile head, a furry tongue and Scobie sprawled in his one rickety chair munching a pie. There was noise, a fight in progress in the next room with a woman shrieking against a man's bullying tones, until Scobie shouted and banged on the wall and the racket died down. Jamie pulled himself up on his elbows to stare at the wall until his dizziness eased.

'I'd say someone fancied himself at Bellamy's being wined and dined by the gentry.'

'Can't I have dinner with a relative without you and your cronies acting like Peeping Toms?' he protested weakly. 'You sat staring at Bennett Muir. Why should you be interested in the man? You don't know him.'

'Ah, but I do know him.'

'You told me you didn't.'

'I told you I didn't know him by name, which was true, but if that was your precious Muir at the table with you last night then I have seen him before.'

'Well, he gets around London a bit.'

'Not London, sure of that. It was back home.'

'He's well-known around Brisbane. Among other things he's a club man, hobnobbing with politicians and the sporting fraternity; you know, the whole social round.'

'Never partook of that round, had to come to London to

find m'true place, know what I mean? No . . .' Gravy ran its usual runnel down Scobie's chin and he licked it off with his unhealthy-looking tongue, his plump face shining with grease and, if there were such a thing, a soft secrecy. 'Thought at first I'd seen him in Brisbane, could have, knew a lot o' folk around the town . . . I did jobs for Pa now and then, real meat Pa had, none of your scrag-ends and offal we get here – takes brass to get the good stuff here – and that's what will drag me home sooner or later, roast mutton and boiled tatties and so on. *Meat!*'

'You do well enough here on pork pies.'

'Best I can get around these parts.' Scobie wiped his greasy hands on a greasier kerchief with a frill of torn and dingy lace. 'We had a sideline in Ma's pork pies, fancy pies dripping gravy; that's how I got a taste for pies, can't get enough, ever. We did a brisk trade in meat and pies so I got to most parts of the city. Even delivered to sea cap'ns and such so thought at first I'd seen your precious Muir around the docks, but no . . .' He paused to wipe his face with the kerchief then drew a bottle of gin from his pocket. 'Nothing like a "hair o' the dog".'

'Muir has a warehouse near the wharves, Creek Street I think.'

'Know nothing of his warehouse. Anyway, it wasn't Brisbane I seen 'im, it was Sydney.'

'Sydney?'

'Sydney. Sure of it. Racked m'brains all night and it's all come together. As I said, I did jobs around Sydney and for a while ran rooming-houses on the Rocks as they call the waterfront there. Sailors mostly, waiting to sign on their ships and living it up while they waited.' With his high little giggle. 'Seafaring men like to kick over the traces but I could always handle 'em, except when it came to settling up for many's the time I had to chase their board through their shipping companies. There was this one cap'n, see, who hated paying up as much as I hated trying to get it out of 'im for he was a big feller, a bruiser, brutal sort o' bastard; used to throw the coins over m'head and get me grovelling in the dirt for 'em while he stood there laughing. Glad he got his comeuppance for he finished up eaten by cannibals in the South Seas. Not the only one of his kind either to go into a cooking-pot for

Kanakas got tired of being kidnapped for sugar plantations. They put Burney in the pot all right, got his desserts Burney did — '

'Burney?'

'Not likely to forget the name. Cap'n Burney he called himself though I wasn't the only one who doubted he was more than a rogue recruiter — '

'Matt Burney?'

'The same. A blackbirder, nothing more certain, but then most traders did a bit of slaving on the side.' He frowned. 'You look a bit peaky. 'Ere . . .' He slopped the gin into mugs. 'Get this down your gullet. Perk you up.'

Jamie gulped Scobie's rotten gin because he didn't know what else to do: there could only be one Matthew Burney murdered in the South Seas. Scobie was warming up, excited, thumping the side of his head as if to jog his memory, rubbing his temples, breaking into his little giggle now and then, a rotund sweating youth padding the tiny room. Jamie cleared his throat with difficulty. 'But what has Matt Burney to do with Bennett Muir?'

'Quite a lot I'd say. I saw them together more than once.'

'Matt Burney and Bennett Muir?'

'When I went to collect at Melanesian Trading in Sussex Street on the docks of Darling Harbour. Burney would go into the back room, most times not closing the door, and I'd hear talk, arguments sometimes, before Burney came out with the cash. "Got it from the Boss," he'd say. The "Boss", that's what he called Muir. Of course your precious Muir never saw me, I kept out of sight and quiet till I got m'brass, anyway I was just the messenger, but I peeked, and it was your precious Muir all right behind a desk piled high with ledgers. Now what would a man like Bennett Muir, as you say Brisbane gentry, be doing in the back room of a shipping office in Sydney going through the books? I'll tell you what I think: he was running the place as a front for slave-trading, with Burney as his offsider . . . Say, you look green. Wouldn't put it past that Muir to serve you up rotten champagne.'

Too confused to count the days Jamie moved in a stupefied fog with only a vague sense of time and place, a haze induced

270

partly by Scobie's gin, which he couldn't seem to refuse, and the fury that was burning him up. He would wake from uneasy sleep to fitful daylight seeping through his cracked window and would turn on anyone who came to his room, usually Scobie with his 'hair of the dog' for in moods of near-hysteria he had poured out the whole miserable story of his years of bondage to Burney and Melanesian Trading unaware that behind Burney was Bennett Muir – the 'Boss'. The man had been laughing at him the whole time, and was still laughing at him, out to trick him once again. To use him . . . In his despair he slapped the women about, something he had never done for he had more subtle ways of dealing with women. When walls closed in on him he would wander the streets daring thieves – what after all did he possess worth taking? – attemping to walk off his urge to kill Muir for condemning him to over five years of stinking native villages and swampy islands and creaking luggers. Lost years. Yet nothing dispelled his rage and he could only seek oblivion in exhausted sleep. Scobie would send a woman with soup, or worse, bring it himself to fill the room with his silky-smooth, persuasive, hateful talk.

'Easy to see, matey, this Muir fellow's got under your skin.' He had taken to calling him 'matey', which Jamie hated.

'Why not? He condemned me to years of sailing around those islands browbeating the natives. I could kill him for it.'

'And finish up on the hanging tree? That's not being smart. No use raving on like a madman, there are easier ways of paying him back. You want revenge, of course you want revenge, you're entitled, but you won't get it unless you keep a cool head. You've got to make plans, see, careful plans.'

'He's still using me. He wants me as go-between, middle-man if you like, in selling his gems.'

'Precious stuff is it?'

'The best. My stepmother's jewellery – brooches, rings and such, though he swears the stuff belongs to him.'

'Well, possession *is* nine points of the law – something for you to remember, eh?'

'All I'll get out of it is commission, a miserable one if I know Muir, and I do. He'll beat me down.'

'He doesn't know you're on to him, does he? I mean, he doesn't know I recognised him?'

'He doesn't know you exist – why should he? Why would I talk about you? Bennett Muir wouldn't want to know any Bart Scobie.'

'No need to get uppity over it. No need at all. I've been good to you, matey, for no one else comes here do they? You're down on your luck and if I left you to the sluts around here you wouldn't have a shirt on your back. If you want your own back on Muir you must set about it the right way; get the jewels into your own hands, I'd say you're entitled, then take off with the proceeds to somewhere warm with good living till it all blows over. Everything blows over if you just lie low. I might even join you; never expected the Old Dart to be so blinking *freezing!*' He hugged himself in his chilly misery.

'The little you pay me doesn't run to fires.'

'Have to make m'profit, matey. Anyway, you won't need fires in Spain.'

'Spain?'

'Warm down south. You can live in Spain on the cheap, wines included. Sherry's the stuff to warm you through. Think about Spain and the gems to which you're entitled; after all you got nothing out o' those years you worked the islands did you?'

'Nothing. Not a penny. I was working off gambling debts, to Burney as I thought when all the time I was working for Muir.'

'Then how do you know they didn't con you over it? I mean, how did you know when your debts were worked off? You didn't, did you? Who did the calculating? Not you, that's for certain, you weren't even consulted, were you? They had you over a barrel, matey, they worked you for nothing. And how do you know this Muir didn't steal his wife's jewels? You don't know. Well, now you can pay Muir back for his – treachery, that's the word – and come out of it all with a nice little profit. Of course you could deal with the Jews in Houndsditch yourself but why should you when I know the right people?'

'You always say you know the right people.'

'Know most worth knowing,' Scobie boasted. 'Can't afford to let the grass grow under your feet in London.'

Scobie was unbearably cheerful, coaxing, his voice beguiling, even soporific. The voice possessed Jamie, soothing him to dreams of warmth and black-haired senoritas and himself lazing on flower-decked balconies with the sun seeping into his very bones. 'Leave it to me, matey, just send Muir to the address I give you where he'll be relieved of the gems without fuss, without him even knowing it, a neat clean job over quick as a wink. I know the pair to do it, see – professionals. Got to have professionals, matey. Then you can be off with money in your pocket, less my commission of course with some expenses here and there, but you won't have to do a thing. Just leave everything to Bart Scobie.'

The voice went on and on filling Jamie's head. He couldn't block out Scobie's voice; it would lull then stimulate, sometimes muffled by a consuming of pies or slurred by his teeth chattering with cold. He was drunk with Scobie's voice and persuasive words; his life was more than ever Scobie's as Scobie dragged him out to music-halls and supper-rooms and the dreadful Penny Gaffes that Scobie loved but Jamie had avoided, as he had tried to avoid Scobie's friends and failed: Scobie knew too many 'buck' cab-drivers for his taste. He couldn't control his life any longer, or Scobie, least of all Scobie's voice in his ear. He couldn't control his drinking. Above all, he could not quell his consuming hate for Bennett Muir and his savage need of revenge.

'It will be dead easy, matey. Arrange to be his go-between, agent if you like. Say you have an interested party and give him the address where you'll be waiting to make the introductions. Order him to take a cab from his hotel – it's important, so tell him it's necessary – and I'll make sure there's one on the alert. The cabby gets him there then drives off and leaves him standing. Easy. Nothing to go wrong. This couple, brothers, and that's all I'll say, are down from Liverpool and won't dare try to trick me, I've got too much on 'em. They pass the gems to me – might take a little time to sell 'em, you've got to be reasonable there – then we share the brass: they get a third between 'em, I get my third, and you get the bulk of it.'

'What bulk? A third is not the bulk of it.'

'Look, matey, if the stuff's as good as you say I can get five, maybe six thousand and you can live the good life on two thousand – good money however you look at it. If you can't live well in Spain you can in Italy so think it over and quick for it's not worth our trouble otherwise. It's the only way the job can be done and there's no time to lose: as you say Muir's waiting to hear from you. My mates are in London now with other jobs lined up; they'll do this as well then be off again quick smart. No time to waste, matey. No time at all.'

Bennett Muir had managed to slip by the doorman, no mean feat but necessary to avoid raised eyebrows at his venturing out on such a night and alone; he knew the man would insist on doing his duty and calling a cab which would necessitate the giving of an address. Discretion was the order of the night, yet even so he hated the necessity to be furtive when he was carrying out a legitimate enterprise, the sale of his own property as discreetly and quietly as possible. He had even had moments of regret at not going to Christie's or some dependable jeweller yet in the end cringed at putting the gems under the gavel. Besides, he couldn't be absolutely certain what Alannah would do if he sold publicly; although she had said nothing concerning her missing jewellery she might in the end make a fuss and ruin everything. Now events had been set in motion and he could not halt them. To date, nothing of his affairs had appeared in the London papers, nor, so far as he could gather, in Australian papers concerning Melanesian Trading, but the sooner he was out of London with cash in hand and on his way to Paris, then farther south to Nice or Biarritz or the Italian Riviera the better, with solitude and time to plan, to raise the funds to buy himself out of the mess . . . Eva would never stand by him, they were hostile kin necessary in each other's life from time to time, but Isabel might be persuaded to be reasonable if not cheerful in helping him put Foxburgh on the market. Foxburgh House was his best bet.

A cab appeared so promptly it startled him until he remembered there was a rank nearby and there wouldn't be many fares on such a night. He would engage the cab for the night, it could wait for him. The cabby on his perch was muffled so tightly in his scarf with collar turned up and his hat pulled down that he was virtually faceless. Bennett ignored him other than to give him the address – Number Twenty-six, Violetta Lane, Holborn, before settling back in the interior smelling of warm leather and cheap perfume. Riggs, Jamie had said, a responsible dealer in precious stones, a man who dealt with many West End gents . . . Jamie would meet him and make the necessary introductions. He'd given himself plenty of time setting out, yet not too much, just enough not to be waiting about, he always hated waiting. He patted his pocket to feel the reassuring shape of his dagger, a stiletto with a fine narrow blade and a distinctive carved handle. There were certain parts of London one never ventured without a weapon, certainly not at night, not even in Holborn. Gentlemen carried daggers as a matter of course and he'd been shown some fancy ones around the clubs.

He felt the satisfying bulge of his jewellery pouch; he was carrying four to five thousand, perhaps more, of jewels and the sooner the deal was clinched the better. It had been spitting rain as he left the hotel, now it had become a drizzle that obscured visibility from the side windows. He closed the curtains before him. Above him the cab-driver was quiet for which he was thankful for there would be talk enough later. They had been driving quite a while when he peered through the rain-spattered windows but all he could make out was the shimmer of cab lights on wet cobbles. Lulled by the motion of the cab he wondered how little he could manage to pay Jamie for obviously the fellow was in a bad way. Interesting to speculate how he would finish up; it was unlikely he would return to Australia, born there but not exactly his scene for there was something exotic and gipsy-like about him . . .

He moved restlessly and glanced at his watch. The wretched fellow must be taking him a roundabout route. Daring rain he parted the curtains but all he could see were narrow streets of little houses with here and there the glow of candles at windows; deserted streets and silent but for the lights of an occasional public-house or gin-palace and raucous voices swelling then dying away. He recognised nothing, it could be anywhere in London with narrow entrances to courts where an occasional fourpence-a-time drab stood staring then smiling as the cab came up with her. He knew Holborn, or rather parts of it, but nothing looked familiar and he tapped the roof of the cab with his cane. No answer, no slackening of the horse. He tapped again imperatively.

'Almost there, Guv.'

It was cheerful and reassuring enough but he began to wish the night over and done with. The cab was too warm, smelling of damp clothes and horse's sweat and he felt quick relief when they slowed and finally stopped. He drew back the curtains. They had stopped squarely in the middle of a narrow street lined with miserable houses with no sign of life and no sound but the champing of the horse and the creaking of the cab. Not a dog or a cat moved, there was not even the scuttle of a rat, just dripping rain and seeping pools between the cobbles.

'I gave you the house number. Point out the house.'

'Around 'ere somewhere, Guv.'

Too vague for his liking but he was glad to alight. No sign of Jamie, certainly nothing of the dealer, Riggs. He had a sudden urge to turn back – but he couldn't go back, he was a potential bankrupt with unpaid debts and a rich wife who had locked her door as well as her money against him. He'd be lucky to escape gaol. He shivered. He was cold and fast getting damp.

'The house, man! Where is Number Twenty-six?' he repeated irritably. The cabby pointed with his whip, Bennett decided, at the house at the entrance to a court and he took a few steps – then stopped dead. This wasn't Holborn, of course it wasn't Holborn, this was Whitechapel and he realised suddenly and sharply how very convenient, how significant it was that the cab had appeared so promptly as if waiting for him – he'd been tricked. Set up! The rattle of harness behind him made him swing about to see the cab disappearing down the street.

'Wait!' he called. 'Come back there!' But the cab was gone and he was alone in a Whitechapel street with no sound, nothing . . . Now there was sound, the pad of feet. Black shadows came from somewhere, black shapes were assaulting him. He opened his mouth to shout but sound was choked in his throat by an arm wrapped about his neck from behind forcing his chin back while another hand pressed hard against the back of his neck. Garotters! He struggled, a violent, desperate and useless struggle for the pressure on his throat increased and with it, pain. He could not cry out, he was choking, strangling, dimly conscious of hands going through his pockets – they were after the jewels, he knew it! Somehow he managed to get a grip on his dagger and with a superhuman twist of his body and arm to draw it out and stab wildly. But he was stabbing air . . . Other hands were on the dagger, struggling against him. An agonising wrench to his arm, his wrist, and the knife twisted back upon himself. Blinding pain . . . weakness . . . The cobblestones came up to hit him in the face . . .

'He pulled a knife on them, matey, they had to defend themselves. He should have let them have the stuff, most do y'see, and when these fellers don't get what they're after quick smart there's no telling what they'll do.'

'You said they were dependable, that there would be no trouble, that the job would be done safely and quietly.'

'I told them no violence, I did matey, but when a man fights back . . . well . . . It was just a mistake.'

'*Mistake?* You call it a mistake? It was murder. Your thugs murdered the man and they'll hang for it.'

'Wouldn't be too sure of that. They're on their way north right now, with something on account to tide them over, and they'll make themselves snug as bugs on a freighter or around the docks; know just where to hide, them two. Anyway, when you come right down to it, it was a matter of self-defence.'

'It was murder and you know it.'

'Don't keep saying that, it makes me nervous. Besides, no sense in post-mortems, it's done and now all we must do is get you out of the country for a spell — '

'Why? It had nothing to do with me. You arranged the whole thing.'

'But it's all over London, matey. In all the papers. There'll be an inquest and they'll ask questions of your family and they might want to question you. Are you going to risk it?'

Scobie was packing for him. Scobie had retrieved his clothes from the dolly-shops but only one valise from his once splendid baggage and was jamming it tight with his few possessions. He didn't like the way Scobie was pushing him out of the country for how could anyone connect him, Jamie Lorne O'Shea, with the murder of Bennett Muir, found dead in a Whitechapel lane with a knife in his chest – except his being related to the man in a remote kind of way? Scobie was making too much of the relationship, in short, Scobie was taking over and he, Jamie couldn't seem to do much about it. 'Coach across France into Spain. Stay in Barcelona if you fancy it – Black Stone Barcelona, some call it. I hear there's a lot of carousing in cellars – you'll like that – and that their *zarzuela de mariscos* is famous . . .' Scobie's Spanish was as appalling as his French. 'That's fried shellfish in sauce you know. When I sell the gems I'll join you – but as I said, it could take a little time . . . Five hundred on account isn't bad, now is it, matey? Five hundred will keep you going for a while.' Jamie's frustration turned to panic – why was he running? He hadn't touched the jewels, he hadn't arranged the fictitious address or the 'bunt' cabby to be waiting, or the thieves – murderers as it turned out – waiting to pounce. He had been fool enough to go along with Scobie's scheme for now Scobie held the jewels; would he ever see the rest of his money?

Bart Scobie stuffed the last of Jamie's shirts into the bulging bag. He'd follow all right but he rather fancied Paris; ah yes, Paris with money to spend on the French cocottes . . . Anyway, safer to sell the stuff there. Jamie Lorne O'Shea was a smart feller but he, Bart Scobie, was smarter, had to be, it was a dog-eat-dog world. Naturally the Smulch brothers hadn't passed over all the loot, too much to expect that of 'em, but they wouldn't risk his displeasure by hanging on to too much: they had convictions longer than their arms and could hang for this job for murder was involved. They were well aware he knew how and where to find them if he so wished – yes, he

278

and the Smulch brothers understood each other! As for Jamie, the feller would write begging letters from time to time and from time to time he'd send him a remittance but there was nothing much Jamie could do without exposing his own part in it. Bart Scobie held the trump card – he held the jewels. As he always said, possession was nine points of the law. He closed the valise with a snap.

'Take the five hundred, matey, best all round. No one will bother about me. I'm nothing here, only a flashy con man from the colonies, but you . . . You're another kettle of fish, you belong to a rich important family and there'll be questions asked of them – and who knows, of you. Besides, a reward might be offered, and if it is there's no saying who might crawl out of holes and point the finger, make mischief, you know? Some folk will do anything for brass! Get out and live quiet for a while. After all, five hundred is better than nothing. Take it, matey, and run.'

Chapter Nineteen

THE INQUEST had been extensive – and interminable. Many had been interviewed but at the end of it all there remained loose ends and baffling conclusions. For instance, what was a gentleman of Bennett Muir's standing, an Australian squatter and businessman, stepfather to the wealthy O'Shea family, doing on a raw winter's night apparently alone in such a dangerous area as Whitechapel? Furthermore, how had he arrived where he was found and where had he been headed? Cab-drivers had been questioned but no one had admitted to driving him that night. No guest or staff member of his hotel had seen him leave, nor had he left a message; indeed, it was not even known if he had been in the hotel that day for no one there had seen him since breakfast. His family had been interviewed – except two stepsons en route to South Africa and another thought to be travelling Europe – but his wife and stepdaughters could give no explanation: yes, Mrs Muir had agreed, her husband could have been staying at a hotel instead of a club for she had not seen him for weeks, and yes, it could have been the Langham . . . Yes, one could call it an estrangement between them . . . Her personal maid, upset at the disappearance of her mistress's jewels, vouchsafed the information that the lock of her jewel-box had not been forced and the master carried the only spare key. It was possible Mr Muir had been carrying the jewellery on him. If so it had not been found, while his personal effects of watch and signet rings (recognised by his wife) together with a wallet containing a considerable sum of money, possibly the withdrawal from his London bank of a few days before, were still on his person. Had the thieves known he was carrying valuable gems and been interested only in the large haul? No such jewellery had turned up in London or elsewhere as yet.

Music-halls, supper-rooms and theatres in the area had

been thoroughly combed: no one recalled a man of the name and description of Bennett Muir. His reasons for being in Whitechapel that night remained a mystery yet the manner of his death did not; he had been stabbed to death by his own dagger – his wife recognised the stiletto by its unique handle – though the marks of a garotter were on his throat: Whitechapel was notorious for garotters, it had been a perfect night for them, their motive in the absence of any other, robbery. No one in the street had heard anything unusual but residents of Whitechapel were notorious for keeping their mouths shut. In reconstructing the crime it was assumed Mr Muir had managed to draw out his dagger in defence only to have it turned back upon himself. The usual suspects had been rounded up but all had alibis, some leading to other convictions. *The Times* came out with strong warnings to visitors to take care in the streets. There was no definite conclusion so no charges could be made. It was the end of the official enquiry although the case would remain open: murder by assassins unknown, robbery the motive.

London was agog. The funeral had been a nightmare with all eyes on the O'Shea family, particularly on Miss O'Shea for apparently the gossipy Mr Bruce Macintosh wasn't the only one to have seen her at Brighton. A steady trickle of callers knocked on the door of Five Elysian Place; Eva frequently, sometimes with a dramatically tearful Lady Constance, but Alannah suffered them all as acquaintances calling from morbid curiosity for there was no one she had met in London she could regard as a friend. Strat McCrae had brought Celine from Brighton, not solely because of Bennett's death for Celine had always hated her stepfather, but to book his passage for San Francisco en route to Canada. There was an uprising in the North West of Indians, English and Scots half-breeds, and the Métis, the French-speaking Roman Catholic half-breeds whose leader, Louis Riel, a visionary some called a madman who flourished a giant crucifix in battle, had united his followers to sabotage the railway, cut telegraph lines, take prisoners and seize arms. The settlers were being terrorised and troops sent from the east must be supplied and provisioned: the Saskatchewan Rebellion had begun. Morgan Hume was useless in such crises so Strat had no choice but to return home. He had put up at a hotel until his ship sailed for there was tension between himself and Celine; in her illogical way she had refused to sail with him yet resented him leaving her. She understood his allegiance to Canada, of course she did, but could she make it hers?

Bennett had left the bulk of his estate to his sister, Isabel, and Alannah had no intention of contesting the will. Indeed it appeared that there would be little if anything to inherit since large claims on his estate had already been filed. His sisters (Alannah could well imagine Eva's rage) could argue it out between them. Bennett had carried large mortgages so it was obvious the Golden Emporium and the Creek Street business would be the first to go. Exactly when Yoolanowi and Foxburgh House would go under the hammer she neither knew nor cared, relieved to leave everything so far as possible to the lawyers Bennett had retained in place of Crutchley and Marr.

There came a further final shock. London papers announced the sensational news, reprinted from Australian papers, of Bennett Muir's blackbirding activities, with one of his captains up on kidnapping charges claiming to have acted under Muir's orders. It was alleged that for many years Bennett Muir had conducted illicit recruiting of natives behind the screen of a legitimate trading firm in Sydney, Melanesian Trading, under the management of one Oliver Hickett, but formerly managed by a Matthew Burney who had disappeared in the South Seas, presumed murdered. Suggestions that Bennett Muir's slave-trading could have been the basis for his murder were discounted by police . . . Brisbane was stunned, or pretended to be, for too many were involved in the importation of natives, legally and otherwise; Muir's activities were of a particularly serious nature and his captains and recruiters were no longer prepared to bear the brunt of them. London met this latest scandal with mixed reactions, in the main staying away from Elysian Place much to Alannah's relief for the house was more than ever her refuge.

All she wanted was to settle her affairs and sail home to try to forget Bennett for too many hazy aspects of his life were surfacing: his long and unexplained absences . . . the sources of his always fluctuating income . . . She remembered with clarity and a new significance her long-ago steamer trip to Sydney with her young children when Bennett had joined her on deck. 'We came aboard late,' he had explained. 'We?' 'Matthew Burney my Sydney manager. I have opened an office there.' Her father's interest in Bennett and, later, Brick's queries when she had quite suddenly remembered Burney's name. Had Brick begun to connect Matthew Burney with Bennett? One such query led to another, all without clear answers, and her confusion and shock were not alleviated by Celine's hostility whenever her stepfather's name was mentioned.

'You must stop talking about him, Mama! You must forget him. Entirely.'

'I don't know about entirely. He was part of my life for a long time and his death was horrible. It haunts me.'

'He was a slaver along with a lot of other things. We all knew of his gambling but how did he manage to keep his slave-trading secret for so long?'

'He kept most of his life secret.'

Celine had settled in reluctantly to Elysian Place, a creature of uneasy moods with a strained look about her that made her dark good looks even more startling. She scorned the few invitations she did receive, refusing to go about socially, a new attitude of shrinking from people, except, her mother suspected, Eva, for sometimes she took the carriage on what she insisted were shopping expeditions. Alannah made no objections, or even comments for if the girl found diversion among Eva's theatrical friends it might help her to ignore the sly whispers and glances that greeted her every public appearance. Unhappy and unsettled she wandered the house staring listlessly from windows at the new spring grass and the crocuses in little gardens.

'It's no use you being angry with me, Mama. I don't feel as if I belong in Canada. I don't know if I will ever belong there. If Strat would only come to Australia with me everything would be perfect.'

'Nothing can be perfect for you. Wherever you go with Strat there will always be people to criticise and outlaw you. And why should he go out to Australia? Canada is his home and where his work is. When you were very young I was afraid of your dedication to him but it's clear you are special to each other so if you want him you have no choice but to join him. You can't have it all your way, Celine. Oh my dear, there is no whole thing, no complete thing, no absolute perfection. We all look for it, I know I did, but all we get are slices of happiness. If you cannot share a marriage with Strat you can at least share his life – it's what you want, isn't it?' She had turned aside with a gesture of impatience. 'You cannot stand still like this, none of us can. You're holding up your life, you're holding up mine . . . I have a right to go home — '

'You're going home to Burrendah. It's what *you've* always wanted isn't it – Burrendah?'

'Eventually. Why not? I must settle somewhere and Burrendah has always been my home. I know I can run it well, Erins Pride too with help, for who knows if Phelim will ever come back to it. Or even if he will come back to Australia. In any case it's in my care until he's twenty-one. I'm facing the fact that you'll all be scattered and that I must make my own life.'

'Go home then! Leave me alone in London if it's what you want to do. Go home!' It was her old childish wail and it infuriated her mother.

'I cannot shelter you here or anywhere else. At the moment it's all I can do to shelter myself. Nor can I let you go on disrupting our lives, yes, Meg's too, for if you do decide to join Strat you cannot make the trip alone. I shall hate to part with Meg, we're used to each other, but she will be happy to go with you. She loves new places, is practical, and has a certain cunning that, believe me, matches your own and that should make you excellent companions through life – I don't have to remind you, Celine, that I have no illusions about you. Just make up your mind one way or the other. And soon.'

Still no word from her sons. The Missionary Society was infuriatingly calm and practical: the party had reached Durban safely but there had been no further news. Patience, Mrs Muir. Patience! Clodagh was all reason: 'They're trekking into the interior and may not get letters out for a long time.' Among Strat's letters to Celine was one addressed to Mrs Alannah Muir – Celine must take her own time in coming to him, he would not, indeed he could not hurry her, but when she did decide to make the trip he would see she had company sailing up from San Francisco. Their Australian mail contained nothing from Will, which was unusual; instead there was a letter from Ran Cowper of Yoolanowi, also unusual for he always sent news through Will. He was writing to her directly not only in answer to her cable concerning Mr Muir but to say that Will had suffered an accident; somehow a wagon had turned over on him and as he was not found for some time he was lucky to be alive. He was being cared for at Hawkes Plains, his broken ribs were healing but his fractured hip and leg would take a long time. He, Ran, had taken over management of the properties engaging more hands and doing his best but she would appreciate that he was no Will O'Shea. When things got really sticky Tod Buxton had come from Jubila to lend a hand. Will was furious at his 'uselessness' as he called it and had refused to write her of his bad luck. Alannah felt Clodagh's eyes on the letter, always hungry for news of Will.

'It's from Ran Cowper. He's writing in place of Will.'

'Will has never missed a mail.' Then as her mother hesitated, 'There's something wrong with him, I know it.'

'There's been an accident.'

'Is he dead? You must tell me.'

'No, not dead – dear God no. But he's injured, and rather badly it seems. Read it for yourself.'

'I don't need to read it. If Will is injured I must go home. He'll be expecting me.'

'He's being well cared for. And Ran has taken over.'

'Ran Cowper can't manage everything. At least I can see that Will's orders are carried out. I should have gone home long ago.'

'I haven't kept you, Clo.'

'In a way you have – that's not fair of me, I know, for I suppose I stayed for many reasons – but now Will needs me.'

'I know how you feel — '

'No you don't – no one knows how I feel. I haven't complained about being here so long, almost a year, but now everything is different. It's different with you too. I know you want to go home so why can't we sail together?'

'There is still much to finalise – finances, the house lease, official matters concerning your stepfather . . . And there's Celine . . . She's still unsettled.'

'She'll join Strat sooner or later, we all know that, she's just acting Celine with a vengeance to make us dance to her whims. And you're surely not bothering your head about Jamie? He'll be as comfortable in one rathole as another.' Clodagh could always startle with apt and succinct phrases.

'I rather think he's travelling in Europe.'

'Wherever he is he'll fall on his feet, he always does. The *Sorata* sails next month. I shall try for a cabin.'

'So soon? With your paintings to pack and ship out and your art lessons to wind up? And can you leave the friends you've made here so abruptly? Particularly that young lieutenant — '

'I'm not leaving anyone I care about, Mama. Everyone has tried to marry me off, for every now and then some eligible man decides I'd make a practical and sensible wife – to say nothing of my money – but I shall never marry and you know it. And don't look at me like that, to be alone doesn't mean one need be lonely. I'll have my art, you know what Chaucer said: "The life so short, the art so long to learn." It can be a wonderful life for me with the whole world to paint. Besides, I should like to open an art school in Toowoomba. I've been considering it for a long time. And of course there will be Will to look after . . .'

'You've made him too dependent on you.'

'Well . . . if he regards me as a comfortable shoe through life that will be something. If I can't book on the *Sorata* I'll go out by the next ship. Or the next. I'm going home Mama, with or without you. But I hope you'll come with me.'

Drifting through her indecisive days Celine would seek seclusion to read and reread Strat's letters. Their final days at Brighton had been stormy, she had never seen him so angry, and on his abrupt sailing she believed she had lost him. But his letters were loving and full of news with no blame or recriminations. He had much sympathy for the Indians who feared the railroad creeping across their former domains,

286

hostile at their rations being cut by an indifferent Government, as he had sympathy for the fanatical Métis who wanted land rights; but the tribes and half-breeds of the North West had been doomed with the passing of the buffalo, ending life as they had known it. He wrote of spring: 'We have a favourite dream (apart from our national dream) of spring that keeps us going through our terrible winters. We do not have many snowfalls on Burrard Inlet but the mountains to the north are snow-topped into high summer and you will only strike winter at its worst if you come with me deep into British Columbia. I hope you will, even though a Selkirk snowslide is a terrifying thing: Malcolm Hume was right that time in Rome, for he's a shrewd codger who knows what he's about and I agree it will be a miracle if the railway crosses the Selkirks. Track still has a long way to go with bridges, bridges all the way and the rocks diamond-hard. It has been a bad year with dry seasons and now the Saskatchewan uprising, but at least troops can be carried across the prairies even if they must trudge from one stretch of completed rail to the next . . .'

He wrote of his house and of a growing town in detail as if she were already on her way; he had no doubt of her, she knew that, so why hadn't she gone with him? Panic had frozen her, panic at the enormity of flaunting herself as his mistress and be damned to all! That, and her suspicion that there was something even stronger and deeper in his need of her, his urge to declare a personal life of his own, not only to himself, not only to her, Celine, but to his legal wife and the world that contained them – she, Celine O'Shea, was the core of his gesture. There were nights she woke in terror feeling for him, aching for his presence, wanting to be drawn close and given reassurance. When he was beside her all was right and well, but he was not there and she floundered, holding her Indian charm tightly against her breasts as if to witch him close . . . Yet still she drifted, hesitant to face a city, a country alien to her, to live with him openly in a socially forbidden relationship, her only alternatives to part from him altogether, which was unthinkable, or adopt a fictitious name and hide away as his side-street *amour* – and this Strat would not sanction. 'You've demanded freedom since you were a child,' her mother reminded her, 'to love then live with a man who is married and devoted to a country that is not your own. Why do you hesitate?' She supposed she was a spoilt woman. Many thought so. Strat thought so. She had not yet learned how to handle herself let alone the life that faced her. In her ambivalence her only comfort was letter following letter:

'The town seethes with expectation as here in the west only twenty-eight miles separate the two ends of the railway. Settlers are coming in wanting more than tents so there is much speculation in land, with houses going up. There are stores – I'm considering opening one myself – with boarding-houses, and of course whisky mills in abundance. There is a bookstore, a local brass band, and even a quadrille club for women are beginning to dress up wearing gloves when they go out and believe me it's quite a sight watching them sweep their embroidered hems over the rubble and around the tree-stumps. Balls are being planned – you love to dance . . .'

There was much activity at Five Elysian Place, a general sorting of possessions that Celine felt had nothing to do with her and was shutting her out. Clodagh's half-filled cabin trunk filling the landing irritated her more every day. 'You're surely not taking those dowdy old blouses and skirts home with you? Even Meg would turn up her nose at them and you know what a magpie she is.' Bored as well as desperate, she would climb to her sister's studio on the top floor, arranged to catch the maximum light and sun, and wander aimlessly, staring from one to the other of the paintings stacked against the wall or on easels. Or she would lean, chin on hand, watching Clodagh sort her art books and small canvases, paintings of her 'London period' as she called it for she always painted what was around her and would go home to transform Hawkes Plains or pickaninnies or the Chinese into paint. She had found her forte in the figurative, her remote and lonely women so vivid in portrayal that for some reason they made Celine ache all the more for Strat.

'Why do you paint them with such long necks and bodies?' she complained as if it were a personal affront. 'They all look like saints.'

'It's a style. One that seems to suit me. The Pre-Raphaelites

288

display all the form and precision that existed before everything went loose in the Renaissance. Do you understand?'

'You know I don't. I know nothing about art despite those frescos in Florence. I don't even know what fresco means. You're not taking all this . . . this *junk* of canvases, sketches, books, home with you as well?' It was spiteful but Clodagh remained unruffled.

'What do you suggest I do? Leave my – junk as you call it, as a gallery for the next tenants?'

'I shouldn't have said that. I didn't mean it. Your work is wonderful – at least I *think* it is.'

'You said it because you're unhappy. And drifting. You can't go on so.'

'Home . . . So much has happened since we left Hawkes Plains I sometimes find it hard to remember details.'

'I remember.'

'All you remember is Will.'

'Don't worry, you'll never lose Will's adoration; no woman likes to lose a lover, particularly you. Will never shows passion for me, in his eyes we're simply brother and sister, companions and playmates since before you were born.'

Celine gave one of her extravagant sighs. 'He'll have forgotten me by now, you'll see, at least in a romantic sense. He had to be attracted to someone at the time and I just happened to be around. For all we know he could be planning to marry that Emily Cosgrove . . .'

Clodagh slammed an armful of books on her desk with a thud and changed the subject. 'I cannot pack, much less paint, with you mooning about my studio like this. Since you were a child you've blocked rational argument regarding yourself and Strat but you can't brush such arguments aside any longer. Not with me. If Mama panders to your feelings I won't. I've booked a cabin on the *Sorata* and I want Mama to share it with me, and frankly I don't think you have the right to put obstacles in her way. This house will be closed until the new tenants arrive so if you stay on in London you'll have to take rooms somewhere or move in with Eva if she'll have you. You seem to like each other. But if you stay don't expect the excitement of another 'season'; there is a fresh batch of débutantes waiting for admiration – and husbands if they

289

can snare them. Besides, you're a notorious woman so you
might as well be a scandal in Canada as anywhere else — '

'You sound like Miss Isabel,' Celine flared. 'Not a pretty
sound, Clodagh.'

'It never was. But it was effective. To quote our Miss
Isabel: "Critical situations call for strong measures." ' For
behind the expressions of panic and resentment crossing her
sister's face Clodagh decided there was relief that her mind
was being made up for her. 'Write Strat today that you're
on your way then start sorting your things. Don't you dare
cry. Not a tear. Nor another word. I'll help you pack.'

At Dover Jamie decided to take a 'breather' before crossing
to Calais. He liked the port with its streets of little cottages
climbing to the heights of the castle and old fortifications. He
liked its energy, its activity of Channel steamers in and out,
its fishing boats and whirling gulls, and even its 'trippers'
on seaside holidays. He thought them quaint. Stimulated by
French accents everywhere he haunted shops with continental
airs and restaurants where he gorged on bouillabaisse and
steak and kidney pie stuffed with oysters. He spent recklessly
on flashy ties and waistcoats and frilled shirts, on jackets
with velvet collars and lapels, on imported boots, and even
jewellery to flash about, all of which made alarming inroads
into his five hundred pounds. Still he could not drag himself
away. The room he had taken reminded him too much of
certain London lodgings, so dressed to kill and fresh from the
barber he chose the Dover Rose, a small hotel in a side-street
with crisp curtains and a fine display of potted palms and
shiny spittoons. 'Cosy' was the word for the place, and 'cosy'
suited the proprietress arranging bottles at the well-stocked
bar, swelling above and below stays so tightly laced they gave
a flush as well as a sheen to her complexion. Her bright red hair
was swept up into a fretwork of combs – dyed hair of course,
but then so was his here and there, though he flattered himself
no one would guess. She was not young but young enough
and attractive in an ordinary way; he'd known many so, the
Channel ports were glutted with such landladies. He asked
questions and made flattering observations on the décor and

as he expected, after setting his coffee before him, she paused to move an ashtray from here to there and brush imaginary dust from the table.

'You'd be a stranger here, sir, since you asked the quickest way to the seafront?'

'Just passing through. On business.' Flashing his white well-tended teeth. 'I like a little sea air on the way.'

'A business gent, eh? Thought as much. And looking for comfy lodgings I'm sure. Travelling men can get lonesome even in Dover, everyone coming and going so much, but I don't let gents feel lonesome at the Rose.' Then added with true missionary zeal in her fake genteel tones, 'Them that wants company that is, for I respect privacy, one has only to say.' He caught a whiff of scent from her armpits as she leant forward and held the pose longer than was necessary. 'Take only select here, no riffraff, and prefer gentlemen, they're polite and easier to do for. Trouble is . . . well . . . I had to let m'barman go . . .'

'Gave him the boot, eh?' A touch of humour mingled with sympathy and he had her confidence.

'Had his hands in the till, that one, so now I'm on the look-out.' She ran a plump hand over her padded hips in a way that drew the eye. 'Cockle's the name, Mrs Herbie Cockle, Flo to m'friends, but in private if you get m'point? Mr Cockle, may he rest in peace, wouldn't have familiarity at the Rose, ah no. I keep nice rooms for travelling men so would you care to inspect? You have the right. Slack time now till tea.' She was a talker he decided as she swayed up then down little flights of stairs, her bustle rolling so provocatively he could scarcely take his eyes from it. 'Hard being a widow,' she murmured. 'Neither here nor there if you know what I mean?'

'I'm sorry,' he lied, knowing an answer was expected.

'Don't be.' Briskly. 'Mr Cockle did his dash – died in me arms Herbie did. Yet always joked he wouldn't mind going out that way, in flagrante delicto, he called it, dunno what it means, maybe he didn't, but it has a nice ring to it. Listened to the travelling men a lot, Herbie did. Many's the time he almost snuffed it, in flagrante delicto or whatever, and finally did. But left me a nice little business to work up.' She opened doors on bedrooms with high beds and thick mattresses and piled velvet cushions, sombre prints of ferocious stags mounting improbable rocks dotting the fiercely-papered walls. Cluttered smothering rooms, rather like herself Jamie suspected. 'Call me Flo,' she said archly, wedging him into a corner of the tiny hall, her breath hot on his cheek. 'And yours?'

'Charles Waverton.'

'Charley! I like Charley, genteel as well as manly I always say. What do you do for a crust Charley?' Squeezing along beside him to open other doors.

'I travel for a relative. A vintner dealing in fine wines. French champagne mostly.'

'There! You'd be right at home with the bar work, not that we have much call for fancy imports, just ale and stout, and brandies and port when the travelling men have a good week. Care to consider the place for y'self, Charley? A good table goes with it, and perks for the right one if y'get m'meaning?' Poking him in the ribs with an excited little giggle she opened the door on a room with a view over rooftops to the sea. 'Me special for them who appreciate. The ones with taste, y'know? There's them what say I spoil m'gents but we all need spoiling now and then, don't we Charley?'

Contemplating a feverish cluster of pigeons fouling the neighbouring roof he heard the key turn in the lock then saw her ring-studded fingers slide over the eiderdown before she turned it neatly to the bottom of the bed. 'I like to take a spell of an afternoon . . . Mr Cockle insisted before taking tea with m'regulars – like to preside over m'teapot as well as m'tureen I do – while he took the bar. A good barman, Herbie, watered the whisky so no one guessed – finesse he called it. Wouldn't stand no nonsense either, always said a man who couldn't hold his liquor couldn't hold anything else worth having.' Her giggle was becoming shrill. 'He liked the curtains drawn did Herbie, all nice and comfy.' With a flick of her wrist she drew the net tight and the room was dim, stuffy and claustrophobic. 'Like to get outa the whalebone for a bit.' Dragging at her jacket buttons. 'In some ways I miss Mr Cockle, he knew how to treat a lady. Not that I said yes the first time he asked me, ah dear no, took me time about that I tell you. "Cockle?" I said. "Don't know that I could answer to "Cockle". But I got t'thinking – it could be far worse.' Loosening garments she scratched and massaged her tortured flesh to 'oohs' and 'ahs' of relief. 'Many a cosy hour we spent here, Mr Cockle and me – though Mr Cockle was . . . well . . . small, if y'know what I mean? Though he did try, I'll give that in. Trouble was, I have a generous nature Charley. Can't help our natures now can we?' She beckoned with an imperative finger. 'Unhook me luv. Men like to unhook. Mr Cockle liked to unhook and get a grip.' Grasping Jamie's hands as in a vice she turned herself about and drew his arms around her waist then his hands up to cover her generous breasts. 'Smooth, Mr Cockle used to say. I look after m'skin, I do. Never let sun or wind touch it. Harmful. "Flo," Mr Cockle often said, "your skin is virginal." Virginal?' Her high giggle again. 'In a cocked hat! But he loved a joke, Mr Cockle did.' Her breasts trembled as she rocked against him with long hiccups of giggles. Abruptly she pushed him away. 'You'll get me excited too quick luv.' She had a good figure he decided, with hips as generous as her breasts and a waist even without her stays pleasantly small; a florid fleshy body to suit a common blowsy sexually generous widow-woman who owned a thriving business – ah, a man could do worse. Much worse. 'Steady strong hands y'have luv. I like steady hands on me. Mr Cockle's hands sweated . . . nervous he was . . . always nervous. "You want too much too often Flo," he always said. Well I do. But mustn't speak ill of the dead. Good intentions Herbie Cockle had.'

She flopped on the bed, her bulk sinking deep, her flesh rippling as she spread herself and waved her scented kerchief over her naked thighs and between her splendid legs. 'One o'me little touches. Mr Cockle loved little touches. Scent, he said, gave an atmosphere. Always a way with words had Mr Cockle.' The bed heaved as she wriggled about settling herself and there was something incongruous as well as ribald, even erotic, about her naked thighs below her ballooning petticoats and her voice issuing from somewhere in the folds. 'Hurry up luv, only got an hour. M'girls waste time down there if I don't keep me eye on 'em. Shake a leg there, Charley boy.' Her giggle became a stifled scream as she heaved herself up on her elbows, scattering combs around her, to watch him undress.

So he was finishing up a 'fancy man' after all, with a lusty widow panting for him; if he kept her so he could soon be running the place – all a piece of cake! Yet it was plain that not only must he service Flo Cockle but must live with Herbie over their shoulders for the sake of a good table, soft beds and this safe sweet corner of life – safe from Lucy, safe from everyone and everything he needed to escape. Even so, as he climbed astride her he was not quite prepared for the strength and ferocity with which she clutched at him. It had better be worth it he thought with a rush of panic as she proceeded not only to consume but to devour him.

Jamie Lorne O'Shea had met his Waterloo!

Chapter Twenty

'THERE IS much talk filtering down to us of gold on a great plateau thirty miles south of Pretoria called the Witwatersrand – known as the Rand – a ridge of low hills pitted with streams in rainy seasons. The farmers have long known of gold there but it has been a well-kept secret, now it can no longer be so for gold is found increasingly on Boer farms and there is much excitement with pressure on the Government to open all up for prospecting. Would-be miners are already pouring in for the old missionaries' road is kept open and well-trodden and the Transvaal, all Boer country, will be rich – providing the money and the skills are there to get the ore out as the reefs lie deep. Boers who have only cared about their cattle are being shaken up but are shrewd enough, those who do sell out, to make fortunes for themselves. The Government doesn't like what's happening for too many strangers – "Uitlanders" as they are called – mean trouble, at the same time the Government likes the resources and the revenue they can bring.

'I am thoroughly bored with psalms and helping in the schoolroom and itch to try my luck but Dominic will not desert his flock, in a medical sense of course for fundamental religion does not interest him any more than it does me, and he falls out with the clerics so often I am sure they'd be glad to be rid of us. Perhaps I can convince him that the flotsam and jetsam pouring in up north need him more even though he cannot set up in practice for himself – yet he's so skilled that no one, including himself, misses his medical degree. Poor Domi, he's pulled every-which-way in this damnably divided country, but he would come, wouldn't he? On the one hand he insists that the Boers, descendants of the Voortrekkers, and an isolated people clinging together for survival, should have their land and the fruits of it. While I find the Afrikaaners a sour lot with too many Old Testament quotes for my digestion and hating everyone with Calvinistic zeal: the British of course (I keep away from the Redcoats myself), the coloureds, as the mixed bloods are called, and the native races as lesser beings in the eyes of God. On Domi's other hand he's so involved with the coloureds here at the Mission they are becoming a Cause for all over the country they work for a pittance and are virtual slaves to the landholders. One feels they won't endure it for ever and are simply waiting. I suppose in the end they will just carve up the country, carving themselves up at the same time, for there's one thing of which I am certain, there will be war here sooner or later as there is much hatred. I tell Domi he should have been a priest though he says a doctor is a kind of priest – not the doctors we know, eh? Where did he inherit such sentiments? From Father I suppose. Even so, we're not a sentimental lot, except Celine over her Canadian and I hope that's turning out all right. I don't want to hang around the human race except a few with whom I can enjoy myself, I want to see the world. Then when I find a part of it I like better than another I'll stay – why not? No one really needs me back in Australia, not even you Mama, now that you have your precious Burrendah. There are plenty of hands to cut the wood, as I've always said . . .'

Alannah added Phelim's letter to the little pile ready to post to Will and Clodagh then rustled through her collection for others that might interest them. There had been a brisk exchange of mail all round this year, for though Dominic seldom wrote, Phelim made up for it by more or less regular chatty sprawling letters that for all his youth showed a growing sophistication. She had placed her desk by the north window of her old room to catch the sun for it was June and even though a fire blazed in the grate the winds off the Snowies were cold. She skimmed through a letter from Celine, an old letter but it would swell the packet:

'In November Strat attended the ceremony among the workmen at Eagle Pass for the driving in of The Last Spike, as they call this historic event. Railway superiors came from the East while a private car went from the West on the completed line pulling the final load of rails to the mountain crevice called Craigellachie where the rails joined. You can't escape the Scots in Canada. I've never felt Irish in my life but here it's a matter of self-defence. Strat says the old Canada has gone and the railway will change everything – an historic day it seems. As for ourselves we manage to be quite gay at times for Strat won't let me hide away and insists I go everywhere with him. I have friends, not that Clo, or yourself for that matter, would approve but I find them as amusing as I found Eva and her friends in London, because they are tolerant, or act so when perhaps like myself they are simply on the defensive. Anyway, Strat knows many people, not that all like him, no, and it does seem to be the same with me. Perhaps it is to be my life that I shock the prudent and respectable. For practical purposes I am regarded as Stratton McCrae's housekeeper, a polite way of spreading it about that I am his whore – and I don't believe I can shock you any further Mama! We are thankful that his wife doesn't come to Kitsilano but every now and then Strat asks her for a divorce, uselessly, for he returns to me with such anger in him against her that I am often fearful for us all. He truly wants to show his devotion to me as his common-law wife, his only wife, when all the time I am addressed as Miss O'Shea; I could do as so many others of course and adopt a married name but I wore a ring in Brighton and in Italy and I don't like the pretence. We are not practical over the situation Mama, so must suffer for it. Perhaps some day a man or woman will be able to get a divorce simply because he or she wants it, and that will be right for there is no marriage unless there are two to make it so, but I don't think that will happen in our lifetime.

'At his most desperate Strat talks about settling in Toronto or New Westminster, perhaps in Victoria on Vancouver Island, but we love the house here, and Vancouver is such a pretty place that even in summer I go out to the verandah each morning hoping to see fresh snowfalls on the mountains to the north. I am learning about a country very different from my own. Meg loves the life because she can order the Indian girls about but she still can't manoeuvre Chin, Strat's Chinaboy. Sometimes we stay in New Westminster, or on the Island, the latter very British, so all in all we don't do too badly despite the fact that here as everywhere marriage is marriage and a man's whore is something else – a fact which lecherous old Malcolm Hume never lets me forget! The friends I've made are suspiciously in the same boat, the women adopting the names of their lovers but I can't do that even if I wished to. Yet through it all when Strat and I are alone together we are very happy though he still calls me spoilt and I'm quite sure that at times I drive him almost insane. But that's me, he loves me as I am, heaven be praised. Sometimes I ask him if I am worth the upheaval in his life; he seems to think so. We can only live day by day though I am often homesick and even with Strat beside me perhaps I always will be. Now to other things . . . Dear Will, is he all healed? I write to him as well as to Clodagh but I would much rather write you long letters and have you send them on . . .'

Alannah put the letter on the pile for Hawkes Plains, pushed everything aside and crossed to the fire to warm her hands. She was off to spend a few days at the Pride, for new machinery was needed and she must not only discuss but bargain with keen, clever and certainly careful Ian McCready, the Pride's new manager. She had found many changes at both stations for paddocks had been ploughed and soil improved, making agriculturalists out of shepherds since Dan Charlton had been persuaded to experiment with crops. There were few left from the old days: Paddy One had been killed in an accident in the town while Paddys Two and Three had taken up their own selections in Victoria. Her six months spent settling into Burrendah had been not only happy but fulfilling after months in Brisbane and on the Downs, first of all arranging the sale of BelleMonte then cutting ties all round. The forced sale of Foxburgh House following her brother's death had caused devastation in Isabel Muir who had finally retreated to her school that was her only source of income. Ran Cowper had taken time off to find Barney Cook settled in squalid permanency with a half-caste wife and a brood of children and resettle them at Jubila, and after much trouble to hunt out Gondola, happily travelling Queensland with a circus troupe; she decided to leave the Neapolitan be for Brick would have decided so, and if ever Gondola did turn up at Hawkes Plains Will would see to him. She made the trip to Jubila to see Fay and Tod, Fay's battered piano now at the mercy of her distinctly unmusical offspring. The Dennings' sprawling homestead was swollen with children coming and going for most of the Denning girls were married.

In Sydney she had spent a week with her father, her stepmother Maria and her Aunt Delia. As the wife of a leading politician and mill-owner, Maria Moynan excelled in her role of Society hostess, manipulating a husband as possessed as any man could be by his handsome if demanding wife who never missed an opportunity to probe and patronise. Owen Moynan ignored his wife's imperious attitude towards his daughter and her bored toleration of his sister, Delia Carney now a sad travesty of the bustling little martinet who had run the Bridge Academy with such efficiency, toying with her bread, spilling her soup and coveting the pudding forbidden her by her hostess as too rich for her digestion. Daring her stepmother, Alannah piled her aunt's plate with cheese and nuts and dried fruits as some little compensation for the situation.

'I remember your younger daughter very well.' Maria's expensive taffeta rustled, her jet earrings glimmering in the strong lights. 'A wilful child. She ran away, as I recall, causing a great deal of trouble. Celia isn't it?'

'Celine.'

'Ah – Celine. Of course. So very Irish.'

'Her grandfather called her spirited rather than wilful – isn't that so Papa?'

'But she's still playing truant he tells me. Running off with a married man no less.'

'She did not "run off" anywhere. She and Strat McCrae simply decided to live life together. An honest decision I think.'

'But a foolish one surely? When women decide *en masse* to civilise a pioneering country they make it such a Holy Cause they will socially and verbally crucify any woman who steps out of line. Celine will need all her spirit, or should we not say, gall, to survive.'

In many ways her father's wife reminded Alannah unpleasantly of Eva Muir. They were both women of supreme confidence before the world, yet women who employed deviousness and contrivance behind closed doors: at least Celine brought her transgressions into the open. She had hoped her father would spend some time with her at Burrendah but since

Maria refused to travel the most he would do was see her off by train. Argyle County remembered her well (would she ever live down those riding breeches?) just as Goulburn remembered her – Goulburn on the Plains they called it now. If she wished she could have quite a gay time of it but she was content to stay close to Burrendah, happiest of all in the saddle; she sorely missed Brick beside her for it had been their greatest joy to ride together. She spent much time at Erins Pride, Hetty Witherstone still happily ruining characters with her tart asides (Can't imagine clumsy old George thumping about amid the fine china and the cucumber sandwiches, can you? Not unless the life of a country squire has tamed him) for the Elstons had long ago sold Wiena and retired 'home'. Erins Pride and Burrendah crowded her with memories despite her resolve to bury the past, for life here now was to be hers and hers alone, her only contact with her family brief visits to Hawkes Plains, and letters: her sons part of Africa's turmoil, Celine working out her life in Canada, Jamie – always Jamie – a renegade but still an O'Shea wandering distant and unknown purlieus, with Will and Clodagh her anchors on the Downs. As she rode the old tracks she was achingly aware of familiar things and places. The black swans on the lagoon . . . The fence, newly mended she noticed, where she had stormed in temper at Brick, mad at each other yet for each other, that summer's day long ago . . . The tree that marked the boundary between Burrendah and Erins Pride . . . The fateful terrible little bridge she forced herself to cross . . . Her 'special place' that turned her heart upside down every time she strolled to the Creek – places where she had been happy or sad or a mixture of both. She would sometimes find herself crying softly for no reason she could name and would scold herself, angry at her softness, a woman of forty-six crying as she had cried when she was eighteen, the way Celine cried . . . And knew she cried for Brick, her only love, and the soft green grass where the old stone wall was crumbling and would soon be no more.

When Will stayed at Hawkes Plains Clodagh served tea of an afternoon on the corner of the verandah where she had made a fernery and where the vines were so thick they gave a soothing green in summer and shelter from sharp winds in winter. During his long convalescence she had made tea together more than a pleasant habit, she had made it a ritual, and even when he returned to Narengee to 'pick up the pieces' as he put it, she would ride over with Cook's pastries for the 'invalid' as Cook continued to call him to his annoyance, while she busied herself about the comfortable homestead. Settlement was creeping out from Toowoomba, cropping was taking hold in the north-west and Will had added to his land, spreading crops over soil he had made the most fertile in the district. 'I'll tell you something,' he had said in one of his rare contemplative moods. 'Growing up I worked with sheep but knew I'd never make a sheep man and fought with our Papa over it. I never could take to the beasts. They chew up the world: worse, they chew down into it destroying the green things I like to grow. And I'll tell you something else. I like to stand here at harvest time, just stand, and see my own wheat giving a sheen to the valley and creeping up the hills.' He talked more often and openly now, at least to her, as if shock had forced the realisation that he was as vulnerable as the next man, for at first there had been doubt that he would ever walk again; he had been lucky, he was as straight and strong as ever. He had never told her, or anyone else it seemed, the cause of his accident and she had not probed, knowing his deep pride in his own competence; purpose translated into action, the need to be up and doing, had always been Will O'Shea's life.

The kettle was boiling and she glanced at the clock. He would soon be in and liked to find her waiting at the small verandah table, just as he seemed to like her to prepare their tea herself. She filled the big brown teapot and set it on the tray beside the platters of sandwiches and thick slices of fruit cake; he had developed a sweet tooth as well as a sound appetite where previously he had taken meals more or less on the run. She bundled up their mail: a package from Burrendah enclosing well-thumbed letters from her brothers, and directly from overseas, a letter for him with a Canadian postmark addressed in Celine's hand, perhaps detailing the terrible fire that had burned Vancouver to the ground. After newspaper reports of a too-hot June with brush ringing the town smouldering away, then the sudden and furious outbreak that left only two houses out of four hundred and charred bodies everywhere they had sent off frantic cables until Celine had cabled in return: she and Strat were safe, they had been visiting in Vancouver and with all those who could, had taken to the water and stayed in the shallows . . . Just time perhaps to finish her mother's letter? 'I fear I will never see Dominic again, you will understand when you read Phelim's letter, he writes in such colourful detail. I have kept back one letter from Domi, one reason being that he writes so seldom, another that I find something historic and a little bizarre about this particular letter out of Africa requesting my permission for his marriage — ' Her start and her heavily-breathed 'Well!' set the letter fluttering and the cake-knife clattering, yet why should she be surprised? She read on. 'Dear Domi, he's too young of course, of course he's too young, but I must stop saying that, mustn't I? I've written my permission with our love, after all how could I refuse?'

Will's heavy tread along the verandah then the creak of his favourite old chair. She swept all on to the laden tray and carried it outside. His black hair shone in the spring sun as he bent over his carving of an opossum; in her efforts to dispel the boredom of his convalescence she had coaxed him back to the carving of the small wooden animals and birds Dominic had treasured. She had even brought out Dominic's collection and arranged it as a reminder and spur. His hair had grown long and a little wild. He looked different yet was the same Will, stubborn, with the same quick but controlled temper, the strong stocky youth she had grown up with since her arrival on the Downs as a child of four with her shattered mother after the death of the father she did not remember to make a new home, to know her stepfather, and soon her half-sister and brothers. He looked up and sprang to take the tray.

'Better put it down or you might drop it from shock,' she warned. 'Mama writes that Domi wants to marry, and she's already given permission – and don't say "Well", I've already said it.'

He grinned. 'I'll just say it's typically Domi. He always did know what he wanted.'

'He's too young – but Mama's already said that.'

'He's getting older by the minute, I'd say.'

'There's a letter from Phelim to tell us all.' She poured tea and, with his cup and saucer, handed him Celine's letter. Glancing at it he set it quietly aside. Unfolding Phelim's letter she skimmed the pages. 'They're in Johannesburg, a place of tents and shacks as yet . . .' She read quickly, her finger running down the closely-written lines. ' "Domi decided we should make the trek north when the Rand opened officially for prospecting. He fussed over farmers selling out with those turned away from agriculture and pasturage having nowhere to go but crowd in here, and believe me he never lacks the starving and the sick. There are some six thousand already in this town with one thousand of them black, so he's getting himself into as much trouble here with his varied Causes as he did at the Mission for he protests even when he sees crowds gathering to watch the morning floggings outside the Court-house. He is working with a Doctor Der Verbruch, of radical medical and political ideas who clashes violently with the Calvinists. Now for the personal news (though I know Domi has written to you). He wants to marry a plump round-eyed little nurse who works with him in Der Verbruch's clinic, but I can't be sure what you will think of it for she is a coloured – and being Domi he might not consider it important enough to mention . . ." ' Clodagh paused to meet Will's steady gaze. 'If he did mention it to Mama she didn't consider it important enough to pass on . . .' She resumed her reading: ' "Domi never seems to notice colour. He was as one with the Blacks back home, all the same to him, remember? But I tell you now, Mama, because of the huge divisions here. Domi can't really understand them and fights against them – and why should he not? For no matter how you rationalise it there is colour in him, in us all, except Will and Clodagh who are not true O'Sheas. Even Jamie shows a bit of the gipsy; we're a mixed lot. Anyway, Domi's love is one Alicia Simpson, daughter of a British soldier, deceased, but once stationed at Durban. She grew up in Durban working as a nurse until she came first to Pretoria then to work here with Der Verbruch. They are waiting for your consent for the Reverend will not marry them without it since Domi is under age – and apart from the legalities Domi's a stickler for such conventions whereas I'm happy to circumvent them when and where I can. He's anxious to get his degree and has a choice of England, or Capetown (very British) or Stellenbosch in Cape Colony where only Africaans is spoken, and it probably won't surprise you to hear he already speaks it well. I think he will choose Stellenbosch as more to his taste, besides, quite possibly Alicia could work near him. He has plans for his own hospital too, so I fear I'll be roped in as boss of some nondescript gang to help build it; can you see me with my own construction firm? Anything is possible here . . ."' She folded the letter slowly, thoughtfully. 'I can see why Mama feels we will never see Dominic again. Nor Phelim. Perhaps we'll never see Celine . . .'

'At least we know she's alive.' He fingered her letter, staring at it.

'Open it,' she prodded. 'You don't have to read it to me you know.'

'I know.' But he did not open it, he tucked it in his pocket. Later he would pass it to her to read, as always. 'Celine will always survive,' he added briskly. 'She has the knack.'

'Is there a knack?'

'Oh yes. While others . . . well . . . I don't believe I would have survived the possibility of being crippled without you around, Clo.'

She did not answer spontaneously, she could not, for the remark was unexpected; Will seldom made impulsive remarks and certainly not flattering ones. 'Nonsense. You were doing well enough under Clara's care when I arrived – except for being sorry for yourself.'

'All the same I took heart when you turned up.'

'Mama says I spoil you.'

'Our Mama could be right.'

'Surely Emily Cosgrove spoilt you a little?'

'Emily demanded the spoiling, and I didn't have the time or perhaps the inclination to do so though I did try to cultivate some response beyond the usual barnyard wanting. It was no use. Perhaps I'm just a clumsy lover.'

'Marriage might have been the spur you needed.'

'Too big a chance to take without the drive, that something more . . . Perhaps I'm a stoic, not meant for the wilder shores of life and love, the adventure of it – some men need to play safe. Anyway, Emily wasn't cut out to be a farmer's wife, she knew it all along for she married Malvern, you know, hardware down the road.'

'I'm not so sure that I could survive intense emotional turmoil, not after watching Celine's agonies — ' She broke off.

'No need to fuss,' he said quietly. 'She has always loved the fellow, she reminded me of it often enough; you know Celine, she never holds anything back. I couldn't compete with Strat McCrae, they belonged from the first and wild horses won't part them now. In any case she never thought of me as a lover, not solid old Will, perhaps I always knew it as I knew that my urge was a growing-up thing, she was there at my side and the revelation we were not blood kin set me on fire – and a great and terrible flurry it was too, all feeling and no sense. Yet I can't be sure how I'll feel if I see her again – which as you say is not likely – but one thing I am sure of, I'll never feel quite that way again for anyone else, wonderful and awful at the same time. I don't think I want to.'

'Don't you?'

'No I don't.'

'It could happen.'

'You've changed, Clo.'

'Older, if that's what you mean.'

'Ah, the ripe old age of twenty-six.'

'On the shelf, as London social circles would put it.'

'I heard there were beaus in London, including a certain lieutenant.'

She smiled. 'Rumours greatly exaggerated.'

'All the same, I never really expected you back.'

'Why not?'

'I believed London would hold you, you know, exercise the mental muscles, provide fresh goals.'

'London was marvellous of course. The river. Galleries with wonderful paintings depicting a European world with its roots in religion – though I don't think all the artists were religious, it was simply part of the world they lived in to believe. There was opera . . . and such wonderful music . . . Even so I felt an outsider, an onlooker, not really a part of it all, not belonging to it. I felt a visitor enjoying an interlude in a fascinating world that was not mine, absorbing it in order to come home and use what I'd learned some other way. To transmute it . . . I understand the boys wanting other places, to be close to Europe where it all began. We are an isolated people, all islands are, aren't they, even large islands? I can understand Celine's excitement at her first experience of London. But I . . . well . . . I hold my feelings close. Sometimes I wish I didn't.'

'Perhaps your feelings only really show through your work; to use your own expression, you transmute. Your painting is different now. More confident.'

'I hope it's confident enough to make a success of my art school. I've had a number of enquiries but need more, it will take time of course and I can't hurry it. But when it's firmly established I can travel again, seek out new backgrounds as well as old. And I want to paint the things I remember, the things that have made an impression on me; you see, I find something . . . well . . . mystical about painting from memory. For instance, at Erins Pride there is a tree everyone calls "the big tree" where children play – Mama told me you played there as a baby. I would like to paint children in its shelter . . .' Her voice trailed.

'You're wearing your distant look. You always do when you talk of your childhood.'

'At least I've grown out of my stammer.'

'You wore the same look – complete with stammer – when you first came to Hawkes Plains. Young and old had jobs then. It was rough living and Papa O'Shea wielded a pretty sharp stick. I can remember stumbling about collecting wood chips . . . You helped me pile them up.'

'My face always did give me away,' she mused.

'It's a nice face.'

'Which means it's a dependable face. A scrubbed sisterly face.'

'More than that. Why denigrate yourself now that Celine's not here to overawe?'

'Perhaps it becomes a habit when one has a good-looking younger sister.'

'You have your own looks – and talent. That's why it's

306

unfair that you work around Narengee as well as here waiting on me, a farmer, a bit of a bore I don't doubt, with no polish, a bushwhacker as some call me. You deserve more than warming my slippers before the fire. It's all wrong, you on a farm.'

'It's what I choose, I never want to be anywhere but on the Downs. Besides, I feel, just as Mama does, that Dominic will never return, that he'll settle in Africa and become a famous doctor, while Phelim will take what comes, even that war he expects . . . So that leaves the two of us caring for Hawkes Plains and all that goes with it. Ironic, don't you think, when it is not ours and we are not even Brick O'Shea's children?'

'At least you know who your father was.'

'As to that, Papa O'Shea always insisted — '

'You're reverting. Haven't you learnt even now to call him simply Papa?'

'I don't think I'll ever learn. Papa O'Shea insisted that Jamie was your father.'

He shrugged. 'All I've been certain of is that I'm the bastard son of a scullery girl, father unknown. As to Jamie, he would deny it, or simply laugh it off. Perhaps he's the true realist in viewing the circumstance as quite unimportant.' He stood, stretched, walked to the verandah rail and stood staring out over the fruit trees to the distant hills. 'I'd better make a start if I'm to call in at Yoolanowi.'

She found something vaguely final about the statement and it frightened her for it was as if everything between them depended upon her — as perhaps it always had. Could she, reserved, shy Clodagh Aldercott, 'that cool, collected lady' as someone had said of her in London, with no pretensions to good looks and with too much sense for her own good, make the first and urgent gesture? She stood up slowly, paused a moment then joined him at the rail. He did not turn to her, just took her hand in his and entwined their fingers tightly, a childhood habit as they ran off together to raid the orchard or burrow deep into the shady strawberry patches or simply wander together exploring the bush.

'I'm glad you're here, Clo,' was all he said. He kissed her quickly on the cheek.

She freed her hand, gripped his shoulders and kissed him full on the mouth. It was not a passionate kiss, it was a hard forced kiss, and he drew back, a little startled she could see, for it had been an awkward and untutored kiss. She had never kissed any man on the lips before. There had been the usual kisses on the cheek, rough pecks from her brothers, from friends, and one awkward fumbling attempt at a kiss behind the ferns from young Lieutenant Groves who had seemed a little afraid of her. She had done a dangerous thing. She had spoilt the old relationship, turning their friendly brother-and-sister world upside down. She had forced them over the line.

'It's late,' he said calmly. He took her hands in his and held them tightly and for an instant they stood close, poised. She thought he was going to kiss her but instead he let her hands drop, smiled his familiar, faintly crooked smile and strode off, not fussed, not hurrying, certainly not angry, just Will O'Shea away about his life. She waited for him to look back. He did not. Yet somehow she knew all would be well.

'Will . . . Dearest Will . . . I can wait.'